TEN SLEEP

Also by Nicholas Belardes

The Deading

TEN SLEEP

Nicholas Belardes

EREWHON

an imprint of Kensington Publishing Corp.
erewhonbooks.com

Content notice: *Ten Sleep* contains depictions of body horror; nature horror; murder; sexual harassment; discussions of racism and abuse (emotional and verbal).

EREWHON BOOKS are published by:

Kensington Publishing Corp.
900 Third Avenue
New York, NY 10022

erewhonbooks.com

Copyright © 2025 by Nicholas Belardes

All rights reserved. This book or any portion thereof may not be reproduced or used in any manner whatsoever without the express written permission of the publisher except for the use of brief quotations in a book review.

Excerpt from *Boy's Life* by Robert McCammon (Simon & Schuster, Inc.: Pocket Books, 1991).

All Kensington titles, imprints, and distributed lines are available at special quantity discounts for bulk purchases for sales promotions, premiums, fundraising, educational, or institutional use.

Special book excerpts or customized printings can also be created to fit specific needs. For details, write or phone the office of the Kensington sales manager: Kensington Publishing Corp., 900 Third Avenue, New York, NY 10022, attn: Sales Department; phone 1-800-221-2647.

Erewhon and the Erewhon logo Reg. US Pat. & TM Off.

This is a work of fiction. All of the characters, organizations, and events portrayed in this novel are either products of the author's imagination or are used fictitiously.

ISBN 978-1-64566-132-0 (hardcover)

First Erewhon hardcover printing: July 2025

10 9 8 7 6 5 4 3 2 1

Printed in the United States of America

Library of Congress Control Number: 2024943942

Electronic edition: ISBN 978-1-64566-134-4

Edited by Diana Pho
Interior design by Kelsy Thompson
Interior art by Brynn Metheney

The authorized representative in the EU for product safety and compliance
is eucomply OU, Parnu mnt 139b-14, Apt 123
Tallinn, Berlin 11317, hello@eucompliancepartner.com

For Jane

These forces could not be named . . . These forces were as old as the world and as pure in their good or evil as the elements themselves.

— Robert McCammon, *Boy's Life*

Ten Sleep

PROLOGUE

Before you hear the stories of all those animals, that's right, animals of the American West—some mysteriously reanimated, others consumed—and how they did or did not fight the mother canyon, or how they helped Greta Molina, because this really is her story, you'll first need to know some "strange tidings" from a hundred or so years ago.

Good an entry point as any is what's been hidden far longer than most been alive, and that's what happened to two families of sheepherders caught in the wrong place at the wrong time, which was some decades after Wyoming Territory become inundated with cattlemen and railroads. Their tale of the high country isn't always clear. But ain't no recollection perfect, memory being what it is when telling the history of a thing.

Now, the Merrills and Johnsons were two strong sheepherder family names—and it's tragic what happened to them squatters, although their misadventures are a pioneer story, and ironic in form for many reasons, foremost because they were unwanted white settlers targeted by none other than other *white settlers*, or in more specific terms, they were unwanted by those cattlemen who been in Wyoming decades before the Merrills and Johnsons set foot in that high country. Even so, take pity on these two families. Multiple members were taken and dogwhipped, then put on a long march led by the cattlemen's hired gun Tom Horn—who was just as deadly *while dead* as he was when alive.

These families knew each other well. Come up from Missouri, though it wasn't their intention to become late homesteaders. They weren't altogether honest about what they done either. They run sheep in a joint-held corporation, which was their shared American dream, though they desperately needed grazing lands they didn't have to pay for. Just before the turn of the twentieth century, this being sometime in the late 1890s, they bought land from one of those fly-by-night auctions set up in Laramie. Those acres were surveyed land the U.S. Government didn't buy up, and those parcels in truth was confiscated from Indians and should have lawfully been kept under treaty, meaning that any way you look at this, those sheepherders were set to become occupiers, *settler occupiers*.

Come to find out, the land they purchased was surveyed from false maps, though not a single Merrill or Johnson could prove this in a court of law, being that both government and legislation throughout Wyoming was controlled by cattle barons. Though bought for less than $1.25 per acre, the land was in a sad state, drowning in swampland drainage from a series of wet years, and none of it was about to go dry. Homes couldn't be built on such wet parcels, nor could any acreage be used for grazing or farmland, which the deal for all late homesteaders was to farm, not ranch, especially any sheep.

Near penniless and landless, both families believed they had to squat, to nest, so they could retain all their sheep. So they did just that, constructed homes on public land, which would become theirs after a number of years, and then ignoring the farming requirements, grazed their sheep on trails used by cattle barons, whose herds were funded by men from England and Scotland, which is to say, some folks wasn't completely all-American as some thought.

Truth was, sheepherders purchasing unusable lots and then squatting in or near cattle country meant serious trouble to those cattlemen. Because they had to take care of the squatting, and that meant in their own manner of violence. And that was a bad way for them Merrills and Johnsons, because not only were they doomed from the outset, but by the very nature of being sheepherders, they fell outside the graces of cattle barons, whose gun-for-hire Tom Horn was nothing less than ruthless, him being a former Pinkerton man of the Pinkerton National Detective Agency and all. He'd once carried their card with the *all-seeing eye* that said "We never sleep" and helped capture and kill his fair share of outlaws. Don't be fooled thinking he was a good man either. Horn, later a range detective, was the cattle barons' "killer for hire," and as a Pinkerton man he'd been allowed to murder more than rustlers, including those who held rights under former iterations of the Homestead Act.

The cattle barons, or cattlemen, having formed a secret society of their own, retained Horn's services both before and *after* he died. During his initial interview with his employers he said directly, "Killing men is my specialty and I seem to have cornered the market." They heartily approved his application. Under their direction, Horn then continued to murder many a late homesteader, leaving notes or calling cards of rabbit or weasel pelts he'd hang from porches as a warning, that if not heeded, led to many a cold-blooded ambush. He'd hide in rocks, or in hills, in tangles of bushes, even up in trees, and would take his Model 1894 Winchester rifle, him being a former marksman for the U.S. Cavalry from the very posse that captured Geronimo, and would lay a bullet in the back of anyone lacking enough wits to heed his threats. He got to being feared, he did, perched on his black horse. That uncanny beast was large enough to fit his enormous frame, and though he tried to disguise himself as a bronco buster, would be seen away from any taming of horses. He sat like some kind of reaper, his mustache and hard demeanor and those piercing eyes half-hidden in shadow. All while that Winchester lay over the saddle horn ready to hurl its venom. Sometimes that sight was enough to scare anyone back from where they came.

Then, on July 15, 1901, Horn committed a murder he couldn't squeeze himself out of, the shooting of the fourteen-year-old son of a sheepherder. Horn had closed a gate that was usually left open, hid among some boulders, and waited for the boy to get off his horse and unlatch the poles from loops of wire. No sooner was the boy done that Horn snuck a bullet into his liver from three hundred yards. Some, including an Indian of renown, said Horn could never have made that shot. But just because some famous old Apache said Horn didn't do it, didn't mean he *didn't*.

Either way, Horn—reason being he either had the gift of gab or just couldn't plain keep his mouth shut—confessed. Something he would not forget was the fact that not a single cattle baron would testify on his behalf, which would have likely spared him the noose. Stranger still was him not exposing a single one of them barons. Was soon after that a date was set for his execution—all his waiting for the noose passed like a short breath of wind. It was a cold fall day in November 1903 when he got jerked to Jesus on the "Julian" gallows. But wait . . . While that flight to eternity was supposed to break his neck, he done cheated again, at least for a short while, because that son of a gun twitched a full seventeen minutes.

Horn had done more killing while alive than anyone ever thought, and that's probably why his corpse eyes got a tinge of green like sea-foam. That and his hanged body, though it been in the ground five or so years, was needed by the same nameless and desperate cattlemen who hadn't defended him, the very same men who'd stole a bit of magic from a certain canyon, a so-called *mother canyon entity* that *they*, meaning the cattlemen, would soon be contracted with for some mysterious reason or other. Said they needed Horn resurrected "not only to take care of our plan for the Merrills and Johnsons, but so that our pact with the canyon is set. *She*, meaning the *canyon*," the cattlemen said, "is about to give birth and we gonna give her all the blood she requires."

It was an elderly Civil War veteran turned cattlehand who pried the lid from a pine box at near two in the morning. Horn's corpse mouth was still blue and bubbly. His eyes flicked like they wanted to come to life, like he'd turned all those nasty thoughts on himself but would soon be ready to turn them elsewhere. That was near to when one of the barons declared, "We need you, Horn. You hear me? We need you now more than ever."

Horn's dull green orbs stared, some say, like he'd been in a short coma with the yellow-*green* fever and not five years in the dirt, dug up during a dark moon. Always did have that midnight personality. They say his own hatred contributed to why his body hadn't completely decomposed before he got dug up. Something in men like that never dies no matter how many times they been hanged. Still, that magic they gave him put some meat back on his bones, though not enough to make him any less rotten.

A little magic paste made from God-knows-what had been smeared on his tongue, though it could have been dripped like sap onto his corneas. Either way, that sorcery done woke him from his time crossing purgatory. No one knows what this magic was or is, or what it been made from, but there it was nonetheless, somehow bled straight from the earth, unexplained, old as the most ancient granite, and learned by tricking both Indians and mother canyon—all of it stolen like them surveyed lands. The cattle barons said they'd stumbled upon this wizardry, something not seen in thousands of years, and in their own way, just like with anything, took it, held it, though they didn't say they learned it in their own foul manner.

Anyhow, some cattle barons said Horn tore himself from that worm-eaten box, started pacing and ranting about like he was gonna get even, but then the cattlemen set loose what they'd planned, an apology for what they hadn't done at his trial, which was to keep him alive. They said this was their way of making amends, *gotta forgive us for what we done* and all that, but damn if Horn didn't still have a gift of gab, he started ranting that with this newfound energy, he might finish off all them cattlemen and settlers, who still been coming in wave after wave by wagons and rails. "I'm gonna be the new terror." Horn coughed up some kind of bile-rot, then told them that's just "the way it gonna be."

That was, until he winked with his one working eyelid and said, "As long as I'm still living, might even forgive the rope for being too tight."

And so, the cattlemen, trying to rein in this living-dead man, and not tell him that he was again their pawn, explained to the corpse out of the sides of their mouths that in plotting their takeover of mother canyon, that this was a deal with her and it required sacrifice, but someone would have to do the murdering besides them. They told him outright that some cattlemen, Horn too, would be rewarded with the very thing them old conquistadores were after, *eternal life*; that there would also be some kind of return from the past in the form of monsters and other critters of darkness, not to mention other things raised from the dead; and that they needed to do this or the canyon, *mother canyon*, would unleash a kind of hell that even Horn couldn't weather. They explained that with his help this could work—all of it. They could spare a number of cattle. They could definitely march these sheepherder families, and could see to it the canyon got what she required, or so they thought, could put man, woman, and child back inside her limestone guts as payment for a birthing she would unleash in a flood of blood and embryo, without killing them with her terror, or releasing it outside the canyon's borderlands.

So you have to learn what Horn gone and done. In fact, he got to being a thousand times more self-important in his second go at living, told all them cattlemen in their midnight gathering at their meeting house in Greybull, every face lit by candle- and lamplight, his breath reeking of spoiled meat and fruit, that if they didn't do him right, hell, even if they *did do him right*, he was gonna teach this canyon mother a thing or two and build an army of monsters and the dead of his own, and set them loose for no good reason on her, on Indians, on last homesteaders, and might include every politician in Washington, D.C., maybe every Mexican and Chinaman too, unless they came to his rally at the steps of the White House and listened to what he had to say . . . That was when the cattlemen told each other that maybe, just maybe, the hiring of this corpse might be a problem.

But that was too little, too late. Horn, dreaming of his army of the dead, tricked them just like he did that boy he murdered, and so went and worked for them cattle barons all over again, made them believe he was chock-full of servitude, though he wanted that magic to himself, yes he did, because after all, *a monster loves a monster*, and *all monsters want to be king*.

Horn though, he could lie when dead sure as he could while living, and acted like he was helping those cattle barons, who reminded him that the Merrills and Johnsons were their sacrifice, to which Horn agreed, not as the cattlemen leader—though he thought himself such secretly—but as their hired gun. He knew they were afraid of the law, afraid of him, that they feared this magic, though they wanted it, craved it, were trying to understand what eternal enchantments could do through such hocus-pocus, and assured themselves that it surely revolved around bargains with this mother canyon. And so, the cattlemen reminded Horn that *she* needed two families' worth of offerings, though none of them cattlemen were a damn bit sure of what they were doing, or why so many sacrifices were required, having stolen, tortured, and killed for these secrets.

I say all this to not only remind you of Tom Horn being a ruthless monster. Or what them cattlemen done. Or of sheep, sheepherders, sheepboys, sheepgirls, sheep everyone eating up all the grasslands. You have to know this is a tale that includes murderous white folks who done their best to bleed the land and bend the will of mother canyon.

And so Horn and some of the cattlemen kidnapped the Merrills and Johnsons, burned homes, and threatened to sew closed some of their victims' eyes, to tie their legs together too, and even have the children dragged. A man of no remorse, Horn said to these sheepherders, "Should never have come to Wyoming with your damn woollybacks. Now you gonna learn why." It was around then he shorn the ears off Stewart Merrill and nailed that cartilage to a tree stump near a main trail as a warning to other sheepherders who might venture north.

It was an unseasonably warm late spring when both Merrills and Johnsons were marched for ten nights. By the end of that first day, feet blistered, eyes turned wild at Horn and his stink. They scraped their arms and legs crossing every rock, only being allowed to graze on day-old hard biscuits and dried meat, while the littlest Merrill sucked the remaining droplets of mama's milk. Stewart Merrill's wife was the mother of that baby, and that mother had a sickness, but tried her darnedest not to hack her lungs right there onto Stewart Jr., or in the dirt, and kept holding that infant tight, swallowing against her sore throat. Stewart himself could no longer hear, not with his head so wrapped, bloody, infected, earless. Their two daughters, Molly and Enola, eight and ten, helped their mother not pass out or fall again, and begged her not to crush the little one, and by the tenth night the ground grew so cold it burned their thighs. That was when little Stewart Jr. stopped moving altogether, his tiny corpse seemed more like something you'd lay under a tree as an offering for some bountiful crop or other.

The grandfather Johnson, along with Michael, his son Richard, his son's wife Esther, their young ones, all tried not to complain, though it would be a lie to say they didn't. Bernice, the youngest, resembled a tiny white imp that might about to leap from her mama's arms. She had the devil eyes, *not lying on this*, she tried charming one of the cattlemen, who, fearing that little thing, made Esther cover the child's face, saying, "Something wicked in that one worse than Tom Horn."

There did come much crying too, mostly before that tenth night. Sometimes the marchers howled like coyotes. But that stopped, all of that, just turned to grim determination, even in Bernice's hidden devil eyes, because while the Johnsons' wrists went raw in their rope ties, the family also sensed something besides malice in their captors, a kind of fear, a kind of pity, a kind of salvation along with that hint of devilry which had been said to them the first night by the corpse himself: "You know how long this gonna take? Ten nights. Just like when cattle get drove, or your damn sheep. We gonna get to know each other. Yes, we are. *Ten sleeps are all you get.*"

And Horn, he didn't stop at that and gave a speech to them captives while they sipped water and fought over a remaining strip of bacon fat. Some say this was the biggest speech he ever gave, since he was used to his guns doing the talking, that something clicked in his head for once, something amid all that rot: that words could be a form of torture too, words that cattlemen often used, and he, of course, was and wasn't in cahoots with the cattlemen, but sure hated every sheepherder there ever was, and might even use them in his army of the dead. Either way, he struck fear in them as their march was coming to a close:

"Someone told you to come take up this new country. Maybe those voices in your heads. Thought you knew the American dream, what it was to come start up all this sheepherding, while we done all the work for you winning over these grasslands, burying more Indians than stars in the sky. But you come to the wrong country, though you hold the Republic in your hearts. These United States ain't but a map and a government that likes to eat fancy in Eastern hotels and restaurants. High-and-mighty politicians who don't know a lick about grazing lands are the kind of men who fill your Capitol. And now you gonna see that it wasn't America in your hearts after all, but cattlemen dreams you wanted to steal. You wanted all we had. And now that you can't have any of it, whatever America you thought you knew gonna bleed right out of your mouths."

Not a thing could stave the fear that every Merrill and Johnson felt at his words. Mothers tried to console each other and their children. They whispered to babies they would go home soon, have a nice supper, that everything would be fine. Said even the sheep was all fine too, though the adults knew every head of woollybacks been slaughtered like the culls that rid southern Wyoming of its swarms of jackrabbits and prairie dogs. Odd thing was, during one stretch of their march, bunch of coyotes howl-yipped as if them dogcritters believed what the cattlemen been saying since long before statehood: "You and your plague of sheep been poisoning this land."

During the earliest part of that tenth night, every Merrill and Johnson been blindfolded, roped together. Some of the men were even gagged after the cattlemen said, "Y'all just won't shut up, ever, will ya? Where you plotting to run off to?" And that was enough to also sew William Johnson's eyelids shut, and for the women and children to talk only in low whispers, to wipe the now-blind man's bloody lids.

Eventually all went quiet except for the whinny of horses, and that endless coyote yip-cry on dusk-lit prairie winds, not to mention teeth chattering around night fires. And everyone, even the babes, thought about ghosts . . . and Tom Horn looked like he'd die again at any moment, incisors dropping from his gummy mouth along the trail.

And soon, well, that very night, they all stood at the entrance to that mother canyon, ghosts welcoming them inside, and Horn smiled through those yellow-green eyes. And then he revealed his new intentions, that he didn't want to only raise an army of the dead. "This place gonna make me young again. Then I gonna live forever and run for president."

Now listen, I got to tell you these other things before I get back to that tenth sleep, that forever sleep, okay? Mother canyon might not recall everything, but it's fair to say she remembers every drop of blood ever spilled. *There's murder in the rocks.* Murder on their granite surfaces. Inside too, in the belly of cold volcanic fury, in every pyroclastic or granite pebble, and every rising pinnacle of limestone. In any mineral thereabouts too, and that rock that formed from mineral sediment so long ago where life itself was ancient, primitive, got killed and remembered. More kiss of death in them than any rock imaginable, where every grain becomes a skeletal fragment. Every coral or ooid or limeclast in them, or string of algae, or brachiopod skeletal micrograin, or tube worm or planktonic foraminifer, and so many, countless *countless*, because *them's* in even the tiniest of fecal pellets shit by marine organisms, god knows what exactly, but those organisms surely murdered, and murdered again, and were murdered, forming entire canyons reeking death and shit and blood, everything compacted into carbonate sediment, and deep inside, so much acid burned at the violence that caverns formed, vast and empty, sometimes with openings to the earth, with air trapped that ain't been breathed since a hundred trillion other exterminations took place, creatures screaming in agony, creatures no white settler or Indian ever knew, or could know of, they could only feel that the canyon knew, her intent, her burn, thoughts like acid, in need of sacrifice, because she was to give birth. And it wasn't ever fair. In no way was the mother canyon being right or just, but she took, so that she wouldn't unleash homicide on the scale of limestone formation, that claustrophobic crush and mineralization, or volcanic formation, or any geologic upheaval into the bloodstream of the world, that epic slice of organic life that had to go back into the land, grain by grain, cell by cell. And then come to find out that every hundred years or so she went through this, you never knew the exact time frame, and that she, mother canyon, demanded blood payment, though she didn't always used to. And her terrors ate and devoured, though was hardly seen, and could be born again and again.

And Horn didn't really understand this, nor did the cattlemen, not yet, and definitely not the Merrills or Johnsons. They didn't realize a thing until after that tenth sleep, when they woke inside the canyon to all those eyes, animal eyes, bird eyes, dog eyes, lizard eyes, dead eyes, living eyes, though every eye was one or the other, or wasn't, because there were hides that rippled, and wings spread, and those legs moved, and teeth gnashed, and they were things that no one had ever seen.

That night Stewart Merrill's wife was glad her baby already died. And that devil child, Bernice—a charmed cattleman took and spared her and she fled with pockets full of magic.

And the rest of those Merrills and Johnsons, they got their ropes cut from their hands, but there was nowhere they could run, not from this, not from mother canyon.

The cattlemen soon retreated, yes they did sure as a gun has bullets, unsatisfied with their new bond because not a single one of them figured out how to live forever besides what they done to Tom Horn. Afterward, they could see that mother canyon had retreated into herself, and knew she would lie dormant for a time, long enough for some of them to pass on what they thought they knew, and what they done to Horn, and wouldn't do to themselves—to make creatures and men live long after cattlemen gone and died—though there ain't been an undead man or woman roaming Ten Sleep in fifty, maybe sixty years. Cattlemen, they say, just don't like seeing their grannies with *dead*-alive eyes.

One day, however, they hoped to learn something new, that maybe the time would come that not too many would have to die to make the magic work, to appease the mother canyon. But that's what this story is about, and you'll have to read on to discover any truth . . .

Horn, however, deserves another mention. Bent on betrayal of everyone and everything he could think of, especially since he'd been betrayed too, Horn went right up to them creatures and rocks to demand of mother canyon that his new eternal life make him king of the canyon, that all of this should now be part of his army.

Been written in cattlemen's logs, and in a few other portions of this story, that this was when Horn lost his head for good, that something fierce took it clean off, making it evident that he would *never be president*.

Some say, if you were to return and put your ear to the cold lips of his decapitated head, he might whisper different. That is, if you can find his head at all.

Many decades passed since the canyon massacre, an atrocity that no one outside of cattlemen and cattle barons had even known. But I gotta say as you enter Greta's story, and the stories of all them animals, that mother canyon has already begun her transformation in ways even she never intended or could foresee.

Blood is again required.

More than a hundred years after the massacre . . .

206 BONES

The calf dragged behind Greta's Yamaha quad and all she could think about was bones.

Cow bones. Human bones. Bones beneath all that sinew and skin, and how many. Both, two hundred and six. Dogs and cats have dozens more. Birds, twenty-five if they're lucky. Cattle have the same number as people, as *her*, she thought, under all that black hair tied up tight, her pierced skin slightly darker than her dad's tatted Mexican American arms ever were. Much darker than Hannah though, whose hair was blacker than moonless nights, who'd been missing for months, though not officially. And this was all gruesome to think about with the dead calf's hind legs roped to the quad, dirty head full of weeds, blood no longer flowing, lungs no longer crying for its mother, bones no longer doing anything, all two hundred and six of them.

Twenty minutes ago the month-old calf dropped dead. That's what Tiller told her. The trail boss who'd hired Greta and Scott, Tiller had been driving the main black-and-white mass of herd across a sea of green and gold, working his quad slowly back and forth, pushing the cattle through prairie and sage, making for distant limestone canyons—still many miles off. This was all part of that grazing ecosystem—that balance between what was profitable and what was best for the land. Not to mention, they had other grazing grounds where this bunch could be made fat and happy, and a proper milking facility. Before that, Tiller had given Greta and Scott the same herding instructions he'd bestowed on them a million times: "Look, this is the way herding goes . . . move slow, some stop to eat, some stray, they advance like a small army, an infestation, eating grass and whatnot, scaring away some critters, attracting others. When animals do what you want, back off on your quad . . . and I don't want to hear anything about a horse being more maneuverable."

And, yeah, that had been the gist of it, the day starting off at the pens outside Ten Sleep, Scott belting out the cattle call that Tiller taught him, *Come on–come on–come on!* with hay bundled to the back of his quad to get them following some kind of prize, funneled out of the pens and on the march. And then, miles later, they didn't use that hay but pushed the herd down the trail, triangulating them with their quads and catching strays, moving the mass of complaints and hoofstrikes eastward with the sounds of their engines.

And then Tiller about that dead calf: "Critter fell like her thin legs were done holding all that weight. Just couldn't take whatever was eating at her."

"That why you came and got me?" Greta adjusted her ponytail, shifted her hips against the quad where she leaned, goggles around her neck. "Poor thing's buzzard meat."

Greta had been creeping along the cattle's western flank, goggles on but not her helmet, *whoops*, ponytail flipping behind her, the breeze ripe with pollen, Greta trying to get a troublesome heifer to keep up. The wide, stumpy bovine, shorter-legged than any other cow, had been enamored with some of the wildgrass amid nearby rocks and a gully of cottonwoods, always wanting to eat where she shouldn't, always wanting to stuff herself even with some of the wildflowers—buttercups and clover around this patch—to chew, regurgitate, chew some more. Greta hadn't eaten lunch, had spent so much time with that bovine, driving over cowshit mounded in the grass. "I'm going to move you"—she nearly poked the beast in a wet black eye—"and then you know what? It's going to be my turn to eat." More than anything, Greta wanted to slap that mess of fur in her hindquarters, get her going. But that could have startled her, made her run the opposite way from the main group eating its way west across the high country. She'd nearly got her interested in rejoining the herd when Tiller called Greta over.

The cow quickly trotted back out to a tasty outcropping of thick emerald stalks.

"You just let the most persnickety cow get her way," Greta complained. "That heifer's gonna eat herself down to Dallas."

"Or up to Billings," Tiller said without cracking any kind of smile. The sun in his face made his eyes squint nearly closed. "Need you to drag a carcass a mile or so back to the main trail and call the renderer. Wait for him and get a receipt. Don't want any accusations of leaving dead cattle."

"Drag?" Greta eyed a lump of hide in the distant prairie grass. "That's a goddam delight. Carrion eaters just waiting for that veal."

"Problem is," Tiller went on, ignoring her, "as you know, phones don't work on this stretch. Gotta head back over that eastern slope, back down to a connection." He wiped his nose with a handkerchief. "Come on with your quad. I'll tie her up."

Greta had known Tiller on and off for several years but still wanted to poke him in his skinny chest for not listening. Why didn't he get that she needed to win out over that wandering cow, chase her down again and teach her a lesson, else the creature would get the best of her. Greta swatted at a cloud of gnats. "I need to move that cow right now." She plopped a remaining bite of jerky from her pocket in her mouth like a prize. "She's going to end up lost in a ditch."

Tiller wasn't having it. "I'm telling you to drag that calf." He scratched at one of the scars near his chin then drove over to the dead calf, not even checking to see if Greta trailed him, which she did.

Greta parked on a dry patch of grass, still positive nature could take care of the corpse, she was sure as anything about that. Flies were already licking at its snot, laying their maggot eggs. "Just who are you wanting me to call?" she asked.

"The dead truck—the renderer." Tiller had already begun winding the calf's hind legs together, leaving a stretch of rope to tie to Greta's quad. "He got a deal now with the ranchers," he said. "Free pickup for dead livestock. He'll come winch the critter into his truck, take the remains to a compost facility."

"Why not all the way back to Ten Sleep? Your dad might wanna turn her into taxidermy. Make her into a little milk shrine." She liked joking but truth was she didn't want to pull that thing ten feet, let alone all the way back to the edge of town where Tiller's dad, *Bobby*, gutted every living thing imaginable, then made that into corpse art.

Tiller lifted his hat, wiped across his head. Greta knew

it wasn't in Tiller's nature to laugh, but he nearly did. "He would," he said, as she cracked a smile.

At the same time none of this seemed good at all. Being ground to meat pellets in a facility sure would be a gross way to end up. And the idea of pulling that carcass? Last thing she wanted was to sound like she couldn't do her job. But dragging it a couple miles or more made her insides squirm. She couldn't admit that to Tiller while she copied the number off his phone, like she also couldn't admit this brought back a particularly messy memory, that after her dad collapsed a few weeks ago, when he weighed all of a hundred and eleven pounds, she saw *him* being dragged worse than this calf.

Cancer had been eating at her old man for the better part of two years. He could hardly walk or breathe, was no longer Gabriel "The Pope" Molina, badass Mexican American truck driver, gun-toter in a black Stetson barreling down highways, picking bar fights just because the pool tables were full, or ordering her and her mother around simply because he thought he could. He'd become a shell, a whisperer, a mutterer. There'd been something both good and tragic in that transition, not having to listen to him butt heads with everyone in the room. There were some parts of him she missed, because she did sometimes love the way he was, the way his voice could lower a notch when he'd say, "Mija, you know I love you." The way he could protect her and taught her to protect herself. And the way he understood the outdoors. He was the first to teach her anything about animals, the misery of nature, the fact that every living thing had to fight for survival. She'd seen it in birds, bears, prairie dogs, coyotes, mule deer, you name it. Sure, there was an order to things. Didn't change the fact that nature had a tendency towards violence, and that made her wonder what would happen to her at the end of everything, even though she'd grown to accept the possibilities. At least she hadn't cried like when she was a little girl and would see a skunk or a possum dead on the side of the road. That kind of loneliness destroyed her insides when she thought about being something small and injured, then abandoned like that. She'd seen a coyote swallow a rabbit in three chews, a bear gnaw on bison ribs, and bovines murdered like the calf, dead and staring. And she remembered sleepless nights, having seen so much death while her old man pointed out each instance, including that gory bison corpse in Yellowstone: "Look mija, that bear is hungry, *hungry*. You don't wanna be no buffalo today."

Her dad died much slower than something on the side of the road or in the prairie. He started living inside himself, having slipped into his own memories, and she and her mom knew he was never going to return. Sometimes he would groan and stare, sometimes laugh to himself, sometimes string words together like he might remember there'd been love in the world. The afternoon he died, he collapsed on the lawn, legs twisted under him. Greta had just rolled up in her maroon hand-me-down Subaru, metalcore blasting from blown speakers, as her mom, like a hungry creature in some slow-motion film frames, dragged his rubbery corpse by one arm across weeds and dirt. Greta turned off both the car and the radio, and her mom said, teeth grinding, breathing heavy: "Don't want your father out in the sun attracting flies . . . Just fell . . . Told him to stay inside today . . . Didn't listen."

Greta couldn't do anything but sit there watching, didn't offer to help at all. She saw her father's head bend back like a rubbery wet stick covered in mud and that dirty brown eye stared back.

So she grunted at Tiller, didn't say what she wanted to say, because last thing she ever wanted was to drag a corpse, and she probably shouldn't have brought up that bit about taxidermy and Tiller's strange-as-hell dad.

She was older now, mature, yeah? It wasn't like she didn't know animals died. She'd driven a few cattle before dropping out of college, occasionally helping move herds near Laramie. But those were only a few dozen cattle over several miles—from one small pen to another. Fifty bucks and free meals. Those days were fun. She laughed a lot, flirted more. She was dating Hannah then, had someone to look forward to no matter what dumb side job she had. They'd seen each for the first time at the Lope, a bar in Laramie, though they weren't on a date, just strangers making eye contact. They met for the first time outside Greta's apartment, Hannah standing beneath Greta's window, smoking. That led to a date, and another, and so on . . . She felt confident those days, beautiful and all that. Not like now with all these heartbreak blues still haunting her, lips all cracked in the sun and wind. She felt like a tomboy, tomgirl, plain, broken, all that shit that she didn't want to think about.

But Greta wasn't so laugh-happy anymore, not about any job. Since abandoning UW two years ago she mostly waitressed, other jobs too, fed horses and goats, cleaned windows with drones, drove a Red Bull car until she crashed it—hadn't told a soul she'd been drunk—just hopped gig to gig after, always hungry for extra cash, for a way to stop dragging her own dead weight. Nothing happy about any of that, really. She knew she made choices that others might not. Those were about all she had, choices not to screw things up, even a simple job like this with a couple old friends. So she had to have this money. She would use it to gas up and get the hell out. Whether or not she'd chase down Hannah—if she was chaseable—or just go work somewhere else, well, maybe this drive would help with all that.

Good thing was, this drive was different than any other. Greta thought it could take her mind off things. A thousand bucks to help move about three hundred and twenty dairy cattle, including ten or so calves, over sixty miles or so to a distant ranch or grazing grounds, she wasn't sure where exactly. Somewhere deep in Bighorn Canyon country, with gas caches stored along the way for the ATVs. No idea why there weren't enough paved roads in this day and age.

Seeing a dead calf wasn't enough to ruin her day. Not that dead things necessarily grossed her out anymore, okay they did, but worse was the tying up of this dead thing that made her uneasy, as if its spirit, or whatever soul-thing it had, was still swirling in its innards, and couldn't be set free, and that felt like some kind of prison that something dead didn't deserve. *Death makes an idiot out of everyone*, she thought, *as if no one can really play the part*, so she promised herself right then she'd never die like that calf and get dragged. And then she imagined herself an old woman and kind of hated and loved the idea all at once.

She stared at the calf's dead brown eye. A line of clear snot bubbled from its nose. "You can't send Scott?" she asked Tiller. She wasn't giving up on this just yet.

"He's a quarter mile away," Tiller said. "Consider this your second test."

She almost laughed at that. "What happened to my first?"

"You couldn't get that cow back into the herd."

"Piece of shit. I coulda moved her."

"How many days you need for that?" he asked. "Look, carcass gonna draw predators sure as anything and that could lead to killing," he went on. "Calves drop dead sometimes, you know that. Your quad can handle dragging her. She was only a month or so old, barely a hundred pounds. And Scott's busy moving the herd in case the prairie grass around there went toxic."

"I can move the herd."

"Whatever, Greta Molina." He said her name with a kind of finality, which she hated, like she was still the same half-Mexican American girl he gave a hard time to before she dropped out of school.

He finished tying the rope to the back of the quad.

She knew right then that was that, she'd have to pull the body.

Though she hadn't seen Tiller in at least a year, he seemed harder, especially so right then, like he'd gone through something he hadn't told any of his friends. He had one scar over his left eye that hadn't been there before, almost like a burn, and another on his lower cheek. She had the sudden thought that a single claw had tried to scoop out his eye and then nicked his cheek. She noticed a limp he'd never had too, like a part of his left foot had gone missing down the throat of a wolf. He'd been emotionally cold even back when they were in college, that was just his personality, though maybe something had happened to further harden his demeanor, something with those wounds, and if she was seeing straight, with his thinning hair. That monotone voice had always been there. The lack of a grin too, and he never hugged, ever. Never seemed excited to be around anyone.

She always brushed that off as him being a loner like her, and, well, a little weird, more than her anyway. Some towns and people around here made you that way whether you liked it or not.

She was hopeful about one thing. He used to loosen up some when he drank, especially if he downed more than everyone in the room. He liked that. It was stupid, but he did, made him kinder, she remembered. She recalled an innocence about him when he was drunk, like he really was a kid inside. For a time that counted for something. Back then she even thought Hannah liked him. She stupidly remembered that maybe she liked him too. One night they even made out, kind of, not really.

She'd been such a jerk afterward, keeping her distance. It was just that the kiss had been off, maybe that whole night had, and she'd done it to make Hannah jealous, and though Hannah said she forgave her, maybe she didn't. She knew she shouldn't have ever slipped. But when you're at a bar, buzzed, and mad at your girlfriend about something stupid, well, it was one of those nights at the Lope that should be forgotten.

All those times doing things they shouldn't have, crossing other boundaries they never should have. Hell, even Tiller's narrow-set eyes and long face seemed cute in that neon bar light, almost normal in the moment. When they kissed, when *she* leaned over to kiss *him*, she instantly pulled away, realized she could find a hundred times more affection in a farm dog, the kind that don't do a thing except lay there and stare at chickens and big white manky mallards named Wingy and Ducklin' all day. And he saw that realization in her eyes, had to, yeah? There'd been no hiding it. And that was unfair, made her a jerk, the fact that she couldn't hide how gross she felt at the time.

And Hannah never cared enough, though maybe she did, that was the problem, maybe what made her leave, though Greta didn't really know. Hannah had even said to Greta's face, "I just don't care about anything anymore." And Greta remembered taking that personal, and then Hannah saying, "I didn't mean it like that," though her eyes kind of betrayed her. And then, because memories all blend together anymore, Greta recalled Hannah disappeared soon after that. Three years together and she just split. Ghosted. Months later and Greta still go'ogled obituaries. And hell no, she wasn't about to ever read her dad's obit. She skipped his funeral altogether. Had to.

Greta and Tiller kept on as distant friends for a while after her flopped makeout, and in a way that surprised her—that they kept any connection at all. He kept on acting like the same cold tap water. Like television static that once filled screens at midnight. And he even was a bit kind when drunk. Or had she remembered wrong? But their distance grew. Pretty soon she stopped seeing him around. He took to working for his family. Grandma's cattle. His dad's taxidermy. And then he disappeared from Greta's life. Until now, until this cattle drive.

Something about those past days between her and Tiller had struck her while she drove to Ten Sleep: *You forgive your friends, forgive their weirdness, forgive not knowing who they really are.*

Then there was that other thing: *You need to forgive yourself.* She knew that. She also knew she was a long way from that kind of self-repair, from letting go of that hot flash of pain still deep from her mess-ups, and Hannah's recent disappearance, and from when Greta refused to help Mom drag the Pope up the stairs to the porch. And then skipping the funeral, yeah, she was a long way from just being happy with things, with processing, with moving on in her present, toward that shiny future that now seemed dull, waxy. She thought maybe it was fading altogether.

When Tiller phoned her out of the blue a week ago, he acted like no time had passed, like their distance had never existed, like they'd just had that ridiculous kiss she could still taste as if something dry and dead had lodged itself in the back of her mouth. He didn't ask how she'd been, instead straightaway wondered if she was available to help drive the herd. And he said it like that too, "I was wonderin' . . ." And that was that. She didn't even ask about the pay. She needed the money, any money. And surely this would pay more than serving at the Ribs N Go.

And now here she was hauling a dead thing, dead like her dreams, the way she sometimes could imagine Hannah dying over and over, though she thought Hannah wasn't dead at all, couldn't be. This deceased same-number-of-bones-as-a-human thing.

She throttled at a slow pace through prairie grass and over ruts, even animal burrows to the anger of everything living beneath. Even the nearby prairie dog town raised its collective fur in an uproar at the macabre parade float, barking and complaining at her, some of their dog bones strewn in the dirt, maybe killed by a bobcat, while a flock of curlews sailed low over the grasslands, calling like scared sky-dogs.

Greta got to pulling the calf faster than she should, in a hurry now along a fenceline to call the dead truck to get rid of the thing. Then she cut across a curve, straight into open prairie to try to save time. It was bumpier here. She didn't care and hauled ass.

She started thinking about the time she busted a wrist leaping off a rope swing. She remembered how the Pope had told her to stop being so damn reckless, but she just swung higher and higher, then flew like some kind of crow, black and diving and twisting through the air. Sure, every kid was stupid at one time or another. She'd leapt from where the swing had been mounted to an oak, tried to get to the moon, a mooncrow taking flight, thinking maybe she could escape gravity. She somersaulted onto her own outstretched hand, came down hard on a root. Then came a *snap*, then hopping up to see the lump that formed under the skin of her wrist. The bone, crunched and jagged, somehow hadn't broken through. She hated that feeling of knowing how broken you could be inside, the shock of knowing how it really was.

Prairie grass soon morphed into repeating memory while she pulled the calf, her family's double-wide trailer somehow transported to the ochre horizon, her forearm floating at an unnatural angle, the young version of herself making her way to their front door, hoping a whooping wasn't waiting just inside the foyer. It *was*. The Pope, having heard her yelp, was just about to wreck her world, grab her by her collar while her unsupported wrist bones ground and jiggled, trying to break free and spill their marrow.

She thought about that door, that thin barrier between

safety and hell, how much she'd dreaded stepping through. It seemed to breathe there in front of her even now, like she could shut off the quad, sneak through to the past. That girl she imagined just stood there, not even crying, arm bent like a snapped broom and wrapped in plastic. She started to think what she'd say to her, how she'd tell her not to be afraid, that the Pope was a temporary shadow, that he'd get dragged across the lawn one day like a dead calf behind an ATV. That middle-aged man so strong then, arms like pipes, finger-vices ready to grip, that black-and-grey beard, the glistening macho earring like the piercings in her eyebrows, eyes like garnets, that godlike baritone voice.

Then her vision shook loose. The ATV's rear left tire slipped into a rut, then a deep hole. The sequence nearly jerked her from the seat when she hit the brakes, and then it was like time stretched itself into infinite uncertainty, a starry hole beneath the quad that could swallow her and the ATV, the calf too.

Fear rose in her throat as the quad jolted to a stop.

She glanced at the stuck, sunken tire. Farther back, a cloud of dirt and fur swirled and faded above the calf.

Moving along this kind of territory was always a stop-and-go thing. Never knew when a tire might slip into a badger den, a hidden prairie dog's sunken town hall or a ditch. Either way, she was now annoyed on top of being annoyed. She didn't want to jump out too fast or the calf's dead weight might jerk the whole quad back on her, then she'd be stuck under the machine with no one to help. She didn't want to untie the calf from the quad and have to retie it, though she knew it might come to that. Better to just throttle slow and steady.

She gave a twist. This rocked the quad forward, sunk the trapped wheel deeper, putting her even more off-balance.

"Goddam it!" she barked. "Scott should be the one doing this." She pulled up her goggles, shook her head—she couldn't be mad at Scott. But, Tiller. Yeah.

"Hell with it," she said and throttled hard, spinning tires, kicking dirt. The exhaust let out a groan along with the sound of ripping and tearing. The ATV jumped right out of the hole. When it did, the rope jerked on the calf and nearly flipped the quad. Strips of tire flew past. The off-balance quad wrenched at such an odd angle that she killed the engine and jumped off.

A shredded mess of rubber covered the ground and axle. Now stuck with a homemade three-wheeler and a calf about to bloat, she pulled off her gloves and checked her phone. Still no cell signal.

She examined the hole, a cut in the earth like something wanted out rather than in. A rusted finger of metal poked from the dirt, having been lodged there a hundred years ago, maybe more. Didn't know what it was, and wasn't about to pull on it or give a kick, the damage had already been done. She just let it protrude like a digit, expecting a metal hand under the earth to pull it back underground someday.

After untying the rope from the quad, she walked over to the carcass. The poor thing lay covered in dirt, weeds, flies, and butterflies slowly flapping pale grey-blue wings. If she'd pulled the carcass over the rut that metal might have split the calf wide open.

"Should I just leave you?" she said, thinking maybe she should have untied it anyway. "Who cares if some coyotes get a free snack?"

She knelt down, not knowing really why, maybe out of sadness that a thing could be so fragile. A wood tick crawled along the calf's white eyelid. Others crept through fur, easily seen in white hair or on pink skin, engorged and blue. One hung on the cow's lip, waiting for Greta to move closer.

She felt bad for the calf, stared again at its dead eye, flicked off the tick. "What would you do?" she said. She could inch along to the trail on three wheels, though she might break her neck in the process. She could just lie about everything, limp her quad back to the herd and say she called the dead truck. She doubted if Tiller even brought a spare. Didn't remember seeing one strapped anywhere.

"I can't pull you like this," she said, not liking either choice.

She decided on a third idea and started walking.

A wind kicked up, whooshing and scratching among grasses, rattling seeds and more pollen, making all kinds of strange noises that Greta hadn't heard over her quad engine. Prairie grass moved like undulating cilia, as if the world hung upside down, could crawl away on grassy legs if you somehow flipped it over. If only she could, she thought.

Some of the land here had formed more than a billion years ago. She knew that, had read about it. While she'd dropped out of the bullshit scam of college and its loan system, she hadn't abandoned learning. She wasn't too shy to check out a library book, and hoarded a personal collection built from one of those little neighborhood libraries run by retired UW biology professor J.A. Maynard. He was always shoving bird guides, novels, even geology books in her hand. "Study this one. There's life all around you, even in the bedrock," he'd say. "You need to understand,

Greta, just how fragile this old world has been." That's how she knew about nature writers like Sibley, Lee, Lopez, and McPhee, and more novelists than she cared to admit. Because of Maynard she knew that distant towering canyons had been carved from shale deposits of Precambrian sediment. They held beads of fossilized algae, some of the planet's earliest known life. She'd read about the end of the world for dinosaurs, fossils found at the asteroid strike, a skin-covered *Thescelosaurus* limb torn at the Tanis fossil site in North Dakota, entombed on an awful day sixty-six million years ago. Fish too that had breathed impact debris. Funny how all of that generated new microbial ecosystems. Subterranean nurseries beneath crater floors, leaking right through rocks fractured by the impact event.

She dreamed of wandering those cliffs, discovering fossils, stumbling into fame for her discoveries, if anyone could be famous for finding anything. Though she would never name anything after herself, that was stupid and one hundred percent ego. She dreamed of the prairie too, those long loping swells, the yellow and green folds, its topography frozen in time, covered with grasses here, sage, coyote, and other brush in other places, all on a land so time-forgotten that Greta thought not even the rocks and dirt beneath could remember where they came from.

The ground sloped upwards here, making the trail in the distance hard for her to find with the naked eye. But with distant rises like purple shadows on the afternoon horizon, she knew where she had to go. Tenth of a mile, quarter mile, didn't matter how much farther—eventually she'd run into the trail.

She trudged up a long slope, down another, and over two more low rolls in the earth, peeking back in the direction of her quad until she couldn't see it anymore. Wasn't like anyone was going to run off with the machinery, though not seeing it made her uneasy. Sure would be a long walk back if she couldn't get a lift with a spare.

The main trail, just over a final slope, came into view. She could see the path stretch far into the grasslands, parallel to sage-covered slopes. Eventually, she knew it turned into a canyon route up past Tiller and Scott, but not for many miles yet.

Her phone now showed one bar—enough to call the dead truck. Starting to punch in the number, she stopped and gazed in the general direction of her quad and saw what seemed a large raptor sweeping low over grasslands, too big to be a vulture. This was the third or fourth she'd noticed, though this bird was the largest she'd seen for sure, probably ever.

Something about its wings she could tell was different—thicker, wider wing tips, long primaries like distorted skinny-fingered hands, maybe some kind of white pattern in the underwings when the bird started to roll away to its right. The angle of its flight was different too, something was off, she could tell.

She'd seen a lot of birds through the afternoon, raptors mostly, hawks and falcons, a few buzzards too, along with the occasional sparrow, a blackbird swarm, several thrashers, a few towhees, too many meadowlarks to count singing along the fences and rattling their exultations in the grass. Sometimes ducks and more curlews flew over, including a lone male Wood Duck. She wondered if she'd ever seen such a duck, maybe? Half the time she could never tell a duck species like Maynard could. They all looked like mallards to her, though some were clearly smaller. This raptor would surely bring others, she thought, the thing having likely sniffed the dead calf on the breeze. What had Maynard told her once? *Species with similar shapes usually have similar habits.* She hated when his voice popped in her head. Better than the Pope when he was mad, though she missed Hannah's soothing whispers. She loathed those fragments of echoes the way she loathed that calf and doing all this walking.

This bird must have been more distant than she thought. Heat shimmered off its wings through the afternoon daylight. Its mostly black wings didn't beat at all, just glided, cut through the landscape, soared like it owned the wind. Then the bird dropped beneath one of the low slopes, and if she wasn't mistaken, somewhere around the quad area, though that didn't seem right, maybe far past it? But then, what if it was past that point? Would it be that large? Sad thing if that carcass got half eaten by a swarm of carrion eaters by the time the rendering truck reached it, then why bother calling?

A moment later the bird's black form shot upwards with big floppy wingbeats. At first she thought a jackrabbit might have been swept into its talons. Then she realized this was too big to be a rabbit, had to be something bigger. And *this bird*. It was large all right, eagle sized, no, *condor* large, jumbo bird sized for sure, though there hadn't been a condor around these parts since Maynard stopped her at his outdoor book kiosk to tell her that Condor 832 had been discovered at the highest point in the Snowy Mountains, that Maynard had seen photos taken of the thing perched atop a rock. She didn't care much at the time, just went on listening. "It was up on Medicine Bow Peak," he said like she'd hungered for every detail. "Disturbingly at peace, staring down at Lookout Lake."

"You know, I just want something to read, something

I can escape with," she told him at the time. "Something I can curl up to with a hot dog and a beer."

Identifying tags on its wings had marked it, he said. T-2. Condor 832. Spit flew from his old lips like he was giving a lecture. "Furthest north a bird like this could usually be seen was Utah. Not this girl. She's been on a five-hundred-mile carrion bender, burning through the American West, ripping through every carcass she could dig her sharp bill into."

Sure as hell, that condor was found dead a few days later near Laramie, probably from eating a dead coyote or deer shot with lead bullets. *Another sad story*, Greta thought when she ran into Maynard again. *Another sad life.* That day he handed her a book on ice floes in the arctic. She tried to tell him she didn't care about ice floes, calving, or how thin polar bears got from lack of food these days. She then wandered off with the book anyway, thinking about big dead stupid birds.

But this bird almost seemed double condor-sized. Almost, because no bird could grow that large, *could it*? And if it was—because it seemed like a small plane racing over the grassland—then whatever was in those talons was larger, much larger than a jackrabbit, meaning that birdplane had dug into that calf. This sent a chill from Greta's stomach into her throat, even into her thighs and arms. She tried to swallow.

As far as she knew, no condor could lift a dead calf. And there weren't any double-sized jumbo condors. If this was such a bird, it would have feasted right there, broke through hide, ripped out organs and meat, chowed like Condor 832 did in her glory days. Whatever this was, if it really was carrying that corpse, then it held on like it was nothing—which meant its wingspan was twice that of any condor.

Her chill continued, freezing up her shoulders and legs

as if an ice wind were blowing from an invisible glacier, even though logic told her that sometimes in the prairie maybe you see what you wanna see. Hell, maybe that ambulance that carried her old man's corpse had been a big metal hog that swallowed him whole. Whatever this was, she felt for that calf like it had been a friend killed out on the dirt. She felt all wrapped up in its hide, that pink skin and sweet dead face, then wished she'd buried the thing, that she'd done something besides walked away to where she was now.

The prairie surrounding her seemed both bigger and smaller all of a sudden, like things even a thousand feet in the sky were watching, could close in any second, like she could run forever and not escape her own nightmares, that even the sky and distant cliffs would eventually press in. Even these grasslands left her feeling on edge, like they might rise up, even in daylight, stuff her mouth full until she choked, that maybe all of this was gonna take her and pin her to that rusted spike that tore her tire to shreds.

She thought all this and watched that bird flap those long wings until it fused into a speck that disappeared into the haze of coming dusk. A moment later, still feeling watched, still chilled, she figured to hell with the dead truck and started walking back to town for that spare and a ride.

The Sparrow

The small birds scattered from their rusted perch when the machine wheeled over a small rise toward them, the dead calf flopping behind. Then came a smash of metal and engine, followed by a roar from the woman sitting atop the machine.

The birds had darted over the wildgrass, their tiny minds aware and sparking as if an ultraviolet cloak had descended around them. They landed on a clump of sage, the prairie encircling them in a wide, large vista. Uncertainty unfolded in all directions. The birds had already been wary of dangers here, a sky that could unleash terrors—hiding in front of the sun, or the grasslands and shrubs that could suddenly release hungry shrikes, snakes, or foxes. The machine was something they hadn't seen except from a great distance.

Before the dust could clear, the birds, though scared as usual, started singing their complaints.

Then the woman stormed off. Most of the little brown birds used this as their opportunity to return to the same wildgrass perch. Some fluttered to the machine's handlebars and started trilling and chittering all the more. A couple, however, landed on the ground, began consuming small pebbles that helped them digest the seeds already in their stomachs.

Then came the warning. A quartet of plump Eastern Meadowlarks chirruped, then a meowing Gray Catbird chattered. Some Brewer's Blackbirds and a lone crow joined the *squawks, tinks, kedekekeks, vreets,* and *trills.* A bawling Mourning Dove cried somewhere close.

Fear of the sky-thing echoed across the sloping grasslands, warning that its shadow was closing in from where it soared in the thermals a thousand feet up.

These little brown birds were mostly a mix of sparrows. One was a bright little Chipping Sparrow with a rusty cap, pale grey chest poufy and soft. The others numbered fourteen Lark Sparrows, each with black, white, and red cheeks and striped crowns reminiscent of veins in wet river rocks. They skittered into the grass. A male Lazuli Bunting joined them—colorful as if a bit of pure cerulean sky lay on its head, tail, rump, even on its back and wings. Its belly and wing bars shimmered white. The bunting *chipped* once in case another was nearby, then along with all the sparrows, went quiet and still.

The Chipping Sparrow had been the first to hide, but was also the most curious. She knew what the sky-thing was coming for, not the little birds like herself, but the dead calf, so poked her head out while every Lark Sparrow hid. She spied and spied, quickly inching her way upward for a better view, head on a tiny swivel, tiny claws clinging to a sturdy grass stalk.

Then an immense shadow fell onto the prairie. The chipper felt a wind from the sky-thing swooping in. It didn't smell good. Air shifted and pressed against the sparrow's tiny striped back. Then a darkness and cold fell from a blotting of the sun, from those enormous spread wings. The sky-thing's talons reached for the calf. And though there came hardly a sound while the chipper held still in the grass, the tiny sparrow felt a scream inside her pale chest. Her little heart raced and shook as if she were flying with all her strength, but still she held on and spied, and did so in the same manner in which she recently watched dead things walk through the grasses. In the quickest of moments, she saw darkness and dust, and as the calf was lifted, four rubbery legs, its broken neck, and the immensity of the sky-thing, its eye many times larger than the sparrow's head.

And then both the dead calf and the sky-thing were gone, and the Brewer's alerts came again, then turned to *chit-chattery* song. And then the sparrows, all of them forgetting their danger, flew to the crash area.

The Chipping Sparrow landed on the handlebars of the ATV, and the Lark Sparrows circled, some of them perched, singing alongside the chipper, while the rest landed and foraged along the ground. And they felt safe again, and this was the way it was, they knew. Dangers came and passed. They knew that sometimes some of them might be taken, and they cried when this happened, because even the little sparrows loved each other and could feel heartbroken at the way of the world.

But they sang now, and the Lark Sparrows ate seeds loosened from the grasses and that had fallen from the calfskin. And then the Chipping Sparrow landed by the rut with the spike sticking out of the earth, and swallowed more tiny rocks. Then each sparrow grew tired, but kept singing nonetheless, because the falling sun brought this out of them, to sing about the end of day, about the coming of darkness. In their songs this time came the chipper's warning, that the next day might bring that sky-thing again, and if so, she knew she would watch closely, she would spy again.

And then the sparrows flew to shrubs surrounding a distant cottonwood, and though they didn't sing, made little *tink*s and *whine*s while they made themselves comfortable. Then the chipper huddled close to one of the much larger Lark Sparrows. And then another chipper flew in, another female, and the two chippers snuggled, their rusty caps touching, they'd known each other since birth. And soon one of the chippers dreamed of the great eye of the sky-thing, and also dreamed of flying above it, and soon in the dream felt her own wings break from a great dizzying wind, and felt herself swirl toward that eye, spinning and spinning out of control, and then woke terrified in the darkness, knowing in that instant the morning would bring songs of fear, and so she sat awake for a while, and felt haunted by the rustling in the distant grasses, by owls screeching in the sky, and imagined the dawn's rebirth as a way to calm her startled heart, and tried to remember a golden light.

Night One

Not a lick of breeze washed over the grasslands by the time Greta neared camp, a new tire on her quad. It was nightfall.

She rode slow, headlights shining across dirt and grass, having cut two or so miles over uneven terrain from where her tire had blown. She needed this week of soul-searching, she thought, just being out under Wyoming stars. This kind of side job should be a paradise for thinking now that the bullshit of a blown tire was over. Besides, no late-night restaurant shifts at Ribs N Go working with assholes, where she got fewer and fewer shifts of any kind, serving racks of baby back to jerks who objectified the same body parts that Hannah used to compliment. The prairie was difficult but different. Just hard, mindless work moving cattle. Long days of weanlings sucking air, some getting at bags of milk in between walking or trotting, cows chewing vegetation, mamas complaining about whatever mama bovines complain about during a long day's push, every cow in a loose herd moving along the trail and tall grass, kicking up dust, complaining, always complaining, but following an invisible bucket of food while the ATVs slowly crept behind, pushing them toward the next camp. While driving them, Greta was free to let her mind roam.

And soon, good times under the stars. She would be glad to finish pushing through the dark so she could lounge under a tent before the early morning push, maybe read a book with her headlamp shining down on a page, maybe gossip with Scott about the world, tell him and that stone-faced Tiller what she's been up to, why she hadn't talked to them in so long, maybe tell them that life was just, you know, spinning in this age of anxiety everyone seemed to be in, that maybe things would soon feel less stressful, come back together, pieced into something, some kind of direction for her future. At least she had on her plaid coat to keep her warm in the cool night air. Even though it was dirty, it was her favorite bit of clothing, having belonged to Hannah.

Then she hit a small rut in the dark and had a minor panic all over again, and that image of the bird played out in her mind. All she could think about was the way it swooped out of the sky, lifted the calf carcass like it was nothing. Though maybe it had just been a buzzard, underwings reflecting weird in the afternoon light, and then maybe had picked up some fat woodchuck she'd run over. The more she thought about it, must have been her imagination.

But what if it had been the calf? She let that sink in, play out, while she burned along the trail, headlight illuminating every scurrying mouse and snake. Even a badger scuttled out of her way, eyes shining like pale blue ghosts.

Thing was, and she really thought about it now, if that extra-large, jumbo, king-sized, double Big Gulp buzzard or eagle or unlikely condor *could* do that to a calf, it could do the same to her, just pluck her off her quad, carry her away to some cliff, rip her apart, scatter each of her two hundred and six bones. No one would know and that made her squirm in her seat. That bird defied gravity, really, whatever it was. And it was enormous, had to be, yeah? Because could that have been a woodchuck it was carrying? *Nope.* Not with legs that long, if those were legs she'd seen. And the real thing was, no eagle, especially no vulture could lift a month-old calf. Maybe an eagle could heave a just-born. Definitely a fawn, a young coyote, even a baby goat. But not a calf that weighed a hundred pounds.

Maybe other birds had already been on the ground tearing in, making the calf a soupy mess of innards, entrails exposed like long pink industrial tubing. Maybe the bird was smaller than she thought, had made off with a strip of hide and meat that dangled in the shape of what her mind wanted it to be, an entire calf. Legs could have still been attached. And maybe she wanted to see that, like maybe shit had been so bad in her mind about Hannah, her dad, and everything, super itchy in the back of her mind, that her mind cooked up a giant bird because she wanted, no, needed to experience something spectacular in her droning life. Goddam, why couldn't she imagine some goth girl bringing her movie tickets, or taking her to a beach house getaway, you know, a way out of this mess. Or Hannah showing up the way she had at the Lope their last night together. Would she just say the same thing all over again? *Don't make all your shit about me. You want America, or your life or whatever to be this really big place. And it's not. It's small. We're not even as big as this bar. We'll be forgotten before morning. When we're really gone, no one will remember anything but all this light* . . .

Why did this thing have to be maybe picked up by a giant

bird? Like, no one wants to hear about giant bird fantasies, or spaceships, or ghosts, or all that bullshit anyway.

Except the entire *thing* was missing. When she got back to her broken-down quad with Tiller's dad Bobby, and a spare, she'd scanned the area with a flashlight. Not a bone in sight. No fur. No fluff. No head. Not even a leg or hoof. Even the rope tied to its hind legs had disappeared.

"What are you looking for?" Bobby had growled. He'd driven her back and said maybe two words before then, those old knuckles tight on the wheel, him sipping a Milwaukee's Best like it was teatime. Thank god she'd approximated a GPS pin when she finally had wifi—though sometimes her map app half worked even without connectivity—or they might not have found the quad until morning. They'd keep their phones off most of the rest of the time, this wasn't the kind of country where you could always keep in contact with the outside world, and that was fine with her for the duration of this job.

"I don't know." She searched the dirt around that rut and finger of metal. "I untied the calf here."

"That skin and bones splayed out there somewhere," he said. "Probably got dragged. Then carried away in parts." He glanced into the evening sky like he'd heard some kind of groaning from the moon, then scratched his grey scruff, or beard, or whatever that mess was on his face that was hiding some serious scars on his chin and neck. His eyes were big compared to Tiller's, two grey orbs flickering with light, black pinpoints in the centers like portals to someplace awful, she didn't want to know where. And the way he spoke, those sentences dripped, lingered too long, like he was pulling a knife along a belly. It was the kind of voice you didn't want stuck in your head, that she was sure of.

"Probably got mostly devoured in minutes," he added. "Should have called the rendering truck before you started walking. Now we might have more coyotes and cats. Maybe a wolf or bear, especially if that corpse still around."

She'd only grunted a reply. Coyotes always around anyway, she wanted to say, though she wasn't going to argue the point like she would with Tiller and blurt out, *What, an entire zoo hanging around out here for a calf?* She wanted to spend as little time as possible with Bobby while picking up a spare, riding around in the dark out on the trail, changing a stupid tire. It was bad enough she had to walk to his taxidermy shop, Creative Creatures. She'd stood outside, seeing that animal blood trickling from a pipe near the front stoop, that dark rivulet puddling in the street, only this time it looked even blacker than when she saw the goopy mess that morning. In the dusk it made her hair raise, that bloodline glistening from creatures bleeding out all day long, for weeks, years. Animal after animal after animal.

Tired from her long day of riding and then her walk to Ten Sleep, she'd slunk through the taxidermy shop entry beneath dozens of dark faux eyes, then down a hall, tracking Tiller's dad to where he emptied the insides of a raccoon. A gutted fox lay nearby just waiting to jump up and haunt the place.

"Heard you come in," he said. In front of him two metal sinks and a counter, all coated in bits of flesh and splatter. A pipe from the right-hand sink ran the course of the room along the baseboards, then disappeared beneath the floor, emptying outside.

She didn't say anything while surveying the room. On the counter lay an array of knives for skinning, fleshing, disassembling—all manner of surgical work: scalpels, skifes, razors, a necker, a smooth-bladed fish flesher, not to mention horse-tail glue brushes, wire brushes, surgical and glover's needles, scissors, a well-used ear opener, a bird flesher, and a blood-splattered staple gun. Besides the assortment of random hides and antlers on shelving behind him, she could see prefabricated molds, from those for the smallest of mice hides to those that could fit possum, badger, or deerskin.

Another shelf had been lined with pigments, tin-catalyzed liquid silicone and urethane rubbers, foams, plastics, and bottles of acetone and lacquer thinner, and several paint kits. All kinds of pastes, adhesives, and glues had been arranged next to those like trophies. Super gel glue for hides, gap glue, fish paste, even a big bottle of KILLER GLUE, a two-part adhesive for damp applications. She wanted to squeeze some of that onto the throttle of Tiller's quad, watch him panic and stampede the herd for causing her this mess. There were bowls filled with teeth: raccoon, bobcat, mountain lion, bear, fox, snake fangs, all kinds, each carefully labeled; and marble eyes of every color, some that promised to glow in the dark. Some looked like obsidian. She imagined them in her dad's skull, wondered what the Pope would have looked like being dragged across the front yard at night, faux eyes wide, glowing in the dark. But then she saw Hannah's face, her eyes glowing, that long hair wrapped around her cheeks, Hannah not able to push the hair away from her chin like she always did.

It wasn't long before Bobby gazed at her. If he was surprised, he didn't show it. "Why you here? My kid . . . He better not have fucked something up."

"You work late," she'd said, trying not to be freaked out by the raccoon's pale tongue lolling out of its mouth.

"I'm always working." He scraped at the inside of the raccoon, hollowing it out. There were those eyes again, so grey, not a hint of white or yellow, she thought. She hadn't noticed how purple and dry his lips were, how spiderlike red capillaries stretched thin across his pale cheeks. And those strange scars in his scraggly neck and face scruff peeking out like little worms.

"Moving the herd, or more like settling in to camp, I guess," she said.

"You guess?"

"I need a spare."

"Spare what?" He grimaced at the dead raccoon in his hands. "This one's about used up. Ain't got any extras. Gonna be made to look scared of a bobcat. Got the cat over there in that pile of skins."

Greta had seen the mound of dead things on a nearby table as if a giant irradiated mass from a monster movie had made its way there to die. Couldn't tell what was what other than possum and bobcat heads poking from the monstrosity of legs and flaps of skin and hide.

"A tire." She wanted to glue Bobby's face to the wall.

"He didn't bring any?" Tiller's dad wiped his hands on a rag, fingers still glistening with water, blood, or both. He popped open a cooler by his feet, pulled out a Budweiser, didn't offer her one, then set it back in the cooler and pulled out a Milwaukee's Best.

That raccoon corpse kept staring.

"Just tell me where you keep them," she'd said. "Happy to do it myself."

Bobby hadn't liked that either, made a clicking sound.

She wondered if he had a raccoon tongue, the way he licked at those lips.

"You're not gallivanting around my sheds and pens unsupervised," he said, draining more of the can. "Go wait in the lobby. I'll see what I got. Take me fifteen to finish up. Can't believe Tiller don't have spares."

When she didn't move, he grew agitated: "Got something else to ask?"

"Why do you call him Tiller when that's his last name?"

"It's what we always called him."

She still didn't move.

"Something else?" he said.

She thought for a moment, didn't want to really say, though she had to ask: "Are there any big birds around here? You know, large raptors."

"Jesus Christ, you want to ask about birds? Got raptors of all kinds, eagles, hawks . . . I pretty them up too."

"I mean, like, larger."

"Why would you ask that? Nothing larger than an eagle."

"Saw one a long ways off. Seemed bigger than normal."

He took another drink. "There was that one bird everyone talked about. Died soon after they found it. Another one like that would be rare as rare could be."

"Heard about the condor," she said. "No others? Nothing bigger?"

He downed the rest of the can then tossed it on top of tangles of loose fur, bloody bones, god knows what else. "Anything like that would be a curse, wouldn't it?"

"I don't know," she said. "Maybe. Depends on the curse."

He got out a second beer but didn't open it, pulled on a light coat. "You gotta understand, a land like this has history bled into the rocks. And blood don't come easy. But let me tell you, any curse there *was* we wrung out of the land years ago." He shoved the can in a pocket. "All them immigrants. All them Indians before that. All them sheep lands too. It was a curse to graze or run cattle on the same land as them sheepherders—you know that, right? We fixed that too . . . a long time ago. So if you're seeing things, that's you trying to bring something back that's been gone long as anyone can remember. Now you go wait in the lobby. Be there shortly."

Creative Creatures, as far as Greta could tell, was a rip-off made to look like a hunter's trophy room with high ceiling beams and damp, log-cut walls. She wandered beneath big cat skins that hung from rafters, some still with paws attached. Every inch of the room had been stuffed with dead things—mounted rhino, elk, pronghorn, moose heads, raccoons, bears—some poised to run for their lives, others trapped in stillborn images from their lives of survival and violence. She ran her fingers along the hide of a moose. It was a young one, and stood tall as her. She wondered what it would have felt like with a beating heart beneath that coarse fur.

She turned to a mountain lion, then a line of possum, feeling uneasy amid these shells of animals, like she was going to be part of some natural history museum herself if she wasn't careful. She sat down on a chair near a front counter, pulled out her phone, and went straight to the dictionary. Still obsessed about words—dropping out of college hadn't killed her desire to summon the etymological origins of things—she googled that taxidermy was a Greek combination: *táxis* meaning arrangement, *dérma* meaning skin. *Pretty gross if you think about it*, she thought. *Who wants to arrange skin?* Is that really what all of this was, the art of skin?

She read about zoologists and ornithologists stuffing birds with spices hundreds of years ago, embalmed birds and alligators given as gifts for kings and queens who wanted to start dead-thing collections, then how people wanted to raise the dead, see an afterworld in diorama form, not to mention preserve, embalm, stuff, hang, put animals in a cage, as if dead things might worm themselves back to life. She wondered how many bones were tossed, or fed to dogs.

The room reeked of chemicals, blood, skin, fur. More molds sat on shelves. Random skulls, jaws, marble eyes, jars of teeth. If somewhere in the world was a lost sheep, here it was literally by the front entrance. She eyed spirals of fat white fluff submerged in a tank of formaldehyde and wondered what possessed Tiller's dad to do this to the animal, like an odd kind of fish tank, let alone put such a thing on display. She never thought the sheep or any of the taxidermy, including the pair of cocker spaniels by the front desk, seemed alive, or were even remotely lifelike. She thought they might hop up and greet her, but like little zombies, like lifeless automatons that wouldn't even smell the back of her hand, because they hadn't just lost their olfactory senses, they'd lost every glimmer of life force, recast in a marble-eyed sick glow, every inch of what they'd been sucked out, gouged from ocular cavities, scraped from skin, poured down drains, tossed in the garbage, sprayed clean, drowned away. She wondered if these spaniels and that chemically drowned sheep had been the family pets, that maybe all of this was like a childish obsession with a jar of drowned butterflies and bits of grass and flowers, as if a container filled with every fox and bear cub and chunks of tree and earth had been filled with water and swirled around, becoming a crude tomb failing at mimicking life at every turn, because nothing felt real, looked real, smelled real—all for this white man's desire to gaze at death, and to further control, to bring his own version of the eternal, which made him what, besides an asshole . . .

Hell, when her cat died, she cried to Hannah, *Put that carcass in a trash bin*, never wanting to see the furball again. But she loved that cat and had just been in a ridiculous panic. She remembered nights where she would tap one of Izzy's white paws and pat her dog Connor, then grab her coat and keys, and say, "I gotta go, piglet," to the dog. "Take care of Iz while I'm out." Then to the cat, "You can sleep on me later, you rug." Didn't mean she wanted to see either turned into taxidermy. And goddam it all if she wanted to face that dead calf standing out by her quad, posed like a happy bovine cherub eating plastic buttercups. Hannah buried her cat for her, at least there was that.

But there was another cat in here, an orange one still with its tag "Catcat," and that one stood next to a chinchilla of all things, as if the two were best friends, or maybe friends with a falling out, the cat running away from the chinchilla. After putting away her phone she'd spied three baby black bears and two juvenile raccoons drained of their insides, made to look like they were trying to scramble onto branches, forever frozen, like that had been their most difficult moment in life, not meeting the hunter's gun that took them down, or the poison that maybe melted their insides.

Trout appeared bent like rubber, having swum through Bobby's creepy imagination onto shelves. A coyote, frozen, seemed trying to sit up, back legs blurred into pelt. Fish bones in jars of liquid, strange heads, and spines too, sometimes in neat rows. Several badgers blankly stared, hopefully at an internal universe of star-glow and colliding nebulae, she thought, externally in fake growl pose, as if death was just an annoyance that no creatures could really understand. Weasels had been glued to sanded and stained branches like they were peeking over pristine limbs. Foxes forever caught mid-leap as if these were afterimages, like they'd been frozen in an atomic explosion, bushy-tailed, playful, dead, missing their hind legs. A bobcat mother and her kittens, animated, all floofy, poufy, dead-cute, spritely, though probably drowned in a bag, or hacked to death with a knife, maybe shot one by one on the side of a trail, each furball crying and confused.

On the walls she read National Taxidermists Association Convention, Competition & Trade Show winner certificates from years past. HUNDRED-DOLLAR WINNER BOBBY TILLER, BEST ALL-AROUND TAXIDERMIST. FIFTY-DOLLAR WINNER BOBBY TILLER, MASTER'S CHOICE AWARD. HUNDRED-AND-SEVENTY-FIVE-DOLLAR WINNER BOBBY TILLER, DISTINGUISHED TAXIDERMIST AWARD. And so on until you got to his biggest prizes, of which he had seven, though one stood out: ONE-THOUSAND-DOLLAR WINNER BOBBY TILLER, THE BREAKTHROUGH BEST OF SHOW AWARD. That one was attached to a framed photo of the front half of a black bear mounted to a wooden column like it was about to maul some hapless hiker and scoop the insides like a breakfast burrito bowl.

Congratulations, Greta thought. *Bobby, you're a goddam champ.*

Photos placed between certificates included a Bengal tiger freeze-framed to appear to take down a water buffalo. Fake viscera spilled from a neck wound. Another, of a lion's mouth on the neck of a zebra, both shot by a hunter who wanted a still-life trophy recreating not his hunt, but one typical of animals hungry for each other. Greta imagined a new scenario. A dead white hunter forever frozen, aiming his rifle at a terrified zebra. In another photo, an elephant stood like it had just finished its thousand-mile-or-whatever trek to a watering hole during a sub-Saharan drought. Nope. This elephant was a goner, all water and blood drained from its corpse, sucked out, leaked onto a street, or down a pipe into a sewer somewhere, maybe even bled into the ground, skin and tusks shipped to Wyoming in a big grey sack of itself. And then a small section titled ART IS LIFE. Beneath the sign, a poster of a kitten tea party, every puffball dead as dead could be and dressed to the hilt, arranged around a table. Not cute, she thought, very dead. Very sick.

It was then she thought she heard a rustle. Could be anything—a live rat caught in this mess, a lonely house cat made to live among the dead. She half expected someone to be standing there. The Pope. *Hannah.* Maybe her grandmother she'd once been close to, still with the senility and that line of drool about to wander from her bottom lip. And then she realized that every single dead thing in the room already looked about to pounce on her, including a long row of mice.

For a moment though, another sound. Not rustling this time. Thought she heard a voice, even turned toward the hall, half expecting someone to hover there, toes pointed down, tips scraping the wood floor. The sound had stopped. It came just once.

Grettaaaaaaaaaaaa.

So faint, so whispery that she wondered if it came from her own lips, something she wanted to hear, wanted to have sung to her. She leaned into the chemical air and thought maybe the sound had been a throat wheeze, but from whose. Her own?

Then something caught her eye. Coming over the side and back of a wolf. She thought she saw something working through thick grey fur, and then she saw skin, *human* skin, bits of wrinkles, knuckles, fingers. So familiar, but not, like Hannah's fingers with tattoos of stars. Dirty, tattooed fingers digging into fur. And maybe, just maybe, there, like the top of a dark moon, the crown of a head, a blackened scalp. Hairs on the back of Greta's neck stood, her insides turned to stone, and she felt that same inner coldness from when she saw that bird.

Then she blinked, and tried to reason through her fear, thought maybe she'd seen the rack of antlers on the other side of the wolf, which she imagined as fingers, then imagined them moving, and told herself that she was seeing things, hearing things, that maybe she was hoping Hannah's face would be there in the room, hovering, dead, alive, she didn't know, but ready to tell Greta where she'd gone—to work somewhere, to the big beyond, the big sky, to another country?

It was then that Tiller's dad, Bobby or whatever, finally appeared in front of her cradling a taxidermy fawn. "Look like you seen the soul of a bear," he said. He held out the creature. "Gotta fix a hind leg," he muttered like he was going to repair an already-dead thing for the afterlife, send it up in a motorboat out back.

"Spare's ready with some extras," he added, set the fawn on a table. "Truck's out front. Let's get you back on that damned trail."

Greta's mouth turned to cotton. Not at Bobby, but that thing he held. Not just any deer, this was a nightmare creature. A baby goat head had been sewn to the body of the fawn. Its left hind leg was bent like the poor thing had tried to stand, forgetting how rigid it had turned the day it died.

The campfire glowed from a low rise.

Greta cut the quad's headlights and engine, while Scott stood by the fire cooking hot dogs. He gave a small wave while she thought about what Tiller said earlier in the day when asked if anyone would be driving cattle by horseback.

"Good horse cost more than a quad," he'd said, then blew snot into a big red handkerchief. "But a horse ain't got headlights."

She wanted to crack that same joke, break the ice, sing: *A horse ain't got headlights!*

But soon as she pulled off her goggles Tiller came out of the nearest tent, face contorted in the firelight, complaining.

"Have a cold beer in town while we busted our asses rounding up strays, bedding down?" he growled. "Watch the Rockies play a double header?"

"You know, might help if we had satellite phones," Greta said.

Scott's hot dogs smelled like heaven on earth. She hadn't eaten a thing since breakfast except that lump of jerky. She could chow down at least three dogs.

"What am I supposed to do with one of those," Tiller said, "put in a dessert order? I don't need a phone. I need you here."

Greta aimed a thumb at her quad. Two spares had been corded to the back rack. "Brought two since this quad is a piece of shit. Not that I needed a rescue or anything."

"What are you talking about?"

"Take it easy, Tiller." Scott handed her a plate with two hot dogs, buns soaking in a pile of beans. "She must have blown a tire. Got no spares, bro."

Greta was a tough-ass Chicana, but she was grateful for this assist. It worked too. Tiller walked off and sat by the fire. Didn't even offer an apology. What really bothered her though? Neither of these assholes had gone looking for her when she didn't come back from dragging the calf.

"You just assumed I went to town?" she said to Scott.

"Yeah, Tiller seemed to think maybe you quit. He was trying to figure out if he had to go back to town, hire somebody else real quick. He was thinking Courtney Sides. Remember her?"

"So . . . you didn't think that maybe I crashed . . . that maybe I got bit by a rattler?"

"That would have been bad."

"You think? Do you also think I can't do this job?"

"I didn't say that. Tiller just thought . . ."

"I know."

Scott wore his usual yellow-and-blue beanie and checkered coat. He was six feet, four inches, pretty much all beard from the neck up, definitely looked wilder than last she'd seen him. Definitely the nerdiest Black outdoorsman she'd ever seen. Besides, she knew if he wasn't making some side cash, he was buying Marvel comic books of some kind and hiding out reading them, maybe digging into some PlayStation devil game in an online multiverse.

Star Valley always did that to Scott, she thought. Made him wilder when he went home. College had cleaned him up for a time. He'd gotten focused, dressed like a student who wanted to impress the boys and girls, trimmed that monster beard. But like Greta, he was done with all that, had gone back to work in his family's furniture shop, took odd jobs too. Looked like he could be in some grizzly bear gang with that facial hair. She wasn't even sure if his parents were paying him. She could see the unhappiness in the dullness of his eyes, a kind of longing to escape.

She hated Star Valley. Drove through more than once. Nothing but a Burger King and dinosaur bones and this vibe that you should get what you came for then get the hell out. "Starvation Valley" Scott always called it. "Can't even get a fish out of Salt River," he'd say. His soul had starved too, and that's really what he meant, that living there made him dead inside. He was ex-Mormon and always made sure to let his friends know how tough he had it growing up being adopted, Mormon, and Black in Star Valley. Not to mention his comic book habit.

She knew why he was on the cattle drive too. Same economy. Similar problems. He didn't want any more than she did to toss the dice and go back to school just to pile up more debt. This job was a way forward. Get paid a chunk of change, maybe get to a new town, find a new shit job, try to figure things out from there. Greta understood that when you burn through a place, you kind of want to try somewhere and something new. She was now thinking Arizona, down by the border, close to Madera Canyon and all those beautiful rare Mexican hummingbirds that cross imaginary lines. Maybe Scott would come with her. There was a town called Portal. She could live in a place with that name. Teleport through one to a new life, maybe try to forget Hannah. *Right.*

California here I come.

Greta took a chair by the fire and dug into her plate of

food. She turned to Scott, mouth half-full. "You like being back home?" She already knew his answer.

Scott seemed to read her mind just fine. "Nah."

"Figures." She was still chewing but already about to start on another dog.

Scott poked at the fire. "Let's just say I need this job."

"Enough to work with Tiller for ten days and nights?"

"I'd work with his grump ass a month if it got me out of Wyoming."

"Leave me out of it," Tiller said, back for another helping of beans. "Lucky we're not night herding."

"You want to move the herd now, let's go," Greta said. "Pack the tents. I can stay up all night. I got hot dog energy."

But Tiller didn't say anything, and Greta, far more tired than she realized, soon slipped into the pit of a dream, hearing herself say over and over, *A horse ain't got headlights*, and didn't realize in her stupor how this was the kind of dream that felt like she'd never been asleep at all, just aware of darkness and stars, of the moonglow casting its milk over everything.

When her eyes opened something startled her. The fire was near to dead, and the night seeped its chill on her. Both Scott and Tiller had gone to their tents. She wondered if she'd heard something but could only grasp the remaining crackle of fire and all the crickets out in the fields chirping love songs to each other. There was something else too as Greta sat there still as could be, something that made the stars feel like they were about to drop their knives, or maybe the earth might kick up dust and howl right there out of the pit's embers. And then she scanned where the stars met earth, and saw an obvious rocky ridgeline lit by the glow of a half-moon. On it, which was clearly above the herd, something faintly lit by the same dim celestial light, someone, *something*, maybe in her dream if she wasn't awake, or maybe in her reality, standing silent. Couldn't make out who or what, and whether or not it had a mouth like a human, a mustache on its face, a cowboy hat on its head, or a pale grey bald lump atop its neck. All she knew was it cast fear into her gut. This feeling told her she needed to run away, leave everything behind, though somehow she couldn't flinch, could only stare back and wait for the thing to move from where it stared. It had to be staring.

It was staring.

Grey light drowned the pale form, its milky skin, or clothes, and long arms, its breath coming like smoke, Greta swore. She wasn't sure if she saw a flicker of wings. She wasn't sure of anything.

Below the ridge, cattle frozen in sleep began to feel something too, she thought, because they began to wake, to stir in their own fear, while Greta, hit by this wash of dread, still trapped as if in her dream, or whatever it was, maybe not even a dream at all, stood and watched the thing take its eyes off her and slip away.

"Tiller's gone," Scott said, shaking Greta into wakefulness.

She didn't know what she was seeing.

Scott's beard and breath hung over her. He was in her tent.

"Get off me," she finally said, heart racing. "Jesus, you're a hairy Sasquatch."

"Sorry," he said, backing up. "Don't know what's up.

Thought maybe Tiller was sleeping outside. When I got up, he wasn't anywhere."

"What time is it?"

"Two in the morning."

"Yeah, well I need sleep," she said. "Why aren't we taking turns watching the cattle anyway?"

"Tiller didn't want to. He thinks they'll be fine, that we can wake fast enough if some bear comes. What happened to your hot dog energy?"

"Wore off."

"Where you think he went?" he said from outside the tent now.

She poked her head outside, then stepped completely into the dark. "Maybe he heard something."

"Like what?"

"A bear. A wolf. I don't know." With the fire dead, she could see the Milky Way hovering close like its thorny starpoints might pour over the land. "Maybe a cow got sick. Maybe was making double sure to lock down the food away from camp."

"A cow didn't get sick."

"How would you know?"

"You think he's all right?"

"I'm all right," came a voice.

Tiller stood between the tents. Greta couldn't tell if he was breathing heavy or not. He sounded his usual distant self. Scott turned on a headlamp. Tiller, pale in the light, looked like his blood had all been drained into a prairie ditch. His scars almost glowed.

"Get that out of my eyes," he said.

Scott switched to a red beam. Now Tiller looked *drowned* in blood.

"Where were you?" Greta asked. "Had Scott worried. He was about to call your daddy. Oh wait, we don't have satellite phones."

"I wasn't about to call anybody," Scott said.

"Checking the next gate," Tiller said. "Sometimes all kinds of locks."

"You walk there?"

"Got two feet and a rifle. Only had to follow the fenceline a bit. Don't sleep all that much."

"Yeah, well I do." Greta headed toward her tent then stopped. "By any chance were you up on that low ridge line?"

"Might have been. You two go on to bed," Tiller said. "Gonna sit up awhile yet."

The Prairie Dog

It had been a week since the monsters came. They tore through at midday, ripped sticky tongues from mouths, pulled prairie dog stomachs apart from their soft belly fur. The monsters left a swath of blood and guts that resembled a stream of fresh rain, but on a second look, the prairie dog Yellowbrown, inspecting the bloodbath, sniffed hearts and entrails, and saw entire livers, bits of lung and brain, bones, even paws, so many twitching paws, many on legs ripped from bodies.

This happened on the other side of the shrub that separated the clans, and lasted only a few minutes, if that. The monsters had made quick work of the prairie dogs, ripping and tearing into them before many of the little ones could even get into their burrows. Some of the youngest had been swallowed whole.

This happened on the upper side of the shrub in the *uphill* clan's territory, and had scared all of the *lower* clan into their holes. Not a single dog from the lower clan ran to their aid, and this haunted many, including Yellowbrown, who now stood watch in the early morning light, a week after the last death-yip rang out. He could name all seventy-two prairie dogs that had died or were carried off, and thought about naming them all . . . maybe oldest to youngest . . . but decided to focus on his one job, surveying the wildgrass for intruders.

The grasses were tall right now, could hide some predators, though in some places the prairie dogs had made trails or the ground was bald. He had to ignore the mostly decomposed prairie dog head that had rolled downhill after some of the little ones played a game with it. The head belonged to Deepgrass, and now Deepgrass was merely a landmark with sunken grey eyes, soon to be a furless skull. But now that Yellowbrown was on guard he thought he heard something, had heard it soon as he exited his burrow, as if something had growled with the first signs of Yelloweye.

Like all his clanmates, Yellowbrown had a dark cheek patch, and sometimes kissed or was kissed right on the patch, or was lightly pawed there, or on the mouth, whiskers in a frenzy, or held that cheek against another cheek, sometimes against Barkbarkwhinebark, because she was one of the ancient mothers, but usually against Coldbrownpaws, because she felt good and made the tips of his paws tremble. He would feel her cheeks puff in and out rapidly, and he usually wanted that ripple through his fur, though he had to be the lookout right now, his responsibility, and besides, he felt something out there in the grasses, and knew that he alone buzzed with this pulse of uncertainty.

It was a low sound that didn't make sense, and came from a patch of wildgrass toward the distant rising Yelloweye, which glowed a dusty orange just then.

The Yelloweye was that burn-fire in the sky. That ball wasn't alive in the same way like the prairie dogs or the big kittiecatty, coyote-dog, bearbearbear, or the squirrelfurs. He'd killed a few squirrelfurs for entering dogtown, and dragged them to the no-no dirt, left them for the flying skyterrors.

He was a kind of sibling to the occasional groundhogger, and not a friend at all to the other dog clan males, well, most of them, though he had a soft heart for them after the monster murders. Sometimes Yellowyellow and Brownbrown would come by, even after those killings, say what they had to say, and they would yipyipyip together, not about the females, well, sometimes, and that would make him jealous and he might ram Brownbrown especially. Maybe they'd yip about a skyterror that swooped in earlier that he'd warned them about, say how high the flyer flew, that it was a redredtail skyterror, and how they'd screamed that it was coming in over the second hole out of six, always in shadow, up on the mound where Yellowbrown now stood. They didn't talk about the monsters.

He did have the perfect lookout over the town after all, like some crater that Yellowbrown had seen on that bright night eye he knew as Greygrey. That's what he called that night eye that was sometimes only a tailcurl in the sky, and was much colder than Yelloweye, and had mounds that Yelloweye didn't.

And anyway, he stared at the grasses, cautious not to gaze at Yelloweye, and the blades moved like something was in them, and all these thoughts came so fast, so fast, so fast, and he watched, and he sensed, or smelled for a rattle because he thought it could be a slitherworm in search of a mousemouse, or a shakerslither in search of a young doggie, but he didn't smell one and that was just fine.

No this was something else, something besides slither-worms or shakerslithers hunting furballs. This *something* had to be on feet, quiet feet, walking toward dogtown. Maybe it was the monsters.

Maybe.

Yellowbrown gave a tooth chatter. But no dog was listening, or no dog cared. How quickly they all forgot. He gave a *wee-oooooo* and a chuckle, though it wasn't so much a warning as it was an anxious read of the morning grassland and all the dangers it possibly held, which wasn't enough to scare all the dogs underground. And again, not a single furball seemed to care, though a couple heads cocked, and a few whistle-tooted from tiny throats.

Then it got quiet while Yellowbrown stood and stared, or he was that focused. He waited to see the scariest black eye beaming back, one of the longlongblackfeet, or some larger eye, that of the widewidesnort, or a smaller dot of an eye, like the shakerslither, or any other creatures, but none stared back though the grasses wiggled again. Eventually as he stared, Redredred, Coldbrownpaws, and Redred all briefly stopped by the crater opening with mouths full of grass, and he gave a happy *oo-eeeee* because seeing Coldbrownpaws broke his concentration. She gave a scent that made Yellowbrown want to dive with her deep into the burrow and wrestleplay and raspy purr in the nest she'd been building for days, but this off-scent that he'd picked up made him stand tall again, and all the dogs ran off and yipyipped into the burrow because he wasn't giving them his full attention.

Yellowbrown figured he would see Coldbrownpaws later. Then maybe the burrow would smell like the both of them, and then the little ones would be born, but even that thought was fleeting because he suddenly let out a string of repetitious barks after picking up the odd scent again.

This time that low sound came louder, guttural, almost like the *cooo cooo cooo cooo coo coo* of the fastrunner that sometimes zipped in for a lizard, or for one of the young baybah doggies, then retreated over the tiny hill and through the brush that separated the two prairie dog clans. Shrubshadow or Stubtail always growled down at him to remind him to stay in his own clan, his coterie, which he always did, and knew where he wasn't welcome.
   But it wasn't the other clan, or the fastrunner fluffering her florfy feathers. He knew how sneaky she could be, and so low to the ground, parallel to the dirt with her long tail sticking out for balance and that crest on her head like a soft leafy brown sail, and the skin around her eyes flaming blue and white and red, and that beakbeak opening to reveal a deep black mouth to snatch a lizard or baby dog, but it wasn't her, nonono not at all, because he didn't smell her and could always smell her lizard-chomping breath when she was around, but it was something. Now Yellowbrown was an uncertain cautious dog and has been known to bark at his own shadow—and so chatter-barked *ch-ch ark ark ark ark ark ark* to let everyone know to stop what they were doing, to help listen.
   But that was right when Coldbrownpaws ran past to pick up more grass for the nesty nest, and she *oo-eeed* at him as she ran past, heading straight toward the sound he thought he'd heard. Redredred zipped past to follow, and Yellowbrown desperately needed to tell them to wait, but his throat locked and now he could only let out a low growl. He couldn't see her or Redredred because he wanted to run deep into the safe roomroom, and wanted to raspy purr more than ever, and wanted to run toward her growl, and keep growling too, and didn't know what to do. So he

snarled, just stood and snarled, before his feet took him straight toward the sound, as if he didn't have any control of his paws any longer, and he abandoned his post at the cratered hole opening, and raced headlong into the grass.

The grasses were thick and terrifying whenever something was in them, and this time was no different, but he knew his way, where every open pocket had been exposed, where a hidden hole went to a shallow burrow, how the little ones liked to play when the grasses, yellow and scrubby-tall now, stood shorter and green, but not too deep in them in case of slithershakers. Sure, he could smell it now, whatever *it* was, but didn't know exactly where it lay, and knew that even a little one could get lost, but was also convinced now of the lurking thing, that it maybe lay half-buried in one of the open pockets, or had maybe circled around for an unsuspecting dog to snatch. And though his thoughts whirled, he now slipped into an angry panic running straight toward the sound and smell of Coldbrownpaws, who suddenly began snarling and yipping and crying.

What Yellowbrown saw next took him outside himself into a primal place he didn't know he had inside his furry tum. It wasn't the entire pack of monsters. But it was a mighty monster, a deathly creature intending to kill, and eat, and destroy dogtown.

Yellowbrown threw his front paws skyward and leapt up and down, then let out a sound that wasn't part of their current dog language, but had been part of it a long time ago, and so, without thinking, made both a warning and battle cry, a kind of scream-yip-jump cry, *oooeeeyahhheee-ee-ee-ee* that made the monster in front of him pause.

Though vaguely similar, the monster stood taller than a fastrunner. Its florf was so different too, not as drabdrab, but more colorful, with a larger, stouter, yellowish beakbeak, now covered in blood, black skin exposed around the pale eye, and long eyelashes that mesmerized, and brown plumage-fur that turned orangey around the face, and on top of its head a bright bluey-green crest that stood and flicked. What struck Yellowbrown, besides the monstrous size of the fastrunner monster, were its wings and tail that shimmered green and purple and flicked side to side. And a smell that this creature was much older than Barkbarkwhinebark, or the great grey bearbearbears that passed through from time to time, as if the creature had been trapped in a pocket of air from a distant land and finally released.

Parts of Redred lay strewn in a mess of fur and blood. The doggie had been torn in two, the rear half likely swallowed, part of the tail stuck in the beakbeak, the unswallowed half in parts, including the head from which protruded a bloody spine with remains of drippy meat. It seemed another dog had already been killed, for there were far too many parts, and a pile of guts and shit that seemed to have spilled from a dog besides Redred.

Two remaining doggies growled and yipped in front of Yellowbrown. Bitebiter, one of Yellowbrown's immediate cousins, and Coldbrownpaws. He knew she would try and rescue any dog in danger, this was why he loved her and also why he always feared for her. But now he didn't have time to think, just wanted the monster to go away, and wanted these doggies safe, so barked for them to retreat to the holes. But faster than Yellowbrown could blink, Bitebiter was snatched by the snapping beakbeak, the dog's throat burst, head tumbling and smashing into the grass. The corpse fell in a spurt of blood, with still wriggling legs, and a tail twitching as if still excited.

Then, just as fast, Coldbrownpaws was snatched and tossed into the air, but the throw was poor, and when she was about to be snapped apart, the monster almost missed, and now she dangled by a twisted and broken rear foot from its beakbeak.

She kicked and snarled in its grasp, dangling mostly, then shivered, nearly out of energy, so terrified, and was clearly about to be scissored into halves or swallowed, until Yellowbrown, filled with a kind of madness, bellowed his screamy yip-jump cry, causing this giant creature to pause.

And though the monster was hungry and fierce, Yellowbrown instantly determined one thing: *This creature had no right to eat Coldbrownpaws.*

He ran straight at this strange, giant fastrunner, with Coldbrownpaws dangling and now hardly kicking in its beakbeak. Yellowbrown lunged at its legs, causing the bird to dance around Yellowbrown, and though Yellowbrown was ferocious in his attempt to fight this superior foe, biting and nipping, he soon felt one of the monstrous fastrunner talons clamp onto his back and shove him to the dirt, pinning him down. His back legs kicked and whirred like pinwheels, all while this foreign, ancient fastrunner was about to fling Coldbrownpaws down its throat. In fact, it flung her up and back as if practicing for the great swallow. Instead, she smacked against its head, her broken foot nearly twisting off.

Yellowbrown, in his fury, refused to believe his poor fighting ability wasn't going to keep them from being torn apart or swallowed, and though he kicked, didn't realize they were both crying now, he to Coldbrownpaws, and she to him, as if neither wanted to say goodbye.

But what he also didn't realize was that screamy yip-jump

cry, the uniqueness of it, its ancient power, had unlocked something within the clan, and not just their clan in dogtown, but *both* clans, because Shrubshadow and Stubtail were the first to arrive snarling and biting. And they were soon followed by two hundred other dogs in a wild frenzy, whose frantic nips and yappy yips caused the monster to abandon Coldbrownpaws, and squawk openmouthed in terror at the fury unleashed toward it. And if it wasn't for the speed of this monster, and its ability to fly a few feet off the ground, it might have been torn apart by the angry doggie swarm.

It was some time before the clans parted ways, so much kissing and whining and yipping, and so many circled Coldbrownpaws and licked at her broken foot. And it was Yellowbrown who came to her first, sniffing at her injured paw, which was a bit warmer than usual, but still cold at the toe tips, and he licked her paw first, and she whined.

Though they never saw any of those monsters again, they knew this was a morning they would remember, and their pups would remember, and both clans too, and even if Coldbrownpaws now had a forever limp, the entire ordeal, and especially their survival, was worth a fearsome jump-yip or two.

Night Two

Greta woke to the sound of a quad engine firing up. By the time she popped out of the tent, Tiller had already began pushing the herd away from camp.

Scott stuffed his face with a breakfast sausage. "Tried to wake you thirty minutes ago. Thought maybe you were dead."

"I feel dead," Greta said. The soreness from riding only part of that first day, then walking several miles, had stiffened her back, arms, everything. Her inner thighs felt bruised. And today would be worse: that Yamaha rattling beneath her would feel like a medieval torture device. "Gotta eat before I can even think." She grabbed what was left of the sausage and a few bites of potato while Scott broke down his and Tiller's tents.

"Ready for a full day of riding?" Scott asked.

"Not really," she said.

"Come on, this is fun. We don't have to deal with anyone's bullshit out here."

"Uh-huh."

"What's that supposed to mean?" Scott asked.

"Means you didn't have to drag a tick-infested dead calf and have a tire blow, then have your co-workers think you quit when you coulda been dead, then . . ." She cut herself off, thinking about the giant bird, then Tiller's creepy dad and his ridiculous awards, all the taxidermy, and how she was still burnt over the whole thing.

Scott wrestled tent poles into a bag. "Try pulling pallet trains around the furniture yard for what feels like an eternity, then not getting paid for it."

Greta poured some coffee, took a slurp, then a bite of potato. "Lucky you in Star Valley."

"Maybe you're just not a morning person."

"Maybe if you didn't wake me in the middle of the night over Tiller taking a piss."

"He wasn't taking a piss."

"How do you know?"

"He was unlocking gates." Scott rolled a second tent, started shoving it into its nylon bag. "Why'd you ask if he was on the ridgeline anyway?"

Greta had forgotten about the dream, the pale form on the ridge. She wanted to tell him but what was the point? Did she even know what she'd seen? A stupid nightmare was all that was, like her waking dream of hearing and seeing things at the taxidermy shop. Waking up just did that thing everyone sometimes does when dreaming: everything blurs, you get confused, reality and imaginary worlds fuse. Maybe there was something about the dark that weighed on these moments too, celestial objects, stars, the moon, a million satellites blinking, the occasional shooting star, everything up there pressing down on top of her anxieties and worries that she wanted outside of her head, not inside swirling around images of Hannah, the Pope, or giant birds.

"It's nothing, thought I heard something," she lied. She was feeling a little spacey from lack of sleep and just wanted to get her head in the game. This feeling though, creeping into the back of her mind. Something felt odd, off-kilter, ethereal, like she didn't know exactly where she was, had slipped back into some daytime version of her dream. She glanced at the ridgeline, at the low shrubs dotting its bruised rise, and suddenly thought she'd be glad to be farther down the trail, that maybe this little patch of prairie had been haunted, that something primordial and awful and maybe even sacred had happened here, and whatever it was, she wanted to get on the move, not feel eyes poking daggers into her back. The same way she was glad to be far from Bobby and that goat-fawn in his arms staring straight toward Hell, that bizarre creation of a man obsessed with death and the power over the shells of the once-living. Of course, many cultures had been and were obsessed with death and ritual. Didn't mean Greta had to give a shit about some guy carving up dead animals for restaurant walls. She wanted to get away from Bobby Tiller's knife and bloody hands, those piles of teeth, that rut where she'd last seen the dead calf, and that jumbo bird like some kind of giant set loose in the sky riding its magic *hide* carpet, that might carry every cloud, then all of the cattle, maybe her too. Yeah, she wanted to be on the move with these dogies, forget all the bullshit. This drive would eventually do her good, help her refocus, as long as she was a little farther away. She was sure of that. "Yeehaw," she whispered.

Scott geared up first: gloves, goggles. Wearing a green shirt, he looked like a lanky praying mantis, if he twisted his elbows just right, he might sprout wings. Greta wore a clean red denim button-up over a tee she'd stuffed into the ATV saddle compartment. She had other items already packed away: sleeping bag, extra blanket, clothes, binoculars. She'd be a pig pen before seeing this through. That was all right with her. She loved the outdoors, loved the mess it created.

They needed to move cattle a few miles at least, get them started up through a long stretch of sloping prairie so they could move northwest of Hyattville. Tiller came back before she and Scott got on their quads and launched into half of the same speech he'd given the previous day, about how the cattle were mostly desensitized to ATVs—but not completely. "A few might get spooked," he said. "Not every cow sniffed this machinery to get rid of their fear, and not all of them will be adjusted just because we drove them yesterday. We'll have to babysit some, try not to lose them. Just keep calm and quiet. Think low stress. Don't constantly gun your engines when within a few yards. Don't wanna freak them out. No one wants a stampede over a cliff."

"You told us already," Greta said.

"You'd be surprised what cowhands forget," he said back. "The whole key to herding is to move slow, ease around the outskirts of the group. Keep your distance. Watch what the cattle are doing—you can't be right up next to them."

"You sure?" Greta shook her head at Scott, who grinned back through that mess of beard. They both knew Tiller wasn't listening again.

"Always think ahead," Tiller went on. "You don't want everything to go wild and out of control. Got that? We got all the permits we need, so let's hit this trail before they expire."

Greta didn't know anything about land use permits. Didn't matter to her. She simply wanted her money. Tiller was good for it. He paid a third up front, "on good faith," he'd said.

"We paid top dollar for these cattle," Tiller said in a hurry. "Need to get them moving."

"Waiting on you to finish your speech," Greta said.

"Weather might sour on us in the next few days." Tiller gazed at some low distant clouds, throttled his engine, started after the herd again.

Before them, late spring hung over the landscape, every wisp of cloud white and rainless. Not a thunderhead in sight and Greta was glad for it. *You ride an ATV, you don't drive it*, she reminded herself, butt muscles sore from yesterday's adventure. She knew it would take a couple days to stop feeling like every bump in the prairie physically poked at a bruise. She knew you really had to be cautious too. Get going too fast and you could literally lose your head, roll your ATV, end up with another blown tire. She had a helmet with her, but didn't always wear it, but promised herself she would wear the damn thing if riding in the dark again, or fast up or down a hill. And like Tiller said, be careful around the cattle. No one in their right mind wants to be charged by a cow, or cause it to up and run. Her entire plan was to keep her distance. She was going to stick to that. If Tiller or Scott were going to be hot-rodding, then that was on them. Let those idiots cause a stampede off a buffalo jump, so long as she wasn't caught in it or blamed, not that she wanted to see any more cows die.

Greta took the herd's left rear flank. For now, Tiller pushed them gently, sweeping his ATV back and forth behind them a few times the way horse riders do. *Nothing like easy money*, she thought. *Just go gently after those strays, especially that troublesome cow from the day before.* She would know her anywhere, that side pattern like some freaky inkblot, those stubby legs. If there was any kind of mental hopscotch to assess her own personality, it was her relatability to that cow, which she spotted right away moving slower than the others, drifting toward the edge of the herd. "Yeah, I got a bad attitude too, Lady Grazer," Greta said.

Greta carried lots of water, planned to stay hydrated over the next nine nights. Snuck two bottles of whiskey too, though she didn't plan to herd the cattle while drunk. Those bottles were solely for campfire storytelling, which she wished she hadn't been too tired for the night before. If drunk enough maybe she would have shared her bird tale, or something about her breakup with Hannah, knowing that the boys didn't have a clue about any of it. She was a little worried about those two. Scott could still likely put the drink away like Kool-Aid—she was sure he'd brought his own supplies. Tiller had been one hundred percent drunk in college and still smelled like a beer can now, like his old man. For some guys, maybe Tiller's dad, beer is a good enough breakfast, lunch, and dinner. You can't change them. And you don't want to marry them. She just worried about working with these boys if they had too much. She had a medical kit and could do a splint, but she wouldn't be able to sew an arm back on if one of them got so drunk that they let a cow or two or three charge them.

Everyone had a rifle in case they needed to scare off, or on rare occasion, shoot a predator. Coyote, bear, wolf, lion, bobcat. You never knew what you'd have to shoot at, or when you'd have to fire off a round when mother to a few hundred cattle. Maybe a thousand pikas would wake from their rocky crags and treeless slopes, descend some mountain peak, scare every cow back to Ten Sleep with their squeak-toy war cries, though that would be a strange day for sure. Invasion of the tiny, cute, round-eared herbivores. Greta smiled, thinking of the absurdity. Carnivores, real carnivores, can smell blood in the air, and carrion if there was no blood at all. And out in the wild, well, Greta knew anything could happen. The pikas weren't likely, ever. But a brown bear? That was a reality. No angry mama and cubs would be welcome on this journey. Luckily, every pre-prepared camp had a bear-proof locker for food, set a ways off from the tent area. Greta wished they had a dog to help out. *Tiller's family must have a herd dog somewhere*, she thought. Sure wouldn't have minded the extra company or the built-in wolf-bear-cat alarm system.

Right now, Greta had to stop thinking for a while and focus—the cattle were moving, and she didn't want any mishaps, especially since Lady Grazer already again had that wander-off attitude.

Over the next hours the weather grew warmer and the sky yawned to full daylight. Still far from midday, they were already rounding up strays, including Lady Grazer, who wanted to forage by herself on a slope, any slope, sometimes over in the bottom grass, and be left in peace. Again and again, that cow complained, her cry of annoyance aimed right at Greta. Sometimes the birds joined in, though the bovine did move her stubby legs and trot back to the herd, sometimes a blackbird on her rump.

Every herder and beast inched along, parallel to a dirt trail that led toward the canyon. Something felt strange, Greta thought while pushing after another stray and calf, trying to scoot them back to the herd. She thought how the quad's constant grinding stole something from the experience of moving cattle. The smell of gas and exhaust, the noise, it felt too mechanical, out of tune with the outdoors. Sure, a horse didn't have headlights. But a horse was a more relaxing ride, that warmth, that movement, that power, sitting so much higher to survey the cattle and the land. A horse had eyes and could smell, could sense danger, and so avoid pitfalls. You start to slip into the sound of the engine rather than hoofstruck beats, and she didn't know how she felt about that partial drowning of sound. You could hardly hear a Red-tailed Hawk any more than grasshoppers and crickets, or the different kinds of mooing from unhappy mothers, lost calves, even the sick or exhausted. And she couldn't hear any distant bellows from four-legged creatures, unless she sat there with the engine off, and Scott and Tiller did the same. So every once in a while, she decided to cut her engine, not only to count cattle when passing over gullies, but to hear if any strays had slipped behind her, maybe if anything lurked over a rise. Sometimes just to swat away a hatching of mayflies, or to pluck a skeeter off her neck. Sometimes the bug spray didn't help. At least they weren't too far from Hyattville. If a quad crapped out on them, or someone got thrown onto some rocks, they could get help. And they had a few spares now if a tire blew.

Crawling along, ATV wheels hardly turning, she glanced back at Tiller weaving back and forth, annoying the herd just enough to keep them moving. Her mind wandered from the plains to Hannah again, to one of the last times she'd seen her. Something had been wrong, she could tell, but Hannah wouldn't say, only that she was off to visit her family for a week. "I'm fine," Hannah said every time Greta had asked.

"No, you're not," Greta remembered saying. "Something's up. Why won't you just talk?" And then Greta remembered seeing Hannah's attention drift inward, turn away. And that's when Greta had said words she soon regretted. "Are you seeing someone?"

Greta played that whole embarrassing episode over in her mind, Hannah crying and saying no, that it was something else, that she would tell her later. Greta just never found out what Hannah might have revealed. Greta still wracked her brain over it, feeling so much pain at the conversation, and afterwards when Hannah ghosted her. What clues had there been? A mutual friend's death. A key she'd seen on the counter that disappeared by morning. A wrong number that Greta had picked up and that hung up on her, and when she called back, it was some retail store in California.

Greta was thinking about everything for the thousandth time, thought she might be onto something, something that Hannah had said weeks before that, that *if we ever aren't together, to remember our trips to the mountains.* They'd taken countless trips to the Tetons, hiking on lower mountain trails, laughing at the birdwatchers who moved like snails so they could see their stupid flycatchers. Greta was trying so hard to recall Hannah's exact words, to see if there was anything she could dig from what already felt like broken pieces of memory, mere fragments. And she was starting to think all over again that she just plain and simply got dumped, that nothing bad had actually happened to Hannah, that she was just done with their relationship. So why bother thinking that something bad happened, that she'd crashed into a lake, or been abducted? She'd have heard about that. Thing was, she knew she was ghosted, though her death fears came back again and again. Hannah's family said nothing, except she never showed up there either. When asked, they told Greta she'd likely ghosted her, that she'd done something like this before when she was in her teens, just left home, ghosted her own parents. Said they found her working at a donut shop in Denver, with fake IDs and everything. Then Greta wondered what kind of name Hannah might have come up with this time, and if she was maybe working for that California retail store, though Greta did call asking the store rep for her more than once, including an attempt to mask her voice, which she tried to mimic her own mother's smoky hoarseness, and was eventually told to stop calling.

"Stop looking for invisible people," some squeaky girl had said. Such an odd thing to say. *Invisible people*, Greta thought. She was still thinking about what squeak-girl could have meant when she suddenly heard her name clear as day over the noise of the ATV engine.

Gretaaaaa.

She didn't know how any voice could do that unless it was yelling. This wasn't yelling. It wasn't identifiably male or female. Definitely not Tiller or Scott. Just strange, *off*. Not Hannah either. Not the Pope coming back from the dead. It came again . . .

Gretaaa.

Goosebumps washed across her like her skin might lift from muscle though she'd been sweating under the spring sun, slapping at flies. She stopped her quad, turned toward Scott just in case, but he was far on the northeast flank of the herd. Tiller was forty yards away still pushing cattle forward. Couldn't have been either of them.

Gretaaaaaa.

Her head was on a swivel now. Why a third time? And why just her name? Just to prove she was really hearing this? Who would call her name way out here? It wasn't a soft pronunciation, not a whisper either. Not calming. Urgent, threatening, more like. Definitely disturbing. Not loud though. A low moan, maybe, and more unsettling than when she heard her name at the taxidermy shop. Definitely wasn't a whisper. More like a gust of wind moaning, or from deep in a pipe underground, like her name had been blurted by the calf in front of her. Almost like whatever, or whoever, had said it was sharing some kind of dark thought, like, *I don't hate you, but I might start hating you.* It didn't come a fourth time but now her senses were on high alert, scanning the terrain for any clue about the voice or its origin.

Then she started thinking about two things in her jacket pocket she'd forgotten since the day before, tiny items she'd stole from the taxidermy shop while waiting for Bobby. Why was she forgetting so many things? *No way*, she thought. Couldn't have been *them*. Two stuffed wedding mice she'd taken from a basket near a line of mice on a counter. They couldn't have been squeaking out her name. Could they? She felt around in her pocket. They were still in their little bride and groom attire, weren't moving, not even a twitch. How would they move anyway? They were only skin, whiskers, and round ears stretched over a tiny mold.

Then her eye caught something amid the shimmering grasslands, a white, coarse furry head, medium dog sized, peering from the grass thirty or so yards away. How long had it been there? On its face a familiar stare, a lifeless grimace, though it wasn't dead, or was it? Had to be. She watched as the head turned and gazed at her, its dark silky neck out of place, like it was two creatures at once, so different in this light. So real. Eyes of creepy dark amber with a slight, but deep yellow glow, surrounded by black. The hairs on her arms raised, her mouth went dry as ash.

She knew what it was.

The goat-fawn.

This was the sick creation she'd seen in Bobby's arms. How did it get out here? That empty, sewn-together thing, moving, creeping, dragging that leg, that broken fawn leg that didn't get fixed after all.

Then it ducked beneath the wildgrass.

She got off her quad, continued to watch the grasses, strained to listen, could hear the constant groan of Tiller's quad, cows moaning from every direction, wind stirring through everything. Even Scott's quad growled in the distance like some angry bear wanting to gorge on a calf.

A moment later she saw the creature limp-crawl into an opening farther to the right, dragging that broken leg. It disappeared the way Sharp-tailed Grouse or Wild Turkeys sometimes duck their heads after peeking over tall grass. Paranoid, she started searching for the creature. Every wind gust working through the prairie slopes revealed a shadow she imagined to be the thing.

She slowly moved forward, examining the stalks and blades where she'd seen it, even thought she'd kept her eye on that spotted hide, but it was gone. She came to a gully, then thought the thing must have slithered its way into the shrub-thick ravine. Or didn't exist at all. Maybe she'd seen some other animal but somehow wanted it to be that thing Bobby held. She wondered if she were that upset about the Pope dying, that his death and Hannah's abandonment, feeling like a kind of death, were both really working double-time on her psyche.

On her way back to the quad she wondered if she'd heard her name at all or something else? She'd read or maybe someone told her that goats can reveal their feelings through their distinctive bleats. *Maaahhh. Maaahhh.* Was that what she'd heard instead of the goat-fawn calling her? Her name didn't sound anything like *maaahhhh*. She imagined those rubbery goat lips bleating. And though she didn't hear that voice again, she thought she remembered the goat-fawn's mouth moving, and so that image played over and over, the thing maybe mouthing her name. Then she had a strong vision of that leg dragging, nearly breaking off—its mouth opening again, somehow forming human-sounding words—that entire body seeming to float in front of her, broken leg dangling.

And that's all she could think about after she got back on her quad, even after they broke for lunch, everyone eating salami sandwiches. She slipped away, pulled out her bottle, which she knew she shouldn't, then took a drink, let it burn her insides, snuck it back. Anything to help take away the image of that thing slipping through the grass, watching, calling her.

The rest of the day she paid as much attention to the grasslands as she did any strays. Every shadow, every bird flying into the sky, some sailing over, some darting from the ochre sea squawking and thrashing, some shooting like fat missiles . . . or the occasional coyote trampling through, a badger snuffling its way, groundhogs, squirrels, prairie dogs . . . even animal-like shadow shapes between rocks or under lone oaks—many of them got her heart rate up. Anything could be moving at any time out in these wildlands, especially deer. She saw lots of those, sometimes herds in the hundreds making their way to favored grazing lands, or just dotting the distance, some leaping and running from invisible dangers. Amid them, she kept looking, and sometimes stopped to listen, in case her name was called again, in case those amber eyes reflected in the sun, goat-fawn mouth hanging open, lips moving like they shouldn't, *couldn't*? Often these were deer and their heads poked above the grasses, and their mouths were sometimes open, and sometimes Greta forgot whether the goat-fawn was a fawn-goat, and jumped at the sight of a fawn eyeing her, or at the thought of something coming up over the next low ridgeline.

And sometimes she crept too slow on her ATV and lagged behind, and Tiller would wave his hat at her to catch up, then hold out a hand like he couldn't make up his mind, which of course really meant to not spook the damn cattle when they started in on a trot. She knew some could be skittish and run hard, and a running cow could make itself a distant stray, or cause others to near stampede, and that could take the herd in the wrong direction a quarter mile or more, which would take some effort to get them back on track.

It was twilight by the time all the cows were tucked in close to camp, including the last two she'd brought over. Even Lady Grazer seemed happy to be around the other cattle. By this time Greta hadn't seen or heard any sign of the goat-fawn for hours. It was a relief to hear only bovines complaining across the folds of green and gold, especially after Scott set up camp, with her helping out, while Tiller counted cattle then drove off to check any locked gates.

"Why so uptight?" Scott asked, getting the stove out. He unfolded a little tray and set a lantern on it, then tried helping her with her tent.

"I can do this myself," she said.

"It's called helping."

"Well, I need something to do."

"Sure," he said. "I can watch."

"I don't like being stared at."

Scott laughed at this, then said: "Cows been staring at you for two days."

"You do realize I don't want to be your *Dear Diary* page?"

"Just thought something might be on your mind. Ever since you disappeared . . ."

"I didn't disappear."

"Didn't mean it like that."

Greta paused like she heard something, and with a spike in her hand, felt like she should clock Scott with it. "You ever think something else is out here watching us?"

Scott ignored her refusal for help and pulled at a loop for her to spike. "Let's see," he said. "Prairie dogs, hawks, coyotes, deer, snakes, maybe a praying mantis or two. They're curious but tend to stay out of the way, don't they? Maybe someone on a nearby ridge watching us through binoculars to see what we're up to. We're not all that far from Hyattville. Can see their lights this evening."

She noticed the town glow from southeast of their position. Still, it bothered her what he said about animals, maybe someone spying. She'd rather he lie and say every damn animal was minding its own business, hadn't noticed her. "I don't want some creeper watching us," she said.

Scott held down a corner of the tent. "You asked."

Greta pounded in the spike. "What about dead things?"

"Now who's being creepy?"

Greta stepped on the corner of the tent, nearly smashing one of Scott's fingers. "Forget I asked."

"Greta," he said. "No one is out to get you. Look at us. We couldn't be farther from anywhere. Ain't a soul in Hyattville wants to see what we're up to."

"You sure?"

He stood back this time, no longer stepping across any tent-building lines. "Just us out here, animals, our old buddy Tiller grumpy as a toad. Everything's cool, yeah? Long days where you can just think. And I got plenty to think about. Don't you?"

"Like what? What are you thinking about?"

"My future. My lady friend. Getting the hell out of Star Valley."

"You have a girlfriend?" she asked. "How'd I not know this?"

"Contrary to popular belief I'm not a bad looking guy."

"But you never have a friend," she said.

"Take that back. I had two back in eleventh grade that I swear I told you about. One in college you never knew about. To be honest, probably dropped out because of her. And I hook up. You just don't hear about those. Not like you send me texts asking."

"This is all new shit to me," she said. "Wow. Scott has a *friend*. Happy fucking day. Fine, I take back my shitty remark, but only that one."

"Times change, Greta."

"Do they?"

"You know, I don't remember you being so uptight."

"Lady Grazer thinks the same thing," she said.

"Who the hell is that?"

Greta pointed to a short plump cow in the dusk light. The cow appeared bluish, a kind of evening glow to her hide. The prairie did that to everything after the sun fell. Greta half smiled at the beauty of it. "She tells me I have an attitude problem. But it's not me, it's *her*. She goes stray all the time."

Scott shook his head, rubbed at his giant beard. "I guess

talking to cows ain't so bad if you're learning something," he said.

"A cow," she reminded him. "Just that one."

Summer knocked on the door of late spring. While the last remnants of dusk still glowed, a warm wind swept across the wildlands, up through the tents, over backs, around the campfire, and carried sparks toward the heavens. Canyons, still a long way to the northeast, loomed purple and orange in the evening dimness, dotted by fir and pine that took shape like bloody timberline necklaces. The coming darkness appeared to be cracking open the prairie. Greta wondered if the night would be an open wound for coyotes to feast on, meaning they might come and terrorize the cattle or even her, and that maybe such dogs would carry her off into the fog of blackness.

Tiller soon returned, said they were a mile or so from the next gates. "Not gonna be optimal food sources for the cattle in the next stretch of prairie," he said. "It's rocky, less nutrients. We'll let them fatten up a bit in the morning, be slow to leave camp. Then push them through noontime."

By dinner Greta felt good-humored, even laughed at one of Scott's stupid jokes about what a jackalope's favorite game is. She laughed so hard she didn't even hear the punchline, even though it wasn't one: *Jackalope . . . likes to jump rope!*

She even thought about telling them about the goat-fawn she'd seen, but was too embarrassed every time she started to mention something so unbelievable as taxidermy dragging itself through the grasslands. Sure didn't need

Tiller harassing her about any possible delusions, or thinking she had it in for his old man. Still needed to get paid that other two-thirds. She was ready for that cash.

Instead, while Scott and Tiller talked and cooked some kind of stew, she secretly brought out the two stuffed mice she'd stole from Bobby's shop. That little bride and groom dead to the world, dead to their marriage, dead to creation. She hoped these mice weren't simply pulled at random, that maybe they'd known each other, were mates, and needed to be free again. Somehow, she knew she needed these talismans, these guardians, sick as they were in their falseness. These tiny gutted and shriveled things would watch over her, and she would watch over them. That was a fair deal, wasn't it? She took them over to her tent, squatted down, gave each a kiss and set them just outside the entrance flap, hidden in a deeper shadow of fold. She was getting to her feet when she felt someone behind her.

"Everything all right?" Tiller said.

Something in her gut fell into a tailspin. "Yeah," she stumbled. "Fine."

"Stew's ready," he told her. "Poured straight from the can the way you like it."

Soon night seeped in and Greta thought she saw a cow with starlight in its eyes. The beast was a shadow in the grasslands, seemed stiff like all the life had been drained out, the Milky Way pressing down on thick shoulders. The cattle had gone quiet though, and over the next half hour, the breeze that had blown in got so weak it couldn't even move the flames.

Scott and Tiller took turns keeping the fire blazing, their chairs set up to triangulate the pit. Greta, lost in thought alongside the others, stared into the dancing flames as if firelight alone could charm her into forgetting the goat-fawn. Dinner was long gone, and so was the water she'd poured from the nearby cache, and now all she wanted to think about was those distant coyotes she still didn't trust. She wondered if those dogs had seen the goat-fawn crawling past, if they were laughing at the creature, her, or both.

To her satisfaction, Scott pulled out a bottle of Jack, offered drinks to any takers.

Tiller didn't seem to mind a nip but deferred. "Greta first," he said, pulling her the rest of the way out of her delirium.

"Oh, now you're going to be polite." She took the bottle, glad it was Scott's stash and not hers, then choked down a gulp. "That should fix the taste of that stew."

"Didn't mean to oversalt," Scott said.

"It came from a can, already had salt," she said.

"What about the hot sauce?" Scott grimaced.

"That part was perfect."

Tiller took a drink next. When the bottle came around again, she doubled down, downed even more. "Easy," Scott said, taking the bottle. "This needs to last me another week."

A few minutes later her head started to swim. She started thinking they were farther along the trail, that those canyon walls were up close and personal, towering over them, that she was wandering, lost in them, that a hundred goat-fawns stared down at her, eyes full of yellow light, every one of them calling her name, some letting their broken legs snap and fall over the ledge. She started to see goat-fawns around the fire too, dragging themselves toward her.

She stood up, almost lost her footing, and the visions disappeared.

"You all right?" Scott asked. "Maybe take a sip of water."

"I have to tell you." She sucked from Scott's canteen, then quickly grabbed for the bottle. "I'm not looking forward to that canyon."

"What's wrong?" Scott said. "Thought you liked hiking in this beautiful state?"

"Nothing's wrong with hiking," she said. "I'm just not looking forward to being in that maze. Never been." She turned to Tiller. "You been in there much lately?"

"Been a while."

"You mean it's not some kind of playground for you and your cows?"

Tiller took a long drink. "That's sheepherder land, or used to be, much of it is private, anyway."

"That why you needed all those permissions?"

"Can't be that bad." Scott took his turn at the bottle, dripped some in his beard, tried to catch and lick it from his palm. "We're just moving three hundred."

Greta had her feet under her again, but wasn't about to let this go. "Sure, but Tiller's afraid of sheepherders."

"It's not like that," Tiller said.

"Then what's it like?" she said. "Ghosts? Monsters? Sheepherders watching over that entrance?"

"There was bad blood at one time. Everyone knows that."

"Was there?"

"Ease up," Scott said to her. "You're getting a little excited."

"Of course I'm excited," Greta said, taking another sip, up now, dancing her way slowly around the fire, moving her shoulders, swinging her hips, some kind of music playing in her head. "Gotta get the spirit out of me, Scott. Look at me.

I'm channeling all these sheepherder spirits. They're gonna come down, take me into those limestone fingers, straight to their hive." She tried to get Scott to join her but he sat back and laughed.

"You know I don't dance," he said. "Not unless I have a long smoke first." Didn't stop him from clapping out a rhythm. "Keep on now."

She moved to Tiller. "Come, get the spirit out of me."

"You're drunk."

"So?" She swayed closer, Scott clapping a steady beat.

"Don't do that," Tiller warned.

"Do what? Call the spirits?" She started waving to the stars, then toward the cliffs hidden in darkness. "Come on down! You hear me?"

"Stop that."

"What are you afraid of? Bad blood? C'mon." She grabbed the bottle again, held it up to the milky strip of night.

Tiller's eyes shone orange coal-light. "Look, people got murdered over this land a long time ago."

"Those sheepherders?" she said. "Or you poor cattle folk?"

Tiller sat back. "Yeah. Them. *They*. Both."

She made her way around the fire.

"So what?" Scott said, still keeping rhythm. "Indians around here before all of them. They got killed too."

"Oh, a contest. I got one." Greta started swinging her body again, this time with the bottle, kicking dirt at the fire. Dust plumes and sparks rose, swirled. "A goddam carbonaceous asteroid smacked down sixty-six million years ago in the Yucatan," she said. "Its name—the Chicxulub impactor. Those billion Hiroshimas came up through a sea that cut North America in half, straight to Wyoming in a storm of wind and fire, killed everything but the birds. Plenty of animal spirits in this dirt. Think I might be dancing on their graves." She danced toward Tiller, handed him the bottle. "Who are *they*?"

He took a drink, eyed her. "Sheepherders."

"Now this is all starting to make sense," she said. "Cattlemen murdering sheepherders, and along with all the goddam Christians murdering Indians and stealing every inch of land, and that mean motherfucking asteroid murdering dinosaurs and all their babies . . ."

"You don't make any sense," Scott said.

She couldn't stop dancing, and at the same time, a kind of dread crept into her bones. "Don't I? If that canyon's as bad as the prairie . . ."

"What do you mean, bad?" Scott chuckled. "The canyon ain't alive."

She looked at Tiller. "How come you never told us this trail was haunted?"

Tiller laughed. He *never* laughed.

"See?" Greta said. "I knew it. This shit's haunted. Can't forget these all been indigenous lands. Crow and Arapaho and Shoshone spirits. And they still play that long game of looking into the future, doing their Ghost Dance, and in their rebelliousness rattle every colonizer nerve. Remember them settlers? Pushing and prodding and murdering? And all them ghost-forts everywhere built for more killing of Indians, for destroying their food sources too? How about bison bones stacked like Babel towers, or colonizers reneging on every single land-stealing treaty there ever was? And, yeah, they're still here. The ghosts, the real people, settlers, Indians, the past, the future . . ."

"I wouldn't call anything haunted," Tiller said.

"What would you call it?" Everything in her wanted to mention the goat-fawn, which hung on the tip of her tongue, to tell him something can be all kinds of things at once, dead, alive, two animals, part of this prairie, and not. She swore that creature was real, must be around, just off the edge of firelight, about to say her name.

Tiller bit his cheek. "Slightly cursed."

"Slightly?" she said.

"You did blow a tire the first day." Scott took another drink.

"I think it's worse than that," she said. "Tell him, Tiller."

"Tell you what?"

"You know."

"No. I don't."

"What about the goat-fawn?"

Something froze in Tiller's eyes, though Greta thought only she'd noticed the spark of a lie trapped in there.

"Is that something like my jackalope joke?" Scott squinted into the flames. "I like jackalopes." He started clapping again. "Why ain't you still dancing?"

"It's not a goddam jackalope joke," Greta said. She started moving her hips, her arms. "It's something Tiller's dad created in that shop. Tell him."

"What?" Scott dropped the beat.

Tiller had a hold of Scott's Jack now and downed some more. He wiped his mouth and set the bottle in the dirt instead of handing it back.

"This is so stupid." Scott laughed, snorted twice. "Shit, I'm more tired than I thought." He got up. "What's that about curses, now?"

"Tell him," Greta said again. She wasn't smiling.

Tiller picked up the bottle, started peeling the label.

"I don't care," Scott said. "You two hash out your whatevers. I need some sleep."

Scott wasn't gone half a minute when Tiller stood.

"What is it?" Greta asked, angry that Tiller was being Tiller, not saying anything, or admitting anything.

"It got quiet," he said.

"No it didn't," she huffed. "Scott just started snoring from the tent."

"Not that. The coyotes," he said. "They should still be yipping and woofing."

"I don't care about them," she said. "I want you to tell me why your dad is making monsters."

"He's not making monsters."

Just then the coyotes started whining and howling. Tiller seemed to relax.

"Why won't you tell me?"

He looked hard at her. "Let's just do the job we were sent to do? We need to move the cattle to higher country. All of them. That's why you were hired. To move cattle. Just go to bed."

The Coyote

The smallest in the litter, she'd been born sixth of seven pups in a hollow tree. A red wash rusted across her haunches and back, even on the end of her snout, more so than any fulvous variations to the pack's black and whitish-grey coats.

When she was abandoned, but not killed, by her mother, probably for being both small and beautiful, a true canine oddity, she was allowed to nurse for just a few minutes each day in a second den away from the main den. But that soon ended, and she was cut off, and left huddling in an old marmot hole surrounded by rocks and broken, sap-covered trunks, blackened and bleeding from a lightning strike. But not for long as it was summer and soon the pack set out, and she with them, though not officially.

In those early days, she followed at a great distance, and often whined and cried, and got nipped and bit if she slipped too close to her mother or siblings. Even the sister with the back scar and thicker teeth like a mother coyote, hip-slammed her into the dirt, though that didn't stop her from longing with a kind of groan while that sister, and other females, groomed each other. She wanted more than anything to feel that kind of love, but could only watch, and yearn.

Sometimes she got bullied by the males, brothers, uncles, cousins, and once got carried around by a brute, the largest of her brothers, his face black and grey, eyes ringed with charcoal-tinted fur, and she was dropped in a stream and almost drowned.

At least she got scraps, rib cages with bits of flesh, though half the time she tasted her brothers' urine, having seen them with other dogs pissing on the remains after their sisters fed. When this happened, all of them stared toward her, laughter in their eyes, a mischievousness she didn't yet share.

At least she could hear her family, their familiar yips and howls and barks, their play-dives and play-leaps, all those raucous spins and dives, and sometimes she'd bark-howl and whine with joy while she watched, her front paws in a shiver, as if she were giving endless *wow-oo-wow*s with the rest of them.

Couldn't exactly remember when, but eventually she found solace in her distant place beyond the far, *far* edge of the pack, and as she grew older, this isolation allowed her to develop stalking skills, watching skills, even hunting skills that her siblings hadn't yet mastered, and she soon could catch voles and mice, then marmots, and on rare occasions, prairie dogs that her sisters and most of her brothers couldn't snatch or grab as quickly as she could—she found she had a zinging, fast bite.

And though she craved deer, remembering so many scraps of urine-tainted fawn ribs, she was more content at the end of that first year catching rabbits, squirrels, and the occasional pika, swallowing entire furballs whole, never even crunching the bones. And though she didn't piss on them, she sometimes left a rabbit for her sister with the all grey-and-black coat and the brightest of eyes, who was the seventh born, and would watch her eat the bunny and trot off with hardly a look, though that slightest of glances led to yips and howls that she could follow, always follow, and knew her sister, the seventh, didn't want her, the sixth, to ever be forever lost.

She found that she could follow her family anywhere, and depending on where she hid amid prairie winds and canyon rocks, her scent wouldn't get picked up. So, she stalked them for fun, and this was her game, her mischievous playtime, and she sometimes popped out of the grass to the snarls of her brothers and sisters, but her seventh-born sister's eyes gleamed with approval, though afterwards she disappeared just as quick as she appeared, laying low in the grasses and scooting off until they lost her scent. And this went on for months, until she found other creatures to stalk, a pair of bear cubs and their mother, a herd of deer, a fox making its way with a badger across the prairie through some of the pipes that allowed access beneath roadways and pastures. They became fast friends, but that didn't last because the mountain lion came and ruined everything, but that is another story.

And then she started picking up on something else, strange death scents. These weren't the death scents she was used to, intermingled with blood and wet hearts and the insides of things slathered in muscle and thin membranes, or the or the fear that could hover like beast-ghosts around the carcasses that sometimes dotted the prairie. Always, *always*, there was a dead thing, something that might die for whatever reason, which vultures would soon dispose of in their silent tearing of flesh.

But these death scents were like smoky remains, washed remains, coated in bits of sticky humanness, and odd parts, bizarre eyes that couldn't see, yet could, and insides that smelled of dust and tree bits.

It was in the tall yellow grasses that she saw one of them, standing and staring at her. She yipped and almost ran away then didn't and stared back. Then huffed. Then barked. It was another coyote staring in her direction, though it wasn't. Its eyes held no brightness, its muzzle appeared frozen. Even its off-pink tongue just lay there in its mouth, no breath, no sound, no yip or bark, not even a growl. She couldn't smell blood or urine. She couldn't smell where the canine had been, other than with humans, or any other strong scent really, only distant life, a faintness to the coyote creature as if it were fading right there in front of her. This confused her and she barked until the dog turned and walked away. She didn't follow, and instead lay down, huddled into a tiny ball, and fell asleep.

Late that night after she'd eaten two sleeping squirrels, came a rustling, and it was death again, only this time she smelled a familiar scent, and it saddened her and she let out a long whine, and realized right away, she just knew, this scent was her sister's fur, those faint reminders in her paws, though those weren't her eyes, and it/*she* lay down next to her and they huddled close. For days her sister, the seventh born, stayed close, so she took care of her, catching her rabbits and squirrels that she wouldn't eat, taking her to water she wouldn't drink. She tried teaching her dead sister how to properly hunt, which she wouldn't, and over the next weeks they hunted together, though not really, and when she slept, only rested half the night and felt her sister's coldness there, so close, and so she sometimes howled at that dead-alive carcass, while distant howls, so very far away, lit the wide, lost nights with sound beacons.

And then her sister was gone and she dreamed about her, every night the same dream, chasing rabbits, until one afternoon, weeks or months later, her sister returned, still smelling like the dead, and lay next to her, still not offering any warmth, yet there was a kind of comfort and fear nonetheless, and no sound, no barks or yips or howls, and her mouth was still frozen. And she howled next to her sister like she did before, hoping they might sing together, though they never would, and would disappear during the day, until one morning she followed her sister when she left in the early darkness, and trailed her to another similar dead thing, only this wasn't a coyote but a creature of two halves, and she ran after them, because it seemed they had somewhere to go, something to watch, to maybe protect.

Then she went to a trail where the two dead things stared at a distant dust cloud that rumbled and roared, where there stepped from the dirt many cows being herded by people on machines with wheels. And so the three of them, the coyote and her dead sister and the creature, which she realized smelled of deer and goat, hid upon a hill, and gazed down to the cows, so many of them making their way, and the machines, three of them, pushing, or following, she thought, toward maybe the canyon, which lay far away, and held a stream, and a path to more cows, so maybe that's where, to the waters and shadows.

Then she realized she could hear something, thoughts reminiscent of her sister, of who she was, and continued to be, and the thoughts of this other creature, which came like needles, but comforting, and she didn't understand any of them, but somehow knew to stay with them, that they were supposed to do *something*, but that they weren't going to do whatever it was.

And this had to do with all the cows and the people, and they really were going to watch over them, maybe be a guide, and that was okay, though she was tired and wanted to sleep all day now, and be awake at night, so fought sleepy feelings until she grew hungry, and then went hunting, and brought back a rabbit after finding and eating one, and could still taste fur on her tongue, even after laying the rabbit at her sister's paws yet again.

But her sister, mouth frozen, still wouldn't eat, or wasn't hungry, and never would be, and hunkered there until the herd moved again, and then the three of them followed after the machines. And they did this until nightfall, when she grew tired again, and needed a brief nap, and woke later from a snore, her sister and the creature and everyone gone.

And though the other two were dead, and though she knew it, though maybe some small part of them seemed to live, she cried again, whining and whimpering, and instead of waiting for them to return, headed east, until she picked up the scent of her family, and as before, hid her scent while she trailed them, and then during this time, hoped she could find one of them a rabbit.

Soon, *soon*, she thought.

And that night she howled when they howled, so they would know she was there, and she knew one voice was missing, her sister's, and that they knew this too, and she missed that voice, and could hear how they did too, and so they howled longer than ever, until the stars shook.

Night Three

The next morning every high-country bird buzzed and sang from nearby willow stalks that lined a stream, while close by grass, seared olive by days of sun, was on its way to turning yellow. Greta could hear bluebirds and imagined them clinging to edges of reeds, and while she did, a Bobolink flock let out a series of cheerful and bubbly warbles. When she poked her head out of her tent, a male Bobolink's silvery bill let out a *chuk* from where the bird perched atop a chair. The back of its otherwise-black head shone the color of prairie grass.

Meadowlarks sang too, some letting out rattles, and Greta, stretched her arms and back, groaned, head throbbing, wishing they'd go back to their melodic notes.

She was pretty sure everyone's head pulsed from the Jack, though wasn't any more day out than a pink-golden hue lighting cloudbellies. She again pulled her stiff limbs then stood in her thoughts for some time. A few minutes later the sun broke from the egg of earth, spilling its yolk skyward, illuminating the same cloudbanks with hints of purple-grey. The dawn song grew louder as if the light were a reminder, and the sound grew muddier because Greta could no longer peel apart what was what. About then, both Tiller and Scott stirred and soon started cooking what was left of the bacon along with last night's beans and prepackaged corn bread.

Here in the grassy slopes the world smelled of earth and clay, and she squatted behind her tent and let out a hot stream, then cleaned herself. Head thrumming a dull roar, she soon downed some water, ate half a cookie, then stuffed her wedding mice in her coat pocket. She pet them with her thumb while making her way to where Scott and Tiller ate breakfast, then stole a slice of bacon off Scott's plate.

The melting glow of distant Hyattville twinkled below them in the southwest but was growing dim, and within minutes, only a few sparkles caught her eye. Along the western horizon, more of that slow beginning to dawn, like maybe the far side of the world was burning, then turned away from its watercolors and muted itself.

Something ate at her throughout the morning, and during this, all brightness turned to gloom, and a greyness settled over everything, over every mood and hoofstrike, and they passed over what looked like ancient railroad tracks, with ties brittle and nearly stripped to dust from the elements, and it seemed like they were marching into a huge funnel of darkness parallel to a long-dead route.

A wind started up too, and more low clouds hurtled westward over their slow-moving army of hide and meat. Greta, along with Scott and Tiller, could see other mist-shapes towering above them, and over the lower plains, as if their blackened undersides were burnt, so they stopped, got out their rain gear, fitted the quads with partial waterproof covers, and steered the cattle toward a gravel trail, rather than just over the grasses and shrubs, because here it was getting more dense, but also, to avoid getting caught in any waxy and sticky gumbo during any downpour, which is what she and the others called some of the mud around these parts. They wanted the cattle and their quads safe and on sturdy ground, so made their way prairiewise to the northeast, then along a side trail toward a distant catchpen. Its narrow chute and large holding pen were still intact, its five-foot fences sturdy, though a half-broken sweep-gate meant the larger cattle had to squeeze through. At the far end, an open shed, which Tiller said would offer some shelter for them and a small part of the herd.

It was midday when the hail came down, the shelter already in front of them. Waterstones big as knuckles fell meteoric, zinging and bouncing, some the size of small acorns, others larger, crashing atop piles of themselves. Cattle continued to funnel. Many crammed the holding pen and half shelter. Others, not even making it inside, ran beneath trees, or fled crying into the low hills.

Greta and Scott aimed toward the shelter with some of the remaining cattle, careful to watch for any lightning, which luckily there hadn't been flashes or thunder, though plenty of ice balls zoomed from the sky. More than one hard *thunk* might have knocked her out had she not worn her helmet. A few hit her arms, legs, and back, those she knew would leave welts. Scott had his helmet on too, and she cursed and thought, *Damn, if we don't all look like idiots.*

Greta drove right in, jumped off, covered her ATV and pressed herself against a cow hiding in the open shed. After pulling out some complaining cows, Tiller also moved his quad into the covered part of the shelter, then stepped out and stared at the cattle, right in the hail with his helmet on, observing the cows moan, scream, and twitch. Luckily they were fairly tight in the pen and couldn't trample each other.

"Get your ass under here," Greta yelled, then ran out and grabbed Tiller by the arm and pulled him in.

"I gotta get the cows," he said. "They're not all in here."

"Not only are you going to get hurt, gonna ruin your quad if you take it back out."

Scott pulled heavier covers over his and Tiller's ATVs to keep them more protected. He hammered a few spikes into the ground so the wind wouldn't blow them away, and had to keep nudging cattle to the side, as man, woman, and beast all sought sanctuary from the violent thrumming against the earth.

Tiller didn't say a thing, just stood back, Greta still holding on. Not ten seconds later a calf ran out of nowhere toward the corral, groaning and screaming, hail slamming against the poor beast. Greta and Tiller watched it fall and knew it got clocked a good one, and she hoped it wasn't dead, and stared out at the mud and gravel, all coated in grey-blue ice, like every eye got stripped from the heavens and poured here, cold and dead, irises turned pale.

The clouds, still angry and low, crawled and screamed, hail dumping along rolls of grassy slopes toward the canyons to the east. Greta watched for any funnel clouds that might touch down, and didn't see any, though she feared the possibility, but now the rains came, and the sky seemed black and ripped upon its long belly, and she briefly put a hand on Tiller's then pulled away, and then those black clouds dumped water onto every living thing, which brought a kind of darkness that felt close to night.

Peering into the winds and rain, Greta thought she could

see something up there even darker than the clouds, something moving counter to their tumult, something that in its immensity easily cloaked her in fear, but the clouds were flying so fast she thought maybe she was seeing firm skybelly edges about to burst, which they were, spilling and rolling and pouring. But then amid the wiping of wet and fog from her helmet, and then pulling it off, and with her rain hood up, she was struck by an even greater weight of fear because she spotted what could have been the trailing edge of a dark wing cutting through the fabric of grey-black, like an airplane caught low in a storm, tearing cloud from cloud. And then she told herself that's what this had to be, one of those storm planes measuring precipitation or something, flown up from the little airport in Hyattville, maybe come in from a bigger city. And she half expected a funnel cloud for real now, and one of those storm chaser four-wheeler armored trucks like something out of *Mad Max* and *Twisters* combined, a man-made monstrosity chewing up the trail, steering straight into the tapered tail of a skysnake, the very thing she feared might land and rip into the open shed.

But there was nothing like that, no armored anything, and she didn't see that wing again, and stopped looking up, and figured if something were there, maybe it would have eaten her by now. And if it had taken a dead calf that first night, maybe it only gorged on dead things, but if there was such a thing as a giant bird, it would come in a rainstorm exactly like this and take every last one of them, saving Greta for last.

A mess of cows spread across the high country in the deluge, maybe a dozen if Greta had made a correct count, some tangled in shrubs, lost from each other and the herd. Some dents in the quads too. Scott had cracked his helmet visor, and Tiller suffered a small cut that was maybe from pulling on his helmet and catching it on the bridge of his nose, that or maybe a chunk of ice smashed him there.

"No good chasing strays in this downpour." Tiller allowed Greta to pull him back. He wiped the cut with the back of a hand, smearing blood onto his cheek like some kind of crimson war paint. "Weather wasn't supposed to be this bad, but you know how summers go in Wyoming. Dry one minute, wet the next, and sometimes deadly wet. Sure was hoping we'd have a clear ten-day stretch with only some light showers."

"Think that calf is . . . ?" Greta pointed. The dogie still wasn't moving. It hadn't fallen in any kind of natural position, and if it were alive, a puddle was forming around it. She figured it might drown, and that made her uneasy.

"What of it?" Tiller wiped at his face again and only made the smear worse.

"Dead—?"

"Want me to go ask?"

"Not dragging it on my quad," she said, also not wanting to help wipe the blood from his face. She kind of preferred him like this, a bloody mess.

"Me either," Scott added. "Not in this. We'll both get stuck in the mud."

"Trail is a straight shot," Tiller said. "If you did."

"No."

Tiller said: "More like you would drag it to a carrion heap near here. But looks like you don't have to."

Greta could see the calf move. The rain really pounded now, and every shadow there ever was seemed to cast grey cloaks onto the corral. A rivulet formed too, tumbling between the shelter and the calf.

"We gonna drown in here?" Scott said. "Looks like a damn flash flood."

"Hope not," Tiller said.

The calf twitched a few times, then twisted its body, struggling to get its legs underneath, kicking and shuddering, then able to pull itself up, shook its head a few times. A moment later, Greta half expected that birdplane or whatever to come swooping out of the sky and snatch the critter, but the calf sloshed through the rivulet, let out a bellow, and came right over to the shelter, leaving deep hoofstrikes in the mud.

"Would you look at that?" Greta rubbed the calf's side as the beast hollered again, then squeezed its way between some of the cows, maybe toward its mother. "Never seen that before," Greta said. "Calf knocked cold from a hailstone. If it could tell stories . . ."

But then the three of them saw a dog-sized shadow skitter into the corral, and because of the grey and shadows Greta considered the goat-fawn, but then this thing's head was long and low in the mud and Greta felt her insides crawl, because this wasn't anything like that taxidermy, and she quickly realized this was a *bird*, not a freak mammal, and more like a roadrunner but *not*. Its coloring was off too, not grey-brown or streaky at all like that of a Greater Roadrunner, more colorful with hints of blue and purple, maybe black, but that could be those soggy feathers once again and the lack of bright sunlight on its plumage, and it didn't have that pale underside she'd seen a million times, though anything wet and soggy would seem dark in the rain, wouldn't it? Though this was bigger, and ran slightly different, more straight up now, but still bent forward, that long tail used for balance, and it jumped onto the middle of one of the fence beams and with a pale eye gazed over to where the calf had lain.

"What the fuck is that?" Greta said.

"Roadrunner, I guess," Tiller said. "Too late for a calf meal. Not that it could swallow one."

"No roadrunner looks like that." She knuckled water out of her eyes. "And they're not scavengers."

"What do you mean *not a roadrunner*, sure it is," Scott said.

"Look at that size," Greta said. "That bird's a good head-and-half-a-neck taller than any roadrunner I've seen. Twice the size maybe?"

"So?"

"That bill is too large and hooked, don't remember a roadrunner's bill being so yellow. And roadrunners don't have black around the eyes. Plumage seems iridescent, blackish."

"Everything looks black in this storm," Scott said.

"I know." Greta shifted against a cow. "But there's orange on its underside, and an iridescence to its wings especially."

"How can you tell?"

"I can tell."

"It's a damn roadrunner," Tiller said. "End of story."

"What made you an expert?" Greta shook her head at his bloody face.

"See the damn things all the time."

The bird stared at them, purple-black in the rain, and with a bit more light now, hints of oranges on its chest and belly, and a purple-green glint on its wings at times, a scaly orange chest, Greta noticed, and along that, a double black chest band.

It clacked its bill and let out a rattle, much deeper and longer than a real roadrunner or meadowlark.

"Roadrunner rattle for sure," Tiller said.

But no sooner than he said those words, the bird let out a shrill sound like a referee's whistle, piercing their ears. It pulsed faster and faster before slowing, like some kind of warning about the rain that made Greta's insides squirm as if she'd just seen a herd of goat-fawns slithering through mud.

"No goddam roadrunner does that," she said.

"Suppose you're right," Tiller said. "Probably seen one or two before though."

"Yeah, it creeps me out. Shoulda brought one of my bird guides." Maynard had given her one in particular, a *Sibley's Field Guide to Birds of Western North America*. She liked the drawings, the details, not that she understood some terms like primary coverts, undertail coverts, malars, vents, supralorals, supercilium, and all that. And though she didn't look at it often, or nearly enough, she'd flipped through it, didn't recall any ground-running North American bird bigger than a roadrunner or grouse, other than a Wild Turkey. This was turkey-sized but sure-as-hell was no gobbler.

Then the bird let out its shrill call again, or maybe this was its song, and either way was like a repeating referee whistle that sped up then slowed. Hardly ten seconds went by before the bird blasted the same noise, while the clouds darkened again and the rain suddenly poured even harder, and the rivulet cut deeper and faster in front of them.

Tiller soon lit a cigarette, his bleeding stopped, and cleaned his face with a rag, and offered them smokes. Both

Scott and Greta declined. "Rain gonna pour a short while," Tiller said. "Maybe . . . should fix supper."

"We're about to get drowned," Scott said.

"Or eaten by that bird." Greta noted the rain scrubbing away hoofprints and any remaining tire tracks and that bird on the fence watching like it wanted to stand atop every drowned cowhand and cowhide, and then feast.

"Suit yourself," Tiller said. "Making a sandwich."

No sooner than he turned around when Greta saw three of the same birds now perched on various sections of the fence. She nudged Scott.

"What the hell?" Scott cried. "Bird been calling its friends over?"

"Doesn't mean a goddam thing." Tiller pulled up the tarp so he could access his ATV, then went to making his sandwich.

The bird didn't sing again, but by late afternoon ten of them perched on the fence, rain-soaked, watching herders or the cattle, sometimes preening or just sleeping. And then every once in a while, one would vanish and then reappear with a prairie dog in its stout bill, a couple times a rattler or squirrel. One bit into a dead bullfrog, let its prey hang by a slimy foot, maybe hoping to trade off for something larger, until it soon got in a fight right there on the fence, and the frog's legs and head got pulled apart like taffy, half its innards spilling in a bubbly red rain-mud. The cows stirred, didn't panic, but trembled nervously. Greta did too, especially when she spotted one of the birds hopping along the backs of cows, while another landed on a calf and started to peck at its head, aiming for an eye, which at least the calf had sense enough to shake the thing off.

"We gotta scare those birds out of here," she said. "Calves gonna lose their eyes to these things, maybe an ear."

"Shoot at 'em and you spook the cows," Tiller said.

"Well then walk over there and shoo them away."

"Across that little creek? Maybe soon, starting to let up already."

Greta didn't like water like this, never did. She didn't like thinking about crossing, or wading, though for all she knew it was less than half a foot deep. She thought of the Pope, and imagined his body floating by, those dead lips moving about things he'd taught her about the outdoors. *Rushing water is more dangerous than starving*, the corpse seemed to say.

She remembered nightmares of floating in the middle of an ocean, of falling into a stream and drowning, of being lost in a rising creek, no one to help. She could hear that voice telling her to stay away from the edge, to not stick her feet in. There was the time they camped by a river, him giving her the same lecture when she was four or five. He'd lost a cousin in the Eel River, said he wasn't gonna raise any kid to be a river rat. When she did play in the gutter during rains, he'd catch her and whip her butt raw, which made her hate him, but sure kept her from messing with rushing water, which is maybe what made her imagine those corpse feet slipping under the fence and disappearing into a distant ravine.

Then Greta heard a groan that sounded close to her name, but with a long vowel sound, similar to *Gretaaaa*, but maybe not, maybe too high-pitched, maybe something else. And she thought for a second that her imagination was real, that she could conjure the Pope and he'd come racing back from the ravine to call her name, to remind her that the dead were watching. It came from the dark grasses, and only once. Everyone looked up. Even Tiller held still, cocked his head like he caught wind of something.

"What the hell was that?" Scott said. "That wasn't from those birds."

"It wasn't." Tiller leaned into the rainstorm, then turned and lifted the tarp that covered his quad, took out his rifle.

"What's that for?" Scott asked. "Think it was a bear or something?"

Greta didn't know what to say or think. She wasn't sure if they'd heard the Pope, the goat-fawn, or something else lurking close. But if Tiller was pulling out a rifle, then she needed to be cautious too, try to figure out what this could be, maybe a big cat for all she knew. She didn't grab for her rifle, but stood listening, scanning.

She gazed at the birds. Half ran off. The rest appeared nervous, eyes on alert, heads cocked. Greta watched the sky now, then the thick brush on either side of the corral, in case something, whatever had called out, hid there. Tiller watched too, flicked off the rifle's wing safety, wasn't going to take any chances.

"Didn't sound like a bear," Scott said. "But maybe that's all it was."

"I think cat," Greta said, not believing herself, still half expecting her dad to perch himself on the fence with those birds and maybe grab one and chew on its neck. She wanted to kick herself for not going to his funeral—didn't want this to be some kind of retribution where he decided to haunt the trail.

"Don't wanna see no bear." Tiller surveyed the scene, watched closely for any sign.

And then something else, a howl, a whistle, not from the

birds, which scattered from the sudden noise, but a sound so loud Greta ducked, while the cows stirred and complained, some kicking at the shelter, tearing away sections of wood.

"Goddam," Tiller shouted, while Scott mouthed *What the fuck*, or maybe did say the words, Greta couldn't tell. And then the sound was gone, and the birds didn't return, and Tiller white-knuckled his rifle. The cows groaned but stopped kicking.

"We gotta save them cows out there." Tiller strapped his rifle to his quad, and fired up the engine.

"That's it? What was that?" Scott said.

"I don't know, but any cows close enough, I'm bringing in."

"I think you do know." Greta's ears rang. "Bear? Monster?"

"Ain't either," Tiller said.

"Then what?"

He pulled on his goggles, the rain having slipped into a drizzle-mist.

"Train whistle."

"What do you mean, *train* whistle?" Scott asked. "No trains around here."

"Look, we got hardly a speck of light out there," Tiller said, "and this little creek ain't raging like it was. If the strays all break their legs, run off, or get eaten, we might lose twenty or so head. And if that happens there's gonna be hell to pay. So, let's roll."

Before he could drive off Greta grabbed at his shirt. She remembered earlier they'd passed old tracks, disintegrating railroad ties, rusted rails. "What really happens if we don't get those head of cattle in here?" Tiller tried to pull loose, but she held tight. "What happens?"

"If you got to know"—he pried her fingers loose—"we're wasting time. Ghost train's coming."

"The wha—" came her words, but then Tiller was off.

The quad engines soon roared, and the three left the catch-pen to push through all the mud and puddles to round up far more cattle than Greta realized were missing, nearly a tenth of the herd scattered in the hills. And no sign of a train where there shouldn't be one anyway, not unless it burst from the earth like a reanimated corpse. No lights, no moving shadows other than distant cattle roaming like ghosts. Only that whistle they'd heard, and Tiller's worrying, which made Greta start to fear every cloud and odd rainsound.

The three made their way into the nearby hills, each taking a separate direction, and needed to be quick about it. In fact, Tiller's words echoed in Greta's ears: "If the whistle feels like it's in your soul, or if you feel a rumble, move off-trail fast as you can."

Mud sprayed onto Greta's helmet as she steered clear of any gumbo-like mud. She swiped across her goggles and was soon able to gather half a dozen strays in the pen area. Turning her ATV around, she nearly ran over one of the strange birds trying to sneak its way back to a calf. The iridescent creature squawked and flapped its waterlogged wings, and ran into the prairie.

Greta passed Scott and Tiller who were bringing in around a dozen cows. Each worked through the slog, when she noticed other of the bovines naturally coming back to the area, pulled by the sounds of cattle bawling for their friends and babies, not to mention, some had been conditioned to gather to the sounds of engines.

Then the whistle came again. The shriek-shrill-blast felt much closer, piercing her ears even through her helmet, which usually blocked out some noise and left her to drone in her own thoughts, like the one she was having whether this Greta, this muddy, scared version of herself, this girl in thick, soupy, drizzly air, helmet and goggles covered in mud, ATV headlight cutting through the mist, was a version of herself maybe Hannah would love. So many times Greta hadn't been wild enough, crazy enough, impromptu enough. But this sound, this whistle, she didn't know how it could be louder than before, but was, and made her nauseous, like all the bile might stream out of her, and she thought, *Yeah, Hannah might love that too*, like that rainy night the two of them shot up an empty trailer way off West Jackson Street. That was something wild that Hannah was proud of her for doing. The trailer belonged to their dead friend Charlie. Everyone in their group of friends had been out there, and that meant Greta too, though she never told Hannah she'd been out there twice by herself, and could still feel something she shouldn't. And that boarded-up window she remembered had been like a shut mouth, and the satellite dish no longer seemed secured to the roof, just wriggled there in the wind like someone been found guilty. And they shot the hell out of that structure, that dish too.

Then Greta wondered if she should turn back to the corral, leave any remaining cattle to wander in the mud, and remembered Tiller maybe said that whistle might enter her soul if she wasn't careful, or maybe she thought he said as much, and because she didn't imagine the sound had completely cracked that immaterial part of herself, she decided to risk continuing to save every cow she could, even though that whistle came soon as it stopped, this time a piercing siren, an *omen*, which made her nearly throw up, and she realized this may have been the same crushing blast she'd heard the first few days after Hannah disappeared, a kind of awful, dead cry that went on inside her head and gut until she passed out.

After that double whistle blast Greta throttled hard up over rocks and gravel, then skidded through mud onto a ridge where she thought she'd seen some cows. Briefly pausing to again wipe her goggles, she spotted a mother and calf already making their way, as if the cow pen had become a sudden magnet to the homing mechanism inside their brains. A moment later the cows pushed past her down the rise. Greta revved the engine, which got them to move faster, and felt glad that the bovines had learned to heed such noises.

The cattle soon joined Scott, who was bringing three himself, and then joined Tiller in the distance with several more.

There was hardly a sound just then except for Greta's quad. Feeling exhausted and wet, she realized everything smelled like mud, shit, or exhaust, not to mention, her ears rang, and stomach lurched. Then, because it seemed Tiller and Scott weren't headed back out, she thought, yeah, any lingering cow could be found in the morning. Hell, that whistle could just keep screaming through the night. Maybe she'd even get used to it.

Then the sky bloomed into darkness again, and she started thinking maybe she wasn't as tough as she thought, telling herself maybe this was something else, not a ghost train or goat-fawn or these birds, but the Pope, his corpse making her fear even a whistle. Then she remembered Hannah doubting her too, *Greta, I thought we were the same, guess not*, and that struck Greta, because she couldn't imagine Hannah chasing cows, though she could imagine her chasing ghosts.

Greta thought maybe Hannah was wrong, maybe they were the same, because though the Pope seemed to be chasing her, maybe Greta was the one chasing him. Then she thought, maybe Hannah would respect that. Maybe this cattle drive would prove just how adventurous and unpredictable Greta could be, now having seen things, chased things, and not having run away from them. Hadn't Hannah always said, *Spirits in the past and present are always trying to talk to us? We should listen.*

And now Greta knew that it wasn't only about her not being adventurous enough, but also about her seeing the world as nothing more than a side gig so she could live more comfortably in the present, that maybe like Hannah said, *Spirits take you down some paths, and you chase them down others*, and maybe there were spirit guides, and maybe there were good and bad spirits, and maybe you had to navigate it all while fighting for the lives of a few damn cows.

She was headed down the main trail to make the short distance back toward the open shed, thinking all this when she saw Lady Grazer huffing her way back on her short legs. *Damn cow*, Greta thought, *of course she'd be the last to make her way back.*

The cow was tired, but determined, legs in a near trot, though she still wasn't much faster than an old hound. Greta almost laughed but nearly got thrown off her quad and hit the brakes. She came to a slide and still felt like she was moving.

Sure enough, something awful came. She heard another engine over her idle, one so loud that it rattled the earth and shook rocks straight from gloopy mudholes.

Ahead, a light, a lone beam illuminating every raindrop, closing in. The rumbling grew into a thunder that shook her nearly off the quad. She started to back up when she realized she had to get away—the light was barreling fast up the main trail. She throttled and pulled left and uphill, and nearly kicked herself off, then powered up a steep incline, her quad groaning, almost slipping.

At the top, she turned in time to see Lady Grazer still huffing her way, only the poor thing headed straight toward the light, maybe unaware, maybe too tired, maybe just too full and focused and rain-soaked to think it was anything other than a quad's beam.

The closing light shot across the earth like a star ready to burn into a nebula and spread its tendrils northeastward. And now the whistle came again. Lady Grazer, Greta could tell, was terrified, as was Greta, the sound smashing her eardrums. The light, as if on the tide of the scream, rushed toward the cow and her stubby, galloping legs.

Greta heaved bile out of her mouth, the whistle now clearly in her soul. And though she wanted to snatch the cow from the train's path, it was too late, there would be no way to get to her.

Greta cried out when Lady Grazer was engulfed. She watched the light and the giant shadow it was attached to, both passing over where the cow had been. Then the whistle came again, but not before Greta could see and hear the carriages on the tracks, and faces in translucent grey windows, the entire train like some kind of wolf pack on its way to devour anything in its path.

Railcar after railcar rattled past filled with ghost passengers. Not Indians, Mexicans, Blacks, or Chinese, but terrified *white* faces, children among them, everyone in suits and dresses. Then the caboose rushed into view, ghost lanterns and a star-spangled banner adorning it with the words CODY DONE DIED. And there on the back holding onto the rail, a horrific ghost rider in a wide hat, a long goatee hanging from his glowing chin, and a mustache for the ages. His wide eyes glowed white, mouth hanging in a deep pit, abnormally stretched like his jaw had come apart.

It was then Greta realized he'd been making that whistle-scream all along. Mouth open unnaturally, unhinged, wide and black. That rider gazed at her and screamed while the caboose whipped into the darkness and mist like a shrinking creature, glowing for what seemed an eternity, then flickered out.

It was only then the rumble within the earth subsided, and that whistle-scream turned into owls screeching close by, scaring up waterlogged field or kangaroo rats, and the darkness and mist melted to a dreary presence, while Greta, shaking, somehow had the wherewithal to ride back down the trail.

The Jackrabbit

The jackrabbit could watch from his place on the shelf, but knew he shouldn't be able to see down into the room. Not that his eyes hurt, or that he'd been blinded. These weren't *his* eyes. And he knew these weren't objects he should be able to peer through, and though deep down he wanted to panic and run and kick, he didn't, and wouldn't, because he was pulled into a calmness by something else. And that created in him a desire to study, to survey, and something else, something he'd never felt, let alone understood, a compulsion to serve, to worship.

These weren't feelings or thoughts he'd had, ever, because what and how would a rabbit serve? And what was worship to him before any of this? He loved the night and the moon and the lights in the sky, but didn't think much of them other than they made the darkness special, and big, and wondrous, and that if anything, the daylight hid it all away while he slept, and he didn't like that. No, not the sun, never the sun. Too bright. Too scary. He didn't talk to the night, to the moon, to the blinky lights, to the night fires streaking

across the dark. But now he felt he was there for them and something more, *her*.

He always craved the nights whenever they burned away, and felt safe in them, except for those hungry owls hooting or screaming, who were also silent in their stealing of victims. He feared them the most, even more than coyotes who would *pounce-pounce* on burrows, trying to make a jackrabbit run straight into canine jaws, which he'd seen happen many times, which always made his heart race and cry and long to be the fastest of all hares.

He'd longed, yes. Loved, played, got angry, constantly feared for his life, wished, desired, though not now, not now at all, because he wasn't completely himself, and in a way this wasn't his life any longer—and there came a soft buzz with that, a hum to his hide, though he didn't have bones anymore, or squishy parts, no tongue, no guts—though he sat upright on his haunches, and could feel he had a familiar shape, it wasn't quite his, as if his rabbitskin had been stretched over something dark and solid. And he could feel that along with having no bones, he had no beating heart, no lungs to breathe through, no brain to think with. Yet he had thoughts. Something captured them and placed his constant wonder inside the pelt-head-whatever of what he was, along with wire and wood, and somehow that wire and wood in his legs and neck had joints, could bend, and had greasy goo in them.

And he tested a paw, and even wiggled each toe, though he could hardly bend, couldn't walk or leap—he knew this much. His new eyes, that weren't eyes, could swivel in their sockets though they shouldn't. And he could see to where a white, two-legged, mostly hairless man held another jackrabbit by the throat, and with wide hands peeled and ripped all the skin and fur away from flesh. And the jackrabbit couldn't tell if he'd known *that* jackrabbit, because he couldn't smell, or kind of could, though his nose kind of wiggled, or thought it did, though his empty chest kind of moved in and out, or maybe not. His plaster tongue could kind of tremble, and anyway, the last he'd seen any of his family it was dawn, the sky was pink. He'd been about to enter the burrow and go to sleep, and then suddenly he was with a dozen other jackrabbits leaping and running down a steep slope, falling over each other, stepping on each other's heads, kicking at air and invisible claws, hearts racing with *blood blood blood*, as they fled a pair of Golden Eagles, talons extended, brown and mottled wings spread, those golden heads so angry.

Those two raptors each grabbed a rabbit by the scruffs of their necks, and carried them screaming to nearby trees, and tore away fur, and unearthed spines, and he'd seen and heard that, and remembered, because he wanted to see who and what and why, and then *ran*-hopped, and fell, and *ran*-hopped some more, until he hid in a bush and sniffed and snorted in fear. And then something happened to him, that loud blast, every pink bit of light turned golden, then everything went dark, until now.

And he watched that man in this room peel apart flesh for some time. Then the jackrabbit saw straight across on another shelf a row of Black-billed Magpies, wings twitching, bills straining to open and close, but also could hardly move, and couldn't coo or purr or squawk, and their abnormal bird eyes, such strange orbs, turned to him because these weren't their old eye-lamps but new eye-lamps. And he wondered what these birds understood, or the tiny, pale, swift fox down below—only half his size—or the raccoons, the beaver, or even the prairie dog on a fake mound, all straining to move.

The birds were watching, and one magpie lifted off and sailed to him, as if trying to recall how to fly, yet still managed to flap straight over, and pecked at his fur, and he was scared all over again, a deeper kind of fear, because though he hardly felt like himself, he didn't want to lose his eyes, or his insides, whatever they had become.

But the bird kept pecking, this iridescent blue-green corvid with its black head like some kind of devil hood, and tail black and long like a serpent, and that white belly beneath white shoulders like a tiny snowbank, and that strange, oblong bill pecking at him, though it didn't hurt. And then something odd, the bird pulled away with a tuft, white like a cloud, and flew back over to its brethren and just sat there, eyeing him, the white fluff in its bill, which he didn't even feel was missing.

For a moment he thought it might have been his white tail plucked right off—but didn't see the bit of black stripe that should be in it, so thought that hopefully it wasn't his tail. Then the room went dark. He realized he could still see, and night was when he remembered he'd most been awake when he'd been alive, always foraging for twigs and root-bark. And he soon felt that bird at his side again, and he could hardly move, so the magpie had its way, pushing its head inside his side, all the way in, like it was looking around inside the moon itself, and instead of searching for rootlets and grass for a nest, was seeking an answer to all of this. But there was no answer, and eventually, after three or four times, the bird left him alone.

When it was light, the man came back, and the jackrabbit noticed a white gleam around the man's neck, similar to the metallic gleam of hooks in all fish mouths, because fish hung there in the room, frozen as if having leapt from a river or pond. And the hooks had feathers and wormy things attached, only this one around the man's neck wasn't metal but white and shiny, iridescent like a shell, and *maybe* it was, and there was an oldness to it that permeated the very room, as if this hook had been pulled from the coast of an ancient sea.

Then he saw that the hook itself radiated something else, a kind of disturbance to the air that he would never have seen with his old eyes. And then he saw the man had begun mixing something, a paste of some kind, in a little stone bowl, and was using a stone to crush the mixture, and the jackrabbit didn't know, didn't know, *wanted to know* what this was for, but then the man left the room with the bowl, and the jackrabbit started to panic that he would be forever trapped in this room-cave, and he sensed that all the other animals seemed to feel the same, this hidden panic, this uneasiness, this collective twitching, this lack of needing to feed, but hunger nonetheless.

They were all anxious to get up and run, he thought, to flee this place, to do more than twitch toes or swivel their eyes, or wriggle noses. And then the man came back in the room with the paste in his hand, a ball of it, grey, like day-old rabbit brains cooking on a prairie rock. And in his other hand, a small, flat stick, rounded at the ends, and the creature, a man, took a dollop of the paste, and walked around the room, and dabbed some in each animal's and bird's mouth. And then, getting a small ladder, slathered gobs in the mouths nearest the man: a skunk, a weasel, a marmot, a bobcat kitten. And then the jackrabbit himself, in his mouth. He felt a wave of fear when the wood and paste entered. And he felt so terribly afraid when the awful taste came, because he'd forgotten what it was to savor. Then he remembered the good things, the grasses and leaves, and bits of root-bark. But this taste was something horrid that had been in the bowels of earth and time, and had festered there, rotting, and was death and life and good and evil all at once. And was a kind of unearthly stone. And was all the sea-life drowned and burned and exploded and distilled. And was a canyon, a mother canyon, and something embedded in her like a tumor.

And the jackrabbit hated the taste, and the way it dragged his mind into a canyon, so dark but not the good kind of dark, and felt a desire to find other two-legged creatures, and bring them, or even just one, to the man, to make one of them like the jackrabbit and all these animals right now.

And the jackrabbit, sensing his body's awakening, could now move and move so much, and wanted to *leap leap leap*. He was able to twitch one of his large, black-tipped grey ears, then the other, then lay them back on his head. Then he watched the man smash all the magpies so that their unnatural lives were stamped out for good.

Then, without thinking, the jackrabbit leapt off the shelf and started running and jumping around the room and into a hallway and back, and while he felt free, he also felt that he must serve, that he must leave this room, and re-enter the night, and watch all the things that are done inside and outside mother canyon . . .

Night Four

In the morning a light appeared in Greta's tent shining right at her face. All she could think about was that star blazing up the trail engulfing Lady Grazer and how Greta had reeled at what charged past: railcar after railcar filled with the ghosts of white settlers in some kind of repeated purgatory, and Wild Bill Cody, AKA Buffalo Bill, if it *was* that bison hunter and showman on the caboose screaming those whistle-blasts. His name *was* on the banner.

She didn't remember getting back to the corral, or falling into her tent that had been pitched onto a bed of rocky, wet dirt. Somehow, she'd been able to sleep on that mess, plagued by dreams she couldn't remember but knew had been cast in a nightmarish moonglow.

And now this tent-light, her realizing this was Tiller flashing a beam at her face, telling her to get up. "Time for herding. Remember how to do that?" And before she could throw anything, or even let out a curse, he disappeared to go do whatever the hell he was going to do, hopefully to make breakfast. All of this was enough for her to wish that train had run over him for not

telling them about screaming ghost-whistles, weird birds, and goat-fawns.

She turned on her side, angry in the dimness, mad at Tiller for everything, at this feeling in her full bladder because she didn't want to move. Though she hated all that morning abdominal pressure, she wasn't ready to release it, or to even look at Tiller's face, so closed her eyes to try to get some sense of the day, maybe of herself.

What she did remember and let replace the image of Tiller's light was something the Pope said to her long ago. He'd taken her outside of Laramie to learn to ride a horse, as well as to teach her the finer points of herding cows. He'd bragged about how the world needed hard men, maybe a few hard women, that being a cowboy of both the road and land meant you had that edge.

"The hard things you do make for a hard life," she remembered him saying. None of this was supposed to be easy, he told her. Those words played like a film reel, the two of them headed up a long slope. "A real caballero, or buckaroo, or in your case, a young vaquera," he said, "must learn to see that cattle are part of the land."

And she did learn this, though she didn't care about his philosophizing, and would never admit how it helped. Eventually, he got her hired on with some friends to help on a few drives, which was never more than a day, just picking up skills up here and there, like learning to keep your head up in case the cattle played hide-and-seek, or riding up on the hip of a cow if you wanted her to move, and talking kindly to them like they were your friends.

"You know, mija," the Pope had once said, "we've been doing this for hundreds of years in our family, and if you trace our lineage, you'll probably see that we were half conquerors, half something else, people of the land, maybe? And that makes all the difference."

"Half settlers in a way," Greta remembered saying.

"Sure. We were the half-breed offspring of those who changed everything about herding. Don't you forget that. We had to become a people. But we also came from the land in a much different way. And while much of that indigenous in us has been lost, something is still in our blood, in our DNA. We inherit the past, mija, not just the present when we experience the world or hear stories. There is a secret part inside that will help you to know how to do this. That's why sometimes you have to close your eyes while you're herding. You'll see the stray by having examined the terrain, by seeing the herd as one large beast that has its own form, that loses little parts of itself, which you have to find, keep safe. You will know this by knowing every rock, shrub, and gully, by the way the wind blows, by examining food sources, the way the sun hits the prairie or canyon rocks to provide enticing shelter in the shade, by the divots in the ground that would make for a nice bed to rest on, you will know. And you will see in your mind's eye where the strays venture, and if you really know the land, you will follow invisible hoofprints as if you're the very creature that has wandered."

She remembered falling off her horse because she didn't tighten the girth properly, and the Pope laughing and laughing. He'd brushed off the dirt and pulled out goatheads, but didn't wipe her tears, and she remembered him rambling into one of his stories. "Your family origins down in New Mexico transformed the West. You had to know, unlike your Aunt Maria who never told her sons about those white sands. One of them works on a damn oyster farm of all things. Forget about those old Westerns I grew up on too. Half the time, John Wayne should have been pushed aside, his characters played by brown men like me. I woulda looked good in the movies, yeah?

"You fall well, mija. Maybe you can be my stuntman." He laughed. "Then again, I don't fall." And then he said that thing that ate at her, that made her hate his every DNA strand. "If you'd been a boy . . ."

The hard things you do make for a hard woman, Greta thought, not a hard life, though maybe she could convince herself that hard lives and hard things and hard women were justified as things that simply happened without any intention, none of which she was certain about, although what she did know, when she finally opened her eyes and got up, still pissed at Tiller, was that living in this world wasn't all about how to be a goddam man.

She slipped on a pair of fresh socks, pulled on her boots, and packed up her tent, which had been pitched alongside the boys' just outside the corral.

Empty-stomached like she hadn't eaten in a week, she greeted her fellow herders with fire in her eyes, trying not to say anything until she had a full meal. Her only plans were to make them uncomfortable with her silence. In the meantime, she downed four slices of bacon, a biscuit, two eggs, and two cups of coffee.

Soon they ignored her for ignoring them, and as she shouldered her rolled tent she could see them whispering the way men do.

The cattle were already antsy to find some food up on

the trail slopes, and complained to get out of the pen for the first time in nearly a day. The night before, some of them had been quivering from their fear of the storm and those strange whistles. Now some of the little ones sucked milk, or tried to, their mothers grumbling and pulling away.

Greta, feeling enough like herself again to talk, said: "What the hell was that last night, Tiller?"

"Good morning," Scott said. "Hope you liked that bacon. Added some maple and smoke."

Greta ignored him and glared at Tiller.

"Cook never gets respect," Scott said.

Tiller pushed up the front of his hat so she could see his eyes. "Told you what it was."

"We have an option to leave," Scott added. "He was just saying . . ."

Greta leaned on an old chute and continued to ignore Scott. Not that she believed what she was about to say, but she accused Tiller anyway: "You been spiking the food or our water? Because I sure been seeing and hearing things."

"Ain't spiked a thing."

"Even the cows been seeing ghost trains." She squeezed one of the corpse-mice in her pocket a little hard, thought she felt it wriggle away. "I want to know what's going on. Why are we hearing and seeing things?"

"Only ever heard about that whistle." Tiller took a drink of coffee. "Always heard ghost trains come east from somewhere south of Wapiti. *Lucky enough to see one, usually not lucky enough to tell the tale*—that's what I been told. But you saw it, didn't you? Couldn't from our vantage point."

"She saw something," Scott said in disbelief.

"Who told you about them?" Greta said to Tiller and eyed Scott.

"That generation's gone now." Tiller gathered all the dishes and a bottle of water and some soap and got to washing. "Never believed them," he said. "Never thought I'd hear that steam whistle, that's for sure. But you seen something, and way back when I was a kid my great-grandfather and his associates insisted this place was haunted.

"They said that train comes in the rain about a day's ride before you enter the canyon, *like it gonna run itself into them Bighorns, push all the way to Cloud Peak*. Said that train swallows every living thing in its path, carriages carry all them men and women who died moving and living West, especially ones wishing they could escape back East to their mamas, all the way across the Atlantic." He dumped some more water and soap on the dishes and used his bare hands to do the scrubbing. "Said them folks ended up on that train as a punishment, got swallowed by that screaming slice of eternal hell because of something every man, woman, and child on there might have done. Maybe Indians cursed them, all these lands, something that can trap you in a long box with wheels, haunt your very ears until you die. They say a thousand curses fell on these parts, maybe ten thousand, that train's just one. Mountain of bones is another. Bison once died around here in unimaginable numbers, and then their remains was stacked into towers and walls. Ain't seen those ghost bones myself. My old man would tell you different about all this. He'd say . . ."

"Something about his taxidermy?" Greta hiked up the waistband to her jeans. "Or ghosts?"

He nodded like none of it could be wrong or right and started putting the dishes into an ATV compartment. "He's known to make strange corpse-creatures special order for those Montana folks who got a big fortress in white-tailed deer country. They used to want to siphon all the geothermal power from Yellowstone."

"Sounds like my old man telling me stories." Greta would be lying if she said she believed all he was saying. And though she didn't think her food or water had actually been spiked, she'd rather this was some sick joke, that she was drunk and asleep in her tent. But this wasn't the case. What she'd seen the night before was real as anything. She wasn't losing her mind, though maybe she already had, which meant she couldn't blame Tiller, could she? Who then? The Pope? Hannah? She'd love to blame Hannah but was past that, past blaming and hating, past wishing Hannah would disappear from her mind. Maybe if she was going crazy, Hannah would just come along for the ride with that goat-fawn.

What still ate at her was why Tiller seemed fine with all of this. How was he so calm about the ghost train, almost like he'd ridden it a few times himself, or maybe his granddaddy did, or was still on it, because you'd have to be dead to do that, wouldn't you, and wasn't his granddaddy in some grave outside Laramie? She scratched at her unwashed scalp. None of this was fine—she knew that much.

"Look, it don't matter what you think." Tiller wiped his mouth then stuffed a handkerchief in his back pocket. "Real, not real, every family got stories. Some true, some false. Can't help that my old man gets hired to make trophies of the dead. All kinds of people contract with him for all kinds of that shit. Hunting and taxidermy just part of life. That, running cattle and building railroads just part of what made America great."

"That so?" Greta said.

Tiller's tight lips curled into a grimace. "And, back to

this business, because we gotta push on, some of the cattle might be out there in a ravine crying to join the herd. I aim to find out while you all move them, if you still want the job."

Greta looked at Scott, and he eyed her, as if each needed the other's approval.

"Thing is, and I get that you're both a little unnerved." Tiller leaned back into a morning shadow until he looked like he had half a face. "Consider this your chance to pick up your things and get back to Ten Sleep and to your lives. You took this job and committed to it. But if you're not feeling like you can handle the work, you can get your behinds out of here. No hard feelings," he said. "I'll be honest though . . ." He pointed to the cattle, all of them anxious to get moving. "I could use your help driving them. Already behind because of the storm."

"That's almost an apology." Greta crossed her arms.

"One other thing," Tiller went on, "go back now, you forfeit the rest of your money. You only earned a third, and I already paid that. Can't see how that would satisfy either of you. So, if you're staying, we start driving. I imagine it gonna dry out faster than the rains came and went. Sun bright already. Ain't no slick gumbo around here to get stuck in either, not like back down the trail a ways. So, yeah, if you wanna stay on, get your asses on your quads, and understand there ain't no explaining last night any more than I already done."

Greta then rechecked that she didn't leave her bedroll and tent behind, that both were secure on her ATV. This was also a gas cache area, so while Scott and Tiller took turns filling up, Greta was lost in thought about her old man again. In fact, Tiller's reaction about the night before reminded her how calm the Pope had been just before he died, like nothing could bother him. He'd given up on most things to be mean about, didn't even care if he lived much longer, though he still had plenty of shitty things to say, mostly about the past. And he said them as if everything he'd ever experienced had been lived by a ghost. He called her frequently during those final days. She entertained his calls, though she never went home anymore. She was done with all that. Didn't matter that he calmed down, or that she could kick his ass if she wanted, which sometimes she wanted to knock him to the ground, cancer and all, for the shoving he'd done to her.

But then, she knew if she'd gone to see him, she might have told him off the way he deserved, might have even started liking him, though she told herself never to like him, never to forget all that machismo, never to forget or to forgive him for ordering her around to pour his coffee and take off his stinky boots. And him always puffing out that chest, making all the women around him feel like servants to an eternal vampire, a Tlahuelpuchi allowed to bloodsuck her at night, who also wanted his TV dinners heated. If he'd been one of those creatures, she thought, he'd leave his legs in the closet, bleeding from where they ripped off at the thighs, then fly over the hills like a stupid vulture-thing, too lazy to hunt, and come back to boss her around some more.

All monsters want to be adored—she could always tell that about the Pope. He demanded fealty, and that was how it had always been. Him becoming docile during those remaining days didn't change that fact, or her memories of him, and only confused her with the idea that men like him could change. They couldn't. Could they? She always thought that men would all be better if they changed when they were twenty, or maybe younger, during their prepubescent years, so they wouldn't become the kind of men who demanded everything of the women holding them up, or who would one day drag them across the lawn. And apart from that, Greta had been hurting about Hannah's disappearance. Felt like shit piled upon Hell's garbage pit whenever the Pope called, and underneath it all, she was suffocating.

Her turn to fuel up, Greta went and grabbed the gas can, now thinking how angry she'd been at her mother too, mostly for not leaving him, for being scared, for saying she had no place to go when he hit her, for when she did have a place to go but wouldn't accept Greta's offer to help her start over. "Mom, get away from him. Come live with me," she'd said. "He's never going to do his own laundry, cook you a meal, or take you anywhere you want to go. When was the last time he was nice to you?"

Her mother said it was too late for that. "Besides, mija," she said. "I love him. You should love your papa too. You don't leave the people you love."

And that stung, because her mother hit a nerve, the same one Hannah owned, the nerve Greta wanted to get angry about and declare, *Hannah really doesn't love me anymore.* Then again, the more she thought about it, the same question popped up that had circled her mind since the day Hannah left: Why would someone say they love you one day, then on the very next day, ghost you? Why would anyone do that?

Greta carried the gas can to the open shed and secured it in a corner for a future pickup, wondering if she loved Hannah too much, or if maybe her love drove Hannah's desire to escape. Maybe Hannah's family was covering for her. She always thought that could be the case, that Hannah needed to have some kind of dark spirit exorcised from her life, and she wondered if that was something only her family could do. Then again, what if Greta had been that dark spirit?

Then her father's image jumped into her mind again as she fired up her quad and let it idle. She pulled on her goggles and remembered how she'd begrudgingly accepted every phone call from the Pope, how she listened to his docile, droning voice. Though she heard echoes of machismo—that pride that would never go away—she also heard regret for not being a better father, though that often lay under a veil of regret for not having done something else with his life, a thinly veiled joke about why he hadn't made himself famous in some way. "I could have been a better man if I'd done something different with my life, mija."

"You weren't an actor," Greta reminded him more than once.

"Used to look a lot like Erik Estrada."

In those last moments between them, his regret not only took over, but warped his mind. He started calling himself *Erik "The Pope" Molina, The Greatest Truck Driver Vato Who Ever Lived*, as if his life was going to be made into a book or made-for-TV movie. He demanded that someone famous play him during his midlife-crisis years, but not to forget his teens or his twenties either, because he'd been irresistible back then. And then, just before he started then quit his chemo, he had his homie ink *The Greatest Truck Driver Vato Who Ever Lived* down his right shoulder and onto his bicep, the one area on his upper body he'd kept free of tattoos, the one place he'd promised to put an image of Greta. The one place there weren't faded images of an American eagle eating a snake, a horse and cowboy roping a calf, a

Harley, six black widow spiders, a thousand-dollar bill, the states of Wyoming and New Mexico, the Mexican and U.S. flags, an orange 1972 Chevrolet Caprice lowrider, his wife (bent over the lowrider), his grandmother's face, the face of some woman he wouldn't say who with long black hair and gorgeous green eyes; and names, all kinds of names: Lupe, Maria, Itzela, Marina, Juana, Barbara, Pokey, Wizbeff, and Chacha. Names he wouldn't mention, who he would only say were "old girlfriends from back in the day."

And while he told Greta stories about the women he conquered, she stopped listening, just didn't care, though maybe she should have cared, but instead would imagine Hannah while they talked. She'd only tune back in to her dad's voice when he started to rattle on about Greta when she'd been a girl, and their horse rides into the hills, and all that he taught her about herding and cattle, trying to always be her trail boss in everything, and then she'd try so hard to tune him out again, and would even start to hang up, and *she* knew *he* knew when she would do that, and that he probably wanted her to, because his stories, though she hardly listened, would always become a lead up to a punch line, the one that had hit her in the face for as long as she could remember, because he really was a broken record: "Now, if you'd been born a boy . . ."

The trail reached a fork, and they took the right, and soon Greta saw they'd turned almost due east, herding the tired, hungry cattle straight toward opaline-lit canyon escarpments ringed with scrub and pines like jade-born neck blemishes. Towers leaned over their eastward flank and would grow closer by the mile.

Greta chased down a stray, guided it back to the herd, then stopped on her quad, examining distant angles of light on ancient faces of shale and limestone. The Bighorns, like Cloud Peak to the south, must be over three billion years old, and that almost frightened her, the idea that anything could be so much closer than her to the beginning of Earth-time.

Though they still had a ways to climb, and would soon venture north again into even higher country, individual lodgepole and ponderosa pines dotted the landscape here and there, sometimes filled breaks in the cliffs, and then lower stood patches of juniper and jack pine, and from Greta's current vantage on the crest of a hill, streams poured alongside trails, cutting through sandy rock beds. Some of those creeks bled from the maze of distant canyons, where she hoped ghosts wouldn't follow, though the entry point still loomed a day or two's ride away yet.

The herd continued to move slow, not always in a tight group, but spread loosely along the hills, willing themselves forward to the groan of engines. A dip between foothills revealed bright pastureland filled with puddles, and much greenery and blossoms releasing the perfumes of spring, which was welcome among the stink of cowhides, and the cowshit that dropped fresh all day long, which sometimes her tires tore through. The cows wanted to stop and eat but Tiller waved Scott and Greta to keep pushing to make up for lost time.

A large flock of blackbirds and sparrows took drinks and baths along the way, fluffed themselves and wriggled and splashed. More birds sang and strutted in the grasses here than ever, and still others darted over wildgrass and pigweed, while above the herd, winged puffballs stood atop rocks and sang or preened, and pikas, mouselike in size, but rounder and tailless, squeaked their disproval of birds, ATVs, and the passing herd.

Greta thought she might have driven this far during the storm-hunt for strays. It had been dark, so she couldn't completely tell, but then she spotted strips of cowhide scattered like highway litter. Some crows pecked at strips of meat. Greta's insides swelled and her chest burned. And then a moment later, she saw lying half in a puddle—a short, half-eaten bovine leg—and up ahead, a host of vultures feeding on fleshy rib bones and part of a skull, taking turns sneaking their heads right in through a broken eye socket. Then she knew Lady Grazer had died here, that the ghost train, no matter how much she'd tried to convince herself that it had been a mirage, maybe was real. She remembered that bright light, Lady Grazer being consumed, a dozen carriages passing one after another. She closed her eyes and felt like she was riding her quad in that dark drizzle again, could hear that scream bellowing from that ghost's throat, and ghost passengers, every mouth open, long-dead settler lungs sucking ethereal vapors, staring while they passed.

Greta thumbed at the dead mice in her pocket and started crying, not for herself and her need for this job, or because she felt like she was losing her mind, but for that damn cow. She refused to make a sound, not that anyone could hear her sobs, but either way, didn't let anyone see her palm away her tears, or glance again at that leg. Goddam Lady Grazer. She wanted to win out over that cow, but now there would be nothing of the sort.

For many hours the cattle weren't allowed to graze. Greta and Scott kept hard on their rear flanks, and quickly brought back any complaining stray. Many cows sniffed at the air and groaned. A few calves bawled.

Earlier, Tiller had driven into the foothills looking for the rest of the missing cows, saying Scott and Greta would find any strays that headed west. He soon returned victorious with all the missing cattle roped together, and had them moving and crying. In the end, only Lady Grazer had been lost, and that bothered Greta even more, that she couldn't save the one cow that needed her. She hated that Tiller was so smug about it, tipping his hat the way he did, giving her that smirk she hated. She wanted to get out of this stretch, not just away from these bits of Lady Grazer, but away from the air suddenly pressing down on her, the residue from that ghost train.

But still there were remnants of rails and disintegrated ties. The land hadn't won everything back. Indeed, the land here also felt barren, like nothing would ever grow where the soil had been gouged from building the transcontinental ghost railways.

Greta didn't want to be here another night, so when they reached a fork, she was relieved that they moved northeast, toward higher elevations, away from the tracks. Even the herd seemed glad there was no more sections of old rail, and Greta hoped she'd never see anything of the like of that trailscape ever again.

Early that evening they topped off their gas and bedded down the cattle. Greta kissed the wedding mice, and she snuck them right back in her pocket, and right after, thought she saw the goat-fawn sneaking along some rocks. She felt something she hadn't when seeing it before, less anxiety about its taxidermy, its *death*, also that maybe the creature wouldn't kill her while she slept after all, that maybe this corpse-thing had something to offer.

Something different had settled upon everything, a slight change, not only in Greta's feelings about the creature, but in the air, the way the clouds here seemed to roll slower, and in the dirt, in the rocks, maybe even in the way the trees bent as if a wind had nudged them to the west, maybe how the grasses had greater pockets of dirt, as if something lay down in them and smashed them beneath a great belly. And then she did see the goat-fawn drag that leg over a rise, and it peeked back a sort of *Hello, come find me*. She refused and went to help make supper, but still thought maybe that creature would protect her from something out there, maybe those roadrunner-like birds, maybe the ghost train, maybe that gargantuan birdplane in the sky.

Hadn't she heard her name just before that whistle, or around that time, and thought it wasn't the goat-fawn? What if it had been? What if the goat-fawn was protecting her from these strange things that were happening? And what an odd thing, because the goat-fawn was made by Bobby Tiller, and she couldn't think of anything good coming out of that man's creations. Then again, she loved the mice in her pocket, and they seemed to love her. Maybe, yeah? *Maybe*. Something she did know: Bobby had created some things that she had to make her own, and that, she thought, was beautiful, because love was powerful, and though she couldn't explain it, she had a love for these wedding mice, and for the goat-fawn, not for whatever they were meant to be, because that had maybe melted away and become something else, but for what she thought they were becoming, or had become.

Other than the goat-fawn, there was nothing here but the faint smell of gas and exhaust, and stars, Polaris and others, constellations in a tapestry, Ursa Minor and Ursa Major and Draco's tail caught between. And bits of Cassiopeia bending and Cepheus like a great empty box, and blinking satellites, and the rare shooting star, and everything above her feeling like a map of her life to be interpreted somehow, to be read like some kind of light-braille, if she could only touch them, if she could only find the secret to their cipher.

At about midnight a screech came while Greta sat with Tiller and Scott around the fire. She hadn't been thinking about anything for once when the sound came like an angry bruja, but then she wished she had some music, though she wouldn't play any from her mostly dead phone. Not only would it kill her battery in no time, but it would make her look at her phone, even though there was no wifi here, and then she would sift through old messages. And she brought no extra charger anyway, didn't really care about a juiced phone she couldn't use, because wasn't it a good thing to be without a phone anyway, even if Hannah did suddenly leave a message? Wouldn't that just teach Hannah a lesson? Be careful what you wish for and all that? Sure, she wanted to look, to peek like she always did when not in the middle of nowhere, to see if Hannah had messaged to finally say she was okay, that maybe she'd even be willing to talk again, that maybe they could start over. Maybe Hannah would even apologize for putting Greta through hell.

And then a screech came again. *Bird.* But not those birds.

Greta knew it was some kind of owl but couldn't put her finger on what species. Not quite a Barn Owl, not a Great Horned Owl. Then it flew over the camp and screeched again, a god-awful night terror that prickled her skin, then landed on an outcrop of serpentine forty or so feet above their tents.

The moon, big and green in the mist, hid just beyond the rise but still illuminated part of the owl, which had ear tufts larger than any she'd ever seen. This night bird seemed a good size too, but she could only see mooncolor, though when Scott shined his light on it, two great eyes reflected yellow as if death wormed its way into a kind of optical glow.

"Why you doing that?" she said to Scott, while the bird let out another screech from being blinded, though now she'd seen its Barn Owl white, a rich buffy brown wash, a heart-shaped face, but also a Great Horned plumage with deep brown and buffy patterned wings, and giant, dark sideways ear tufts. And instead of a Barn Owl's black eyes, when not reflecting yellow revealed red-orange flames. And the bird was tall, real lanky if she thought about it, like an alien with gargantuan feathery probes.

"We're not alone," Greta whispered. Then told herself, *I'm not afraid of a goddam owl, no matter how big the son of a bitch is.*

Scott heard her and laughed and turned off the light.

Right then, Greta thought she saw a flash of the owl beginning to spread its wings, and in the dark before her eyes adjusted, heard it flap several times and knew the creature had flown because the wingbeats quickly faded into distant coyote song. Wherever the bird went, maybe the thing had perched close to spy on the camp, to observe, maybe to judge them and every rodent and coiled reptile in the brush and grasses and rocks, because wasn't that what owls did when not hunting? Didn't they watch everyone and everything, maybe hoot or screech or whatever? Maybe they were always hunting, lurking, waiting, listening, judging, drinking you in with their golf-ball eyes.

Greta downed a lot of whiskey as the fire started to die. Everyone drank too much, and hardly a word was said. Finally, she got up, felt that heaviness in her step, that buzz going on in her head, tunnel vision too, then made her way behind her tent, and saw maybe fifty yards distant, was hard to tell, the same kind of white glow she'd seen illume the ghost train. For a second her heart went wild in her chest, thinking the train was on its way to consume every last cow and tent, her too. But then she realized the shape wasn't right, it wasn't a bright round center light expanding like a star, and along with that, wasn't moving, or making a sound, was just there, a ghostly mountain in the distance.

And this wasn't solely fear but something else . . . something she couldn't quite say what it was, or could be . . .

It was then she felt a distant pull. She didn't want to run like she had with the train. That urge wasn't there. This pull was more than curiosity, maybe was that *need to know*, not just what might be threatening the camp, but what else could be supernatural out there, and what this could all mean. So, yeah, it didn't matter if this was a threat. Anyway, there was no voice warning her, she knew that much and even listened for the goat-fawn to tell her so. This was an instant consuming desire, which included not telling Tiller or Scott, because whatever was happening was revealing itself to her, not them, and like so many things prairiewise, was for her alone, and so she knew right then that she had to see.

And she was scared, her shoulders gave a brief shiver, so she took a cleansing breath, though it didn't help her fear. She was scared of what the glow could be, what it might say, what it might do, how it might have eyes larger than she could imagine and gaze on her like that owl. Maybe this, whatever it was, would suck her into its phosphorescent death-light, because that's what this light said to her, death, eradication, eternal cold, futility, a warning, a siren with no sound, corpses, and more corpses. She thought that such cold and light must radiate its own burn and fury, and whatever that was . . . well, that caused her a moment of terror and panic . . . that if her body were to be absorbed by such light, that there might be no comfort, ever, that she might become twisted, eternally damned, and yet a part of this place and seep into every grip of rock and soil and blade of grass.

But that terror passed, though the fear didn't subside, and she felt the pull again, even harder this time, and left the darkness, which was replaced by her focus on this apparition, and started walking towards those distant white-blown towering lights, and switched her headlamp to its most dim setting so she wouldn't fall into unknown crevices, and also so she might see a big cat or bear. They might be watching like that owl, like the eyes she imagined might be hungry for her in that deathglow.

It took a while to navigate the nearest tangles, shrubs everywhere like sentinels maybe not wanting her to go this way after all, leading her into dead ends of bushy labyrinths, where in between, swaths of dark grass could hide any number of rattlers or badgers.

But nothing struck out, latched on, hissed, or growled, and the only creatures angry were crickets and toads. The singing bugs went silent and skittered away, and while the toads grew louder at times, there was nothing dangerous about their territorial *ohhp-ohhp*s and *plink-plink-plink*s and angry wet eyes.

She could see when she closed in, the ghost form took up more and more of her vision and overpowered her headlamp, which she soon switched off and could see where to plant her feet, and the thing began to take shape, and was mountainous, and she craned her neck, because whatever it was grew taller and took clearer shape the closer she got. And soon, she realized this was a kind of wall, that it had towers or spires, and it stretched for maybe a tenth of a mile altogether, and its phosphorescence was cold and dangerous. Nothing moved up or around any of it, the land here unmoving and silent, though she could hear a few distant coyote barks, and more tinny honks from toads, and along with those, the pianism of crickets that ably performed a kind of musical drone that went along with a slight pulse in the light.

And then finally she was close enough to realize this wall had been constructed from many millions of ghost bones, not of men, or coyote, or bear, but something else, which she had a hunch even in her drunk tunnel vision. She didn't touch any bones, feeling its potential danger, and smelled nothing but grass and dirt, though this was dead, *all dead*, everything about this construction—and what would marrow smell like anyway? She then turned and spotted a great many recognizable bones toward the northern end of the wall, where individual shapes had been piled and piled. These were more rounded and large, not legs and spines and ribs, and so she walked along where the photoluminescence seemed most powerful, emanating its forbidden cold energy, and reached out her hand, still not touching, not daring to, only to feel its intensity, because *this neon bone-light*, she thought, could suck her in, and so kept a hair's width away. And then her suspicion came true when she neared what she now knew were skulls, and examined them from a safe distance, and stared at their endless height, because they had been built into spires.

These weren't ice age creatures, nothing like that, she realized, but millions of bison slaughtered by white men, some by the hands of those riding the ghost train, especially that whistle-man Cody who she once read would hold contest after drunken contest, and slaughter the beasts, shooting them to death, just because he could, and like many other cold-blooded killers, would leave their corpses for all the bears, cats, birds, maggots, so many vultures, including maybe some condors, who knows, maybe this deathrealm rivaled the age of fallen dark primitive asteroids from the outer belt. Though likely not. And she knew that these skulls and bones marked this land, and maybe could only be witnessed on a night like this, not long after a storm, when they might appear to an inebriated Chicana in the middle of what she'd thought was nowhere.

She shivered again, this time from cold and wonder, imagining what these bison might say if they could speak. She leaned as if to listen to their whispers. And though she feared touching them, got as close as she dared, and could feel the bone-light on her skin, a coldness she'd never known, but had imagined even while walking over, how frigid that light might be, like touching the metal deathskin of the ghost train, that might have fused her to the eternal damnation of the passengers' plight, trapping her there, unlike Lady Grazer, split into a dozen pieces or more, which seemed all the more merciful now.

And this wall, she heard no whispers, and none of them pulled themselves back together to haunt, but she felt a power and energy, and knew this *lapis solaris* was borne in both earth and decayed life, from this ancient place, that this was the land telling her something, though she wanted these bones to speak for themselves, and more than anything, to tell her what she needed to do.

So much for the ghosts being gone.

The Buffalo

Greta, *listen*. I need you to hear me.

I speak for the bones of my kind and have much on my mind about horror and history, things I wish to say to you only this once.

I am the bones, all of them. I am the Buffalo, the mother bison, the mother of offspring, the mother of inheritance, who can see far into the past, and was with the last remaining hundred many *many* dozens and dozens of years ago, and was with the millions and millions of my kind before that for a span of centuries that I can't form into words.

We were killed so they could be killed. This was not the way it was before the slaughter. We were connected in death and in life, in a cycle with humankind. Yes, some of us were eaten, our skins used for tents and clothes, yet we continued in great numbers. But then the slaughter came, and now I remember this cull, this *murder*, as if happening now, all the shooting, the endless gunpowder smoke in the sky, the slashing knives, blood draining into fields, our corpses skinned, left rotting. Guts steaming into a morning cloud-mist.

I remember how *it* came and fed because

somehow the contract had been broken, how the mother canyon released it and them, so many in the dark, unseen in the midnight hours. They fed for years, mostly the hungry *little things*, because this happened over and over until our numbers were nearly gone, and the white men wondered what had come and cleaned so many bones. They didn't know we'd become a greater sacrifice, bleeding and bleeding, cull after cull, murder after murder, so much blood.

I am the lone mother, gathering all of this knowledge, *all of this*, my fur deep and coarse, and I am these walls and towers, stacks and stacks of bones a prairie mausoleum of consumption. I know how leg bones and skulls and ribs get piled, and you must know this too . . .

I know the country of the buffalo was the country of the monsters and *is*, and how this country now consists of white men and their new pact with the mother canyon, and that we, the buffalo, must have our own country, and then we must be shared again only with those who take according to the cycle.

This is our way.

I snort cold air, remember how white man before the pact would not taste our flesh, how they falsely made buffalo into the people, as if we were one and the same, how none of that was right. As if every bison skull was Little Crow's head on display, similar to those buffalo stuffed and made to stand next to Little Crow's milky dead eyes.

I know the shipping of our beauty to London—that in this destruction, our death also became *the way* to separate the people from their land, a way to make tribes dependent on white men, on colonizers and settlers, on treaties and capitalism. I know all these words as darkness and mockery, those "town destroyers," the gun-toting military might, and their greedy-eyed starvation of both Indians and buffalo.

And I know the forts, the invasions, the lies, that white men are "a people who possess a mysterious power," that they are the "fat takers." They are from a country which has no relatives, so they took every hide, and every Indian that they could get away with killing, and every child and calf they could murder, and sent some calves away to a farm or other children to a boarding school to forge into docile, assimilated, head-shaven automatons. And many of them were killed and buried for looking the wrong way, for dancing like bison, for a rebelliousness that couldn't, wouldn't leave their blood.

I spit and snort and shake my head. Because I've seen the rapes, the infants used for target practice, mothers' wombs cut open, eyes aghast while babies got shaken and whipped against trees and sides of cannons, or fort walls, or just the cold ground of an ice-packed winter, beaten and beaten as if each soul needed to explode into thin air, mother canyon unable to protect them or us.

Still, she and I know of the warriors, my kind trampling white men into dusty yellow pollen, or the fearless people, some of them ugly in their smallpox scars, rebelling and resisting white men, haunting colonizers in their sleep, like Inkpaduta, frontier bogeyman cutting throats, shooting settlers in the head, others warring with Lincoln, who needed his ears widened because he would never listen. And I know that sometimes the people made wrong assumptions, thinking they and the buffalo might finally be left alone. But they weren't, and we suffered, and the people often starved, just as the buffalo often died, and the people were owed everything from land to money, and some of us too, and at least one white man said about us, Indians, maybe all animals, "Let them eat grass and dung." And so, I watched resisters stuff grass in that white man's mouth and leave him for the flies, and I remember refusing to trample the body for fear of filth on my hooves.

I remember the Crow. And I know that word and have heard it many times, including about a Crow woman, who I once saw long ago. And she said, "This Buffalo isn't good meat, she deserves to heal and be a mother. That's what she deserves. To be a good mother, to be the mother of good meat, and good hides, and the land. She is a mother of us, of so many, and she's the mother of the prairie, and she obeys the mother canyon."

And I remember the words Wind River, and know the words Arapaho and Shoshone, just like so many other peoples' names. I know the land was theirs to roam and live and hunt on, and then not theirs for anything, but also not the white man's, though they still thought so, but really the land had to belong to the people and the mother canyon, or it would become something awful. The things that come from the mother canyon have been seen by you carrying a calf into dwindling dusk light. And I hope that in the meantime, the mother canyon, in her anger, will feed on something else besides the carcasses of my offspring, or you.

I want you to know I've heard the words *American* and *America* and know them and others, and know these people who still resist, that they have never been those words. And neither have the buffalo. I know this, and wait and wait, and play the longest game, the *mother's game*, the way I know that every rare white buffalo has been the embodiment of the Ghost Dance, the resisters' dance, and a promise of prophets to us and to the people, for I know those words too.

I will continue to be bones, to be born, and will remember more the next time, and more the time after that, and want you to know you play a part in this and won't be forgotten.

NIGHT FIVE

It was midafternoon when a breeze washed in from the west. Greta and the others hadn't made much headway since the day before, around six or seven miles was all, the cows grazing only during brief stops, and then slow to get moving in their mass of complaining hoofstrikes, as if wanting to push their dust cloud in the opposite direction, and whining every time Tiller fired up his quad and sang, "Come on! Come on! Come on!"

Driving slow and northeastward, Greta thought about the night before, all the whiskey she downed by the fire, then her inebriated stupor, she wasn't sure, maybe a dream she'd slipped into about wandering through scrub and prairie to a wall of bison bones, spires of glowing white skulls reaching toward starry banners of milk, and wanting to touch them, but so wary of their power to exact revenge, and fearing their cold-spell or death-charm or ability to kill. Such dream-bone magic was surely deadly, she felt, and so she kept her distance, while wanting to hear the bones tell their own tale. She thought she heard whispers, maybe in her sleep. What had the mother bison said? Why did she know those words?

She felt those bones were alive somehow and part of this entire strange landscape that seemed to be talking to her, and then she remembered a story from the bones, no, from mother bison, who was in the bones, yes *yes*, about mother canyon, told to her, white men and the bison and peoples those settlers slaughtered. She remembered feeling cold, wanting to touch the bones, then hearing that story-voice in her head like some kind of ancient goddess speaking about the beginning and end of things, and couldn't remember the story's end, or walking away from the bones, or somehow finding her tent and falling asleep.

If all of that had been real and not a dream, she wondered why Scott and Tiller hadn't said anything. They would have seen that big white prairieglow? They would have wanted to know what it was. Maybe joined her, maybe apologized to the bones, to the Buffalo Mother, for their drunken fire-and-cold-bone night. But then again, though she'd seen that ghost train, she couldn't be sure she'd seen a wall of bones. She couldn't even be sure she'd seen a calf or a marmot dragged into the sky. And she sure wasn't bringing any of this up to Scott or Tiller. What would they say? All she knew was she needed to drive the quad, steer a few more strays back to the herd, and make sure the mice in her pocket were tucked in tight, which they were.

By late afternoon a smell came to the rolling prairie that disturbed Greta's sinuses, making her sneeze and develop a slight cough. This wasn't cowshit or stagnant pond water wrinkling her nose, but sulfur blowing from the open-air bentonite mines outside of Ten Sleep and Hyattville, a stink that sometimes wafted across dozens of square miles within Bighorn Basin.

Open quarries from bentonite surface mines, Greta knew, could be found far downslope, west of the trail and prairieland they'd navigated, accessed by private roads owned by a single mining company. Thanks to discussions with J.A. Maynard and an illuminating study and investigative report that he shared, Greta knew more about these pits where absorbent clay crystals were extracted. It was about far more than just seeing piles of yellow-and-green machinery dissecting the landscape into an ugly brown mass. She learned that the area had been saturated with volcanic ash from ancient geologic activity over in Yellowstone. While the area had last seen rhyolitic lava flows as recently as seventy thousand years ago in the Pitchstone Plateau, there had also been caldera-forming eruptions 631,000 years ago, and dozens of eruptions since, not to mention three massive explosions over a little more than two million years. Turbulent eras upheaved entire mountains of pyroclastic material into ash clouds, including one 173,000 years ago that resulted in a collapsed caldera forming the western end of Yellowstone Lake. Those immense clouds from the three gargantuan eruptions poured over much of the western half of North America, mostly southeastward, and settled on an ancient seabed that had become the entire Bighorn Basin, though ash had blown as far southwest as Mexico, and southeast as far as Louisiana, where it lay upwards of three feet deep. Those ash layers eventually became part of a sedimentary geologic process that formed the absorbent clay known as bentonite. Most Wyoming folk, Greta too, called the clay gumbo, but only after it came in contact with water, expanding interconnected clay crystals to more than fourteen times the size of their dry mass. Contact with the sticky and hazardous mud could make moving the herd near impossible. Their trail wound far from any massive deposits, though small gumbo patches appeared, which were slick, sticky, and waxy, and for a short while trapped two of the calves.

Maynard brought the bentonite mining problem to Greta's attention one evening while they talked out on his front porch. He poured beers, shared some big helpings of elk steak, asparagus, and mashed potatoes, having invited her to share supper after seeing her poke around for his latest contributions to the little library box. She'd pulled out another book on geologic processes in Bighorn country.

"Those sons of bitches act like there's no environmental impact," he said about the mining company, "but everyone knows that around Ten Sleep over in Washakie County, grouse habitats and big game wintering areas get screwed over by the company. On top of that, they sell most of their clay to cat litter companies."

Greta had seen plenty of open mine pits, warehouses, and processing plants, not to mention endless convoys carrying the minerals down highways. Maynard told her that one bentonite plant had a huge sign tacked to its processing plant for everyone to see: AS REGULATIONS GROW . . . FREEDOMS DIE. He called it "the usual corporate bullshit vying for complete control of environments they don't care about ruining."

Greta hadn't known a thing about the clay other than it was nasty, and if you got wheels stuck in it, would leave deep ruts that dried into scars. "It's the most absorbent natural clay out there," Maynard told her. "But these corporate stooges don't care about birds, elk, or mule deer. They'll ruin topsoil too, so forget any reclamation of open-pit mines."

"But it's just clay," Greta countered, chewing a piece of steak. She didn't think it was her fight and he picked up on that.

"You should care," he said. "Ecosystems are dependent on plants, geology, weather, animals. This stuff isn't made up for textbooks just so kids can say *oooh* to nature. Ecosystems are more fragile than ever. They've been encroached on, destroyed. Lax enforcement of regulations in bentonite mining means lack of proper oversight, rules violations, and that translates to more environmental harm. Aren't the particulates and gasses bad enough? Who wants to smell sulfur? Who wants to get asthma from this garbage? It's a regulatory mess, Greta. The Wyoming Department of Environmental Quality needs to do what's right, enforce laws, train their inspectors to take note, and not let these companies mine year-round, or be lazy in how the land gets reclaimed once they're done ravaging it.

"Not only that," he went on, "when these reclaimed mine sites erode, they destroy all surrounding vegetation along with the topsoil, and around here that's prime Greater Sage-Grouse habitat. Never been a finer bird. Their courtship displays come from the age of dinosaurs. *Look how old love is.* And goddam if the Paintrock mule deer herd east of Ten Sleep isn't feeling the impact. That's thousands of animals at risk. Their herd already decreased from nearly twelve thousand to less than eight thousand. Doesn't help that oil and gas gets extracted in the same areas."

If there was one thing Greta missed besides Hannah, it was J.A. Maynard and his rants. She missed their conversations, the meals on his porch, and all the free craft beer. They always got those funny looks from his wife when they got to arguing. That meant his wife knew he was wrapped in one of his retiree lectures again. Sometimes Hannah would pop over then whirl back around, just leave the two to their debate. Not that she didn't care, or didn't know anything about the environment. She would just say she didn't need a lecture from some old white dude, and then wouldn't talk about it.

"Why not?" Greta remembered asking.

"Because I'm an Arapaho," Hannah said.

"Okay, I give, what's that supposed to mean?"

"Means, *I know*."

"Then why don't you ever talk about this stuff?"

Hannah's eyes held opinions that turned to black knifepoints, but she wouldn't continue the conversation, and Greta as usual stopped pressing her.

During their recent discussion about the mines, Greta asked J.A., "Why do you care whether or not some grouse has to find a new home?"

J.A. only had to think long enough to set down his beer. "Let me put it to you this way, what else is there to care about? You can either be on the side of the grouse, or you can be on the side of men who exploit natural systems, who get rich off our dwindling wilderness. Their paths all lead to the same end. We know how sick people get in their pursuit of wealth, the endless corporate cover-ups. Many of these cover-ups are about what men have done to the land. Look at that superfund site in Butte that will eventually drown that town in toxic water. When the wild places become uninhabitable for even the animals, when the wilderness gets churned to death, turned toxic, or turned to asphalt and palm oil plantations, when wars never end, and those conflicts destroy not just the people who inhabit cities, but parks, forests, oceans, grasslands, waterways. And when everything that could be working together to feed the health of the planet, gets transformed into hazardous waste, and literally becomes an unimaginable toxicity in the earth, in its water, then our ecosystems rot. Then the world slips beyond the knife's edge because it has already sustained deep, irreparable cuts. And that means even up here in Wyoming, where bentonite mines may not seem like a problem to you, they are. Lines have to be drawn that corporate industry cannot cross."

Passing through the shadow of a limestone cliff, Greta couldn't see or hear any mining machinery—that was all miles and miles away. But those toxic fumes, that sulfur, filled her lungs as if a skunk had strapped itself to her quad. She tied a bandana around her nose and mouth. It didn't help much, and definitely didn't help the stinging in her eyes, or the fact each lung felt like a hundred-pound sack.

She started to think she should have stayed in school just so she could earn a degree, maybe could have found a job where she could fight the origins of this stench. Maybe she could go back, get one of those gigs, or maybe become one of those protestors she used to make fun of, maybe take down an oil rig while she was at it, climb like a warrior of the Five Suns, hang a flag of shame. Didn't even need a degree for that. She did know that she hated pollution, fucked-up mining camps, all the occasional gaseous smells in general, and wished yet again they'd taken on this cattle drive on horses, not quads. The exhaust could really stink sometimes. Who gave a damn if a horse didn't have headlights anyway?

What she wanted was to get through these last few nights, get paid, and never come back to this part of Wyoming again. If she'd known what this landscape might do to her, that she would start seeing enough ghosts and creatures to fuel an entire reboot of *The X-Files*, she would have never come. She would have found some other way to make an extra buck besides the late shift at Ribs N Go. For the millionth time, while these thoughts rattled around her head, it came down to a simple truth—money talks, and she needed that green whispering in her ear so she could get out of the state for good, maybe all the way to sunny California to find more clues about Hannah.

Earlier that morning, when she was thinking about bison ghost bones and ghost trains, Scott finally brought up Hannah, asking why she never talked about her. He hadn't even known Hannah had completely disappeared, which was no surprise to Greta. Greta never told anyone anything, not even her mother. She hardly talked to Scott after dropping out of UW. Sure, she ran into him a few times at bars, even once at the Lope, but those were short discussions followed by promises to stay in touch.

"Because she's gone," she said to Scott.

"What do you mean, gone?" Scott scratched the ear of a calf that would never leave him alone. It took a liking to him and wouldn't ever let up unless he hid for a minute. But even that only worked temporarily. The calf eventually would come trotting back, and always followed his quad.

"Dead in a lake somewhere," Tiller said.

"What is it with you?" Greta felt her heart rate skyrocket into her throat. "I'm seeing ghost trains, and you're denying things even though you heard and told me it was a train, and on top of it, you gotta go and say Hannah's dead? And why does it always have to be a lake? Oh, *she's dead in a lake. She's fish food. She's haunting a reservoir along with her stupid old Trans Am.*" Hannah's car wasn't that black 1976–1977 *Smokey and the Bandit* mashup version with the rectangular quad headlamps Burt Reynolds drove, which was similar to the 1980 carcass Greta's dad had out in the garage and never put an engine in. *Nah*, this muscle car was one of those third-gen brown jobs with the gold trim, circa 1986, a much sleeker, somewhat shorter car, with headlights that folded up and down like it had real damn *robot eyes*. And every time she thought of it, she did not want to think of it at the bottom of a lake, especially with Hannah still inside.

"Haven't you ever missed someone, Tiller?" Greta couldn't bring herself to mouth what she really wanted to ask, if he'd ever loved, but was sure he caught her drift, about whether he'd experienced anything in his sorry excuse for a life. Furious at his silence, she wasn't done, and was about to ask if he'd ever been loved by his own mother. "Where's your mom, anyway?" she asked. "Didn't see her at the taxidermy shop."

"You wouldn't," he said.

"She even around anymore?" Greta asked. "We met her when you were in college. Remember? Before we became the Three Musketeers of Wyoming dropouts? Not that we hung out more than a few times. But damn, we sure turned into the biggest losers this state has ever seen. She probably doesn't ever want to talk to you. Probably hounds you for not having a girlfriend, or boyfriend, or dog friend."

"She's around."

Greta searched behind the calf that Scott was patting. "Here? Under this calf? Under a rock? Next to one of your roadrunners? Up in a tree?"

"She might be."

Greta wanted to spit fire. "Do you ever say anything about *anything* besides telling us how to herd cattle? Not every topic has to be a mystery."

"Your girlfriend is."

"Ex."

Tiller lit a cigarette, offered her one. "I think she's around too, in your head, a lot."

She grabbed the one from his mouth, took a deep pull then handed it back. "Don't act like you know what's going on in my head, Tiller. You don't want to be in here. It's dangerous and full of monsters. And do me a favor?"

"What's that?"

"Don't talk about Hannah." She turned to Scott. "You either."

Scott gazed at Greta a hard second, then went for his quad and fired it up.

She and Scott soon teamed up to reach a stray agitated by the quads. A handful of cows were so skittish they probably needed to be around an idling motor in a pen for a month before they got used to the noise. Greta thought the cow must be cousin to Lady Grazer, albeit with normal-sized legs, because the beast didn't want anything to do with the herd once Scott throttled a bit too hard. It became a devilish game of hide-and-seek, which made Greta laugh because Scott now had problems with single cows, and she didn't, though she continued to miss Lady Grazer.

Scott's rebellious cow wandered onto a wide, rocky plain that appeared to slope downward into a narrow valley between the trail and the distant canyons and mountains, and was nearly out of sight when Scott went after her, his throttling terrifying her even more. Problem was, Greta soon observed while following thirty yards behind, neither he nor the cow anticipated a cliff. Scott's hands let go of the quad, arms suddenly wide like an eagle taking flight. Greta's throat felt like it dropped into her stomach as he and the cow sailed off.

She raced toward the twenty-five-foot drop, heart wild and erratic in her chest now, then thumping into her throat. She wanted to yell but couldn't, could only drive in a panic, trying not to crash, trying not to groan though she thought she must be doing just that.

She skidded to a stop.

Down below, Scott's quad was a tangle of smashed parts, and the cow's neck had broken, legs twisted. Blood and brains had splattered on the rocks.

A puddle of red bloomed around the bovine, and Scott . . .

Then Greta heard a familiar voice.

"Fuck me." It was *him*, Scott, that pendejo. He paced on a small rock shelf where he'd landed, checking to see if he seriously hurt anything. "I almost died," he added.

"You coulda been a buffalo jumper back in the day," she said, almost couldn't say. She'd thought he'd died, was gone.

"You think?" he said.

"You have the skills." She tried to smile. "Let them chase you while you're running in a bison hide, entice the herd, then dive onto a ledge while a few sail over your head." Suddenly her voice broke. "Good way to get meat . . . just don't . . . kill . . . the entire herd."

"Yeah, maybe I don't wanna do that again," Scott said. "You all right?"

"Yeah," she said. "*You* all right?"

Scott brushed off some dirt. "I got so much adrenaline, not even sure if I crapped my pants."

"I don't smell anything," she said and let out a big breath. "Come on, better climb up so Tiller can kill you."

"Not looking forward to that," Scott said. "What are we going to do? He's not even around."

She reached out a hand to help him scramble up. "Tiller's going to have to live with one less cow. Then he's going to have to go to Hyattville for another quad while we do our best not to let any more fall off this old buffalo jump you discovered. Wonder if anthropologists even know about this spot. Kinda off the main trail, isn't it?"

Scott wiped at his face and beard. "He's really gonna kill me."

"I know."

After Greta tracked down Tiller, who'd scouted ahead for the next cache and pasture, he tore off his cowboy hat and threw it to the ground. "What the hell else gonna happen with you two and the quads? I shoulda had another hand or two follow behind in a truck for when shit goes south. Didn't want to spend the extra money, guess I should have."

"At least Scott isn't dead," Greta said.

Tiller gave her a look and she knew not to push. So much for trying to convince him of anything positive. She was beginning to realize just how disorganized and dangerous herding with Tiller was. They hadn't even entered the canyon, some cattle might get caught up in the rocks where they might never get them down.

"Am I gonna have to forfeit my pay?" Scott said after Tiller and Greta arrived to the crash site.

"Son of a bitch is insured," Tiller said. "But losing the rest of a day like this means we're gonna have to push hard before first light. No more waltzing through this shit." He'd been smoking more often and now lit a cigarette and let it hang from his lips. "Well, enjoy that sulfur stink. I'm gonna call my old man when I get wifi service, maybe meet him outside Hyattville."

Greta turned to Scott as they watched Tiller ride off. "Help me round up the herd, then we'll get your shit."

It was just about the worst afternoon Greta could imagine. She had to do most of the rounding in the sulfur stink, which she told herself that at least her ass wasn't so sore anymore and she was sorta used to the smell. She also hadn't seen the goat-fawn in some time. Added to that, her mind had been off Hannah while pushing the herd, winding back and forth behind them in endless zigs and zags. They moved the herd to a grassland uphill a ways, a patch sure to be consumed in no time. She then chased down no less than a dozen strays, though Scott helped on foot best he could.

Late clouds rolled over by the time Greta and Scott set up camp, the sulfur having dissipated a good deal from shifting winds, though it still felt trapped in her lungs, and left her throat somewhat raw.

A short time later she and Scott were back at the wreck at the base of the cliffs, having rode double on her quad. It was an uncomfortable ride and they almost crashed several times, but made it.

An entire herd of deer had moved in, and in the far distance several elk roamed. None skittered away, though a few kept careful eyes on Greta's quad.

Down at the wreck, Scott pulled out an unbroken bottle of gin, along with his bedding, spare clothes, and tent. They packed it up, then managed to find a trail of sorts up the cliff, though they had to toss up their bags before climbing the rest of the way. Scott heaved himself up first, and when he did, hollered out a curse word, before stepping out of sight.

Greta stood below, waiting for him to help pull her up.

"Scott?" she said. "Give me a hand."

Finally, too impatient to wait, and knowing she didn't have the long reach or long legs that he did, she strained her way out, though nearly fell. She was in the middle of brushing herself off when she realized Scott stared into the dark eyes of a bison.

"How the hell that get here?" he said in a near whisper. "Thought all the Plains bison were at the Ten Sleep Preserve, you know, that nature conservancy?"

The bison stood about thirty yards away, broad-shouldered, shaggy, and dark, that head so large it seemed to have no neck. Greta wasn't surprised by any of this. Buffalo were in preserves and on ranches throughout Wyoming. Wasn't so odd to have one show up where they hadn't seen any, though she instantly thought of those bones, and for this moment considered maybe that wall and those spires had been real, as had the voice of Mother Buffalo, and that for all Greta knew, this creature was *her*, or part of her?

And then something strange and wild shook Greta, because Scott pointed:

"It ain't alive?"

The bison didn't rustle that shaggy fur, swing her horns or thick jaw, or flick her tail. She seemed stuck in position, Greta thought, like she wanted to turn and look, but couldn't. Her eyes seemed out of focus, and her dark mouth appeared glued firmly shut. And then Greta knew what this was, where the bison came from. She stroked the double talisman in her pocket, each furry little mousey forehead. She'd hoped there wouldn't be others besides the goat-fawn, though she did see a coyote nearby and suspected it wasn't alive. She wondered if she'd seen this very bison at the taxidermy shop, maybe that same small patch of white on its left shoulder.

"This thing isn't breathing," Scott added.

Greta took a deep suck of air. "It's taxidermy," she said.

"What the fuck?" Scott said. "Can't be taxidermy." He took a hesitant step forward.

"She is," Greta said. "But don't get close."

"Okay, okay." He stopped. "Why not?"

"Because I think she's alive."

Scott let out a laugh that wilted into a gurgle. "You just said it was taxidermy, which means the thing's dead. Taxidermy is *dead*, Greta, which means, someone put this here as a joke."

Greta shouldered one of the bags. "No one put the bison here."

"It didn't walk here on its own."

"What if she did?"

Scott let out a bizarre laugh again then wiped his mouth. "It can't be alive and dead at the same time."

"What if I told you, she was?"

Scott took another step back. "Tiller's dad is one fucked-up white dude."

"Why don't we get back to the cattle, forget we saw her," she said. "Might be a stray or two to track down."

"Think I can forget this?" Scott said.

Greta packed and tied down most of his things onto her quad, no room for Scott this time, then set off slowly, making a wide berth around the bison, its brown back humped skyward, that thick dark mane like something on a lion. When the creature was finally behind her, she stopped and waited for Scott to catch up.

"What's wrong?" he asked.

"Wanted to see if she was following us."

"It can't," he said. "The damn thing is dead. I'm telling you, this is someone's sick joke. Just like that ghost train you claim you saw. You or Bobby messing with me?"

"Yeah, I'm messing with you—I made this materialize with my high-plains witchery." Greta wanted to say more, tell him she was the Blair Witch or something, but then sped off again, while he walked behind her to camp. Thirty minutes later he arrived and helped set up tents.

The rest of the evening she counted at least ten times that Scott scanned outcrops and the trail itself for the buffalo. For someone thinking this was a joke, he sure was paranoid, damn head on a swivel. She didn't ask why he kept looking over his shoulder, assumed he'd say he was watching out for Tiller, or trying to keep an eye out on the herd. But she knew the truth, could feel it, *he was scared to death of that bison.*

She was too. Not that it would hurt her, just that the bison's appearance made this all a little more real, and that's what scared her, made her look more than she wanted for the goat-fawn, for the bison, for anything of the sort.

Greta wished she knew what all this was about, why taxidermy might come to life, because they shouldn't be animated and following a cattle drive. *No way.* Maybe it was time to consider whether she and Scott might be sharing a hallucination somehow, or that yeah, something supernatural was going on. Scott was right about one thing when he mentioned Bobby Tiller along with accusing her, if there was something going on with the taxidermy, it was because of him. *What a mysterious pain in the ass*, she thought, *his son too.*

Tiller hadn't returned by sunfall. Coyotes howled in the hills, and there came a few growls, stirring some of the cows to complain. Bear or cat, neither she nor Scott knew. Greta grabbed her rifle and both she and Scott stayed alert, but the growls never came again and soon the rifle lay against a chair while both got half-drunk on whiskey by the fire. They seemed hesitant to talk about anything. She didn't want to mention the ATV crash, the dead cow, bison, ghost bones, goat-fawns. She wanted to point out how annoying it was that Scott acted like he didn't trust her, that he was paranoid about some cruel taxidermy joke that she had no part in. Hell, he didn't want to believe there'd been a ghost train even though she knew he also heard that cruel whistle. And what about the weird roadrunnery birds at the corral that weren't roadrunners? She wanted to beat into his thick skull that those birds weren't from here, not that she knew where or when they were from, or whether the bison was enchanted taxidermy that showed up on its own. Of course she wanted to tell him the kicker too, that a goat-fawn had been calling her name for days and a mother bison dream-talked to her. And though she wanted to rip into Scott, and chewed her tongue in the process of not doing just that, she also wanted to sit and drink, and not talk, and not go looking for ghost-*anythings*, and to simply not say shit to someone who clearly didn't want to talk to her either.

She found herself thinking about Hannah again, and what Tiller said about her being drowned. She knew Hannah wasn't dead in a lake, couldn't be. Nothing in Greta's bones told her that Hannah was gone in that way. But was she really alive, either? There was only one person she could ask about Hannah, and that was *Hannah*. And while sitting at that dying fire in the middle of nowhere,

Greta decided that she would find Hannah if it was the last thing she did. And then after that maybe she would save the world from bentonite mines, or help preserve some habitat on the far side of the world that men, *because it was always men*, were about to destroy and turn into a housing tract, hotel, or parking lot, or factory.

She hoped she could remember her promise in the morning, and told herself this a few times while nodding off in the chair next to Scott, who had already started snoring. Maybe he was conjuring a bear, she half dreamed, imagining that growl again.

What woke Greta an hour later was a feeling.

Something in the camp. Something watching. Something out there beyond the remaining orange glow of campfire coals. Whatever was lurking, it wasn't Tiller. She'd have heard him come back. Maybe it was whatever growled earlier. Bear, if she put money on it. But now, only seconds later, she realized she would have lost that bet because she could hear walking, like hooves, but not, and not normal, not in any kind of synchronicity, nothing smooth and natural about these steps. More alien, unfamiliar to walking, maybe to life.

A shadow moved past that seemed too big to be one of the cows. Didn't move right either, kind of slow, but hurried, taking strange steps that made unsettling sounds in the dirt, like the wrong parts were touching.

Too big to be a bear too, and not shaped bearish? She heard Scott startle himself awake, like he'd heard the sounds in a dream.

"Did you hear that?" he said, more alert now, both of them quietly watching, both of their heads swimming with booze.

Greta's heart started to hammer in her chest, as if her

every cell knew that whatever crept in the dark would soon reveal itself. She wasn't sure she wanted to see what that might be, but grabbed the rifle though she didn't trust herself to aim straight.

"Shine your light on it," she said. "My lamp isn't going to reach that far."

Scott felt around his feet for his light. She could hear a rattle, then the light flicked on.

There it was, the buffalo again. She didn't aim at it.

"No fuckin' way, man." Scott got out of his chair, dust swirled into the light beam. He exhaled loud and heavy, like he'd forgotten how to breathe.

Greta didn't move from her chair. She could feel herself wanting to run, wanting to get on her quad and get the hell out of camp, ride all the way to Ten Sleep, hope her car battery wouldn't need a jump, just leave and never look back. She had enough gas money to get somewhere.

The bison didn't move again, not at first. She pawed at the dirt, legs stepping too high, bent too far, some kind of robotic jerking movements, like her legs were too long, like they'd forgotten how to stride, quivering at each joint, maybe even some extra leg joints in there. And then she stopped, turned her massive head toward them, only they didn't see the head turn. She was just . . . *facing them* . . . as if that movement had been faster than any eye could see. And then the buffalo came toward them, to the edge of the fire, only she moved so fast, so quiet, and instantly was where she hadn't been, her massive head and beard flickering in the firelight, dark eyes turned to glowing embers.

Scott fell away from the bison and yelled like some kind

of prairie ghost, though before he could get up, the buffalo was gone.

"Where's that rifle, Greta," he said in a panic. "Where's our goddam guns? I thought you were holding yours?" And then he seemed to see something else, something she couldn't. "Oh my god. Who are *they*?"

"Who?"

"Those *people*?"

"What people?"

"Running through camp, running past us, and the hunters with them," Scott said. "Are they hunters? Why do they look like that?"

"Like what?" She strained to see.

"They're wearing skins," he said, cowering. "Their eyes, I can't see their eyes. They're pits. I need that fucking gun. I need to kill that thing."

Greta, terrified too, tried to calm herself, tried to take a deep breath. She sucked air then blew out in an awkward cleansing breath, and refused to hand over the gun. "You're going to shoot something that's already dead?"

"Damn right I am."

She held her gun close while he tore into his tent for a rifle he didn't have.

"Shit, I left mine on my quad," he said. "Fuck. Give me yours? Jesus. God. Fuck."

"Go to bed, Scott," she said.

"What are you talking about? I can't go to sleep. Where did those people go? Give me your fucking rifle. Oh my god there's another one running through camp."

"Another what?"

"A person. A goddam person. Those eyes . . ."

Greta couldn't see or hear anyone besides Scott. Even

the buffalo wasn't around. "There isn't anybody running through here." She took her rifle to her tent, though she was still frightened, and before she went inside, said: "Leave me and my rifle alone. We're going to bed."

"There's a goddam monster out here, Greta. And people sneaking around. Don't go, we need to kill it."

"None of them hurt you," she said.

"They might. It might. It will."

"She didn't. They didn't. Look, I'm scared too," she said. "But we're halfway through this drive and I want my money. If you want to leave because you're scared, then leave, take my quad now or at sunlight. Go. But I need the cash. Just a few more days. Like you said, this is probably all in our heads." Before she entered her tent she said one last thing. "My old man was scarier than this."

Greta lay on her bedroll and started to think that maybe the Tillers conjured spirits in the middle of the prairie to go along with their weird taxidermy. Then she thought, *they couldn't materialize prairie ghosts, could they? And why would they?* Not that she could see what Scott claimed to have experienced, making her wonder if this was all in his head and hers. Besides, that ghost train was something far beyond anyone's comprehension. There was just too much going on. Tiller had proven a poor excuse for a trail boss, and his dad, she concluded, was probably a dumbass cowboy in over his head, maybe even messing with things he shouldn't, after all it was his taxidermy shop, though none of this weirdness necessarily meant these ghosts or even the taxidermy monsters were caused by the Tillers. Maybe it was just this land? It had suffered, she knew that much. Didn't everything have a breaking point?

Either way, as scared as she was, the more she thought

about it she kind of liked the bison—it was that birdplane she feared. That bison was curious, sure. It seemed to look at her and she wondered why. Why did anything look at anything? Maybe she should have petted it the way she stroked the mice. Then again, probably best not to touch something in the dark so massive and dead.

At just past two in the morning Greta opened her eyes. A vehicle was outside camp—had to be a truck, maybe a Jeep or Land Cruiser. Downhill, seemed like. She poked her head out of the tent, expecting the head of the bison to be next to the zipper, maybe one of the hunter-ghosts Scott had seen, maybe waiting to toss her into the remains of the fire for not sabotaging that ghost train.

But nothing was there, no ghost men or women, no bison, no train disguised as a Bronco, so she slipped outside with her headlamp on, expecting Tiller's dad might be driving drunk, pissed to all hell and back, ready to cuss at them for being reckless herders.

It was an older-model Ford truck, some kind of eerie pale color, and it bumped over dried ruts and rocks, then came to a stop, as if driving any farther would either curse those inside the cab, or worse.

She could hear coyotes in the distance again, then heard Scott rustling around, fuming about the flashlight he couldn't find and the rifle he shouldn't have forgotten at his crashed quad. He even grumbled that maybe he'd be sent home, or should have left. Soon enough he was next to her, swinging his flashlight in every direction, dust kicked up by the tires swirling around the camp.

"Took them long enough," Scott said in half a panic.

"Maybe you shouldn't say that since you drove Tiller's quad off a cliff."

"Yeah, maybe not to them."

"Maybe not to anyone. Jinxing and juju and all that."

She wanted to give him a pat, then didn't, never taking her eyes off the truck, and soon could see two faces lit by yellowy dash light. Tiller and someone she'd never seen. From the distance, his eyes were soulless pits. Shadows, she told herself. And then a third person, the back of a head silhouetted of someone sitting in the truck bed.

She didn't feel like waiting around, so slipped into her tent to get more rest for their long push in the morning. One more day and they'd enter that damn canyon. She kissed the mice, held them tight, and they all went to sleep and didn't hear a thing.

The Bear

For a long time, the bear could remember flashes of his earliest torpor dreams. The sweet scent of cubs filled his imagination during those light hibernations and wintry snores, and when he woke there really were dozens of little and medium-sized cubs, and adults too, and they all gathered around trees eating fallen apples, so many apples. And all the cubs had apple breath, and this was funny, because he'd dreamed that too, and especially remembered when they snorted at each other and let out huge exhalations. They wrestled amid the fruit, and sometimes kicked and tossed them, or held them in their mouths and ran around the trees, and up others, and played hide the apple, even with the rotten and wormy ones, or chased one another until the apples accidentally crunched in their jaws.

And the bear would remember eternal springs and blue skies, and slept deep and rich every night, a kind of rest so lovely back then that he'd become golden spring light, a sugary apple so brilliant. Sometimes when young he dreamed he was at a stream, fish everywhere in thick, slippery schools leaping over each other's scaly backs. He could see himself and other cubs in these visions, mostly his sisters though, all in shallow waters.

During the mornings, sometimes he ate fish his mother caught, though he tried to catch them too, and would forget how hungry he was, always so starving, and he would splash and play, sometimes trout leaping into his paws, and slipping right back out, or sometimes, wouldn't even fish or play in the still, quiet portion of the creek where the water felt like an upside-down sky, lying there, letting that cold water rush through his fur as he stared at the other bears on the banks chewing on the long strings of berries they dragged over.

Then he'd want berries, that squishy sweetness pouring down the back of his fat tongue, and would rush out of the stream dripping wet, and right in the middle of it he'd want an apple all over again, and would rush into the forest and eat and play more apple games.

He slept lighter and lighter each winter, and found himself dreaming less of playtime and bobbing in streams and splashing. And then the world got more difficult and serious and he followed his mother into the mountains, to the places where snowmelt ran like mountain tears, into the canyon where she sometimes stared at a hole in the cliffs—a big cave entrance—and would growl for them never to go there, and they wouldn't stay long, but always stopped to stare and *growl-hum*, and they'd eat deer and elk, always seeking the livers and entrails, and sometimes berries that grew thick in pine meadows.

It was a rugged stretch of mountainous landscape where his mother met their father, and was also where his father threatened to kill them, because every time the bear and his mother and siblings returned, the father would fight his mother, especially if she'd birthed a younger brother or sister right out of torpor. And the bear remembered her body shaking frantically, her moaning, and the baby bear coming out of those moans like a blood shadow, and her becoming weakened, and this happened over and over, the birthings, the fights, until his mother was so exhausted and injured that she walked crooked, and he licked her back and neck wounds that never seemed to heal.

He wanted to fight his father. Anger in him grew into a kind of restlessness, pushing him as if toward a cliff. That troubled feeling went beyond the ripping of deer flesh, or lying in the sun gnawing on thigh muscle and bone, and taking sweet naps after, his muzzle still bloody and smelling of iron. And sometimes these feelings were more turbulent and spasmodic because he did find himself sleepless some nights and nipping at his sisters, thinking they were his father come to torment him. Even picking up the scent of his father's fur or shit or urine turned the bear's eyes red with hate, and he would feel a growl deep in his belly, which rumbled and rumbled until he would roar at any bear that got close to him, and even lunged at his mother who ran and hid for a time. And sometimes he blamed his anger on that hole in the canyon that he could never get out of his mind. Always that hole, that cave, like his father's breath he imagined poured out, though when he thought about it, something did pour from that hole that he sometimes remembered, and it was nothing he wanted to eat, a kind of ancient rot far worse than a decaying apple or an old deer carcass.

Then during late summer, they were somewhere below Cloud Peak, and he saw his father, that thick brown coat, his many scars glistening like silvery bark, and saw how wide his father was, like three of himself, but when his father threatened his mother again, and worse, meaning to eat their youngest sibling, a tiny cub with the brightest golden fur, so fun to nuzzle, a brother the bear loved so much that he couldn't wait to show him his favorite apple trees, who their father now wanted to kill because he was small, so teensy furry and small.

His father was consumed with a kind of monstrosity that could only inhabit such a formidable and hateful old creature in the Cloud Peak wilderness. And so, the bear stood up to his father on two thick legs, and felt like he was dwarfed by that immense size, and his father growled in a way that said, *I could kill you right now*, and the bear, he knew, and growled back anyway, meaning, *Okay, do it, I don't care*. And his little brother cried and squealed, his golden fur standing on end, so terrified, and along with his sisters, ran away and hid, and his mother roared in a way the bear had never heard from any of his kind ever, and knew this could be the end of something, then she hid too.

He didn't know how long the fight lasted. He'd wanted this battle for so long, then hadn't wanted it to ever start and stood growling, but then it began, and kept going, and there was so much blood, and his mother came back out and joined in the battle and lost an ear, and the bear afterward, realizing his side was torn so that a rib was exposed, went and lay in a berry patch for days and days, and slept and couldn't move, and felt tongues on his wounds, and that soon turned to numbness.

His father lay nearby in a dirty, bloody fur mound that hid punctured lungs which no longer sucked air. Coyotes, vultures, and other animals feasted on the flesh. The bear didn't care about that, because his golden brother was okay, and had a chance at life now, though the cub and their mother and siblings soon left to stare at the hole in the canyon, leaving him behind. And that was okay too, but sad because somewhere in him he knew that sometimes you had to move on, and he was ready for that, he knew, because that fight . . . his mother must have known something he hadn't known about himself, and they had to get away though they loved him.

And afterward, there came hard years where the bear didn't know himself anymore, and he roared at every other bear that crossed his path, even those he sensed were miles away, and didn't want to know any of them, even if they were his family.

Seasons came where he couldn't sleep an entire winter anymore, so foraged for food in the frozen mornings, and grew so thin he thought he might die and be eaten like his father, and could hardly hunt, or eat anything anyway, and sometimes when he did get the urge, feasted on bark and ants, sometimes deer killed by lions, and that meat made him shit and shit, until he found a sleeping beehive, and ate all of it, every bit of wax and honeydrips and squishy stingers, and soon felt hungry again, and so ate roots. And eventually another spring came. And another. And he wandered down slopes, and into the canyon and found that he would stare at the hole too, and breathe in its scents, nostrils vibrating and wet, and once thought he could hear stories in the breeze wafting down to him about protection and sacrifice, that he had a place in this, but not yet. And he remembered turning away and letting out a disconcerting huff, and put one paw in front of the other and made his way to the basin.

In summers he found his way across wildlands that he'd never seen, never knew existed, and saw those great, long, black freeways, and car eyes that terrified him, red, white, and yellow-orange, and those roars of the eighteen-wheelers made him shudder like when waking from a long sleep, the kind of losing control of muscles that came when he hadn't had water or food for months, and hadn't pissed or shit for months, because his body had forgotten what it was to work that way.

And in those days the bear saw a great city, towers and homes and people, and climbed through backyards, and ate dogs, even the tiny ones, but didn't like them, and stole food, and thought some of that tasty, especially bowls of dog food, and then because someone shot him in the leg for eating all of their chickens, he left the city, and aimed for the mountains again, limping and licking his festering wound, bullet rubbing against bone. He stopped one night at a corral, and after eating a sheep, fell asleep in a pile of hay, dreaming, surprisingly, or maybe not surprisingly, of apples.

His fur had turned a kind of silver brown by the time he was again in the mountains. He walked slower, his side and leg hurt, and other bears much smaller gave a wide berth, and he could hear in their voices, the story of the bear he and his mother killed, his father, though they all said he did it, he killed the great bear so long ago, and he must be a great bear too, and the bears wondered why he wasn't the father of bears, and no one could guess, until he roared at them and spotted the loveliest creature, a bear with golden-brown fur like his little brother's hide, so shiny and brilliant. He loved her scent, and she cried at him, terrified, but he wasn't going to do *that*, he swore, he wasn't, not ever, never going to do *that*. No, he told himself, he wouldn't, never ever never, until he found himself with this golden-brown bear, her crying beneath him, and he loved on her, he thought, for nights, days, because she reminded him of everything he'd known and loved, though she held nothing but fear in her eyes the entire time.

He didn't bite or snap or roar at her, at least he didn't think so, and she had a wound on her back, and it wasn't from him. He licked at it, and she was still afraid. Then he realized she would disappear for the winter, and like his mother, would give birth soon as she woke, shuddering, shivering. But he never saw her again, and never knew what happened to his cubs. That winter he slept in a cave and dreamed of her over and over again, and kept waking, kept thinking she was about to give birth nearby. His muscles would shake when he tried to stand—he wanted to search for her so bad—but it wasn't time to wake, and had only been about thirty days the third time this happened. Then he fell asleep again, and weeks later woke from the same dream of her birthing golden cubs.

He left the mountains and wandered the canyons again, hearing moans, not from bears at all, something else that groaned from limestone crevices, and sometimes, from strange bird flocks he'd never seen, which eyed him hungrily, including one so large he thought he was dreaming again. Its wings made an awful sound, and he knew this bird had something to do with that canyon hole and those stories he breathed when he stared. And he didn't see any bears, and couldn't smell any, but found endless berries and hornets' nests to eat. And here, he heard human voices now and then, voices he didn't think were alive, yet were human, and this angered him, because this confused him, and he felt threatened when he was frustrated, and the voices in the hole told him nothing. And so he wanted to leave this canyon, maybe find his way back to Cloud Peak for a third time, a final time, to be with bears again forever, maybe find his offspring, maybe sweetly nuzzle their mother, that maybe he could beg the fear to leave her eyes, that maybe he could again see a sibling, maybe his mother, if she could recognize him through that one cloudy eye. But those voices, they kept at him.

Day and night he heard them, couldn't understand their thoughts, and there were many, and he saw forms now too, so many up in the canyons, humans, as if guarding this place, because they had been near the hole and peered at him. And he saw animals, and they weren't alive, but they guarded this place too, and one was a deer with a beehive inside of it—bees swarmed around her neck in clumps and flew in and out of her mouth. And there was a dead walking possum covered in toads. And a badger with wheels for feet, a wolf with spines like a porcupine, and an ancient dog with a bone necklace, and they angered him, especially a jackrabbit with a white tail that would sit and stare at him through strange eyes that appeared more like shiny creek rocks. He would growl at the rabbit, which broke away from the others and followed him, and the rabbit would sit still as a shadow and stare. And sometimes the rabbit's neck bent as if broken and it would take a moment for its head to pop back into place. And then he thought maybe he'd accidentally stepped on the hare's neck, and wondered how the jackrabbit could still be alive.

And then one day, while making his way through the tangle of canyons, hoping he could find a path toward the old peak he knew, the bear craved more than anything, to see the bears again that lived on those old mountain slopes.

Soon, he found that he was followed again by the jackrabbit. Then it seemed that the jackrabbit wasn't trailing but leading him through a maze, and he felt so lost and thirsty, so followed and realized the jackrabbit was taking him maybe toward Cloud Peak, that maybe this rabbit with the stone eyes knew the bears he knew, and so he redoubled his efforts, near to starving.

Days went by, and his side and leg hurt more than ever, including where that bullet lodged years ago, rubbing against bone, and where his rib still crunched along with forever-broken cartilage where his father clawed him open. He found grass and roots, and mostly didn't care that they didn't fill him, and licked the dew off rocks in the early morning because the streams here had dried, and then ate bark, and the sky was lit grey, and the clouds seemed like the death he'd seen in so many eyes. Those voices from the canyon hole seemed to follow him, maybe even came from the rabbit's lips, so loud now that he would swing his great head side to side when he marched, hoping this would make the sound go away. Then he wished he hadn't eaten so many hornets through the years, that maybe they were buzzing inside his belly, until finally the jackrabbit took him into a clearing, one like nothing he'd ever seen.

So many animals with stone eyes had gathered, including the badger, the deer, the wolf, the possum, a buffalo, and many others. A white man stared at the bear, and slowly lifted a rifle, and the bear, he knew, oh he knew what would happen as the man lifted the rifle, and in that instant rushed headlong, like fire *reaching burning stretching* through the scorched sky, flaming at the white man with his teeth bared, jaws snarled wide, paws set firm in a galloping rush, that silver-brown fur thick and bristled, everything in him ready to destroy, for all the years of loneliness had cooked inside the bear, and he hated this man, and now hated this jackrabbit and all the dead animals with their stone eyes, except that instead of the man, it was the bear that felt the crack of death.

A long time passed before the bear got used to his dead body. The jackrabbit was close, hopped at his paws, and the bear knew that the jackrabbit didn't fear being eaten, and the dead bear wasn't hungry anyway, and instead sought to protect the very place he feared, and made his lonely way back to that clearing where he died, and for a long time stood there and stared through two stone eyes, thinking about the bears he once knew, trying to remember dreams of apples, and their taste, and what joy felt like.

He learned he could open and close his jaws again, and wandered about, and protected this place, including that hole in the canyon, and he desired to be here, and knew that this land was *so so so so so* old. Then the voices became one and said that it loved him because it, *she*, was mother canyon, and she needed him to help protect during her next birthing, and that the canyon controlled the dead animals and to a degree, the man too. This was a bargain not meant for this man, but he had stolen *the way*, the ancient way, and the bear didn't understand what any of this meant, and somewhere deep in the bear were feelings of disloyalty to the man, though the bear felt love toward the wilderness, and thought the mother canyon shouldn't have done what she had done, whatever that pact was which allowed death to protect a promise.

The bear soon resisted the canyon, tried to break a kind of spell, and could not completely. And then one night, he wandered from the clearing, and the jackrabbit followed.

The jackrabbit understood, the bear knew, and the bear liked the jackrabbit again, and they never slept, but pretended to, and the jackrabbit would huddle in the bear's fur, and they made their way, lost amid the canyon of spirits, wishing they could feel hungry again, until one morning they found a stream that crossed the mother canyon's jagged mouth through jade-colored slopes, where for a time, the jackrabbit stayed.

The bear descended, where it met a two-legged skin-thing that crept up to him, and was one of his kind, so he allowed the grey creature to climb on his back, and it rode the bear for some time through high-country forestlands, and that was fine, because this softened the bear's loneliness for the jackrabbit. But after a while the two-legged skin-thing made the bear turn back toward the canyon, which the bear reluctantly did, and after some time the skin-thing bent to the bear's ear telling him of a new purpose, and the bear could understand because they were the same, though every breath from the skin-thing irritated him: *We have broken the pact because of a young woman's love for our kind, We must protect her, We can use her to correct this, The mother canyon cannot on her own, We must break her spell so all of us can be free, We must . . .* then the bear shook off the skin-thing mid-sentence, and ran away, confused now, confused about what it said to do and how to do it, and who to do it for, and retreated to the stream that crossed the mother canyon's jagged mouth. It was there the jackrabbit appeared again and sat, its neck broken, then not broken. The bear sat too, trying to reason out this jackrabbit, and what the skin-thing said to protect, and why the bear would have a purpose besides what it was already doing by protecting that hole it never entered. Was it the skin-thing the bear needed to protect? Some other two-legged creature? What young woman? Definitely not the man with the gun who killed the bear in order to remake the bear as a protector.

It was while the dead bear was thinking these thoughts that something tore into his hide that neither he nor the jackrabbit expected. Something silent from the sky while the bear stood in wonder, a sky-thing so much larger than the bear had ever seen. It happened so fast, and when it did, the jackrabbit scrambled away.

The bear realized then that the mother canyon, like him, was angry, confused, that its pact had somehow been broken, and now neither the bear's creator nor this ancient mother canyon could control him. All of this somehow angered the canyon even more, and whatever the mother canyon was protecting in herself, maybe there was something far more dangerous if the bear were to be set free, something that could end the world.

Dead things could end the world.

Though the dead bear felt no pain, he knew his body had been pulled apart from his head. It happened so fast, yet the bear could see that the giant sky-thing had flown away with his body, his fluff and fur and legs that had been so much lighter than they used to used to be. Even so, the bear could still see, still think, but could only see dirt and grass. Then after what seemed days, felt his head lifted, then being set down so sweetly, and heard a kind of hum and whisper, and saw pebbles and water that rushed around his furry cheeks. For a while he opened and closed his jaws wondering what had set him there, but the water kept coming and washed his dead, hardened tongue clean.

And eventually the jackrabbit came and sat next to his head, and together they lay in the water, if a head could do that, and this was peaceful, until the jackrabbit heard a sound, and like everything else the bear had ever known, the hare fled into the wilderness, and then before the bear stood a young woman.

The bear immediately loved her, and for the first time wasn't afraid of a human, and welcomed her, and wanted to be able to talk, but couldn't. When the woman picked him up, her voice was like the music of the plains, of the mountains, of everywhere, and she set him up higher where he could see, and he knew he had so little time left, but that he would do everything to protect her, even if that meant simply watching the world. And that realization reminded him of shiny, golden apples. And for the first time in a long time, almost felt like he could taste one.

Night Six

The tent zipper ripped open in the morning darkness. Greta knew who it was before the light flashed her eyelids pink.

Tiller told her they needed to talk.

She held up one of her hands to block the beam. "Can we stop doing this? And try knocking, asshole. You're in my sanctuary."

"Uh-huh."

She'd been dreaming about an argument with Hannah, who'd sat across from her at their old kitchen table, crying. She'd been made into taxidermy, a seam up and down her arms, neck, into her hairline, which now resembled a plasticized wig. The scent of hair spray permeated the dream. Hannah's eyes seemed fake, her brown irises too red, the pupils small green flames. Then Hannah said she was tired of not having a heart, intestines, a uterus, bones, muscle. "Even my brain is gone," she said. "I want my old body back, everything that was inside that made me, *me*. We have to find my lungs."

Greta cried that they got smashed down the drain like everything else. "All of it."

"My bones too?"

"Yes. They turned rubbery. I watched them slide into the hole."

"My heart?"

She nodded. "It was still beating."

"What's inside of me?"

"A mold, a form."

"That's just a shape. That's not who I am. Who I am is gone, so gone," she cried.

They were no longer at the kitchen table. Hannah sat in the corner of the tent with Greta's mice, holding each up to her nose. "We're the same, little friends," she said to them.

Then one of the mice spoke, the bride: "Are we the same? Did you just recently come to dead-life like us? We were originally born in a big tank with dozens of other mice, and hardly knew our mother, and then we were dumped wriggling into a bag and frozen (much of this told to us later by other mice and a raccoon)—that was really c-c-cold—and it was probably with Ma and half our family, then we were shipped to Ten Sleep, and then thawed in a sink by some greasy fucking *hoo-man*, pardon my French, then hollowed and de-everything'd, and little costumes were put on us, and somehow magic not intended for us got on our fur, or was maybe accidentally sprinkled onto our tight wedding clothes, unintended we think, and we suddenly felt we had to protect the sacrifices, whatever that meant, but we are so small, can you tell? and didn't understand any of this, and so we tried to go to sleep, and we don't know how but then we knew we were stolen. Scandalous! Then we knew we were in a warm place. *A pocket!* And we felt warmth, and love, and whatever magic binding was inadvertently put on us kind of drifted away, replaced by a desire to help others like us to break free. So, right from that pocket we radiated our new *love magic*, and can't explain how, but then the goat-fawn became one of us, then a coyote, then a jackrabbit, a Mother Buffalo, a skin-thing, and others . . . Who do you protect?"

"What the fuck is that mouse talking about?" Hannah said.

Then Greta found herself holding the bride mouse to her own nose, the mouse still pleasantly talking though now it was all squeaks and chirps in mousey gibberish. Hannah was no longer in the dream or had maybe become the mouse. Then the mouse cocked its head to the side and Greta saw Hannah's eyes—those green pupils—and jolted awake to the sound of the tent zipper.

She stared into the dark after Tiller left the tent, dream fragments still firing through her. After a long minute, she threw on a fresh shirt, whispered, "Thanks for protecting me," then tucked each mouse into her coat, careful to check if they'd changed poses. They hadn't. Or had they? A foot on the bride was slightly askew. Five seconds later she stepped into crisp morning air, the ground still nightcool.

"You both look chipper," she said to Tiller and Scott. She glanced over to the truck that had arrived the night before—the entire thing was piss green. The driver lifted his eyes, yellowy dash light illuminating the angles of his jaw, his cold stare on Greta. Hair greying and ash-like hung over his ears. He looked away from her toward the morning dawnsong rattling from meadowlarks. The back of his neck was covered in hair. The man with him was slightly taller, with a small round beer gut, eyes like dirty pond water, receded red hairline, the kind of face that may have been freckly when a kid, but grew out of it, and hardened into the mug of someone who Greta thought probably spent a lot of subzero days during that North Dakota oil boom getting his balls frozen. *Being with these two at the campfire at night without wifi might be a shitshow*, she thought.

"They get any shuteye?" she added.

Tiller ignored her, eyes on Scott: "You were in charge of counting cattle."

"Not me," Scott said, bags under his eyes from hardly sleeping a wink. "I didn't have a quad, remember?"

"Don't need one to count 'em."

"I was." Greta was surprised to see Scott still at camp but gave Tiller the stink eye. "That why you woke me?" She expected Scott would have trekked halfway to Star Valley, or that he and Tiller would still be arguing about the taxidermy buffalo, why it passed through camp, whether or not it was Scott's imagination, Greta's too. Then again, maybe Scott hadn't said anything about all the Indians he claimed ran past their fire, either.

Tiller continued to ignore her, though he clearly included her in his blame game. "We're missing two cows."

"Maybe wandered off a short distance?" she said. "Lots of little gullies around here. Make any coffee?"

"Calves don't wander off," Tiller said.

"Sure they do, but you said cows," Scott jumped in. "She counted the calves too."

"I need coffee," Greta said.

"I didn't make any damn coffee." Tiller turned back to Scott. "Two calves are not fucking here."

Scott crossed his arms as if warding off the coming dawn. "I'm telling you they wandered off."

"What about coyotes or wolves?" Greta asked.

"We'd have heard," Tiller said.

"Sure about that?" Greta thought again. "You weren't here half the night, and we heard lots of coyotes. Bear?"

"I don't like this," Tiller said.

"Miscounted?" Scott said.

"I can count calves," Greta groaned. "They're either playing hopscotch out in the forbs or Tiller here can't count."

"That's not the problem," Tiller said. "We need those calves."

"They have to be around," Greta said. "We'll find them soon as we make coffee and pack."

"Find them now," Tiller said to Scott. "Check those gullies. I don't want to delay any more than we have to."

"I'm making coffee first," Greta said.

The cattle stirred soon as Scott fired up his new quad. Several cows bawled at the noise as Scott headed toward a gully they'd avoided the evening before. Greta made herself a big cup of joe, took a drink like she was filling her soul, then broke down the tents and packed. She noticed their guests hadn't said more than a few whispers, and were standing next to that truck, watching her. That driver appeared near to fifty, greying hair, buggy eyes, squarish face—puffy around the cheekbones—that seemed punched too many times in bar fights. *Looks like he should be in prison somewhere*, she thought. *That other guy too.* Then again, she thought that about a lot of men who stared.

Anxious to get going, Tiller sipped from a thermos, then said he was going to start driving the herd.

"You should have told Scott." Greta watched as Tiller grabbed his gloves.

"I did tell him. Told him to find those calves."

"Not that. You know there are things following us."

He slipped on his gloves, wiggled his fingers. "What, a wolf? A bear? You know something I don't?"

"What are you playing at?" she said. "Want me to say it?"

"Don't want you to say anything," Tiller said. "I want you to find those calves. We got cattle to move. So, forget about coyotes or whatever."

She guessed Scott really hadn't said anything about the buffalo, so just said, "Yeah, coyotes. Or whatever."

Twenty minutes later Scott returned empty-handed. He pulled up next to Greta, who was packing her bedroll and tent onto her quad. She'd piled Scott's personal effects for him to pack.

"Find anything?" she asked.

"Nothing out there. No calves in gullies, or downslope, or up the trail. Nothing."

"Tiller's gonna want a corpse at least."

"Ain't going to find them back the way we came." He shifted his weight on the seat. "Maybe they're up by the stream we're pushing toward."

Greta leaned on her quad, then swung a leg over. "Maybe."

"What's that supposed to mean?"

"I don't know. Just, maybe." She fired up the engine.

"Two calves dead or missing out of more than three hundred head?" he said. "Still a good haul. Wanna know my opinion?" He didn't give her a chance to answer. "Maybe you don't need the money as bad as I do."

"And you wanted to leave last night after your furry friend visited," Greta said, burying in her what the bones had told her. "Maybe I should have counted *her*. She can join us. I like the way she walks."

"I don't wanna talk about that," Scott said. "I was drunk as hell."

"Sure, that's what it was," she said. "Shared hallucinations."

"Oh, I'm sure we saw a buffalo. But that weird walking shit? Those Indians? That was just something I ate or drank. Had to be."

"They were headed to a buffalo jump. They just wanted you to help—saw you were good at it."

"That's not funny."

He was about to drive away when she stopped him. "Who are these guys with Tiller?"

"Hired hands. Bill Cherry drives that piss tank. His friend is Pinkie Zollers. Not sure he's getting paid. Just wanted something to do."

"Something to do? He looks thirty-five."

"Maybe he wants free meals and your company. Maybe he likes our stink. How would I know? Supposed to follow in that truck in case we have any more mishaps."

"I don't like them," she said. "They don't talk, they . . . stare."

"Sounds like most white dudes. Welcome to Wyoming."

Tiller told her to maintain the herd while he went off somewhere, where, she didn't know, probably to find the calves, though for all she cared he was still taking a leak over some cliff-rock. He'd been gone a few hours and that vomit-piss-*whatever*-green truck, a late-1970s Ford F-100 filled with tools and whatnot, had followed. She hated the damn thing. Big tires. Big exhaust. Gas-guzzler. Never a good experience with men in a truck like that. Even clean-cut boys in similar wheels could be trouble, and these were farthest from the kind of boys you'd bring home to meet the Pope.

Seemed like all morning she could feel Cherry's and Zoller's eyes on the back of her head while that damn truck bumped along. Cherry floated a greasy tan Stetson onto his wide head, pushed those wheels up behind her, bounced that squeaky chassis through ruts while Zoller grinned, that truck sometimes staying a quarter mile back. Other times Cherry pushed that bumper right on her heels, revving like he might wanna stampede the herd, or crush her under the front end. She waved him off each time he did that, turning and glaring the first couple times, catching Cherry's eyes on her, and Zoller grinning and laughing, seeing whatever he wanted to see in her, which couldn't be anything good by the way those beady black pinpoints undressed her.

At lunch she walked up to Cherry. Zollers was off relieving himself. Cherry was also the new cook, he pulled meat from a cooler, tossed some kind of steak onto a portable grill. The meat reminded her of fish market tilapia too long in the sun—all bloody in the eyes.

"You gotta stop following so close," she said. "Gonna startle the herd."

"That so?" Cherry's voice bent like some kind of floorboard about to snap.

"Where you from?" she asked.

"Around."

"Ah, another Tiller," she said, blinking, face against the sun.

He leaned against a rear fender and eyed her. "What's that?"

"Answers questions the same way."

"Live in Thermopolis. Tiller needed help. Said I'd do it. Happy now?" He moved to season the steaks.

"More than I expected, chief. Hope he's paying you."

"Not really your business." He turned the steaks, seasoned the other sides.

"Just stay off my tail, all right?"

Then came another voice behind her. *Zollers.* "Not a bad tail. Seen better. If I was getting paid, maybe I could afford it. Just here for the fun."

"Fun?" Greta thought about giving a little wiggle, what it would mean to creeps like these. But never would, not in a billion years.

"Just saying. Maybe you need some. Seem high-strung."

Greta wanted to laugh. "That why you're here? Wrangling up some good times with your pals?"

"Yes and no," Zollers said. "Since you're asking, I make indie films. Here for research."

"Forget your camera?" Greta asked. It was then she realized *Pinkie* was missing his left *pinky* finger. Most of it anyway, there was a hint of a nub. Seemed whatever had been there slipped off long ago, and that other fingers might slip off any second. She wanted to ask if he lost it in a lawn mower accident when he was seven, or if he'd been born that way and his parents had been that cruel to nickname him Pinkie. Or maybe the nickname had been cuter at one time, something like *Pinkiepie, Pinkieboo, Pinkiewoowoo.* Couldn't be his real name, could it? Maybe his friends just started calling him that and it stuck. Either way, she wasn't about to ask, wasn't ever going to call him anything but Zollers.

Even Cherry laughed at her comment, which got Zollers to squint. "You might've seen my viral short film *Nude Camp Zombies?*"

"Good film," Cherry added.

"Got a bunch of naked cattle here," Greta said. "Some of them can act. Though you might have to find a bull for those money shots."

"Not what you think," Zollers said. "Bunch of people got no clothes on during the apocalypse, is all. Cherry got a bit part. Put all my friends in that film. Know what I mean? Won all kinds of festival awards. Bakersfield, Austin, Roswell."

"Not the Oscars? Must feel good taking sleaze onto the home movie indie circuit." She then did her best impression of a director: "*Let's put some tits in here. Maybe some the size of Cloud Peak—is that what you say? Nothing makes a movie scary like topless girls.*"

"Ain't pornography." Cherry flipped the steaks again. The fire was awful low.

"We met on a previous shoot if you wanna know," Zollers said. "Friend of mine made a Civil War era film short. Cherry was Confederate Major Edmund Kirby Smith, you know, before he became a real general and all that."

Greta eyed the steaks, which weren't looking edible. "Can't say I recall my Lost Cause generals' history."

"Alternate history," Zollers said.

"That right?"

"South wins. Called *The Real South*. Should see it," Zollers said. "Cherry has a big moment. Crying scene after he kills his Yankee aunt."

"You kill a woman?" Greta wanted to fake puke.

He and Cherry both nodded as Cherry said, "Cryin' ain't easy."

"I play a blockade runner who has a motorboat from the future," Zoller said. "Anyway, had to have Cherry in *Nude Camp Zombies*."

"Here's where I'm confused . . ." Greta leaned against the truck. "Why not *Naked People*, since, you know, these are nude people running from, I'm guessing, clothed zombies?"

"They weren't naked zombies . . . yet."

"But why give the end away?" she said. "Where's the mystery? If you're selling an idea based on genitals, why would you want dead . . . you know . . . Kind of gross. Guess if you're gonna use wilted genitals, why lead your audience astray? Here's one even better, *Dead Parts*."

"She got a point," Cherry said. "Better title."

Greta tried to nod but couldn't quite get her chin to move.

"Too goddam late for that. Anyway, I'm taking notes out here, gathering ideas for my next film," Zollers said. "Thinking, action. Cartel deep in the heart of America. Popular genre right now. Drugs, you know? Maybe you could be in it, be one of my girls. Gonna be feature-length. Big cattle drive. Shootout with the drug lords. Lots of Mexicans and stolen weed, that sort of thing. We'll hire a crop duster for the gun battle . . ."

"Thing is," Greta said. "I'm not your girl."

"Time to eat," Cherry said.

Slopped onto plates, Cherry's still-bloody steaks glistened like they'd just been cut from bone. Something smelled off so Greta only chewed one bite and spit the meat when no one was looking. She slung the rest into the waiting fingers of hungry buttercups and steer's head blossoms.

The rest of the day continued in a lengthy push alongside towers of limestone, over hills bursting green, with cliffs and mountainous terrain to their east, covered in various lodgepole, ponderosa, limber, and juniper pines. And there were more grasslands around them now, some areas dropping into fens, marshy and reedy. A few ducks dabbled or dove. She wanted to call them all Mallards, but there were probably some Goldeneyes and Ring-necked Ducks. A lone Trumpeter Swan bent its slender white neck into a half heart shape, and some elk traipsed through like they were late for a party.

Greta pushed the cattle through puddles and thin streams. Then they wound upward again, where every forb imaginable brightened hillsides in reds, whites, yellows, and blues. The land here swarmed with bees and wasps, more species than Greta had ever seen. Flies too, some big as her thumb, bit at the cows, and tried to chew on her neck, while red dragonflies with orange wings darted and perched like trophies on patches of cheatgrass and houndstongue.

A pair of male Wood Ducks flew overhead and slid into the water. She knew those. Too weird-looking to be Mallards with their greenish crested heads, strange ornate white lines, and chestnut breasts. Frogs bawled and chirped, some trilled like crickets, and a few small herons snatched those into their bills and swallowed them whole.

All this time, the cattle seemed less tired, maybe even eager to get to the canyon, as if pulled by the shadows that lay hidden within those cliffs. Cherry revved his engine now and then, still too close to Greta, and every time, she thought it seemed like a game to him and Zollers. She'd wave him off, and if she did manage to turn around, they'd give her a wicked tongue waggle, or Zollers would lick his fingers then pretend he was working an imaginary camera, which grossed her out even more.

Always on the lookout for the goat-fawn, she finally spotted those side and back spots dragging through a fen. Greta was pushing hard through a mud puddle, and had only a quick view, and wondered if the taxidermy had lost its voice. Then she thought about that buffalo in its herky-jerky steps, in near teleportation the way it moved, or didn't, or couldn't talk, or even look at her through real eyes—though maybe that was the very beast that talked to her in her dream. Somehow, the more she thought about everything, she felt strangely comforted. Why was she in such a good mood? Why wasn't she terrified? Had the goat-fawn really turned into something protective like the mice? No monster could be good, she thought. But she hoped, and her hope always seemed to get her in trouble, though right then she wished Cherry and his truck would go tumbling into a ravine, Zollers with it.

When Tiller finally showed up later in the day, he drove two calves up the trail and Greta laughed at that. Tiller didn't even act furious, smoking one of his cigarettes, his black hat pushed back, slowly moving the critters. He later said he had them roped to his quad for a while, just to make them go faster, but didn't want to kill them after all that work finding them. He seemed quite proud of himself, and tipped his hat at Scott and Greta in an I-told-you-so. Cherry didn't say anything either, and started up another round of blood spatter steaks, while Zollers scouted the location by taking pics with his phone.

All Greta would eat was a peanut butter and jelly sandwich that she slopped together, claiming she didn't want all that red meat in her gut.

"More for me." Cherry chewed gristle while he stared at her. Scott and Tiller didn't seem to notice, or couldn't, because Greta knew men couldn't see what women could. Whether plain as day across a bar room or in a glimpse of a passing car, a woman could always see what men were thinking while the gristle was being chewed.

Late that night, Greta grew hungry again. She'd hardly eaten a thing besides that sandwich, so talked Scott into making some fried potatoes. "They're world-famous," she said. "Besides, I'm switching to potato energy."

And that put everyone in a good mood, even Cherry, who tossed his hat into his truck and leaned prairiewise as if he might go sleep in a field. Zollers generally seemed less of a creepy grump and was more talkative, but Greta wanted nothing to do with his film lectures. She wondered if Scott felt something strange about Cherry's meals, about Cherry and Zollers altogether. Those two wouldn't even sit by the fire while they ate their potatoes. She noticed after a while that both slipped back into the truck with a little electric lantern, maybe fearing every mosquito and moth, maybe the bats that had been squeaking overhead, maybe talking their stupid movies. Or maybe they'd seen the goat-fawn, she didn't know, and maybe didn't want to know, though she couldn't stop wondering what they were really all about, if she had to worry about them more than she usually worried about dudes.

Scott dumped a second helping of potatoes on her plate, and she drowned it all in gooey ketchup and pepper, then chowed, and afterward the two of them drank gin and stared at the flames of yet another campfire, neither willing to bring up the buffalo, maybe because they'd had a good day for the most part, not having lost any calves after all. And with Cherry, Zollers, and Tiller keeping their distance, and that goat-fawn creeping around the perimeter maybe offering some kind of watchful eye, things seemed to be getting behind her, all that *ghost*-whatever that happened in the prairie. And then she thought how that prairieland and wildgrass been haunted for millions of years, that it must be so filled with the dead, with ghost trains, ghost settlers, ghost bones, and whatnot, that she thought maybe it all congregated behind them. Then she considered that for once on this godforsaken drive maybe they'd risen above all of that spectral atmosphere, like getting above the mist or cloud line, that it would be smooth sailing in these hills where in the darkness she could smell the fire, and every petal blossoming all round, and could hear the soothing buzz of cicadas and crickets, and the occasional territorial toad or frog.

Later, while she sat trying to read a novel, spinning her wheels on the same paragraph over and over, a series of growls came, not just from coyotes, but from the cattle themselves, aware of something out there in the milky night where all those smells of flowers and camp ash had drifted. It took away some of her day's joy, but she wasn't rattled out of her skin like she had been a few times on the trail. Both Cherry and Tiller set rifles against the truck, that dash glowing the entire night, and she wondered if that drain would kill his battery. That constant LED-pale yellowy-green bled onto Zollers's and Cherry's skin, made them look like those men and women she'd seen on the ghost train. And then she wondered, when yet more growls came, if Zollers and Cherry might be dead after all. Maybe Tiller too. She'd kinda be fine with that.

"I'm tired of this growling," Scott said.

Greta had a great buzz going and tossed her book in the fire.

"What the hell you do that for?" he asked.

"I don't even know what I read," she said. "I'd rather read the planets. I see Venus, I see France, I see Martians in their . . ."

"I hate my parents," he suddenly said.

Greta poked at her half-burnt book with a stick, got it to catch fire again. "Good to know." Occasionally, a strip of ash floated into the air like a butterfly wing.

"Can't go back," he said.

"All right."

"I mean it." He took another drink. "Don't care about their stupid fucking furniture store."

"Me either." Greta half laughed at her own response. "I mean, can't see myself going in and asking to see the sofa collection."

Some time passed before he said, "Don't want to walk to the dinosaur museum. Don't want to go fishing. Don't want to stare into the flatness of Star Valley and watch cars pass my bedroom window. Don't want to know that they're just passing through, hating every second of what they're seeing."

"I doubt they hate every second."

"There's nothing there." His eyes glistened with fire. "I hate our neighbors. They hate that I'm Black. They hate that I'm tall. They hate that I'm different. They hate that I live in their valley. They hate that I read comics. They hate that I don't listen to their music."

"Always steer clear of creepy white unaccepting neighbors."

"I won't go back."

"Then don't."

"I can't."

She took a drink this time, trying to push the buzz back in her head. "What about your stuff?"

"Some clothes, my Marvel shirt and hoodie collection, my comic book collection . . . shoved it all in the trunk before I left . . . it's over in Ten Sleep . . . hope no one breaks into my car."

"Oh good. Tiller's dad will have something to read when he isn't bleeding out bear cubs. What about your girlfriend, or boyfriend, or *friend* friend?"

Scott stretched, poked at the fire. "Lied. Don't have one."
"It's okay. Me either."
"Should have stayed in school."
"Sure," she said, wondering the same thing herself. "Then what? Where do you imagine you'd be? In debt? Or I should say, besides that?"

"Graduate school, maybe. Finding a job. Having a steady life away from here."

Greta watched more paper wingsparks lift from the fire, flutter toward Venus. The planet blinked in the night sky. "Think you'd miss this place. Imagining you teaching at some community college in Los Angeles is kind of funny. Might find cities gross."

Scott cleared his throat. "I actually think I'd like it. Truth is, I feel lost when I'm outside. I want to live in a tiny apartment in a big fucking city. I don't care if it smells like shit. These cows smell like shit. I smell like shit."

"True."

"Thanks."

"We're just lost for a while. Think of this as a temporary thing."

"Maybe."

"You could always be in one of Zollers's films. Be an action star. Lots of scenes in Jacuzzis, naked zombies with their balls dripping off."

"I . . . don't think so."

"Me either." Greta suddenly felt a chill along the back of her neck. "Hey, do me a favor."

"What?"

"Tell me if that freak Cherry and his buddy are staring again. Bitches got eyes that need poked out."

Scott turned around like he was grabbing his shirt off the back of his chair, then stared at the fire again. "They're talking to Tiller."

"Can't believe they say more than three words to each other."

"But Cherry's still looking over here."

"What is it with that guy? I wish Tiller hadn't brought him."

"Neither would have showed up if I hadn't tried to buffalo jump my quad."

"Maybe you shoulda stuck with sports."

"Too boring."

"If I'd been great at soccer I woulda taken it far as I could. I was decent but average. Maybe a little bored."

"See?"

"*Maybe?* Could be a problem we share. Not meant for sports. Not meant for trails, I mean, if you think about it, why the hell are we out here? Meant for bars for sure." She thought of the Lope again. She loved the beers, the prices, but hated the place and its Rolling Stones *Tattoo You* vibe, "Start Me Up" and all that, too smoky and loud even for her, and every guy a tough cabrón. Not even all bikers, just the *tough-as-nails club* from around Laramie who worked every dirty job imaginable—at those bentonite factories and shit, or in construction—or just those day-laborer types who needed rent cash and endless beer credit somewhere. They would fight in the bar, or in the parking lot, and ate women with their eyes and would pass you free beers even if you didn't want one, which meant Greta could have one or three and not shell out too much. And that lot was filled with every revving truck, car, and bike engine you could imagine. Everything happened in that lot, sex, shooting up, whatever, just smoking out sometimes, just like almost everything happened in that bar. But damn, she would kill for one of those beers right then. "Only three or four more nights then we're done with this shit," she added.

Scott nodded. "You gonna tell me what happened with Hannah?"

Greta wished the conversation hadn't made such an obvious turn. "Still working through it," she said.

"Through what?"

"Through not talking about it."

"All right."

Greta didn't apologize. She couldn't. Truth was, it wasn't his business. Hannah left, and while the mystery of where she went and why ate at Greta, she knew that as long as Hannah was okay, and not dead somewhere, which she still didn't think was a possibility, then it might not be her business either. Then maybe she could let go of all this, let Hannah go her way. But then Greta thought for the millionth time, because she, Greta, wanted to be needed: *What if Hannah needs my help?* Then again, Hannah had never called or texted after she left, so maybe Greta could learn to leave her be.

She stood up, felt toward the fire to warm her hands, said she needed to get some sleep, let the crickets soothe her dreams. Scott grunted in reply. She turned, Tiller had gone who knows where. Cherry was back in the sick light of the truck, eyes on her, eyes that she pretended not to see, though she knew he caught her looking. It was the kind of glare that made her feel like she was the outsider here, not him. That she didn't belong, that she was an alien thing, more so than the goat-fawn, more than her mice, the buffalo, those bizarre roadrunnery birds, that wall of bones, that owl. How could she forget the owl? Or that huge birdplane? Where the hell did that thing go? Perched on the ghost-bison bones? Or the fact that she was still hearing those growls from beyond the perimeter, beyond the cows, which were still somewhat restless. Maybe Tiller told Cherry to stay awake, protect the herd. Maybe Tiller was out there on the perimeter, just waiting to kill some wild dog. Zollers was in the bed of the truck asleep. At least he was out of the way, for now. And she was glad for no wifi after all, wouldn't have to look at any of his film trailers.

She didn't know what the morning would bring, but knew the canyon loomed close. Earlier she'd seen a kind of opening, like a pair of gates, rocks, cliffs, towers, an illusion the way time upheaved rocks and formed through hundreds of millions of years of rivercut erosion.

Then a cauldron of thousands of bats swirled past, like they'd been released from the darkest pocket of earth, like they might do more than eat every flying bug they could echolocate, maybe take away every star, drink every bit of night-milk. She saw herself with them, spreading her rubbery wings, a little thing consuming her way through the night, insignificant, but driven onward by hunger and *something else*, she wasn't sure.

In a way, she felt trapped outside the canyon, then thought maybe this wasn't a trap but more like a slide, like maybe all those bats had been on an invisible sky-slope, slipping toward the night, toward whatever they might gorge on in the dark, and maybe she and every last bat and cow might tumble through those gates.

The more she thought about this on the way to bed, she wondered if the canyon might offer respite from their days and nights in the prairie. She wanted to ask her mice but instead just kissed them and hoped that maybe one would kiss her back in the morning.

The Skin

At first, the skin lay in a pile in a locked room within the taxidermy shop. It had been there for at least a year in a trunk. Then the skin lay on the floor covered in dust. A mouse gnawed away two toes. A rat ate most of a hand. There was no form to the mess, though there was color for a time, pink and olive hues that slowly turned greyish and pale. And there were tiny, near-invisible hairs, and freckles, age spots, moles too. And a face. Thin eyebrows, lips, a waxy nose, and earlobes with tiny pinholes. The chin came to a bulbous point.

The skin waited to be stretched again, pulled into a familiar shape, only, it didn't know it was waiting, not yet. Something had to be smeared onto the no-longer-soft skin, onto the paper coarseness, before it could know. It soon knew many things, including details about the pact with the mother canyon, how this was a crucial time, how monsters were unleashed, that the past would flourish for a time, and wanted to flood the world with living fossils, but couldn't because of the pact, that men had corrupted and trapped the canyon, that its resources were used, that the monsters would only live a short time, that they would rot, and have to wait yet again, for another brief time.

The mold that the skin would be pulled over had taken some time to create, the joints too, which weren't of a fine construction, having been slapped together from wood, plastic, and screws, each bendable enough, every part slopped with grease, so that the legs, arms, and neck could be moveable. The skin could hear its construction, the hard, aggravating work that went into the parts, but also knew the lack of care, the hurriedness, the panic. It sensed much panic from its creator, a fear of losing the land.

The skin felt happy when given fake eyes and some magic on its skin even as a lump so that it could be aware. The eyes were taken out and implanted again after more of the magic paste had been applied, which felt like a sparkling sunrise. The skin could now see even better, and this was before its slow stretching over the mold, though that pulling sensation came right away, pinpricks along every ripple and crease. The skin vaguely recognized the one who made its form, though all people seemed familiar, no matter who the skin saw passing the windows. Their voices blended together, which the skin sometimes imagined as melodies it once knew.

The outside appeared familiar too. The skin hung by a window from a hook where it craved the shops across the street, to see racks of clothes hanging like hides, to see plates of expensive food, though the skin wasn't sure what it would do with them. It knew this life as a separate reality from past delusion and entitlement. Still, the skin yearned to drink from plastic cups with green logos, though the skin would not drink or eat again.

Some time passed while the skin continued to get stretched over the mold, inching its way over hard rounded blobs and joints. To be stretched over a new shape was to be filled up, which made the skin feel swollen and whole. This was the shoe and not the foot for once, and the skin somehow loved this.

Now more paste was applied, and the skin could feel its shimmering consciousness growing with new knowledge pulled from a deep core bored from the past, from both the mother canyon and descendants of the People, which it also knew and accepted had been corrupted by colonizers and settlers, and it knew about Tom Horn, and knew how he and the cattlemen sacrificed the nesters, and drove them like cattle for ten sleeps until they were torn apart by the mother canyon, who was duped into a new contract, and how before that, the People's descendants in all their many forms and tribes were manipulated and killed, or moved, and their children sent to reformatory schools, and many of the little rebellious ones were murdered and buried by their proctors, and all those tribes, their contract with the mother canyon, stolen, ripped from them, manipulated the very month the settlers spotted a giant bird and tortured a Crow for his secret knowledge, who took them to an elder, and the elder was tricked, though the elder rebelled and nearly killed all the white men holding him down, and would have ended the settlers' trickery had it not been for a sudden heart attack, or perhaps some supernatural intervention that took him away to the big sky.

The skin soon felt new ripples along its legs and torso, ebbs along each fingertip, pulses in each palm, electricity up its arms, vibrations in its remaining fingers and the half stump of that partial hand. It soon remembered the idea of touch, though the skin couldn't feel the way it used to. The skin missed having a tongue. Something black and slick had taken its place, been sewn into the skin's throat.

The skin was uncertain how many days, weeks, or months the process took until it could feel the mold, to finish stretching, for it to sense each bendable joint, for it to know many more things. Everything had to be stretched and pulled, more paste had to be applied, the process needed to be repeated. The creator who did this grumbled while he worked. At first the skin felt like he might be cooing, but he wasn't. The skin never saw tears in his eyes, and several times witnessed his fingers shake, and watched him leave the room as if late for something. He also exited the room whenever the front door rang, and he hurried to double lock it in the dark. And then he'd come back, and his hands were warm, and there was a coldness in his eyes, an infinite piercing that didn't go away, and those coo-grunts turned to curses, and the skin cocked its head to the side, because it suddenly realized it had heard them all before, and then remembered the day it fell from whatever struck the back of its head, before it was mostly peeled from who it had been.

Soon the skin's seams were closed by the man, who used mostly glue for this, though other times stapled in places, leaving long tracks up the neck into the hairline. Grotesque callused and glue-covered hands trembled against that stubbly scalp with the scar that made the skin's head appear as if two halves of entirely separate faces. Most of its original scalp had been destroyed, that hair now gone. It remembered tickles to the back of its neck. The man's hands shook as he examined his creation, then he choked on spit, or maybe vomit, and left the room. The skin tried to smile but couldn't.

Time had no meaning to the skin. Days, hours, even seconds fused together as it learned to stand, to balance, then walk. It was glad when it was finally lifted off the metal hook. Soon the skin could stumble around the shop, and then almost walk with ease. One night, the skin was given extra paste on its black, greasy tongue, then was told to leave, to protect the family from the mother canyon, to make sure the sacrifices were taken to the hole. The skin was told it would die again there.

The skin imagined all those canyonlands releasing the past onto the present, especially those beating wings that soared, and those that scuttled in the dirt and grass, or crawled from the waters. The skin was told to travel to the great den of mother canyon, to seek the help of others like itself from the shop, to ready for the great sacrifices. It was told that if sacrifices didn't happen, mother canyon would set loose something else, along with a river of hot blood, and lift new mountains, and release an earthquake that would set new courses for rivers, and swallow lakes and towns, and fill the land with a choking mist. The skin didn't really believe the mother canyon about that part, and especially didn't trust the man, though it couldn't kill him, and somehow knew that mother canyon and the world could survive side by side, that the age of ice had ended long ago, that another new world could be created, one that would not rot, that wouldn't need the skin, or the dead creatures, or boundaries.

The skin set out from the shop, northeastward, on private property, moving like a partially stuck windmill, like it didn't belong on the earth under such a big sky, amid so many moths, flies, and spiders. Its arms needed to whirl, to wind up in order to start walking, sometimes while stumbling, though not completely, maybe it could just swing them, the skin thought, and tried to bend both elbows. It soon tried to bow at every joint, making each step strange and frightening to any creatures that saw it. Nothing felt right to the skin. It could feel grease dripping inside itself. And maybe that was okay.

Driven forward by the magic on its tongue, it slithered under a back gate, stepped onto a trail, began walking into the high, lonesome country, into the dark, across grasslands, and wildflowers, hiding some days behind rocks, or cottonwood trunks in ravines, in pigweed and sagebrush, sometimes in fields of buttercups where it lay and tried to hum like bees. It walked at night, slow, ever so slow, though never tiring, feeling a kind of alchemy inside, and when seeing the little creatures in moonlit pastures, it knew that the enchantment within itself had somehow made them scatter into the dark places.

It had been given clothes but after the first night and second day, tore them off, leaving them scattered across the prairie. One evening the skin spied the great bird with the calf and feared the bird's giant, pale talons, and enormous sharp bill, so hid in a bush where it was repeatedly struck by a rattlesnake. The deep bites felt soothing. The snake eventually roped away into a borrow pit, no longer threatening.

That same night the skin stood naked on a ridge, and saw both the goat-fawn and the broken-necked jackrabbit, and felt their magic. And through whatever hard black bruises the skin had for eyes, it gazed, and didn't feel naked, though was, and stared down on a camp, its skin having turned a deep moongrey from some kind of magic-rot. Though it didn't have wings, skin loosened from its sides from all its slithering during the mornings. Sideskin-flaps opened in the spring night breeze and resembled wings, though it didn't care. It could see a young woman staring up at its mooncolored form, and from her emanated a new magic, for she was friends with two dead mice in a way that went beyond guiding her to the mother canyon, which struck and confused the skin, because it knew that she was one of the sacrifices.

Feeling like it shouldn't be seen any longer, the skin hid, and yet peered over the ridge and spotted another form, a young man, and knew that he'd come out of the skin's womb at one time, that he'd grown over the years, and the skin retained memories of that young man, how he never had childish laughter, but had been a child nonetheless, and had done something unforgiveable to the skin along with the man.

And then the skin snuck downhill, around all of the cows, and walked and walked to a gate, and waited there for the young man. He arrived, and fiddled with the locks, and cursed at his slowness of unlocking them, and the skin witnessed his hands shake. It knew he didn't see the skin at first, because the skin stood so still, like the night itself, like an invisible dream, until he pushed the gate in a wide arc, nearly hitting the skin, and said, "Jesus, fuck, Mom," then, "Thought I wouldn't see you for another day at least. You need to protect us, all right? Make your way to the goddam canyon. Protect us from the bird, and whatever else is out there. I think there's an owl now, and some smaller birds. God knows what else. Can you do that?"

The skin was confused about the young man's fear and anger. It reached out to touch his face, to pull him close so it could whisper in his ear. The skin's mouth opened and closed, and its black swollen tongue made a clop-slosh wet sound.

"What the fuck?" he said. "Don't . . . Don't ever touch me. You'll be gone soon. And then you can rest, or whatever it is you dead things do. And then we won't have to do this again for a hundred years or more. You will be long gone by then. Okay? Dad wants me to live forever. You're doing the right thing to protect our land. We'll build you a nice mausoleum. Now go."

Again, the skin reached for that face, to touch scars it didn't remember, and to whisper-whisper its own thoughts, maybe forgiveness, this time stretching with its half hand. But he smacked it away, breaking a finger that snapped and hung like a broken stick, and then he stormed into the night, back toward camp, while the skin watched until the moondark swallowed him. After an hour of being stuck in that position, the skin struggled to move, then was able to bend at the hips and knees and turn away. Its loose finger fell as it walked toward what it felt was the direction of mother canyon.

Eventually, hail and rains made walking difficult, as if water and ice took away more of the magic. During that time, it knew to hide or that it would be destroyed by falling ice, and found nearby a mountain of bones and carrion: halves of horses, hollowed-out elk, dead sheep, dogs, cattle . . . Everywhere, *bones bones bones*: rib cages, femurs, hips, meta-everythings, skulls . . . And god knows what, the decomposed halves of things. The skin wriggled and burrowed alongside a bull, slipping inside its gutted cavity, worming to escape the falling ice, and then lay still and stared from between torn hide into a whitened corpse-dog eye, and after the hail stopped, let the rainwater wash away every bit of bull, goat, and horse death that lay above it, and the water turned its skin a more mottled grey-green.

When the moonrise came, the skin made its way up the trail, and passed through streams, then after several miles, wandered into a fen where it submerged itself in a bog next to several sleeping turtles and Mallards. It considered staying where fish and crawdads nibbled and poked, but then the morning light brightened the pond like a green lamp over its head and beckoned the skin to lay under the dusk sun. But it made its way, even in the daylight now, and the algae coating its skin dried and flaked and made it reek like fish guts, and the skin's joints started to become even more difficult to bend. It lost several toes to the crawdad.

Soon the skin saw a bear, and knew the giant furball came from the same creator, and knew the bear was aware of this too, and the skin crawled onto the back of the bear and whispered in a fuzzy ear, and they traveled along escarpments up into the timberline, and down into other fens that tempted the skin to go lie in them and never come out.

And then, near the mother canyon entrance, the skin flopped off the back of the bear, and the bear indicated he was going to come with it, but then the bird came, that giant vulture-thing that made even the skin scared of light and dark, and the skin hid next to the broken-necked jackrabbit that had been following, while the bird tore the bear's head away.

The skin hid even after the bird took off with the bear's body, and then the skin went and picked up the head, for the skin somehow knew the young woman was on her way with the dead mice, and so it placed the head lovingly in the stream, and whispered into the bear's ear, and then beckoned the jackrabbit, which came and sat with the giant bear head, while the skin hid for a time until the girl and the herd passed, then wandered into the canyon.

It was a dark, starless night when the skin stood before a hole in the limestone cliffs, the great entrance, a place it was told to never pass through, where it thought of the jackrabbit, and the young woman, and the bear head, and decided to stop protecting the family, the creator man and him, the young man who'd come out of her womb.

Something had transformed the skin, something with the young woman and the mice and bear, and besides, something else must have happened in the prairie, because it sensed the pact had been broken, and the canyon's power over it was nearly gone. The skin then remembered whispering to that bear, because the skin had sent much of its remaining magic into the bear head.

The skin thought it might cross the threshold anyway. It could go reason with the mother canyon before it was too late, whisper in her ear, though the skin knew that might not be a good idea, that maybe it should hide there, see if the creator followed, or maybe that young woman, and was feeling conflicted about everything. And so the skin slithered into the cave hole, *the den*, the mother canyon's sweet rotten mouth, and in the dark, waited.

Night Seven

A quarter mile from the canyon mouth Tiller stopped. Scott was off his quad and checking out a cow or calf. Greta couldn't be sure and drove downslope next to Tiller, thinking that since he wasn't driving over to Scott, she wouldn't either.

Cherry gunned the truck engine behind them, which made the entire herd twitch and bawl in unison. Zollers laughed in the passenger seat and snapped pics of cows and scenery.

Tiller turned toward Greta soon as she stopped. "That SOB better cut that noise before we lose the herd to a panic."

"Why you telling me? You're the boss." She wanted to call him a dumbass, that he brought those creeps, but then cut herself short. "Why'd we stop?"

"Cow come up lame," Tiller said. "Scott's trying to figure it out."

"Thought you were the expert."

Tiller pushed up his brim, the hat unclean and misshapen from having been slammed into the dirt too many times. "Let's see what he comes up with."

When Cherry gunned his engine again, Tiller turned and waved his hat. "Cut it out, you stupid fuck," he said. The truck went into idle, then Cherry hung his elbow out the window and killed the motor altogether. Zollers let out a *whoop!*

"Why'd he gun that?" Greta said.

"Don't know," Tiller replied. "Maybe wanted to piss you off."

Greta sure as hell wasn't going to let Tiller think that worried her. She'd get some digs in at Cherry sooner or later. "Everyone wants attention."

"You think?"

She and Tiller got off their quads and watched Scott check the cow's back left hoof for a third time. Still watching, Greta pulled off her goggles and slugged water, thinking Scott might get kicked in the balls. Nothing so interesting happened, and he soon wandered over, shaking his head.

"What you got?" Tiller asked.

"Can't figure it out," Scott said. "Can't see anything trapped in the hoof but sure has a smell. Ulcer? Warts?"

"Said the hoof stinks?" Tiller said.

Scott nodded. "Like something dead."

"Goddam." Tiller turned to Greta. "What's your diagnosis?"

Greta wiped her mouth, could see Zollers pretending to film them. "No clue. But hold on." She didn't like that she was being tested but then remembered that maybe the Pope told her something about cattle catching some kind of lower-leg infection that caused them to quickly turn lame. Had to do with inner bones and whatnot, though she couldn't remember any more than that. "Hoof rot?" she said.

Tiller clicked his tongue. "Bingo," then started over to the cow.

"Well, how about that?" Greta said.

"Yeah, how about that," Scott replied.

Tiller was already at the beast and lifting her lame hoof by the time Scott and Greta caught up. "Thing about foot rot," he said as they watched on, "bacteria gets caught between the toes, all up and around the bone that's encased in the hoof like a casket. Called a coffin bone."

"Like a *casket*," Greta repeated.

"Everyone gets one eventually," Tiller said.

She groaned at him, and at *coffin bone*. What a stupid name. Been too much death lately with all those ghosts, the Pope, dead animals following them, and Lady Grazer torn to shreds. She didn't want to think about coffins or graves, let alone bones. But there they were again, those two hundred and six, just like her, like the Pope rotting underground. Probably nothing but two hundred and six pieces left of him anymore, some of that matted with hair.

Tiller showed them the sole of the cow's outer claw. A smear of yellowy blood drained into a drip. "Look at that. All bloody. Now, isn't always just smell, but this girl was quick to come up lame. And here, that's a deep wound plenty swollen above the foot. Got all kinds of pus in there too. Coffin bone and coffin joint both in trouble."

"Damn," Scott said. "Now what?"

"Ain't got antibiotics." Tiller stood up, wiped his hands. "Wrap won't do no good. Just gonna get worse. Good chance a few might pull up lame. Highly contagious. Gonna have to put her down, take our chances this don't spread."

"Jesus Christ," Scott said. "You don't have to do that, do you?"

Tiller looked at Scott. "You're right. Ain't me that's gonna. You're gonna take her down the trail and take care of it."

"Me?" Scott said. "You got the wrong guy for that job. This has to be treatable."

"She'd slow us down," Tiller said. "Been stalled enough. Like I said, don't want this spreading. You found her lame, you kill her."

Scott looked at Tiller like he had to be joking. Greta did too. "I'm just a herder," Scott said.

"That all you are?" Tiller said. "So am I."

"And a trail boss," Scott pointed out. "You do it."

"Trail boss says what to do," Tiller said. "Now take my rifle since you lost yours, take her down into that gully, and put her out of her misery."

"I won't do that."

"What are you doing, Tiller?" Greta said. "Don't you want to spare the cattle? Thought you were gonna lose profits if we lost another one?"

Tiller ignored Greta, locked eyes with Scott. "If you want a ride back to town, now's the time. Cherry and that dumbass filmmaker will take you back. You can forfeit your pay."

"Why are you always giving ultimatums?" Greta said. "This is bullshit. What's wrong with you?"

"I'm not doing it," Scott said. "I don't kill cows."

"Then go."

"I'm not going." Scott stood a head taller than Tiller. Greta had never seen such a fury in either of their eyes. "I'm finishing this drive," Scott went on. "But I'm not killing anything that doesn't need to be."

"It needs to be," Tiller was quick to reply.

"It doesn't," Greta said. "Tiller, stop this. Quit trying to prove how tough you are."

"Ain't stopping nothing," Tiller said. "Best to get your friend to go do what I say."

"Now he's not your friend?" Greta said.

Scott tucked his chin into his chest and eyed Tiller even harder. "Gonna have to make me leave . . . *boss*."

"I'll make you leave," Tiller said. "That ain't a problem."

"You going to shoot me, white boy? Your rifle ain't over here."

"Oh, I'll shoot you."

"Go ahead."

"Take a step." Tiller started to reach in his coat like maybe he had a hidden shoulder holster, though Greta couldn't see anything of the sort. "I'll call it defending myself," Tiller added. "Got plenty of witnesses."

"Who?" Scott said. "The cows? Greta? Your friend Cherry? Zollers?"

Tiller didn't move, didn't flinch. "God is enough witness."

"You're both stupid," Greta said. "It's a fucking cow. You're going to die over a cow, a half-dead cow, a cow that Tiller isn't going to rescue, and neither are we at this point. Quit being so stupid."

"It's my cow," Tiller said, "and Scott's gonna shoot her or go home. Or worse."

"I'll die first." Scott refused to move.

"You're not going to die," Greta said.

Tiller blinked. "He's going to die."

"Shoot me, asshole."

Just then, a voice came from behind Greta. "You got five minutes to move the herd before I shoot this damn cow once and for all and send every last living one of these bitches stampeding across kingdom come." Cherry held a rifle and rope. "I'm all for ending this now. If you don't get to moving, this will be a hell of a day."

"This is great material." Zollers snapped pics with his phone.

Tiller and Scott seemed unwilling to budge, while Greta turned and said, "All right, Cherry. All right. I'm going. These idiots better follow. If they can stop fucking staring at each other." And she was off to her ATV, burning at men, at the stupidity of maleness, at male ego and machismo. Though neither looked like the Pope, or had that toughboy Mexican American accent, this all reminded her of her father, who would stare at any stranger and act like he would fight to the death if someone looked at him or his wife the wrong way. It was the same machismo that demanded she go and cook a meal, or clean the house of every bit of dust or scuff mark on the linoleum, or wash dishes like some kind of domestic servant, and pull the boots off his smelly-ass feet. She remembered having to do that for her dad while listening to his storytelling, those grandiose tales about nothing as she slowly grabbed the heels. Then she was expected to heap praises so that he—like other men who needed their very auras worshipped—could go mentally masturbate, empowered by their maleness, their deeds, their reek of sweat and aftershave, their opinions all rotting like the inside of that cow's hoof, because so many men were just coffin bones trapped in a casket of maleness, rotting on the marrow.

By the time she fumed her way to the back of the herd and started moving them, she saw Scott and Tiller had gone in opposite directions. Scott drove to the outer flank as

Tiller caught up to her and called out, "I got this. Go scout ahead. Find the best place to cross the creek at the canyon mouth in case it's too deep at the trail crossing."

She was never happier to burn her way past the herd and up the trail, out of sight of their dirt clouds and shadows. She hoped they wouldn't kill each other before she returned. Last thing she wanted was to dig through a dead man's wallet just so she could get paid. She considered whether she would and left it at that.

Then a shot rang and she knew that Cherry had killed the beast with the lame leg, and though she hadn't been attached, not like Lady Grazer, she felt a kind of pain for the cow losing its life, and imagined a quivering heap, blood and spit oozing. She wondered what else was going to afflict these cattle, and hoped no more had to die along the way, that she wouldn't have to ever see more cow bones and hides.

Soon enough, she was at the stream. Thrust faults, eroded cliffs, and pinnacles towered above the waterway from where she could see the canyon entrance open like an angry mouth. Limestone palisades and granite teeth ringed with fir and pine in every direction, more than at any point in their drive thus far, and in between those folds of green, shrubs, small caves, boulders, many with pictographs. The banks, lined by willows, coyote bush, sage, and sparse cottonwoods, wove a heavenlike spell releasing pollen and starry seeds everywhere that floated like snow onto Greta and the creek. The water here bubbled and gurgled over rounded stones, having churned far longer than she could imagine.

The trail was clear of brush at the ford. The stream itself flowed wide and shallow, winding along cliffs, and from where she stood, the waters swept deep into the prairie along a line of riparian woodlands that huddled close as if from the will of some unknown force. Ahead of her, only sparse patches of wildgrass in the canyon mouth, a few clumps here and there. Tiller was right, the cattle might not get their fill once in the canyon. Either way, the stream was fairly shallow and easy to cross, so she headed back toward the herd, which was already closing in on her position.

Scott and Tiller steered clear of each other while Cherry bumped the truck through ruts and gravel. She didn't want to talk to Tiller, not after what happened, but told herself she still had a job to do, so went over and grumbled that fording the stream wouldn't be a problem. He gave a nod and put Scott on duty to push the cattle through. Greta couldn't tell if that had been Tiller's half-hearted apology to Scott or not.

Greta then drove to the water's edge with Tiller and parked, hoping to deter any strays from slipping up- or downstream. She was already shaking her head about all these men and their problems when something large in the creek bed caught her attention, Tiller's too. "What the hell?" he said.

It was round and nearly black. Water swirled past.

Greta recognized the dark matted and soaked fur, that wide face staring upward, jaws agape, teeth like pinnacles above a canyon mouth.

It was a grizzly head.

No body, no legs, nothing. Just a head.

"This some kind of joke?" Tiller eyed her. "Because that ain't funny."

"Oh sure." Greta thumbed the mice and walked into the stream, water rushing around her boots. "I always keep a bear head in my pants to run and drop into a stream."

Considering how on earth a bear head could have

appeared, she gazed up and down the stream for any sign of the body, which there was none. There was no way she'd missed this, was there? Then her eyes caught something that ducked under a cottonwood across the stream. A jackrabbit maybe. Something grey too. Almost looked like part of an arm, like an elbow pushing away from something. Then again, maybe a grey squirrel, a dove, a young coyote. She wasn't sure. Her mind focused again on this woolly dome staring at her. "You just don't just find a massive bear head lying in a streambed," she added, then to the crop of shagginess: "How'd you get here?"

She bent closer. Something about its eyes. Why so glassy and black? Mouth too, teeth and tongue shiny in the light. She pulled off a glove, leaned over, slowly reached toward the sclera with an index finger. She didn't want to touch it but didn't have a knife on her. She felt her insides shift the closer she got, then finally, though still hesitant, she pushed on the left eye, then tapped. There was no give, nothing squished. Felt more like a marble. She pulled her finger away and grabbed the head below each ear. Felt strangely light except where water weighted the furriness. She rocked the head and lifted until she spotted a line of thick sutures like tangles of wild rice waving into the water.

She set it down with a bit of a splash, then walked over to Tiller.

"Trying to send me a message?" he asked.

"Got one better for you," she said. "Notice how easily it lifted? This is from your dad's shop."

Tiller turned away but she grabbed him by the elbow when several cattle started making their way into the water. "Tell me what the hell a bear from your old man's lobby is doing out here?"

When Tiller didn't answer she grabbed harder. "Where's its body?"

"How would I know? Just watch for strays," he said.

Greta shook her head. "That's how it's going to be then?"

"That's how it's going to be," he said, not watching her.

"All right." She sloshed toward the bear head. This time she picked it right up, cradled the massiveness to her gut and carried it dripping over to her quad. Her jeans got soaked but she didn't care. She took off the two spares she was carrying and stacked them on the bank, picked up the head, and strapped it to the quad's back rack.

By this time, the cattle entered the creek, hoofsplashed, snorted, bawled, and groaned, undersides steaming and white.

Then Tiller caught on to Greta. "What are you doing?" he called out. "Stop that."

"Don't you think your daddy will want his bear head back?" she asked.

"You don't know that's his. Just watch the cattle."

"What do you think we're doing?"

"You and who?" he said. "You ain't watching a damn thing."

"*We* are. Me and Think Tank here." She aimed a thumb at the bear head. "We're watching the goddam cows."

Suddenly the canyon seemed like it couldn't be a bad place as long as you had a bear head strapped onto your quad. Greta wondered how long they'd be passing through. Was it three nights or four? Ten sleeps seemed so far off. She'd already forgot how many nights she'd slept in a tent. And what about after the canyon? More prairie? A dirt road through hills? She thought about driving away with Think

Tank, just heading back to Ten Sleep, dropping the keys to the quad in the mail slot then hightailing it home with the bear head in her car, hardly enough cash to get anywhere. What a way to start a new life.

It took longer than expected for Scott to get the herd across the stream. Greta and Think Tank had to gather several strays, Tiller too, and each time Greta went back to the main trail she wondered where the bear's body had gone, why Cherry would continue to stare like he had nothing better to do than shoot things dead with his eyes. Think Tank was already a goner, so what was the big deal?

"He can't hurt you," she said to Cherry.

"This is gonna be my movie." Zollers marveled at the bear head from the passenger seat. "Shooting cows, big arguments, now this? I'm going into script development tonight."

Cherry licked his teeth at Greta. "You got emotional problems."

"And you drive a piss-colored truck," she shot back to Cherry and zoomed off.

At least her stolen mice had company now. She liked that.

And then she saw Cherry take his truck too fast into the streambed, like he wanted to prove something besides being the man who could cook foul meat and shoot a cow in the head. What a mess that had been. The truck hit down hard on the front axle, and though it didn't break, the engine stalled right there in the creek. Zollers was having the time of his life.

Cherry got to cursing right away. "Goddam son of a bitch."

The truck wouldn't restart.

Greta thought Cherry probably flooded the engine but didn't say anything, and heard him say to Tiller to go on ahead, he'd catch up when he could.

And then Zollers's enthusiasm waned, she could hear him complain: "You're shitting me. We need to get this started. We can't lose sight of that bear head."

"You want us to push it out of the stream at least?" Tiller asked.

"Goddam right," Zollers said.

Cherry just shook his head and ignored Zollers. "Nah. It'll start. See you up the trail."

"We'll be pushing hard," Tiller said. "Nothing for the cows to eat for the rest of the day—there'll be a patch in there to eat by this time tomorrow. Follow the main trail, don't take any forks into side canyons."

"All right, all right. I get it. I'll see you."

"No way, we gotta fire this up," Zollers said. "Give me one of those quads. I need to follow this storyline. It's writing itself. Come on, Cherry."

"Will you stop your talking for once, Pinkie?" Cherry growled. "It's flooded. You wanna walk, *walk*. If not, shut your goddam mouth."

Greta could still hear them complaining even as she fired up her quad and took off, though their voices soon gave way to the canyon.

Once inside the canyon mouth, Greta felt claustrophobic, like the walls and all its colorbands squeezed her field of vision into a tunnel. Even her thoughts seemed thrown back at her. The quads roared, growls bouncing off every eroded cliff face the way the limestone trapped every ATV grunt and rumble. Felt like these weren't machines at all but monsters telling her to get out or else the cliffs would rip apart and bury her under a rockslide of ancient fossils.

Twice the walls narrowed to where only three or four cows could squeeze through side by side. She thought Cherry and his stupid truck would be lucky to navigate the narrows, maybe if he took off his side mirrors. Glad he and Zollers weren't on her heels for once, she half hoped they might never get that truck out of the creek, or might angrily turn back. Maybe Cherry had enough of cow stink. And maybe Zollers had enough research to write his next film. Maybe there would even be a Greta lookalike and a bear head in it.

Tiller seemed confused when the walls narrowed, though he didn't say anything of the sort. Greta caught him scratching his head, swiveling around now and then like he didn't recognize the place.

Trees disappeared from this area, the landscape dotted by shrubs the deeper they went, though there would likely be more pines up ahead. She could hear a roar besides the ATVs, which she thought must be echoes from the creek they followed, though it seemed mostly a trickle. Greta wasn't sure the name of this waterway, and didn't ask, since they all looked the same. She remembered names like Devil's Creek, Crooked Creek, and Deadman's Creek far to the northwest by Yellowtail Dam. She didn't want to learn any more white man creek names anyway, and instead wondered what Indians called this, if it even had a name.

Something then twisted in her gut, reminding her that she'd never been anywhere near here with Hannah. She'd never taken her to Yellowtail Dam, partly because Hannah didn't want anything to do with the drowning of the land that took place up at that reservoir and visitor center, not to mention all those tourists camping everywhere, who probably didn't give two shits about Indians or history, or what the land was intended to be. She remembered an argument over this where Hannah said:

"They just do whatever they want to the land, drown it, poke it full of holes, suck out oil and gas. They let that gas burn all day every day and seep into a nasty wind. You can see some of it from space, this lazy burning of fuel from the oil boom, and all the scars on sacred land, like nature got ten thousand million lashes just for being beautiful and now it's time to punish it for something else undeserved. And white men still hurt all this land, and will keep punishing the very rocks and rivers until those wounds won't even heal anymore. Yeah, I don't want to go there."

Greta tried to understand, she really did, or thought she did, maybe, and said she just wanted to go camping, and thought all the trail maps looked like something special, but Hannah acted like every single trail around there had a ghost on it that would point a finger in your face just for using it for recreation. They never went, and Greta never brought it up again. And now Greta felt like she understood something about place, about anchors in the land, where people took root and had community, and why they stayed, especially the people who came before, not the settlers and colonizers—everyone knew the settler story, how white men and their fellow colonizers held onto a form of collective amnesia and denial about what they'd done to people and the land—and Greta knew that she'd been so hardheaded about everything, had just been living in the moment, whatever the moment was, and was again right now, and maybe sometimes was part of the forgetting.

Still confused about everything with Hannah, Greta at

least felt better with Think Tank behind her and the mice in her pocket, whose tiny heads she might rub raw of fur if she wasn't careful. She had them and their silent marriage. And she protected them. And she thought, for the tiniest of seconds, they were protecting her too, that they might have wanted to come on this journey. And here they all were. One damn happy broken family.

Both the herd and its herders seemed inside a sickly throat. There were few squirrels and not a single goat or ram on these rocks. Flocks of birds darted through but didn't land. The sky turned a dismal grey, and the cattle, bunched up and wailing, swished their tails and shook their heads as if agitated by every hoofstrike, though strangely none cried when seeing the bear head on Greta's quad.

Then something rotten seemed to slip from deep in the canyon's gut and settled over the trail. "Not again," she complained. Greta picked up on the putrescence as they moved the herd along a wide bend in the meandering course. There the cliffs were cut with many crevices and dotted with holes that bats had likely turned into homes to hang upside down in during the long days. The smell weighed heavy, and never let up, filling nostrils and lungs with a wretched scent that wouldn't let go, settling in the back of Greta's throat in a kind of phlegm that she couldn't cough out.

The trail soon cut left and right so often she'd lost her sense of direction until noticing which way the shadows leaned. But that stink was everywhere, even cut through any exhaust, seeped into every fold of her clothes, and—as she learned when she leaned over and smelled a calf during one of their food breaks—even the thick hides of cattle.

Think Tank seemed somewhat resistant, hadn't started reeking any more than his matted fur already did, including hints of formaldehyde that she picked up on when she buried her nose in his fur after squatting for a pee behind her quad. This wasn't that flammable organosulfur spray from skunk scent glands. This canyon stink was far stronger, deeper, smellier, settling in her lungs as if a kind of death had slipped inside. Nor was this sulfur from the bentonite mines. Couldn't be. Smelled different, worked sinuses with less sting, was heavier, and had more of a nauseous effect. Felt like it emanated from fissures in the canyon walls, from bat caves and undiscovered caverns that wound through limestone tunnels to the surface. This was mustier, rotten, *dead, dead, dead*, like a perseverating corpse voice, like the mountain of carcasses she'd once seen, only a hundred times worse, like half the world had died and got jammed somewhere amid all the canyon pinnacles. Made her think of that asteroid all those millions of years ago forming far beyond Jupiter, packed with ruthenium so it could leave its mark—all six miles of it smashing into Earth—and then piles and piles of obliterated flesh, corpses stretched from land to sea, that filled everything, not a mountain of carcasses or mountain of bones but a *world* of a bones, a planet of rot, seventy-five percent of every living thing decomposing, sloughing off skeletal masses. Planet Earth, long before it had any name, had become the ultimate rot farm, a sick world of carrion for birds, small animals, and every kind of slippery and multi-legged scavenger that survived the blast, to eat and gorge.

And then another thought. She hadn't seen the goat-fawn

for some time, and started scanning, expecting it might peer from over a cliff rise, then thought that maybe it alone could handle this pungency, lead her and the cows to safety. If it would only appear.

Vultures and the occasional raven now sailed overhead, less apt to disappear from the stink. Once in a while a curious Red-tailed Hawk circled. A few times, when the smell lessened, came the howls of Canyon Wrens and the bubbly flight chatter of swifts, though she only glimpsed their narrow boomerang wings when they swirled and darted along the tops of cliffs into the thermals. And still no sign of the goat-fawn.

Along the ridgeline where spires seemed to grow like fingers she thought she saw a flock of dove-sized birds, shadows at least, then not shadows, skittering in a flock, running, maybe bigger than doves now that she tried to get a better perspective of them against some prickly pear leaves, but still couldn't really tell, other than a herd or flock of them running on two legs, though she only had glimpses at best, and when she stopped, couldn't find a single one because of their brownish plumage camouflaging them when still. She suspected more roadrunnery birds from the corral, though these weren't dark-colored, so maybe something else? It was always something else.

Not ten minutes later she again spotted the flock, or maybe another, and slid the ATV to a stop, and they stopped as well, what seemed like more than a dozen, she wasn't sure, since counting anything as a group, crows, sparrows, finches, elk, deer, whatever, was always only a guess, like you couldn't really count fast things, especially when moving, unless you're that good, which she didn't really have that kind of expertise or practice—like you had to count by fives and ones and tens all at the same time—and when she reached for her binoculars and scanned the talus, couldn't find them, maybe because they stopped moving and didn't make a sound, which made finding them impossible amid the engines and cattle cries.

Half an hour later she stopped and cut her engine, having seen some movement on the escarpment. Then came noises that weren't from hooves smacking on occasional stones, that sounded almost like the pops of a campfire, maybe the sizzle of something cooking in a pan, and then, Greta thought, almost like she'd opened a can of beer or soda, a kind of *fizzing*.

She surveyed just below the ridgeline, still couldn't see anything even with her bins, wasn't a lick of smoke anywhere for there to be sizzles. She listened for those weird roadrunnery whistles she'd heard in that storm, any sign of the goat-fawn maybe making new noises, but there came nothing of the sort, and no more strange sounds of any kind, just occasional birds and cow complaints over the quads, Scott yelling some curse, Tiller doing the same, calling for a break. Frustrated, she kept her bins close, then remembered something J.A. once told her: "Sometimes you don't see something until you're prepared to see it."

"Well goddam it, I'm prepared," she said.

By the late afternoon the cattle slowed, then about the fifth wave of nausea hit Greta. A sort of lethargy took hold from the foulness which seemed to quiet the herd into a silent procession. Every beast hung its head lower, and moved as if climbing steep hills, not the steady low incline of the canyon, which should have been easy for them to navigate. *Then again, maybe they're just hungry*, Greta thought. She'd hardly eaten a thing all day and couldn't decide if she wanted to eat or puke. At least Cherry wasn't around to cook his lousy meals. She could be happy with scoops of peanut butter on crackers and an apple.

There was plenty of water here, and she noticed that even when they took a break the cattle wouldn't take a drink. Greta noted that the stink wasn't in the water. "Nothing wrong with it," she told Tiller, the bandana around her face hardly cutting the stench, not that she would drink from the same stream and risk any bacteria. When she asked what he thought the rot was, he told her he had no idea.

"Never smelled anything like it," he said. "Like entire whales got dropped in here, decaying and dripping into fissures. Then again, sometimes things just smell in this world."

By the time they set up camp alongside a stretch of stream that fed a pond, the stench dissipated but still lingered, as if coming like tides. Greta had by then eaten half an apple and was still chewing when she wondered if Scott and Tiller were again on speaking terms.

"I wish this stink would go away altogether," Scott coughed. "And now I got something in my throat, like deep in there that won't come out."

"I got the same thing stuck in me," she said. "You and Tiller okay? Done trying to kill each other?"

"We're not about to sit down and play cards or anything. But I think we're all right. A lot of stress out here for all of us. More than anyone expected. I want to finish this, you know? And not get charged for the loss of his quad or that rifle."

"Not like we signed anything that made us liable," she said.

"I'm ready to get in my car and drive."

"Let's just get this done," she agreed.

Scott laughed when she set the bear head outside her tent. "To ward off evil," she told him. She snuck her mice into its fur.

"Think Tank though?" Scott said. "Not Concha or Maria? How about Juanita?"

"Think Tank is not a Juanita—I think he's a *he*," she said, and left it at that.

And then not two seconds later, Scott said: "Where's Tiller?"

"Jesus Christ, Scott," she said. "You two won't talk and you still have to know where each other is every minute of the day?"

"Yeah."

"Should be wondering about Cherry and Zollers."

"Figure they went back to Thermopolis, or wherever."

"Guys like that not really from anyplace," she said.

Scott grinned. "Wisest thing you said all day."

"I'm full of 'em," she said. "Expect they'll show up. Zollers will love the smell though I don't know how he'll recreate that in his next B movie. Or maybe D movie?"

"Hey, what's wrong with cattle drives and cartels?"

"Please tell me you're not interested in being in his film."

"Maybe I'll play you, put my mane in a ponytail, cart around a bear head, take charge of the herd. I'm cool enough."

"Good luck."

That evening a cacophony of trills, squawks, barks, growls, and hisses filled the canyon while they sat around the fire. They heard sizzles and howls too. Sometimes that fizzy sound like soda being poured or bacon being overcooked. The cattle moaned, sometimes three or four at once, restless long after the sun went down. Some of the noises had to be coyotes. At times those doggos could sound like they were dying. Then they'd sing all over again. At times the fizzes seemed close, somewhere on the talus slopes on either side.

"What *is* that?" Scott asked.

"Animals make all kinds of bizarre noises," Greta said. "Could be anything echoing in this canyon."

"Don't know anything to sound like that," Scott said.

Then Tiller was behind them, asked if Cherry said anything to either of them about turning back.

"Must have," Greta said. "Not sure if his truck could have fit between some of those walls without getting scraped. Guy like Cherry might love his pissy-flavored truck too much to risk extra dents."

"Goddam it."

"What?" Greta asked.

Tiller seemed to think for a minute. "Nothing. Just expected the help."

"He already did you a big favor with that cow," Greta said.

"Just stop, Greta," Tiller said.

"I can stop. When I feel like it."

"Feel like it."

Greta wished for more smoke to come her way from the small fire they built. The rot stench was so awful that she could hardly think. She thought about crawling into her tent, dragging Think Tank inside with her, snorting into his fur rather than breathing that godawful canyon stink.

And then she heard something in the small pond next to their camp. Everyone did. She flashed her light on bright reflective eyes, dozens of them glowing green. Birdlike creatures barely above the water gazed from small mostly brown heads. Each had grey beak-like mouths, white eye-rings, and pale cheek patches, and from what she could see, were covered with short fuzzy feathers or fur. One of them opened a gummy mouth. She could see spittle and rows of teeth like short saw blades, as if they might slash with their entire heads. Even the sides of those blades seemed serrated. One thing she noticed was how much they salivated. Out of their mouths came carbonation sounds, fizz-hisses mixed with something more pronounced like Pop Rocks candy bubbling under a tongue, a kind of simmering with spit and mucus.

"What the hell are those?" Scott said.

"I don't know." Greta stared, not knowing if she should yell out, throw a rock, or what.

"Ain't goddam squirrels." Tiller stood up.

Scott leaned forward. "Yeah, look hungry either way."

Greta had hoped these were roadrunnery bird creatures, but they weren't. No way. Their eyes were large and yellowy-green. And they had claws, all of them started to reach out of the water with them, long two-fingered talons at the end of mottled brown wrists about to cast spells, and knobby elbows. And then she thought of that phrase again: *Sometimes you don't see something until you're prepared to see it.* And then she knew:

"These are monsters," she said.

Scott was on his feet now. "No such thing. These gotta be raccoons with mange or something."

"Maybe they're what's dying," Greta added. "Maybe there were ten million of these monsters and they're caught all over this canyon just dying and rotting everywhere. Not enough food."

"We'd have found 'em."

"Not if they're in the cracks and fissures, in every cave and hole."

"Bullshit."

And then Greta jumped, her hands brushed something she felt crawling, pinching her thighs. "Some*thing* is on me."

She shined her light and couldn't find it. She checked her pants too. It was clinging there and hungry as anything, raised a mouth about to bite. She squealed and knocked it off then did a full body wiggle and shudder while it scurried away.

"It was tinyish, green, had a pink mouth," she said. "Maybe a lizard? Thought it had spines. Do lizards come out at night?" She waved her lamp like a wand, could see more of the little things moving near the cattle. Some of the cows appeared restless and jittery, were maybe shaking the creatures off their legs, stomping at others.

"Jesus. They're all over," she said. "Look, another one."

Scott crunched one with his boot before they could examine it, and almost forgot about the creatures in the pond. He whipped his light back to the water. The fizzers continued to stare and now hissed, smacking their lips and drooling until they sucked themselves underwater into a stream of ripples and bubbles.

"Where'd they go?" Scott said.

But then something else. *God, something else*, Greta thought, the hair on the back of her neck raised and her stomach flipped inside out. "Guys, we need to leave." She had her light on something large slithering across the surface of the pond.

"Just hold tight," Tiller said, going for his rifle.

This creature moved back and forth like a gator, gliding through a mat of floating grass that it dragged like hair.

Slimy and pale, the thing was about three or four feet long, with a scaly back, and oozed rather than crawled out of the water when it reached the bank, sliming itself out until it was completely exposed.

"Doesn't appear to move fast on land," Tiller said, clearly hesitant to shoot the thing and risk a night stampede.

Scott continued stomping more of the little creatures. Greta got one on her hand that was about to take a bite before she peeled its jaw from its head. She punted another one deep into the pond.

The creature on the bank, maybe more salamander-like than fish, lowered a large triangular head, throbbed its gills, and had a scaly reddish-pink underside, close-set black eyes atop its pale head, and a long tail that tapered to a point. The creature slapped its tail against the ground then waddled on four cleaver-shaped fins along the edge of the pond, ignoring Greta and the others.

"Too big to be a mudskipper whatever it is," Tiller said.

Greta thought she was dreaming, had to be, this primordial *nightmare*-thing with a white tongue and no teeth, black-gummed ridges of some kind and a strange smile that widened when its huge mouth closed.

"I think we should wake the herd and go." No sooner than Greta said this, the fish-thing turned its massive head toward her, making her skin crawl from head to toe, and before she could yelp, a whitish tongue shot out, snagging one of the little creatures crawling in front of her.

The tiny thing disappeared into the fish-thing's cavernous mouth. And then the creature opened wider, made a gloppy *croak*, and its throat puffed into a massive slippery pink bubble that seemed about to carry it away. Then, as soon as the bubble appeared, it wheezed away into a flap of mucusy skin, the creature glopped its mouth several times and slithered in the water.

"See, doesn't want to eat you," Tiller said.

The fizzer heads reappeared just then, opening their mouths and began to hiss and slurp, some of them squawking, then *fizzing* some primordial hiss that made Greta wonder about any kind of venom in their spittle.

Then as if in unison, they all submerged again in a swath of bubbles, and not five seconds later a roar bellowed from southeast of camp, deep within the canyon trail's twists and turns.

Greta shuddered, thinking maybe the canyon had released something even more foul than the smell of death, walking fish-things, fizzers, and little buggers.

But then Scott said, "It's the truck, that goddam truck. Cherry's on his way after all."

For a second, Greta was relieved.

Only, when the truck pulled up, Cherry was alone.

The Little Creatures

The truck sat in the stream like a huge piss-green rock. Water swirled around bald tires and over creek pebbles where the bear head had been lifted then carried away.

That bear head.

Nothing like it, Pinkie thought.

That girl.

A movie had been playing out in front of Pinkie starring a hot, dirty, sassy, outdoorsy, *wild*-child cowpoke of a girl. *Voluptuous*, he thought. *Mesmerizing*. Those lips. He couldn't stop thinking about those full lips. And her eyes. What color were they? A kind of brown, a sort of greenish hue in certain light. Brown-green? Hazel? And rosy cheekbones, and that figure, he thought again, yeah, slim, long legs tapering to those ankles. Yes, he could see that figure, imagined that olive skin against his, those warm fingers on his ass cheeks. He'd keep working on her to be in a movie, any movie, that's for sure. He was always discovering talent. Not that he needed actual talent. He just needed a pretty face. She could be an extra, sure. Might even give her a line in a film. The talentless loved that, thanked him over and over. She reminded him of that twenty-something extra in *Nude Camp Zombies*, different color hair and everything, which was fine because weren't they all interchangeable? Blonde if he was remembering right—who sucked him off in the back of his PINKIE FILMS white Ford van (big sticker on the side and everything), who begged to be lead actress in an upcoming short film. He kept telling her, *Yeah yeah, of course. You'll be the first to try out*, so happy there were still girls like her. Most of the ones with talent were way too fucking professional, wouldn't flirt at all, steered clear of his van.

But this Greta. Her and that big Wyoming sky. Cows all lowing—that kine bawling thundering moos—he learned kine and other words from Cherry, who said only his granddaddy used that *k*-word. Pinkie loved every cowpoke saying thrown his way, kept jotting them down.

And now that bear head was gone. The girl was gone. The cattle were *long gone*.

Fucking Cherry. Fucking piece of shit truck stuck in a creek while the story, cinematic masterpiece, the bear head, that girl got away. Pinkie needed more than anything to follow her, see what she and that decapitated monstrosity were all about. It was a wild stunt for sure, strapping a grizzly head to a quad. Greta had balls. And he loved that, flexing his hand, feeling that phantom finger, the rising dull pain that sometimes radiated as if the finger were still attached and slowly squeezed in a vise.

She must have grabbed that bear head just to get in my next film.

He saw no less than potential movie magic in Greta's wild act—it was an act wasn't it? She couldn't really be that weird. Then again this was Wyoming and people were different here, like they sometimes did strange things with animals. Murdering for fun and whatnot. Right? You never really knew what to expect. Wasn't Cherry always shooting something on his property just for fun? *And not with a camera.* Birds, cats, deer, skunks, and, when in Idaho at Cherry's second trailer, some dumbass curlew with a radio attached . . . and almost got one named Dozer that slipped past all the way to Morro Bay, California. Sometimes Cherry'd take those kills to the Tillers, pay to get them mounted, put them up on shelves and all that. Even that curlew with the radio, though Cherry wasn't smart enough to take out the battery until Pinkie noted that the GPS coordinates ratted them out on some website. *Whatever.*

But that girl, that bear head, was much more than picking up roadkill. There was a kind of affection in taking it with her, something sick, an emotional truth, something beautiful in the act that made Pinkie feel more than a little jealousy, like she and that bear had already been best friends, and he could only get there if he offered her a part in a film. Goddam, girls loved him.

And more than that, he imagined a major streaming content sale, maybe to Amazon or Hulu. His makeup crew could make a bear head. Sure they could. Wouldn't be easy, but if monster magic could be created, they would die trying to make their alchemy.

He immediately began writing scenes in his head thinking maybe this was more than a cartel film though he didn't know what else it could be. Wild girl on a cattle drive who needed to be tamed? *The girl who talked to bear heads?* Her need to cart around the dead would be formidable on screen. He could sell this, finally sell something. Maybe there would be many dead things. *Maybe this was a cartel-horror mashup.* He had to find her, stay on her tail, creatively feed off that inspiration.

Cherry made no attempt to turn the key and appeared deep in thought, smoking a cigarette, elbow out the window.

"Been fifteen minutes," Pinkie said. "How much longer?"

"Shit, I dunno. Thirty minutes? More? *Green Sonja* gets temperamental when this happens."

"Jesus Christ, Cherry. This is my movie you're fucking up."

"Says the director who owes me ten stacks."

"You know you're getting that back."

"Do I?"

"Told you a thousand times."

"A thousand?"

"Those coffeehouse owners gonna foot sixty for this next gig."

"So, you gonna make your cartel film for fifty? You said it would take more."

"I'll find two investors, maybe three. We'll cut corners, dodge permits. Film on the fly. You know how I get shit done. Guerrilla filmmaking done dirt cheap. Maybe your friends can loan some cows, get us on this trail."

"Ain't promising anything. Told you the Tillers are hard nuts to crack. Best to CGI them critters, use more actors who'll work for free. How about that AI? Ain't that big these days? Maybe some website chatbot will write your film for you?"

"Don't tell me how to make movies, Cherry. Just don't. Fed up as it is."

"Wasn't telling you how. Okay maybe I was."

"Can you at least try the engine? Jesus."

"You got boots on, get out and walk if you need to catch up so bad. They drive slow most the time."

"I will if you don't turn that key."

"Ain't gonna flood it again, or we may be here even longer."

"Goddam it."

"Go on then."

"You go on and turn that key."

Cherry, in a huff, opened his door and splashed into the stream. He walked around and opened the passenger-side, grabbed Pinkie by the elbow and dragged him face down in the water.

Pinkie, spitting a mouthful of gravel and water, cursed and jumped to his feet, wrung out his soaked hat. "Goddam . . . what the fuck . . . You son of a bitch . . . just ruined your chance to be in my game changer film."

"Probably only gotta walk three or four miles or so before you catch up." Cherry tossed him a bottle of water.

"Yeah, what about wild animals? There's goddam wolves and cats out here, Cherry."

"You'll be fine. Thank me later."

"Gonna thank you right out of my next film. Fucking worm."

"You called all your ex-wives worms too. Now get on. Tired of your mouth and don't wanna talk about your wiggler."

Pinkie walked toward the opposite bank, stopped, and flipped Cherry the double bird, who through the windshield glare gave him a nod.

Goddam Cherry, see if he gets his money now, throwing me out of the truck like that. Son of a thankless bitch, thankless for being in my films, thankless for making him a celebrity. Is this how you treat a guy? Goddam Cherry.

Pinkie walked the canyon now, the sound changing right away, more muffled, quieter, a couple birds, a lone pika, the gurgle of another stream. It might take forever for his jeans to dry though the sun struck the trail. At least his socks didn't get wet. That would be the end, *wet socks*. Didn't even have a chance to grab his backpack. *Fucking Cherry.*

Pinkie was more than ready for this cattle film. He'd finally acquired all the right film gear, high-end Sony HD cameras, lighting, expensive laptop used for an editing bay—three other editing bays had died—none of which he paid for himself, because if there was one thing he could do along with fake murder on set with fake blood and body parts, it was talk businessmen out of surplus cash, make them feel like they were investing in Hollywood by investing in Pinkie Films, and that meant coercing anyone who might listen to his overblown ideas for low-budget straight-to-YouTube filmmaking. After all, anyone around him over the past ten years was made to feel like he was on the verge of a big hit.

Sure, success could happen.

A rash started burning his upper thighs. Wet jeans, wet boxers. Balls and thighs smashed and rubbing together. It stung down there and he'd only walked two miles. He tried not to think about it though he started to amble bowlegged. If he could only get out of these wet clothes and let his junk hang in the sun while he dried on a rock. These canyons were filled with lots of places he could air out and wait for Cherry to come by. Didn't care if Cherry saw his dick, was so used to being nude on set, and though he was supposed to hide those parts, never did. Maybe he could talk Greta into some nude sunbathing.

Then the air started to reek. Pinkie immediately let out a cough and covered his mouth. *Fucking skunks.* Had to be, right? *Megaskunkasaurus.* He pulled his tee up to his nose and breathed creek stink. At the same time, he could hear the stream letting out a faint whistle or hiss, like air slowly being let out of a tire, or maybe wasn't even that at all, like gas rising to the surface. Yes, *that.* Had to be a spring-fed creek, all kinds of fissures deep in the watery earth, all those underground rivers and lakes, of water, oil, oil-like substances, created over unbelievable spans of time. Goddam, Pinkie felt smart for reasoning that out, practically a Wyomingite. Like a meteorite. *Wyomingite. Here I am and there I go.*

And then he started to think about Cherry again, that ten grand Cherry'd sunk into *Nude Camp Zombies* had only seen a return of three hundred. Pinkie promised to pay him back with whatever he raised for his cattle film. And he offered Cherry another starring role, which *okay*, maybe getting tossed out of the truck *could* be a scene in the film. Cherry had that bad boy Wyoming*ite* quality about him, could maybe be a trail boss who sleeps with one of the hired hands, though not the Greta character. No, there would be two cow-guys, three cow-girls, herd hands, or whatever the fuck they're called, and Pinkie would own the main love scene, one where the spray bottles would come out to spritz his oiled-up pasty white ass.

Damn, he couldn't wait to drive his van on a trail like this with a crew. And anyway, Cherry wrangled an extra thousand from Tiller on the downlow for Pinkie, which Pinkie was gonna give to Cherry, but now *fuck it, never.* He was pissed at Cherry. And hated this stink, this fucking stink, and still no bear head or Greta in sight.

Couldn't even hear a damn cow.

And what on earth were those noises?

And then a shadow above him, dark and cold, filling him with instant terror. He thought it would be a cat or wolf, something on the ground that would scare the shit into his pants. But the sky?

Pinkie heard maybe two wingflaps as if an entire ocean of air was being displaced, and felt an instant rumble beneath his ribcage. Then he saw the monstrous thing, and was shaken to that inner place where nerves and guts seemed wrapped together, and felt his bladder turn loose a stream of piss right in his pants that had nearly dried out.

He tried to pull out his phone, aim at the belly of the thing, which was wide like a plane fuselage but covered in dirty feathers and blood smears. And then thick legs textured like scaly tree trunks passed too. Its talons folded like overproportioned mechanical crane claws ready to carry steel beams.

Pinkie wasn't sure what this thing was besides some kind of monster bird. He mumbled or thought, *Holy shit*, wasn't sure which, and at the same time realized, *This IS my fucking movie, this thing is my film, a horror flick, fuck that cartel shit.*

Then the bird soared past and he dropped his phone while trying to pull it out to film the thing. But the bird started to bank and now he felt himself vulnerable out in the open, so reached down, and while trying to pick up his phone, pushed it into the dirt, and couldn't get ahold of it because his ass was on the move, so sprung for the rocks on the other side of the creek.

He splashed into springwater which hissed at a fever pitch, and couldn't find a crevice small enough to squeeze in to. And then the bird crossed again and he stopped cold.

This time the bird's eye was on him, a giant orb, and that yellow bill, and the most beautiful head feathers, nothing like anything he'd ever seen, and wasn't sure but maybe that bill opened and one of those talons flexed.

Pinkie *ran.*

The bird flew out of sight as he made for larger rocks farther upstream. He sprinted for his life, angry that he dropped his phone, that he maybe lost it for good. Then the shadow crossed a third time and he felt some relief that it hadn't plucked him off this earth because he found a dark crevice to hunker in until the thing left him alone.

He squeezed himself down between two boulders and flexed his phantom finger which radiated stinging pain, always a warning, and as usual came too late, like the time his ex-wife caught him in his film van giving movie make-out lessons to a *Nude Camp Zombie* actress, and though his phantom pinkie started throbbing a warning, it had only been seconds before she pulled that door open.

Too late. Always too late.

Thing was, that phantom pain worsened, had really started burning. So he sat in the cubby and waited what seemed like forever, until his knees couldn't take it, until he couldn't hear those wings anymore or see any bird shadows from his vantage point.

Peeking his head out he caught sight of the bird-thing far in the sky, as if about to wrap the sun. He followed the shadow upward into the thermals, which was a relief, it seemed far enough out of range, making him think that maybe the bird had been merely curious rather than hungry.

Standing now, Pinkie had to shake his throbbing hand, and even put the tiny pinky stump in his mouth like when he was a little kid, and sucked the pale pink nub, still watching that bird-thing swirl higher and higher until it was the tiniest of dots. And still standing there half in shadow, sucking the throbbing ghost-digit, thinking now about how much giant bird CGI might cost, he felt a sudden sting in his other hand. Something so rapid and biting, yes, so literally biting that he felt it up through his palm, into his forearm and into his bicep.

When this happened, he leapt out of the shadow, through the stream and onto the trail, thinking he'd smacked his right hand on a cactus, or got stung by one of those rusty-winged tarantula hawks he'd seen only once before. When he checked, he *groaned*—the pinky on his other hand was gone—his hand oozing blood where the finger had been.

And worse: the digit had been sliced off at an angle below the first knuckle exposing a ring of flesh, stick of bone, and wiggling spaghetti of tendon.

Pinkie cursed and stumbled back, could see on the rocks some kind of creature spitting and drooling, hisses emanating like fresh carbonation, and realized *fuck no* this wasn't noise from a spring revealing itself like a fresh can of Starry at all. It was this thing, this monster that reminded him of all the dino drawings he'd seen as a kid, only now he knew how far off those illustrators' imaginations had been. The reality was vivid, striking, terrifying—the way they stood, full of muscle, poised to strike. These bird-lizard-monster things weren't something anyone would want to see except in one of his films, and damn if he wouldn't get it right after seeing this. He just needed this thing dead, then he'd drag it back to Cherry, and they'd be off to moneyville, recreating the monster movie of all monster movies, because this shit was real.

Nude Camp Zombie was child's play compared to this.

And then he saw the tip of his finger, just the very bloody pink tip, protruding from its mouth, and as it hissed, the finger hung there on its black tongue. Pinkie felt like an angry out-of-body spirit witnessing his own missing digit, until the creature swallowed and licked its gloppy mouth, wanting more.

Furious and in pain, Pinkie picked up a rock and made an awful throw. It hit near the creature's feathery clawfeet, though the little monster didn't budge. Pinkie already had another few rocks, one in his bloody hand, including a sharp piece of obsidian that he stuffed in his pocket.

He felt like he still had both pinkies so much adrenaline furiously pumped through his veins, and threw more rocks, hitting the creature in its chest feathers, making it hiss louder and snap at him. The thing still wouldn't leave that rock.

"Gonna smack you in your monster bitch head." Pinkie zinged another rock which clunked off its cheek and dazed the thing, and then running over, pulled out the obsidian, and now making guttural noises himself amid all the stink and blood, slit the creature's throat. It gasped and thrashed and vomited his pinky along with a pile of blue-green bile, and Pinkie plucked his goopy digit from the muck and stuffed it in his wet pants, then tossed the creature over his shoulder and turned back. Damn if he wasn't gonna drop that digit into a bottle of tequila, or wear it on a chain around his neck as a badge for surviving Wyoming's version of *Jurassic* fucking *Park*.

It was sunset by the time he closed in on his retreat back to the canyon mouth, having not heard any more of the creatures like the one now draped over his shoulder. And then *goddam no way*, could finally hear Cherry's truck fire up and idle. That sound echoed through the canyon, bouncing off wall faces, growling and growling. Hot damn, Cherry was a godsend after all.

Having downed his water long ago, he was dying to get back, his hand starting to swell and burn and throb. He could already feel the dollar bills piling up from the thing over his shoulder, and thought *fuck it* about his lost phone. He'd fund his film with this dino-monster alone, maybe sell the film rights to himself. *Hell fuckin' yeah.* That's the way to do it. Tell his story. Forget that girl and her bear head. This was *Zollers Chronicles Part One: Dinosaur Canyon.*

Then he felt himself suddenly in the air.

He could hear those wingbeats again, so loud *so loud*. And something gripped him tight, as if hooks had entered his flesh, even into his organs.

The little dinosaur monster on his shoulder went flopping through the sky, and he watched it tumble like some kind of rubbery thing meant to be in the dirt.

That grip on him was indescribable, so painful, monster talons piercing his back and shoulders. He couldn't move or scream while he was lifted, feet nearly smacking the top of a cliff. And it only took moments to gain incredible elevation, and he marveled at seeing the ground and canyon like toys, and glimpsing Cherry's truck bumbling along, and then scanning farther, seeing a bunch of dots miles to the east that must have been the cattle, where that goddam girl was with them, probably hugging that bear head.

Pinkie tried to reach up, touch the bird. But it was too painful to move, so he just let his arms dangle, that phantom pain in both pinkies now felt more like a tickle. Then he felt something hit against his head, *hard*, and that must have been the bird's giant bill, the side of it anyway, a gentle nudge maybe? And then he realized that in a way, maybe that bump had been a taste, and he again saw the truck far below heading farther into the canyon. Goddam Cherry wasn't getting his money back, that was for sure.

A thousand feet up, the wind chilled Pinkie's skin, and he could see a cloud, and then just when he thought he saw an angel flip him off, it was as if Pinkie had never existed at all. He felt the tremendous pressure of his head being pulled away from muscle, tendon, artery, and bone, and before all feeling disappeared, sensed his head rolling around in the mouth of the thing, and thought, *This has got to be in my movie.*

They came pouring from the billion-year-old limestone, little creatures having been trapped in crevices millions of years, encased in eggs, egg sacs, egg rows, and those rows encased in membranes, many of which never dried or broke, held together by the jelly of time.

To be clear, these creatures weren't embedded in the limestone like fossils or there would have poured trillion upon trillion, all these lifeforms melting the very canyons, creatures slopping over every surface, coating and consuming all that could not fly. And thank time itself for these little things slipping from deep cavernous fissures still in large numbers, where air and life awaited this perfect moment, which like the great cicada broods emerged crawling, skittering, buzzing, fizzing, only these the size of rats, mice, small dogs, cats, prairie dogs, pikas, porcupines, converging in hordes as if spiders emerging to swarm across a city on the same day, the same hour. Many crept from holes, and some of those creatures galloping into the canyon were only the size of large stick bugs, and sort of resembled them, though their exoskeletons shone bright green, and each had four thick, black veiny legs, and teensy pink mouths with teeth, and long orange tongues they used to snatch at gnats and flies. Their narrow backs held rows of needlelike spines, and next to those the smallest of furry blue feather patches.

Thousands of these little creatures poured straight to the main canyon trail like a plague of frogs, swarming around rocks and trees while other animals devoured their heads and legs. Many would be consumed by birds, toads, even martens and coyotes. Roadrunners, kestrels, and merlin dined on them, even smaller birds like vireos and wrens and flycatchers made every thin bone of the little creatures into crunchy snacks.

Ancient life feeding modern life. Modern life derivative of ancient life.

And there were larger four-legged creatures too, though still small, and covered with fur, some feathered but with teeth similar to rodents', or birdlike bills or mouths, which these weren't birds at all but something in between, and hadn't been logged in any science books, for they, like the littlest creatures, walked on fragile bones that dissolved with time, and thus had never been seen by human eyes except Pye'ta'wa'wawi's sixteen thousand years ago. Her dog Mo'n saw them too and ate them while roaming the canyon, and buried the bones, as some dogs do, which of course those also dissolved.

And there were also smallish creatures that slithered closer to the ground, the tiniest of walking fish, and others more like lizards covered in both scales and feathers, with greenish bellies that scraped the earth. Two-legged varieties came in many hues of green, and yellow, and blue-green, and midnight blue, and rosy-hued, and every size variation imaginable.

Some had blocky heads, and some small, rounded heads, and some were very thin-toothed with snouts that could easily be bird bills, and some had actual doglike snouts and serrated teeth on saw blades, and some had mouths that could only slurp at juices of nearby creatures, even their own kind like lampreys or strange monstrous leeches with tongued fingers that drank the blood of everything in every direction.

And there were insects that hadn't been heard by humans, that had never been found in cavern walls, tar pits, even in drops of sap turned amber, because they came from a time when there were so many varieties, that their innumerable species dwarfed what had actually been found by fossil hunters, and had never been lucky enough to find their way into globs of syrup.

And mother canyon held back from flooding the earth with every species from all the eggs hidden in her limestone innards, for she preserved many hundreds of species, billions of creatures, stashing eggs in secret crevices which meant she was waiting, waiting, and had been for so long, or was prevented from unleashing them because of her pact, the pact that was now close to being completely dissolved.

Mother canyon in her current pregnancy birthed clouds of winged insects, storms upon storms. Unless you were some biologist studying microchanges in species adaptation and evolutionary gaps, many of these arthropods looked exactly the way they always did: so many gnats and flies, so many tiny blood-feeding organisms, that adapted quickly, that evolved at astronomical rates, that could live in land crabs and fish gills, in thermal spring algae, in pockets of petroleum, and feces of other insects, birds, and mammals.

And bats swarmed too. They were of various sizes and species, some with tiny frog-like faces, others with doglike profiles, catlike round stubby grins, some like newts with gills hanging mid-air, dripping fluid, with round eyes, so large and front-facing above tiny snouts.

At night they swarmed other creatures mother canyon released, and in turn these were prey to owls and carnivorous relatives of nightjars and poorwills, which were only a third larger than their descendants. These craved bats and small rodents, and so from the passing of dusk until morning twilight, would gorge on them, and flew alongside screeching owls and night creatures this world could not remember, because they'd never found the wing bones of such flying creatures that have four legs, or two hind legs and two shorter front legs, and layers of wings, and were covered in fur, but weren't bats. No, these had feathers for wings, and mouths, such large mouths that their heads appeared all mouth, more so than any Tawny or Papuan Frogmouth or nocturnal Oilbirds, or Owlet-nightjars, or Potoos. Those monstrous poor-me-ones, or ghost birds, with cryptic plumage and gaping nyctibiid maws that open wide to release those haunting, descending screams as if a ghoul—*right behind you*—was letting you know before feasting on your neck veins; and their heads, already flying mouths, were *so so* big, too big for their bodies. But these even wider, that didn't sail over oceans, but over land, once in schools, flocks, herds, these large ones born to devour even a dire wolf, and one or two of those once-extinct wolves now roamed the *mothercanyonlands*, though not anywhere near the cattle or where some of Pinkie's remains fell to be devoured bite by bite until only a few bones and patches of skin remained.

Below these were the night-fish, some of which crawled out of the creeks to dine on spiders and things of the past trapped within webbed foliage and deadfall along creek banks. And there were ground-dwelling birds molting, transforming, baring teeth in their bills, razors in their mouths that could slice off their own tongues. Razor teeth that could sever fingers and hands, tails and necks, so some birds hid in pines and scrub and perched and feasted while their rubbery tails drooped onto branches.

As the stories went, anyone who traversed these canyons, who was assailed by similar plagues, had been sworn to secrecy by the mother canyon herself, starting with her indigenous inhabitants. The canyon spoke to travelers and nomads in their heads, the same way she could have with Pinkie, and made them think they'd gone insane, or that they had made a pact with nature, and would be whole with nature, and would be doomed if they reneged.

And the dead things, which were never supposed to be taxidermy, would soon be no more. Mother canyon had never welcomed them, built from corrupted magic to protect the sacrifices for a time, to prevent Tiller himself from becoming mother-blood, allowing him to watch death unfold like a kind of voyeur, though everything was changing, would change, because of the *mousefriend*.

Greta.

Mother canyon awaited her choices, and in the meantime more of the little creatures would be born. She pushed and pushed them into the world.

Mother canyon was dying.

Mother canyon was alive.

Mother canyon birthed past into present.

Mother canyon, born herself before one of the great cataclysms.

Mother canyon awaited sacrifice nonetheless, to die or transform the world.

Blood would spill and that liquid would tell the story that was to come.

Night Eight

Greta dreamed a fish-walker gulped its way up her left thigh. Its mouth widened, neck folds undulating as it swallowed its prey, then *slurp-squish-slurped* toward her hip.

Half-awake, Greta kicked at the imaginary fish-walker mouth, then at long tongues snapping at spiny-backed bug-things crawling up the walls of her tent.

None of this invasion was real, but she wasn't fully aware and kneed Think Tank in his fuzzy snout, then again in the side of his head, spilling her mice from his fur. A few seconds later she realized the smelly bear head wasn't a fish-thing, that no creatures clung to the walls or were eating her leg.

She rolled over and righted Think Tank, scooped her mice and cooed. *Sorry guys. You know how it is out here in monsterland. Thought we'd slipped away from all the shit—the ghosts and ghost trains anyway. But this isn't a canyon, is it? It's nightmare alley and now we have monster bugs and dino-things and weird fish with triangle heads that walk on their fins, and now everything haunts my dreams. But you know what?* She tucked the mice into her coat. *I know this sounds insane, but what's a few fish faces? We got cows to deliver and money to make.*

She'd only slept an hour, her lids heavy, her limbs rubbery, every part of her feeling like it should be in a five-star hotel tangled in clean sheets, not here where she smelled no better than Think Tank. Better at least than that reek in the air.

Last she remembered, she was helping Scott stomp bugs. They kept watch while Cherry and Tiller took off to look for any sign of Zollers. They weren't gone long because of all the things crawling around the cattle and trail, and soon returned without Zollers, saying that farther south were thousands of those bugs, that they'd driven over plenty, and many tried to get in through the windows, and so they figured that Zollers had been scared off, was already making his slow-ass way back to Ten Sleep, and was sleeping outside the canyon somewhere.

Everyone crushed the strange bugs with their boots the night before, Tiller with the butt end of his rifle, and kept an eye on the crawly fish-things slipping out of the pond, including one large enough to swallow all of Greta, not just her leg. Lucky, the thing kept its distance and preferred to eat any nearby buggers or fizzers, which kept them away though gurgle sounds could be heard throughout the night and even now, as if calling from deep in the creek brush, and beyond the pondwater.

Greta packed her bedroll and could hear Cherry and Tiller arguing about turning back.

"Told you, Zollers gonna be starving," Cherry said. "Can't blame him for wanting to leave. He ain't the only one who had enough of all this."

"You mean just you," Tiller said.

"No. Both of us. Maybe the others."

"Said yourself you tossed him from your truck."

"Zollers has a mouth sometimes," Cherry said. "Got tired of it. Besides, he knows better."

"What's that supposed to mean?" Tiller asked.

"Means he owes me so should know better than to talk too much. Either way, we gonna find him on the trail farther back the way we came."

"Just turn the cattle around?"

Cherry grumbled. "Yeah, turn their butts south and get them out of this stink hole."

"Can't do that," Tiller said.

"Can't be serious," Cherry said. "This canyon crawling with things I ain't ever seen. What if worse things sneaking around? Ain't got enough bullets to shoot all of 'em. I say if you don't turn around then leave them damn cows."

"Cows worth too much," Tiller said. "Not leaving."

"I would."

"Couple more nights is all," Tiller said. "We can handle a few bugs."

"Did you not see the goddam longtails creeping around last night? Those were goddam dinosaurs if I ever seen one. Big as goats."

"Not a single thing we saw bothered us," Tiller said.

"Don't want to be here when they do."

"Name your price," Tiller said. "We need you backing us up, helping with meals, watching over these monsters so they don't attack the cattle. Could use your help."

"Ain't no price," Cherry said. "They need to send the National Guard and some of them bone hunters and biologists or whatever. Might try and grab one of those things myself to take back, but my luck some kind of Gila monster version gonna bite me."

"Here's the thing," Tiller said, Greta now out of the tent, surveying the pond and cattle, and not a bug in sight or a fish-walker, as Cherry ambled to his truck. "If you go, you need to keep quiet about it."

"Keep quiet? Ain't nothing to keep quiet about." Cherry squeaked open his truck door, slipped inside, and rolled down the window. "Matter of fact, I'm gonna tell everyone and then I'll be on one of them talk shows. Got a video of one running alongside the truck like a goddam turkey. Never seen no Tommyboy looking like that. Crazy goddam feathers and teeth. Had short arms instead of turkey wings. And another thing, Zollers ain't gonna be kept quiet. He gonna want to be on a talk show too." Then he eyed Greta. "And that girl worse than you thought. She got a damn bear-head obsession."

"Tell me something I don't know," Greta said, wondering what *worse than you thought* could mean.

"I can," Cherry said, "though I wasn't talking to you."

"Tell me anyway, big shot," she said.

Cherry fired up the engine, then leaned out. "You all gonna die out here."

Next thing Cherry's truck rolled over gravel and dirt and bug carcasses, then turned around and roared back down the canyon.

Greta shrugged and packed her tent and bedroll and attached Think Tank to his ATV perch so he could see the canyon trail through his black marble eyes. There was gas here, so she topped off her tank, all the while searching for any sign of strange creatures. A few blackbirds blurted their dawn chorus while a couple thrashers chattered atop scrub then disappeared. Otherwise, nothing.

Oddly, none of the cattle had run off.

The morning sky hung mostly grey, while the bright eastern ridge gleamed like a pearl. Below that every surface lay cloaked in shadow—bruised and cold. The pond's surface shone like a dull mirror, unmoving as if nothing had ever crawled out or fizzed or shot white tongues across the surface, while the stream bent away from this area and whispered over rocks.

Everywhere it stunk worse than cattle, worse than those bentonite mines, worse than any carrion hill and Think Tank's breath, if he had any. The rot lay heavy in the morning air, so Greta tied a handkerchief around her face while one of the cows watched her with its big brown eyes. Another stared toward the pond as if something might come crawling out, and even walked over, but wouldn't take a drink. Greta suddenly remembered her vision of Bobby's taxidermy shop, of hands reaching over hide, and that bit of human scalp, and thought, some dead woman might lift herself from the water here and chill everyone to the bone.

That thought was replaced by an image of the Pope also rising from the murk, his frail legs shaking and covered with bugs—some with wings—all those tattoos on his arms and naked torso warped by death, him staring from sunken eyes, facial hair dripping, yellow-green teeth in a permanent grin. Greta turned away and kicked at one of the squished bug corpses. She thought about picking one up, then remembered how some creatures can be poisonous even in death. She poked at another with a stick. The little creature fell apart. She noted tiny slick-round heads, pale green skin, some feathers, veiny legs and spines, lots of goo and blood. She thought about taking a photo but was too lazy to dig out her phone. Might be dead anyway. She didn't care that much.

"What do you think these are?" Scott said. "Got pieces all over my boots. Didn't run too fast. I think one bit Cherry."

"Monsters, dinosaur-bug-lizard things. No idea. You tell me if all these things even come from the same era or epoch." *Maybe that's the thing*, she thought. *Maybe this canyon remembers its entire history.* Maybe pulls at random from what once lived here. Maybe the past was just a big file cabinet, or one of those old Rolodexes her mom used to have sitting on the kitchen counter. Maybe the canyon could unleash anything, anytime. Greta didn't even know why she was thinking about the canyon as a kind of living thing. Where'd that thought even come from? Canyon couldn't be an entire living being, yeah? She went on: "Doesn't explain the taxidermy buffalo, or Think Tank, or . . ."

"Or what?" he said.

She noted a distant dust cloud, likely from Cherry tearing down the trail. "Cherry got better things to do, huh?"

"I was gonna ride back with him." Scott piled bags on his quad. "He took off before I could get back from counting the herd."

Greta took a bite of sandwich for breakfast. "You'd leave me and Think Tank?"

"I'd leave you and Tiller, yeah, but prefer if everyone left together."

Greta looked for Tiller. He was out of sight at the front of the herd. She thought she heard his voice. "What about the cattle?"

"I'd leave them," Scott said.

"You and Cherry. Thing is"—she shoved a large bite in her mouth and continued—"Cherry didn't understand, and maybe I'm wrong. Wouldn't it be quicker to keep going forward?"

"If we brought the cattle," Scott said.

"Even if not. You would leave them?"

"Shouldn't we?"

"And let them starve? That would be cruel," she said. "Besides, nothing attacked us, except maybe the one on my leg. Those creatures"—she pointed to a bug corpse twisted in the dirt—"are just ancient things, maybe that haven't seen or been seen by humans ever, just doing their own thing. They're *afraid*. Animals fear other animals, Scott. Like *us*. We were like that all the time, before any of this, because we had to survive, you know? But now we got Netflix and chill. And cities. And safe streets with no fizzer herds roaming them. And clean showers without murderers, mostly, and without dino-bugs inside drains. And I'm kind of generalizing, but you get it."

Scott finished packing and now leaned hard. "What if they stop being afraid?"

"We have Think Tank. And your buffalo."

"You're talking dead things again."

"Yeah? So let's just go, all right? Cherry's gone anyway. We can handle a few lizards. Two more nights. Let's roll, okay?"

"Here's what else I don't get," Scott said. "Why are you okay with this?"

"You mean *we*. Me and Think Tank."

"Why are you acting so weird?"

"Like what? Like I got friends all of a sudden?"

"Are you not aware of what you said last night about monsters?"

"What do you want me to do, Scott? If I walk, I don't get paid. If I don't get paid, then this was all a waste of time and I'll be right back at the Ribs N Go working paycheck to paycheck. No guarantee I will get rich off seeing a monster or whatever. And yeah, maybe . . . *okay* . . . We're all sure these monsters are something that shouldn't be around. But then, neither should Think Tank. And neither should the roadrunners, or the ghost train." She still hadn't told him about the goat-fawn or that bison skull tower, and though she hadn't heard her name called, felt in her bones that it was somewhere close, dragging after her, watching over her along with Think Tank.

"Are you even with me?" he said. "Never thought I'd hear you side with Tiller."

"You never know which side me and Think Tank are on," she said. "Maybe we'll be on yours next."

It was late morning when the shadow first appeared.

This was long after Tiller called the cattle to "Go on, go on, go-o-o on!" rather than his repeated "Come on!" and revved his ATV to threaten their tail ends if they didn't get on down the trail. That was after they'd all bunched up and bawled and groaned, hungry and awful, and hoofstruck angrily against the dirt, and swung their heads, even the little calves, and this was way after some of those calves cried because of near-dried milk, and after they all moved toward Scott's quad as if led by their own echoing trail cries and hoofclomps.

Fingers of sunlight had reached over the edge of the canyon when the shadow passed through in a flash that caused Greta to look up.

She didn't see anything specific, not even a wing, and thought maybe an airplane passed over. She noted contrails now and then, and at night, satellites and all kinds of bats and owls. During the day an occasional plane, maybe a passenger jet swung past at a high altitude or was simply heard, not to mention soaring hawks and other raptors. Sometimes smaller birds darted between shrubs, though she hadn't heard or glimpsed any in a while.

After the shadow passed again a few minutes later, the groans and fizzes began their panicky chatter. First on the western talus, then the eastern slope chorus joined in. Only a few bubbled at first then gurgled over the quads and hoofstrikes. But then the noise ratcheted up, and the fizzers seemed to hiss and glop their mouths in unison. Greta didn't know what some of the deeper croaks were though she imagined fish-walkers could make such sounds. They lurked in the stream like big slippery rocks, flapping their fin arms, throats gulping air, maybe belting territorial or mating croaks.

Eventually they stopped for lunch and Greta made another peanut butter sandwich from her now-stale bread, though she began to wonder whether gulper meat tasted any better. She and Scott hadn't said much to Tiller but now he came over while the cows bunched and cried or sniffed the air and chewed their regurgitated bile.

"I know you don't want to be here," Tiller said, "but them things can't touch us."

Scott appeared more nervous than ever, could hardly eat the jerky in his hand. "They better not. I'm ready to kill."

"I might move faster than one of those gulpers," Greta said, "but their tongues are nasty and quicker than anything. Saw that last night." She thought about her dream again, how one swallowed up to her hip. "Then again, Think Tank gonna eat any that gets close." She patted the bear. "Aren't you, big boy? Sorry for kicking you earlier, ya big grump."

"Funny," Tiller lied. "You need to get rid of that."

"Or what?"

"You're stinking up my quad, for one."

"Hear that, Think Tank?" Greta said. "I haven't had a shower in more than a week, and he's more worried about your ass than mine."

"Just get rid of it," Tiller said. "We got other things to worry about."

"Why don't you go find Cherry?" she said. "Scott could use a ride out of this place."

"Damn straight," Scott said.

Greta went on: "You hearing those things?" She motioned to the buzz-pops and groans emanating from cliffs, crevices and stream, a cacophony like a hundred bottles of soda shaken and twisted open followed by humanlike groans and grunts. "They're saying Scott's not welcome."

"Seriously, Greta."

"I'm gonna up his pay, yours too," Tiller said all of a sudden. "Cherry's share. He forfeited. That's five grand. And I'll double your pay."

Greta, who was tired as hell from lack of sleep, woke to that and knocked Think Tank on the snout. "Good thinking since I have to split mine with my new partner. We're good to go." Greta couldn't believe she was going to make so much cash. Things were looking good. Maybe if Scott bolted, she'd get his leftover share too.

"I'm tired of this noise, whatever these things are," Scott said.

"See that?" Greta said. "Boy's gonna run."

"Greta. Stop," Scott said. "This whole thing has got on my last nerve."

"They're just critters," Tiller said. "More afraid of you than you are of them."

Scott looked down at the ground and shook his head. "Greta said that too."

"Telling you, I'm doubling your pay," Tiller said. "Two more nights. Would take a lot of solo riding to get back from here. Anything could happen on the way back. Fewer miles forward."

"Greta said that too," Scott admitted. "Be much happier if we called for some rescue though. And don't tell me we're in a no wifi zone. I checked. I know. Just saying."

"Not a single cow been hurt," Tiller said.

"Seems like they would be the buffet before any of us." Greta was tired, scared, and plenty worried. But she could deal, especially for this kind of cash. Once she got paid she could go wherever she wanted, start a new life, get things on track again, whatever that meant, which, if she was being honest, probably included tracking down Hannah in California and getting an apartment. "Those fizzers aren't anything to worry about," she lied, hoping the creatures would keep their distance. "Besides, I'm telling you, you got me and Think Tank."

"Why doesn't this make me feel any better?" Scott said.

"How many times can anyone almost quit a trail?" she said. "This has to be a record."

"But Cherry said . . ."

"To hell with Cherry." Greta fired up her quad. "He had a staring problem anyway. He may have taken care of that cow. But he abandoned us, nearly stampeded the herd multiple times. Quick to arrive, quicker to leave. That goes for Zollers too. Let's show them we're tougher than some guys from Thermopolis and wherever with a piss-colored truck and a fake movie deal. *Let's go.*" She held out a fist and waited.

Hesitant, Scott bumped fists and soon they were on the trail, moving the crying cattle, ignoring fizzers belching and hissing from the scrub, small herds of them leaping over rocks, scrambling up slopes. Greta counted seventeen perched on long, needleless branches in a dead pine, all soaking sun and making their awful noises, which still didn't startle a single cow.

One fizzer hung lifeless over a branch, picked at by a darker brown one that snatched at an eyeball. Vitreous fluid squirted and a long optic nerve stretched and snapped from its optic chiasm.

The cattle didn't seem to notice, didn't stray onto any slopes, and kept moving forward, hungry and complaining, still several hours' march from a patch of grassland where they could feed one last time before their next day's final push to canyon stalls and interior grasslands.

Late in the afternoon they reached carpets of wildgrass interspersed with thick bunches of prickly pear and wildflowers. Some of the cactus blossomed with yellow pear-shaped blooms that bees pollinated, buzzing and darting. Their sweet scent over the rot drew Greta to inspect them, maybe cut one of the pads, scrape the needles, put the fruit in a pan and cook it up.

All around her cows were happy eating grass, chewing and crying less, hardly complaining except when they heard the occasional fizzer that went running for the upper slopes.

These cows were tougher than Greta, and she was okay with their lack of fear of fizzers or ghosts.

She wandered up to the cactus, and when closing in, an actual roadrunner leapt to one of the paddle-shaped pads. Startled, Greta cooed at the bird: "You're handsome. But you better get out of here."

Then a fizzer poked its head out of the cactus patch and bared its teeth. Greta half ducked behind a nearby cow. The roadrunner rattled its bill at the creature. But the threat didn't take. The fizzer snatched the bird by the neck and soon another joined in and tore feathers from bone and flesh, and head from body. Both fizzers soon ran off with their prize and joined others far up the slope.

Greta nudged the cow away, stepped back to the cactus, made sure there weren't any more fizzers, then cut off a round pad and scraped at the needles, remembering how her mom would harvest only the smallest, non-floppy leaves. Inspecting the fruit-meat, she imagined the hot, sweet fruit on her tongue. She had shimmers of gathering them, of being in the kitchen scraping spines away. They'd place the leaves in a pot, and Greta imagined the scent here as if her mom boiled them right there in the canyon. They would eat nopal salads year-round, and the jars always disappeared from the pantry shelves one by one until they fought over the last helpings. Some fruits would get canned into jams, and those jars went quicker than anything. She wished she had some to add to her gloppy, dry sandwiches, also so she could smell something more than this canyon stink.

Rounding the cactus, wary of hidden fizzers, knowing they were skittish and afraid of cows, maybe of her and her mice too, she was surprised to find a boot tangled in the cactus.

She'd seen other trash. Wooden boards, part of a homestead chimney, a few bits of rusted mining equipment. But those were on the ground. This was half in the cactus as if someone had dropped it right on this spot.

The boot was black, worn, but wasn't damaged by the seasons. She bent, not too close, spied the shadow of a muddy sock inside. The boot was low enough that she could knock it with her foot. When she kicked it to the ground a mess of ants came pouring out.

Scott called out: "Greta. Quit messing with the cows. Made you a sandwich."

"Be right there," she yelled.

The ants poured in a frenzy up and around the boot's insole lip, swarming the pull strap. She wondered why they swarmed. Because if they were feeding, that meant they'd been eating . . . *meat* . . .

Greta started wondering about Zollers. *Could this boot . . . ?*

He hadn't walked this way had he? They would have seen him.

Maybe this was some random off-roader who owned this land passing through who tossed an old boot. Then she remembered that Zollers's boots were brown workboot types, nothing fancy. Pecan brown. Hardly scuffed. Probably made his feet blister. So, not his. That was a relief.

Cherry though? What color were his kicks?

Maybe black? Had to be.

Gotta be nothing, she thought. Cherry'd been heading southeast—he hadn't even driven this direction.

Thing about Cherry's boots that she remembered, that

was coming back to her in fragments, they were Laredos. And there was that one detail about them she suddenly recalled: *silver tips.* Not thick silver tips, just a thin line of metal, kind of easy to miss, which she hadn't noticed on this boot.

She didn't want to touch it, but thought maybe she didn't have a choice. The boot toe was pointed away from her, and even so, there was no silver on the heel, which some boots had that maybe? From this angle there didn't appear to be any silver on the toe, which was a relief so far.

Weren't any sticks around, so she got a hold of the heel and lifted quickly, just to flip the boot around. If there had been silver on the toe, it was gone, ripped off, because the entire boot toe box was missing right up to the vamp that covered the top of the foot. And now another clump of red ants came falling out.

Then Scott yelled again and that got her attention:
"I'm gonna eat your sandwich."
"It's fine. Jesus. One second," she replied, glad to be over her paranoia. She turned to walk back when she heard a thud nearby—sounded like a calf tripped in a rut or gopher hole, though she thought she'd seen something else, maybe a raven landing on the other side of the nearest cow. Didn't do one of those gurgle-croak *kraaahs* or twangy sounds, or *brrronks* or anything the way ravens do, and the cow took a few steps, but not enough so she could see what it hid.

When Greta nudged the cow's hip out of the way for a better look, she bit her lip. This something didn't resemble a raven at all. It was another black boot, the toe aimed right at her.

A silver-toed Laredo boot.
Dropped from the sky.
Immediately she looked up, saw nothing. No airplane.

No birdplane. A couple clouds. No flying cowpuncher missing his shitkickers. *Nothing.* Yet in front of her was this other boot. And that silver toe burned at her retinas. And she swore, no—she *knew*—this boot had fallen from the sky.

And so she moved to it, slow, like the boot might be attached to an invisible foot, and that to an invisible leg, and she feared it might kick at her, though it didn't, *couldn't*, just sat straight up like a cat that landed on its feet. And even though it stank to high hell around there, she swore she could smell the leather, the mustiness of cowhide against human skin, though maybe that was what she wanted to smell.

Then, just like with that other boot, she got close enough to peer inside, and didn't touch it, but slowly inched her gaze into that leg hole like some rattler might strike from its depths, sink its venom into her throat. Right away she saw there was no snake at all but something *was* in the boot, something solid, something that told her that someone had pulled this boot on that very morning, or maybe wore it all night, and was still wearing it, because there was a lot of meat, folds of pink-white skin and hair from part of a leg that must have been twisted and pulled apart above the ankle joint. She assumed the entire foot was still in there, maybe toes wriggling and everything, and she started to get sick, but fear took over, and uncertainty, and questions. She had so many questions she wanted to ask this foot, because the only way she could imagine this severed leg and foot appearing was that giant birdplane she swore she'd seen carry a calf, and if that bird did this, then no one was safe, hadn't been safe this entire time.

And then fear took hold and she examined every part of the sky, and she also wondered if she should still feel protected, and surveyed the cliffs for the goat-fawn, and every shadow too, and then she saw something in one of the cactus patches upslope, and it wasn't one of the fizzers. It was a face, that familiar goat-fawn, those eyes, and it said her name, *Gretaaaa*. And she waited for it to say something, anything else. But that was it, just her name, once, as if to say it was there to look after her, to keep the peace between land and sky, *her* and canyon creatures.

And that's when she saw something else. Part of a human torso was all she could think, or what had been one—mostly ribs and folds of skin and spine left, no arms or legs. What was left had been fairly picked over, was now swarming with those bug-lizard things and the smallest of all the fizzers, a fresh one still fuzzy like some kind of *fizz*-nestling. It not only picked at the bones but snatched some of the bugs and, eating as if with a stuffy snout, opened its maw and exposed a mouthful of yellowy guts or pus-blood, or maybe that was simply the spittle of this cute fizzer with its doe eyes blinking, now hissing toward Greta, dripping some of those innards from its glop-tongue.

And then she walked back to Scott and Tiller, and they asked what she'd seen.

"Nothing," she said. "Not a damn thing but roadrunner feathers."

That night the fizzers came out in full force. Greta kept a rifle loaded at her side, but didn't have to use it. She was glad they camped nowhere near the stream, that they'd set up tents at a distance near the base of a cliff. She waited by the evening campfire until darkness slipped its cover over the canyon, thinking something else might fall from the sky, maybe the rest of Cherry. Maybe an arm. A hand. An eye. A tongue.

But nothing fell from the heavens, and she heard *Gretaaaaa* twice, which took away some of her anxiety, and so did the mice in her pocket, just knowing that they were there, and that big warm bear head at her feet, and warm thoughts about Hannah for once, who she wished were in the tent. She'd keep Greta straight, would somehow know what to do.

And then Greta thought about that second boot, and knew the ants had found it, maybe some of the fizzers, probably some of those other smaller things. And she knew that soon Cherry would be nothing but foot bones and part of a leg bone, and the number of bones in what was left of Bill Cherry, because so much of him was missing, when she thought about it, might be somewhere around fifty-four.

The Owl

The owl, stomach growling, flew straight toward the wood rat, but the plumpy rodent was too fast and disappeared into the deadpile, perhaps having sensed a shadow, a stillness, a form among the dry branches. And though the tangle collapsed some from the owl's sudden landing, that round-eyed murderbird could hear the rat had found passage to a safe space deep within, and the owl could even hear the furry thing cower and shiver.

The owl didn't really want to eat the rat, just kill the thing with her abnormally large talons. She knew the rodent wouldn't taste good. But killing wasn't always about taste. Besides, there were plenty of fish in mother canyon's streams and lakes. The owl then took flight and silently crossed the waters toward the shadow of what she wished was a giant mouthbreeder from the past, though this was cartilaginous, that long, sleek shape visible even at night through dark water, then sank her talons into the fish-spine and sides, and lifted while the slippery thing wriggled and gasped.

The owl devoured a young sturgeon, leaving behind fins that in the morning glistened on the deer-colored earth. Later, butterflies fluttered at the head, drinking water from around its dead eyes. The owl next plucked out a walleye, and then the day after, gutted a bass that made popping sounds with its fishy lips while its intestines were pulled like stretchy worms.

After hunting, the owl slept deep in a pine. While she tried to rest, crows, more than a dozen, perched and flapped, making all kinds of racket. Two brave crows dive-bombed the owl, cawing and swooping. The owl did nothing but turn her head and blink. She sat like a puddle in what felt to her like the oldest tree, thickest in a stand of ponderosas, wood black as night, her tucked on a lightning-scorched branch, and was able to half sleep even when bumped by those noisy, acrobatic crows. This went on for an hour before the owl finally decided to fly parallel to an escarpment, deep into a small natural cave, where she could peer out to jade-colored slopes and nearby canyon streams. The ravens that chased the owl didn't fly in after her, and soon took to chasing and diving and looping around each other a few miles away.

The owl didn't know how she got to mother canyon, or if she'd even been born there and forgotten then returned because of some instinctive pull. She could hardly recall being young. Images fired of an owlery, of fuzzy owlet-siblings and adults, but nothing in detail. Sometimes at night she perched there and sang, hoping for a response, her notes a deep, resonant conch-like bellow, a distant foghorn that came slow and methodical, a lovely curse over the night. She only knew to duet, and always sang her lonely part. His response was always missing, because there was no *him*, though sometimes she imagined a partner singing his portion of the conch-hoot. The owl found a kind of peace when she did this.

She heard other owls, different species, all smaller, the non-fish-lovers, some so tiny she could swallow them whole, and knew all their songs and calls, though she couldn't repeat them. Even larger rodent-hunting owls didn't have her husky girth, which was twice the size of Great Horneds and Barns. She also had a longer bill, one suitable for catching fish. Her wide head harbored a pair of large orange-red eyes, and her plumage, which she preened regularly, coated her in reddish-brown tones. Darker patches adorned her long wings, while primary fingertips appeared dipped in black ink. And she could hear better than other owls though her hidden ears were similarly asymmetric, one higher than the other for better sound triangulation. Her sideways tufts, both long and rounded, as if godlike headwings, were often mistaken for ears.

The owl soon felt she could roam from mother canyon. She only flew several miles before she felt the pull to do something for her, so found a place to spy the creeping things coming from Ten Sleep. Even that large bear, which she'd seen more than once, and that skin riding him, and then when the dead bear lay broken and torn, the owl had watched from a pine and stared at the bear head before the skin placed it in the stream. The owl liked to observe the dead things and sometimes flew all the way to Ten Sleep, where she sat upon the taxidermy building to watch the hollow creatures come out and slither or skitter into midnight hills. Sometimes the owl carried a fish all the way to the building and picked at it all night while waiting for the next dead weasel or marmot or deer to come slinking out, smelling of death and skin and fur and nothing more. Even a dead orange cat and chinchilla made their way toward the prairiedark high country. The chinchilla led the way.

Soon the owl realized that some dead things had assembled near a carrion hill, while others encircled the cattle that were moving to the canyon. She knew this had to be a kind of protection from the violence of ancient creatures, most older than the owl. And the owl knew she couldn't go anywhere that the dead things didn't want her to go.

Though she could fly to Ten Sleep, she could never fly out of the basin, but could explore the canyons, where she felt safest—because it was always about desire and feeling safe or afraid, or hearing mother canyon's voice in her head—and she couldn't always get close to those cows, not really, though a few times she'd been able to perch close on rocks.

One night the owl spotted at least a hundred dead things in mother canyon, dotting rocks like statues, all of them facing a chasm that smelled like some kind of ancient rot. Not just the dead, but redolent as if the oldest form of death was in there, had always been there, and the heart of mother canyon was in there too, and her womb had incubated a bird egg, one special among thousands, maybe millions of others. Not an owl egg, but something else.

Somehow the owl also knew that mother canyon had been held back because of a pact, not with the dead things, but with the creator of the dead things who lived in Ten Sleep, and which at one time had been with those who came before. And now she knew that people from Ten Sleep had traveled to the chasm now and then, always with more dead things, and had in whispers somehow talked to mother canyon and could understand her ancient voice, though she cracked and rumbled as if her language echoed the cryofracturing of granite.

The owl could listen in, and the mother canyon expressed that the pact she'd made with humans had been warped many times over, stolen from the People, who themselves had lost sight of some of her intentions.

Sometimes the owl felt weakened and sick when the dead things came in great numbers. They stood so still outside the birth-chasm, as if to keep the rot inside other holes and fissures, to rot and rot some more, and die and melt and scream in the dark places lost to time. The owl didn't eat until they left two days later, because this was near the old trees that the owl loved so much, and there was no fish there.

Sometimes the owl thought she might die when the dead things came, and realized this was a reminder to fear even the tiniest dead mouse. The owl had seen two of them near the cattle, sometimes set outside a tent. Sometimes she could hear their movements while the human with them slept.

The owl wondered if another of her kind maybe lived beyond the basin, maybe that's where another owl sang, and so the owl desired to ride the moonlight, maybe moonstars to a new place, though she didn't know how.

And then before dawn one day the mother canyon talked directly to the owl. It was through the giant bird, which flew to the owl's favorite area with the old ponderosa and the scorched birth cavity, and the two birds stared at each other—the owl into the giant eye of the bird which seemed to be a cavern that reached deep into the core of everything.

Mother canyon said: *You and all the little creatures have always been sacred to me. But you should be afraid of magic, even on the eve of when the world may be about to transform.*

As they spoke in silence, mind to mind, the owl knew mother canyon was the bird more so than in herself, but that she was the canyon too, and she also knew something was about to change, as mother canyon said, and felt deep in her heart what she had to do to help with this . . . which was to choose, and it was a good thing to be given a choice, which was to protect creatures, not the dead, and the owl liked that because she feared the dead.

The owl knew what she had to do, and so the giant bird flew off, while the owl continued watching the dead things, singing her deep, lonely duet, spying on both the cattle and the people, not to mention the little creatures making their way through the grasslands and canyons. She watched how the creatures often hid from both people and dead things, afraid of touching something in the air around them, the way the owl was also afraid.

One morning right after the owl went to sleep, she again felt something calling to her and again knew what she had to do, to follow, to observe, to protect as best she could. She opened her red-orange eyes and preened and nibbled at her long wing feathers—pulling above the calamus along the rachis, picking through barbs and barbules—then after her huge eyes adjusted to the filter of early sunlight, ruffled then took flight, making big floppy wingbeats, her primary feather tips like obsidian. She gained altitude, sailed from the timberline over emerald slopes and endless wildflowers and imagined flowers and trees from another time. The owl somehow remembered their shapes the way she recalled the sugary fragrant smell of petal oils, or the way thorns rubbed against stems, and how petals tasted in the mouths of the rodents she killed. She remembered megafauna with so much hair, and armored backs, and large antlers, and horns, and humps, and long bendy trunks, and slow-moving creatures the size of enormous boulders, with long claws for scratching fruit from trees, and snorty wet black sniffers.

For flashes upon flashes the owl could see into this other time and remembered the owlery too, and how she yearned to sing duets one after the other all night and into the daylight, sometimes ignoring her hunger so she could sing and sing and let the deep, sonorous *hoootooooots-hoootooooots* soothe the endless death of those ancient nights, a time when terrible nighthawks with saber fangs ate snakes, rats, and giant hares in their dens, and monstrous cats and dogs prowled, and martens the size of jaguar snuck into trees and feasted on owl eggs. In this blood-filled darkness, quieted screams of the nightkills dueted with the owls' nightsong.

She flew over the prairie now in the great basin, and then started circling, having located the man from that taxidermy building in Ten Sleep from where all the dead things originated. The man barreled along a trail atop a machine, and so the owl easily circled without him noticing, even though it was daylight.

The man, she could tell, was determined, maybe on his way to carry out more of his portion of the contract. Closing in on the canyon, he stopped on his machine, slurped from a thermos filled with soup and chicken parts, and paced and ate, then pulled down his pants and took a shit, then pissed on the prairie, and didn't bury any of it and stood with his pants partly down, sipping his soup again while the owl circled silently. And then she saw some of the ground-dwelling roadrunnery birds that shined like blue-green jewels, so tiny compared to her. They had strayed far from the canyon, though they weren't supposed to be able to. They ran along the ground, and soon closed in on the man.

When the man saw the birds he fumbled with his belt but gave up because he panicked when they saw him. And because there were no dead things around, these birds surrounded the man.

The owl knew the birds were merely curious, though she also knew they probably wondered if they could eat him, whether he'd taste like lizard meat, or toad belly, or maybe like prairie dog or gopher hearts.

The man hurried to his machine, buttoning his pants as his belt flopped, and found a stick, or something like it, and aimed it at the birds, and yelled, saying things the owl didn't understand. The owl knew the stick was harmful, had seen them before, knowing they could destroy life, could kill deer, elk, bison, owls, anything.

The owl also knew somehow that the man aiming that stick at those birds was taboo, that the contract strictly forbade the destruction of mother canyon's creatures by that man, that it had always been this way, that the man's son was also not allowed to kill her creatures, that they would kill their own, bleed their own, rot on their own.

Then the owl thought, what if the man was merely trying to scare the birds? But then smoke came from the stick and one of the birds flopped and flopped in the dirt and grass and then hopped up, and luckily had merely been grazed by something hot and stinging, and the owl could smell its blood, and the herd grew angry instead of afraid, and rushed after the man who ran toward his machine, and then instead of getting on and driving away, again aimed the stick.

And this was when the owl knew, really knew that she had to preserve the birds because even though it was good that the pact had been in some way broken, this was the way for the owl to play her part, to not simply observe, to not simply hunt fish, impale rodents, and sing her half of a lonely duet, but save something of mother canyon. She cut through the air and knocked the man and the stick to the dirt, and he let out a yelp, and was clearly afraid, scrambling.

And the owl didn't stop. She saw the man as if he towered at the edge of an owlery with that stick, as if he would murder every fuzzball owlet. And so she clawed the man's face, pulling out one of his eyes that snapped and gushed, then went for the other with a snap of her bill and missed.

Now the owl knew what she must do—she aimed to tear open the man's neck. But he had wormed his way from the owl, squirming and screaming, and was somehow on his feet with the stick, blood gushing from his eye hole and arms, and faced the owl. The bird landed and screeched, beating her wings in defiance, snapping her sharp bill at his soft flesh, dirt flying, limbs dodging. Then she released a *call*-screech this world hadn't heard since ice filled every crevice of those nearby canyons thousands of years ago, her feathers agitated and ruffled, raised like spines along her head, chest, and belly, making her seem like the largest of her kind the world had ever known.

Then the man, crouching and bleeding, fired the stick, and the owl felt a hollowness inside her chest and throat in a way she'd never known. She felt hot and cold and shivery, and so turned away and ran and flapped and tried to fly and tried to cry out but the stick had severed her syrinx.

Her insides pounded and pulsed. Her heart, so large in her body, felt erratic, squeezing, pumping, then weakening. Then the owl's life, she knew, was leaking away. She again flapped her wings, this time having just enough energy to flap along the ground, and felt another searing pain, this time in her shoulder, and though she kept flying and was far from the man, quickly ran out of strength, and skidded into the prairie a mile away, and though she wanted again to fly, this time to her pine where she could hide in shadows, could only yearn.

She struggled and struggled, still on her feet, trying to find strength, but everything that made her hungry for flight was now leaving her body. She felt cold and hot and angry and sad, and even so, a peace began to fill her, because the roadrunnery birds had gone and hid, and were safe. And soon she lurched and stopped thrashing, and in the few moments of her struggled breaths, wanted to sing but couldn't, and this was hardest on her weary soul, because she knew she would never duet again, so simply tried to remember.

She bowed her head into her wings remembering duets with her family, and huddled in her own self-made night, and it seemed she could see the lovely fuzzfaces of young siblings, and her parents, and knew she would come back to them, *soon*, so soon, and knew at the same time that everything had changed, that this world would be different, that mother canyon might spread like clouds rolling and thundering.

Then she silently cried, and the daylight felt warm on her back and wings, and she took comfort in that over the throbbing, and in remembering the final notes of a duet, one sung long ago in a dark pine lit by a warm blanket of moonflame.

    She felt a final coldness in this memory, but even so, would coo if she could, because somehow, real or not, she heard the other half of the duet she'd been waiting so long for, and the song rang throughout her body while she drifted toward forever sleep.

Night Nine

Greta was sick of the tent, sick of her smell, sick of the stench outside, sick of not having a shower, sick of dirt under her nails, sick of Tiller's voice and his lack of deodorant, sick of mama cows and their two hundred and six bones, sick of baby cows blubbering like sad weanlings, sick of trails, sick of peanut butter sandwiches, sick of thinking about the Pope, sick of headaches, sick of herself for being sick of everything. If she could, she'd go for a walk so that the part of herself that was sick of everything would maybe leave her the fuck alone.

She wanted beer for breakfast. She wanted cake for lunch. She wanted pizza under each eye to make the bags go away. She wanted an entire slab of beef from the Ribs N Go. She wanted to tell her old boss to get his ass over to the kitchen and bring her some goddam bread and butter. She would drink to that. And then drink some more. And she wanted Hannah, she had to admit this, didn't she?

She. Wanted. Hannah.

And then came her only hour of sleep for the second day in a row. Felt like she hadn't slept in a week. Felt like she'd been

hit with a sack of bricks. And then there in the tent, after feeling sick of just about every fucking thing in the world, came the most pleasing thought. And it felt really good.

Bill Cherry was *dead*.

What struck Greta, and she didn't have to think twice about this—was how fine she felt with the fact that Bill Cherry was now merely a couple of dismembered feet in boots and a meaty rib cage. One hundred percent she was totally fine with the fact that Bill Cherry had his boots ripped off, feet and all. She no longer had to think, *There goes another starey man boring his eyes into the back of a woman*. No one had to deal with his truck grinding on their heels. No one had to look into those eye-pits and wonder what he might be capable of doing behind closed doors. He was *dead*. And she was okay with her secret that he was never coming back. The son of a bitch didn't deserve a decent burial. And would never ever get one. And Pinkie? He was probably terrified out of his mind, still walking, hungry as hell, and hopefully, with some luck, completely lost.

Greta kept Think Tank close. The mice had been snuggled in her pocket since before daybreak. She thought she felt both move—their little broken whiskers twitched or their torn ears wiggled—and then she noticed that two legs, one on each mouse, *had* changed positions. They didn't seem broken, still stiff. She cooed at them like she always did, though neither twitched again. She thanked them for their protection, said she would protect them in return. And, so Think Tank wouldn't get jealous, she patted the bear head and told him he was a good bear, a *very good bear*. Then, a little while later, to the disapproval of Scott, she strapped Think Tank to her quad.

"Why you still packing that?" Scott asked.

"Take a look around," Greta replied. "I need my talisman."

Scott's voice went up a notch. "That's not a talisman, it's a bear head."

"Think Tank has a name," Greta said.

"But not a body."

"Maybe he can have yours?" she said a little too quick. "Look, you get through this your way. I'm going to keep on doing what makes me and Think Tank feel safe."

Greta didn't care about Scott, not today, not like she had. She'd been burning a while now knowing that he would have easily cut out with Cherry. It wasn't like she wanted Scott to die. Only Cherry deserved to be remembered as swollen corpse feet being parted out to the local ant colony. Pinkie came in a close second. She did care about Scott not being eaten by fizzers, fish-walkers, and that giant bird.

She didn't want to be eaten period. And she didn't want to be ridiculed by Scott. She wanted to survive this moon-cold morning, then like Cherry's big dead dream, maybe tell the world what she'd seen.

J.A. taught her about logging birds, so she'd recorded the fizzers making their odd noise, shot video of one of them running, some of the dead small things too, then her battery died. Oh well. She'd show J.A. He'd know what to do, who to talk to, how to get the word out. Even if she came out of this alone . . . maybe there was still a way to make a few more bucks, yeah?

What she also cared about at the moment was her sudden sighting of the goat-fawn peeking over a ridgeline. It was dawn, the canyon steep, shaded. The grey-blue sky hung rose-colored around the eastern edge where the creature, *my old friend*, she thought, said her name, *Gretaaaa . . . Gretaaaa . . .*

That sighting put her at ease, because as long as that creature was around with Think Tank and the mice, she had a fighting chance at getting through all of this. Didn't matter that the goat-fawn was likely a voice in her head, it made her feel lighter both inside and out—protected and uneasy.

She began suspecting that maybe the canyon was dying, that its ancient heart might be slowing, but why? How did this all work? Weren't there enough fizzers for the bird to eat? How about fizzers gobbling each other, getting slobbery mouths on those long necks? Which should she fear more, birdplane, fizz-fizz . . . *Tiller*?

Though she'd only glimpsed that condor-like thing, she knew how high it could fly, how it could soar within the edge of stratocumulus, and watch her, *them*. Then again, what did the bird want? How could the canyon be dead or dying when that giant bird, the fizzers, the fish-walkers, birds and bugs, and whatever else Cherry claimed to have seen with long tails, were everywhere? Just what was going on?

And what was that ongoing rot? That mephitis, as far as Greta could tell while checking her quad for any bugthings, had really got to all of them, seeping into lungs and clothes, and maybe had gotten to the cows too, heads tossing low, breathing hard out their slavering mouths. This place was rotting from the inside out, had to be. Maybe the canyon birthed all of this and there just wasn't enough to eat, so they rotted, melted, sloughed away. Maybe these fizzer things and whatever couldn't handle the changed atmosphere of today's world, maybe that did something, was doing something to their biology. Maybe they were on a timer, had so little time to feed, to mate, to lay eggs, the way mosquitoes had so very little time to bloodfeed and create chaos. And when they died, they stunk up the place.

Also, the cattle hadn't eaten enough, their muzzles and lips caked with red dirt from picking at sparse weeds in the early morning light. And they cried, as if to the drum of their own anxious hooves. And they bunched up closer than ever, head to tail, flies swirling around their ears and backs, tails swishing, eyes turning inward. And though they'd yet to set out, it already seemed they'd been running all day and were exhausted, though maybe the cows had their own expectations, maybe they knew they were going to be dead tired at the end of all this. Maybe even they'd lost some kind of hope. And this bothered Greta, because so many bovines in that state of mind made her think the crew might not even get them safe to their destination.

And the cows weren't alone in their lethargy. While Greta herself was noticeably slower, she observed Scott and Tiller moving as if in slow motion, as if they also hadn't slept in a week. But also, something in Tiller had changed most of all, or was changing. Seemed that every fizzer startled him. Even Tiller's lips were slower to part, and his voice had a slight slur. Maybe he was drinking too much on the job, wouldn't surprise her. She'd taken some nips herself over the past week, though not enough to make her fall drunk off her quad or to tire her any more than she was. His skin appeared clammy too. Purple half-moons formed beneath his eyes, curtained his upper cheeks, and he sweat even though the air was cooler, even downright cold. He hadn't even counted the cows that morning and mumbled to Scott not to bother, that they needed to get going, finish this job.

Then her thoughts drifted to Hannah, because Greta remembered using Hannah's plaid coat as a pillow, and then leaving it hanging on Scott's quad while she grabbed breakfast, some biscuits that he cooked up. Now he was off relieving himself, and Tiller staring off into the cliffs, smoking a cigarette. When she grabbed the coat, about to crack some joke at Tiller, she almost dropped it. Her hand slipped along the lining, felt something hard and thin inside. Whatever it was, she quickly realized, wasn't in a pocket but in the actual lining. Feeling the object now again, she had a weird thought, and with that a sudden shot of adrenaline. She got out her pocketknife and cut right through some of the stitching, which she hadn't noticed wasn't original but some hatchet job on the poor coat.

And then there it was, not just a funny feeling making her feel more disassociated than ever from this strange canyon, her bizarre life . . . but something tangible. Something she'd seen before. A clue to Hannah's whereabouts, one that she thought had disappeared with the girlfriend who ghosted her.

It was the key.

The key from the counter—from when she and Hannah were still together. The one she thought about countless times. Did the key belong to a trailer? Did it open a shed? Maybe an RV door? Why had the key been on a counter? Why did it disappear? Why hadn't she asked Hannah when she had the chance?

That key had disappeared. Like *Hannah*. Just. Gone.

And now it was back.

The *key*.

In Hannah's, now Greta's *plaid coat*.

Sewn inside like a riddle.

A riddle Hannah must have expected Greta to solve all along.

One that would have given Hannah time, so much needed time alone.

And there it was, not just the key, but on the key . . . a phone number written in permanent black marker.

Only, there was no wifi here, no juice in her phone.

Just monsters. Everywhere.

The cows groaned more than usual as if they might wanna fall down and starve. But Scott belted out and repeated *Come on!* about seven times—they followed his quad slow and uneasy like sad dogs.

Greta soon felt like she was losing her senses. She couldn't hear her quad's drone. Couldn't feel her thighs, couldn't feel her hands on the brakes. Couldn't feel if those late-season Chinook remnants swirled any kind of warmth into the canyon. She could hear Hannah mostly, though she wasn't sure what was being said, as if distant memories slipped into a repeating pattern.

She tried to make herself aware of her surroundings, spotted cliff detritus breaking and crumbling. Rocks loosened, tumbled, like the world might fall in on itself if she breathed too hard, though maybe unstable erosion had been loosened from fizzers zipping along steep upper slopes and rock faces. When she briefly stopped to pull on her helmet in case loose talus came zinging toward her, she had the sudden thought: What if rocks were falling because of the rot?

Soon a breeze made the cows stir and moan. Greta tightened her coat, realizing her own hunger for Hannah, the dirt burning in her eyes, which when she lifted her visor and knuckled at the corners, made them water even more.

Her thoughts went right back to that *key*. Couldn't see anything but Hannah's face hovering in their old apartment, both sitting across from each other, staring into those brown eyes, but somehow, she continued driving slow in the rear, Tiller thirty yards ahead, her sometimes dropping off to stop to listen to the sounds inside herself. Somehow, she didn't crash into the creek bottom, or the cliff walls, determined to stay on the trail, drone on to the cacophony of fizz-pops.

And then Greta stopped again. A feeling to hit the brakes? It was always intuition, a feeling, yeah? She had Hannah's coat back on, had stuffed the key in there with the mice, but now shoved a hand in her pocket to check, and then realized the mice in her pocket were *alive*, or some kind of *dead*-alive or *alive*-dead like the goat-fawn, though these betrothed taxidermy mice wriggled and nuzzled against her fingers when she reached in. And she knew—or had she already known—this canyon had a magic, that it wasn't only from Bobby Tiller, couldn't be, that some kind of enchantment emanated from here, and maybe that augury shimmered inside her too, had been inside her lungs, hands, throat, and that it might have something to do with, or was triggered by, love, or compassion, that those feelings had some kind of magic quality here. Couldn't they? Didn't they? Because the mice were loving her back?

She felt their death and their life.

When she caught back up to the herd, Tiller had stopped, was letting out a whistle. Then he threw his hat to the ground. Greta wasn't sure how much more that hat could take. Far ahead, Scott stopped too. The herd seemed eager to rest, though they'd hardly traveled. They cried as they always did, but something sounded off in it, a different pitch, a different sincerity in it. Greta, having pulled up behind Tiller, realized that her grip on the quad had been too tight, shoulders and neck tense, so was slow to let go and slip off. She half-heartedly tried to stretch a little when she finally did, picked up Tiller's hat, smacked it against her thigh, and set it on his ATV.

There was no food for the cows here, and they still refused water, besides, Greta could see a few triangle heads breaking the surface where the stream backed up. Then the cattle started complaining as if taking turns, whining, blubbering even more than they already were. Greta had no idea how long they'd pushed the herd, maybe only a few hours. Possibly less. She recalled eating some trail mix, and all those thoughts, not much else. Hannah, she recalled those *Hannah* conversations in her head. And a shadow, maybe even the tail of the giant birdplane, and still, she'd told no one. She did wonder if more Cherry bones might fall from the sky. Maybe she could catch one, twirl it like a damn baton. *Nah.* She'd pound it on a handmade drum and chant the warrior power of bear heads and mousefriends. She slipped her hand in her pocket, felt the mice tucked in a ball, heads nuzzling. She rubbed them, tickled them. They moved then went still. Think Tank was silent as usual.

Scott tightened the bandana around his face, the stink particularly rancid here. "Why'd we stop? Why'd you throw your hat?"

Tiller cursed. "Figured out what was wrong and it's my own damn fault for not counting at daybreak."

"That why you were smoking and staring at the cliffs before we left?" Greta said.

Tiller accepted his hat back. He dusted it himself a little more, then let out a sigh. "Half the calves are gone."

"Gone?" Greta said.

"Smells worse here." Scott covered his mouth and nose, while the fizzers popped and buzzed, gurgling louder than ever.

Greta agreed and tried to cover her breath with her shirt and jacket but it wasn't helping. Her head throbbed and sucking air felt laborious, like slurping air through a snorkel. Everything became a weight, bore down on her, her thoughts, the coat, Think Tank, the mice, sunlight. Even the key in her pocket felt heavy and painful like it might sink through her coat into the flesh of her thigh and fuse to bone.

"How'd we not notice?" Scott asked.

"Maybe they're up on one of these cliff trails," Tiller said. "Greta, where's your binoculars? Maybe them cows know something we don't. They're making an awful racket."

Greta had a feeling the cattle weren't crying about the missing calves, though some of them, maybe? If they sensed that birdplane, they might get uncomfortable, especially if that monsterflyer snatched them away in the night without any of them noticing. And that, of course, could lead to a panic here in daylight, a stampede that could kill every head, maybe drive them up a trail and over a cliff in a waterfall of hide and hoof.

She dug out her binoculars, whispering to the mice not to be afraid. She and Think Tank wouldn't allow them to be gobbled by any giant stinky bird. She was sure of that.

Noon light turned cliff faces and pinnacles a deep blue. All the lodgepoles and ponderosas in them, dark knives. Boughs lifted and dropped here along with remnants of a sour-smelling breeze. A few birds passed through, anxious to keep going, Greta figured, to escape this rancid air. A pine marten scampered up a trunk running funny, but still no tree or ground squirrels. No pikas. Not to mention, no deer, no goats, no little carnivores. None of the usual hooved moonfeeders or their sounds either. No squirrely warning barks. No pika squeaks. Mostly those fizzer Pop Rocks, sometimes more like the release of airbrakes. Then she spied the yellow forecrown of a male American Three-toed Woodpecker high in a burned-out pine, and thought, *Good, not every bird wants to leave—some even prefer a little disaster.* The bird seemed to be pulling out grubs, then started in on drumming. Greta was sad thinking many birds might be lost to the monsters here. Then again, weren't many birds eating and thriving? Though in decline as J.A. Maynard told her, birds might be the final rulers of this world. For all she knew, right at this moment, some baby woodpeckers in those pines might be chewing on regurgitated fizzer bits.

While she scanned near the ridgeline, Greta's bins fell to another dead pine, this filled with rosy and brown hues. "Now that's an odd tree," she said. "Looks to be made of stone." The massive glistening trunk had fallen against a crack in the cliff wall, and had atop it, at least at one time, a nest the size of a shed. Built of sticks and narrow trunks, its contents resembled the pine, which to Greta might be a petrified tree fallen against the scarp, the likes of which she'd never seen. She wished J.A. were around to help reason it out.

And then she saw near an opening to a cave or cavern a string of seven blackish dots.

"Hold on," she said. "Might be seeing our missing calves. All lined up too. How the heck they get up there?" She pointed to her one o'clock. "They're to the right of that fallen tree." She handed Scott her binoculars. "See them?"

Scott grunted his agreement then searched to pass the bins to their trail boss. "Where's Tiller?" he said like a broken record.

"Maybe with the cattle somewhere?"

"He was just here."

Greta tried calling the calves down. "Co-o-me on! There calf! Co-o-me on! Co-o-me on! Here calf!" She repeated and yahooed, but the calves only cried, and the cattle on the main trail grew more restless and bawled.

Fizzers popped, wheezed, and hooted.

Scott tried calling the calves too—the results the same. More fizzer fanfare.

"Guess we better get them," Greta said.

"Up there?" Scott said. "With those things? Send Tiller."

"You send Tiller when he comes back. I'm going. These cattle aren't going to move without them now that they know they're up there."

"Too bad Cherry isn't still around to help."

"Maybe he'd fry up some bloody fizzer oysters." Greta checked her pocket for the mice. They wriggled, which made her less afraid of going after the calves.

She gave Think Tank a pat and told him to watch over the herd, then climbed ahead of Scott up a steep set of switchbacks that cut through limestone cliffs. The natural trail had likely been maintained by deer and goats, though seemed like maybe indigenous people created the original path eons ago.

"You coming?" she said to Scott.

"Do I have a choice?"

Wisps of clouds moved in, dulling some of the light, though the sun's white eye still stared through as if the sky might catch fire. Greta blinked at the sun-eye, then coughed from a strong whiff of miasma. She thought if she choked to death on this air, no one would ever come find her, so better keep her head, her lungs, everything under control. What she wanted to do was turn around, because the smell was getting worse. She was so ready to be done, to shove this cattle drive into the past, or up Tiller's wherever, but told herself for the hundredth time to finish out, make that double pay and bonus. Besides, she couldn't leave those calves, had to bring them back to their mothers, even if she'd been the only one to make the climb, even if there were monsters everywhere.

With all her gasping she was surprised to be ahead of Scott, who she now saw labored to keep up. When she turned, a pair of fizzers crossed behind him. She didn't say anything, though he seemed to sense he wasn't alone.

"What was that?" he wheezed.

"Nothing."

"*Nothing* about to eat me?"

Below him the switchbacks appeared steep and treacherous, and below that a long brush-choked ravine and the creek and trail with the cattle grouped tight, bellowing and crying. Greta hoped they were telling the calves to make their way back down since the yahoos didn't work. Up here the wind came up hard and bleak and the burbling of the creek waters swelled up into the canyon, echoing amid pearled limestone ridges. Several switchbacks above her, the line of calves moaned for their mothers.

"One of us really needs to speak cow," Greta huffed. "Would make this much easier."

Scott grunted. "What are they doing up here anyway?"

She pushed on, the switchbacks steeper, a trail of vertigo-inducing drop-offs forced her to look up rather than down, while the grime from the rot made her increasingly nauseous. Her legs burned, and by the time they neared the calves, she could feel herself needing a long rest. She took a sip of water and pointed: "Look at that." A spot of trail fifteen feet ahead was blocked with a young lodgepole. Ripped from its roots, the tree trapped the line of bawling calves.

Beyond the dogies, an oblong cave mouth. A putrescent wind blasted from the depths. And the hint of a moan, a voice so distant, she was surprised she could hear it at all. She said nothing to Scott.

"Someone did this," Scott said about the fallen tree.

Greta didn't think a person did this. "No man can rip a tree up by its roots."

At that moment, some of the branches of the fallen tree twitched. A fizzer jumped atop the trunk and let out of string of buzz-pops that amounted to some kind of angry shriek. The calves fell into a crybaby panic and wailed louder than ever.

Greta found a rock and slung it, but the fizzer was too fast and bolted over a calf, hopped across several rocks and disappeared. It was joined by others making a collective hiss similar to grackles, power lines buzzing and crackling. They also jumped into the shadows.

"These things are like stray dogs," Scott said. "Just gotta scare 'em off."

Greta climbed up and around rocks, glancing skyward for any sign of the bird. She soon ran a hand along the rump of a skittish calf. "Easy now," she sang. "You're going back to your mamas."

She then thought about how they might move the fallen pine. It lay at a diagonal from a patch of earth between boulders where its torn roots spread outward into a tangle of deadfall. The tree rocked but wouldn't budge otherwise.

"This is going to be a bitch," she said. "Just let me catch my breath for a minute."

"I'm all for resting." Scott leaned an elbow on the trunk, wiped his face with the handkerchief that was around his face then stuffed it in his pocket. "Is it just me or is it more stifling up here? Something foul coming out of there." He pointed to the cave. "Can hardly breathe."

Greta examined their surroundings. The petrified stick-rocks that made up the nesting material had been built a dozen feet high at one time, it seemed, and may have been twice as wide, though even now it still formed part of a giant spilled cup.

"I thought it looked big from down there," she said. "This is enormous."

Detritus of all kinds spilled out, and most amazing to Greta, lengths of petrified wood, splintered from its source, a tree still partially upright at its base, though split in the middle by a seam that reached half of its height. It had become rock, and what was stranger still, this decayed wood-turned-stone nest structure may have been used even after the tree died so many million years ago, and was partially filled with old, rotted wood. She wondered how an upright tree could ever become petrified. Had this area of canyon been covered in mud and ash, and then a lot of that same muck eroded away? She picked at the nest, including a web of bones. Thin lengths of hide had become so weathered they seemed like webs.

"When do you think this tree was standing?" Scott asked. "Fifty million years ago? Twice that?" He pulled out a knife, chipped off a fleck of loose quartz-like stone, turned it in his hand.

Stranger things had been found, Greta knew. Some of the nest wasn't millions of years old. Whatever that meant. She thought about the extinction day find in North Dakota at the site dubbed Tanis. It revealed an entire dinosaur leg, exploded off its body. An ancient turtle at the same site had been skewered by splintered wood. Everything indicated the moment of impact, the Cretaceous period, sixty-six million years ago. She wondered if this petrified tree had withstood that event, even as the extinction storm barreled up ancient seaways to this very spot. She wished she had some juice in her phone for a photo.

The hole where the nest collapsed seemed a natural opening, though something about it felt alive, breathing, still releasing its ancient, or maybe recent, stench. Maybe both. Air blew out disgusting and rotten, as if this subterranean entrance had been exhaling death longer than the petrified tree had been rock. It reminded Greta of something J.A. told her, that fossilized remains trapped in parts of Wyoming's ancient basin included beads of algae. He told her how he'd wandered hillsides, cliffsides, had even been shot at, all while discovering tiny strings of beads frozen one and a half billion years ago. That algae prospered at one time, lit the planet with a kind of bioluminescence, provided building blocks for more life to come, then froze for all time, snapshots to the past if you could find them.

Beneath the opening, the calves shuffled, trapped. The entrance to the hole, where the mavericks also couldn't go, had been piled with sticks and shrubs. A couple fizzers jumped past and darted within the cave. Greta couldn't make sense of any of this.

And then something happened. Which didn't shock Greta because if there was one thing she knew:

Something . . . always . . . happens . . .

The *birdplane*.

The *mother-monster*.

The giant *bird-thing*.

It came faster than she imagined anything could, the way it blurred over rocks and steep drops, coming on dark wings, a slight greenish-purple iridescence to them that caught the light. Its vulture-like primary wing feathers alone must have been longer than Greta's legs, maybe her entire body, while the span of its wings easily stretched twenty feet from wing tip to wing tip.

Somehow, she'd caught the greenish hue of its dark bare neck and head, a misshapen grimace where the base of its giant decurved bill formed a gape toward the fleshy corners of its mouth. Even then, the bird flew like it would blanket all the switchbacks with its wings. Then something else struck her about the monstrous bird . . .

Goddam, it's quiet.

In that same sweeping moment, the lead calf was snatched by dark greenish talons so large that one claw could have grappled Greta's entire torso.

Lifted off its hooves, the calf let out a shriek, something Greta hadn't thought possible from a young bovine, and was swept with hardly a flap of wings into the cliffside hole.

The bird must have been soaring at such a height that at any glance upwards, it would have appeared a vulture or hawk in that sun-glare. And that's the thing, Greta had glanced, and that's all she thought she'd seen—three or four buzzards searching for carrion, for any living thing to drop and stop breathing, so they could tear flesh from bone. She'd seen them eviscerate a fresh roadkill deer in minutes.

Then it hit Greta . . . *This is something this bird has done before.*

It must have flown into that hole hundreds if not thousands of times—the seamless result of its inherited movements—its ancient DNA somehow conspiring with the present. Those wings spread as if mother nature had given the bird two enormous sails, gone now into the depths, a hole that swallowed both bird and calf, and every hopeless cry the calf could make, as if nothing had ever cried at all in the history of crying, though now every remaining calf kicked and leapt at their makeshift gate.

Greta and Scott jumped out of the way when one calf, having seen the path they'd taken, leapt onto a rock, nearly taking Greta's head off. It then slipped, and in a crack and snap of neck and legs, fell onto a rock twenty feet below their steep switchback. Its body went instantly stiff, mouth pouring blood.

Whatever summoned this bird, Greta didn't know, couldn't know what had brought it. She could only think: *When is this thing coming back? Is there more than one?*

Then adrenaline kicked in. Greta wanted to get to her quad, needed her rifle. She should have brought it anyway, wasn't thinking, was too wound around that double pay, the bonus, that *key* and *Hannah*, even leading the calves to safety like some superhero mom with a zoo of dead animal sidekicks.

She scanned for a place to hide in these exposed rocks, and without telling Scott to run, swung over the trunk, followed by a calf that somehow miraculously made the leap, and started hauling ass down the switchbacks.

Greta nearly flew down them, taking one of the corners so tight she scraped a portion of her chin, lip, and right cheek on an exposed branch. She tasted blood, and when she did, the calf came tearing past and nearly stampeded her off a steep drop.

"Go go go!" Scott yelled behind her. She didn't stop, couldn't stop, until in front of her, leaping and scurrying, stopping her dead in her tracks, was that stuffed thing again, those goaty eyes staring from above that speckled body, dragging that broken leg in its awkward jump, scrambling out of nowhere it seemed.

She and Scott put on the brakes and almost toppled to their deaths.

"What the fuck is that?" Scott yelled as if to curse the thing away.

Greta peered over her shoulder, heart throbbing in her throat, to see if the bird had exited the hole. "Something I met a while back." She tasted blood from her lip.

"You're shitting me. Come on, go past it," Scott said. "I don't want to be here when that bird-thing gets hungry again. Jesus Christ. Jesus fucking Christ."

"Just wait," Greta said, thinking she could hear those wings stretching from the cavern from where it entered. She wasn't wrong. There came a shriek from one of the remaining calves.

She and Scott could see the bird's wings extend and retract, having perched above the calves, plucking at its next victim. It dove its bill into hide, ripped and tore, sending innards flying while the calf shrieked, and as the others leapt and bucked.

"That thing is just killing to kill," she said.

When she turned back around, the goat-fawn glanced

then slid into a cavity between rocks. She could hear her name. *Gretaaaaa*, just like before. This time she knew it was telling her to follow, to crawl in there with it.

Terrified, she knew in these seconds she had to make the kind of choice that could leave her drowning in blood, or drowning in fear. Though she knew the taxidermy creature protected her, the idea of crawling in after the goat-fawn unsettled her to no end. She wondered what she could be seeing, if this could all be a dream or illusion, this second calf dying, this giant flying condor-thing, aka prehistoric bird monster, aka birdplane, and the stuffed goat-fawn, that deer body and goat head and broken leg. Was it really even calling to her, wanting her to make a choice? Could she be imagining those cloppy hooves and devil eye? Maybe she was imagining Scott imagining it. Was she dreaming even being here on this trail? She felt like her own life had become the *story*, the *tale that lived or died on the trail*, the one that people would talk about. She could be the hero who saved her friends, or the victim who should have done more before being carried away, ripped apart, who maybe would be found barely alive, or never seen again. Maybe she was on the verge of becoming a set of bones discovered a hundred years from now that would have to be DNA tested, even if there were only a lone tibia.

She wasn't ready to be any of that, and before she could act, felt the mice in her pocket kicking up a storm. "*Right.* I get it," she said.

"Get what?" Scott said.

"Follow me." She trailed the goat-fawn into the darkness, hoped Scott would do the same.

Cursing, he scurried in behind her.

Greta felt her way through a maze of rock, a faint scent of formaldehyde lingered. She glimpsed the goat-fawn, slinking ahead of her, dragging that broken leg through slivers of late daylight, wondering where the taxidermy was taking her.

This tangle was an even tighter fit than she realized, her chest squeezed against the ground while her forearms and hands pulled against rock and dirt, searching for fingerholds. Felt like she wasn't getting anywhere. Scott grunted behind her, having an even harder time. Everything felt labyrinthine. A memory flashed of her old house, of crawling beneath floorboards, slipping through spider webs, around beams while she could hear the Pope complaining, *Where's that Greta? She getting an ass whipping when I find her. She sat on my motorcycle again and tried to start it. Where's that goddam girl?* The memory soon vanished, though it was replaced by another, one of Hannah saying, *We don't have sex because you're a spider when you're like this. When you're uptight, I can't relax. So what's the point? Let's just watch TV, cuddle. It doesn't all have to be this kind of venomous pressure.* Then that memory vanished too, and when Greta thought she couldn't squeeze through any farther, the hole opened into a dark room with only a few sunlit cracks.

She lay there, lungs heavy, rolling onto her back, spiderweb-angry-Hannah-Pope memories flashing and waning, then flashing again, making her want to return to her earlier numbness. She fought the desire, pinched herself, probably made herself bleed, told herself to be present, to just be *present*.

Above her, something unexpected slowly came into focus: constellations had been painted on the ceiling, petroglyph stars dotted them, each an eye in a wash of milk, all part of one giant mystery in the heavens, bisected by a swirling line of fire. That portion stood different, a falling star, a comet, no, an asteroid maybe, shooting toward a double line. *Earth*, she thought, or some version of it.

Scott squeezed in by this time, grunting. "Didn't think I was going to fit." His voice carried dull in the room. "What the hell?" he soon said about the glyphs. "Our night sky? Where's that thing we followed? And what the fuck was that out there? Jesus. I can't see anything but these stars. Why are they kind of glowing?"

"Will you shut up a minute?" Greta said. "Your eyes will adjust." There was something about this place, something familiar that calmed her while she caught her breath.

"Where's that goat?" Scott asked.

"You know what *shut up* means?"

"I think so."

Greta examined the ceiling and walls, eyes slow to adjust, wondering if this was where indigenous inhabitants came to understand the stars, the night, the sky, cosmic relations between things. She felt *she, Scott*, even the goat-fawn, didn't belong, that this was far more sacred than they ever could be. Then she thought about Hannah, how she should be here, then about ancient knowledge, how the past was collected, how it was remembered, the question of how anyone could just know that an asteroid had fallen millions of years before they arrived, though maybe this wasn't that at all, but another *something* that crashed into an ancient civilization, that cratered a culture so devastatingly that others had to remember, to record, before the colonizer apocalypse spread its disease and hate and some other false memories. She was part of that. She then wondered what could be read in the rocks, what the story of this place might be, who had been here, what ancient woman might have stared at this painted night sky, what kind of music and fire and smoke might have played a part, made the stars dance, and the asteroid fly from its belt of ruthenium. She wanted to know if that woman hid from monsters too, or welcomed them, or made all of it, everything.

There's murder in these rocks.

Greta could see more now. She could pull out Polaris. She could see the dippers, other constellations, and some squiggly lines of dots she wasn't sure about. She could see a story here, and knew she was a part of it somehow, that others had known this, what had been out there, because there in the corner, a crude drawing, a kind of giant bird sweeping low over human figures, drawings reminiscent of those in the Cave of Hands, or the cave art in France: Chauvet, Lascaux, Arcy-sur-Cure, Gargas. All remnants of picto-language, of storytelling, of lives that could see through time and space. She wondered how the goat-fawn had unlocked this, or maybe someone had unlocked a part of the world and sent it here. And then she wondered about an even stranger connection, if those decades-old murders in the canyon between sheepherders and cattle drivers Tiller once told her about had really been something else, a cover-up of some kind . . .

And then she saw them, not the stars, or the painting of the bird. *Them.* Just outside a beam of broken light lay the goat-fawn staring at Greta, mouth closed, body tucked into a ball, broken leg jutting at a sad angle. It was difficult to see, but behind that sliver of sun on the creature, even farther back in the room's darkest shadow, she could see someone.

Him.

Tiller.

"We wondered where you went," she said.

"Who's that? Tiller in here?" Scott said. "I thought his ass was eaten by that bird-thing. Man, I still can't see shit. Is that goat bitch gonna eat my face?"

"You knew everything," she said to Tiller.

"Never thought I'd want to go back to Star Valley," Scott interrupted. "Furniture shop ain't looking bad right now. Can hide out in the office, read the latest *Spider-Punk* and *Savage Avengers*. Anyplace better than out here in this shit."

"Stop it," Greta said to Scott. "You're not going to Star Valley or anywhere if we don't figure this out." To Tiller she added: "Tell us what that thing is."

Tiller, cold as usual: "What *what* is?"

"I hear you now," Scott said. "Can kind of see you too—cold motherfucker."

"Both," Greta said. "The thing in here. The big thing out there."

"The bird is death and the canyon. The goat-fawn is your protection, but wasn't supposed to be as helpful as it has been," Tiller said. "Like the bear head and those things in your pocket."

"My stuffed mice?"

"You knew it when you stole them. Those weren't even supposed to be your protection. No magic . . . in them. No spell laid and chanted into their hides. You turned them."

"I didn't." She suddenly remembered her dream of the mice and what they told her, and how magic had touched them, and maybe . . .

"Something in you did," he said. "Saw them crawling in that bear fur when you were asleep."

"What are you talking about stuffed mice?" Scott said. "We've got a fucking goat-deer and a giant-ass condor. I'm not worried about a damn mouse."

Greta took a long breath, the kind she wished was filled with smoke, not the grime of this canyon. Her adrenaline was still running hot, but she needed to preserve energy, to think.

"Tiller's dad Bobby made the goat-fawn in his taxidermy shop," she said to Scott.

"You're telling me that thing is alive and isn't?" Scott pointed. "I thought it was some goat with mange. Can goats get that? That thing's stuffed? *No.* No way."

Greta spoke to Tiller: "What's happening to those calves?"

"You saw what happened," Tiller said.

"Look, you better tell us this shit straight," Scott said. "If you know something, tell us."

"Or what?" Tiller said. "There's something worse out there. You can't stop it."

"One of those rifles will change that."

"I took the bullets," Tiller said.

"Cold-ass motherfucker," Scott said again. "What did you do with them?"

"Tossed them in the creek."

An uneasiness hit Greta, something even more disturbing than what was happening, the idea that Tiller had been a willing participant. Something about his voice was off too. He'd been wounded.

"You knew the condor was here," she said.

"It only wants you," Tiller said. "And all the cows."

"All of them?" Scott said.

"So you brought us here to die," she said.

"Wait, there's a giant fucking bird out there, and you talk to it?" Scott said. "Nothing you two are saying, or that I've seen in the last ten minutes, is making sense. I must be high right now at the campfire. That's where I am, right? High as a damn kite with that buffalo still staring at me."

"Why does it want us?" Greta asked.

Tiller was slow to answer, and wasn't budging from where he sat. "That was the arrangement," he said. "People and cows. At least two humans, and cattle."

She could tell his breath was coming with some effort. But she still had questions, so kept him talking. "So, everything was an act?"

"Not everything."

"What wasn't?"

"The calves disappearing outside the canyon. The fact that I kind of changed my mind, wanted to save the both of you. I tried to get Scott to leave. Then I . . . offered those bonuses. These are tough choices."

The Pope always said that kind of garbage right before he slapped me across the room, Greta thought. This was Tiller admitting something. "We don't want your charity," she said. Right away she regretted saying that, knowing that if anything, she could have used this moment, though she didn't know for what.

"Speak for yourself," Scott said.

"You don't have to believe me," Tiller said. "It is what it is."

"All right, you lovers can stop all that right now," Scott said. "I don't give a fuck. I can do the math. And this ain't looking good for you two, because I'm for getting the hell out of this canyon. You can fight over who else dies."

"Yeah, why don't you just look out for yourself," Greta said.

"Why not?" Scott barked. "No one else is."

"The canyon isn't going to let you go," Tiller said.

"You mean the bird," Greta said.

"That too. One and the same."

"Watch me." Scott turned to crawl back through the same hole they'd come through. "I'm out of here."

"Don't." Greta grabbed Scott. "Don't you leave me here."

Scott pulled away but didn't slip into the hole. Instead, he turned and sat. "You done asking that fool questions?"

Greta turned to Tiller, still ignoring his labored breathing. "What about all those stories you told us about the Sheep and Cattle Wars when we were in school? You talked about a few in specific: the Ten Sleep Murders, the Spring Creek Raid, all those missing families. Cattlemen murdering sheepherders or something like that. You always said your great-grandpa had been involved, that he was let go by county sheriffs. You were almost proud of it. Was that really what happened a hundred years ago?" she asked.

"What do you think?" Tiller said.

"I think that was probably around the last time there was one of these birds," she said, "the last time dead creatures came to life. Maybe the last time this canyon was filled with monsters."

"Thereabouts."

"And there was an arrangement then?"

"And an older one from before," he said. "Before my family took over."

Greta could only imagine who the arrangement was taken from. "And?"

"We made a new contract."

"With who?"

"He already told you," Scott said. "He talks to a *bird*—a giant fucking dinosaur bird." Then to Tiller: "Do you sit down, drink beers with the thing, chat about baseball, then write up a contract? How does that jumbo feather duster even fit into a chair? Or is it all done in a hot tub? Sounds fun."

Tiller ignored Scott. "The mother canyon."

"What do you mean *mother canyon*? Is someone else here?" Greta asked.

"It's not like that."

Greta remembered how Tiller's dad acted after she asked about seeing a strange bird, how he said a land like this has history bled into the rocks: *Any curse there was we wrung out of the land years ago. All them immigrants. All them Indians before that. All them sheep lands too. It was a curse to graze or run cattle on the same land as them sheepherders—you know that, right? We fixed that too . . . a long time ago. So, if you're seeing things, that's you trying to bring something back that's been gone long as I can remember.*

"Where did the bird come from?" she asked.

"Remember the condor that died after being seen on Medicine Bow Peak?"

"What condor?" Scott said. "What are you two even talking about?"

"That was a different bird," Greta said. "And it died. They found it near Laramie. This other one must be an ancient species." She tried to remember any field marks she'd seen as it tore apart the second calf. It was obviously condor-like or vulture-like, though this was way out of her expertise. Surely, nothing like this was supposed to exist in the current world. Then she remembered more field marks. Not only was this bird gargantuan, it had a toothlike ridge in its bill that she glimpsed when it passed. The head and cheeks were mottled dark green and yellow. Same on a neck that had blue feathers here and there. The side-facing eye, she could now remember, had glanced her way, bore witness to her in its canyon, like some kind of night heron, the color of blood.

"It laid an egg," Tiller said.

"You're shitting me," Scott said. "A condor laid a damn dino egg?"

"That's why she came all the way from California," Tiller said. "And that's why she died. Everything in that rare bird, every ounce of life, transferred to that egg. Everything she was, everything her past was. No fertilization happened between her and any other condor. She just came and laid an egg, her DNA somehow connected to that of a creature five, six million years ago. Maybe even older than that."

"I thought you two were buddies," Scott said. "You mean, she didn't tell you her age or social security number?"

"The past never wants to die," Tiller said. "Not all of it. The mother canyon won't let go of her history. She has a supernatural connection to our prehistory. That's how this thing keeps on."

"Keeps on what?" Greta asked.

"Doing what she does for as long as she does. Until the next egg comes, or she lays one herself, or dies. Or some other creature is born. I'm not sure. Maybe I'm supposed to take an egg back home if there's another, freeze it for a while. A relative of mine was around the last time, one of the only survivors, a little girl. She inherited all of this, passed this on to my grandfather, then my dad, prepared the way. She was my grandmother, Bernice."

Scott shook his head. "I knew your family was fucked up. But you're telling me this thing was created by a condor out of thin air? This thing that's nearly the size of a Cessna."

"Condors can do that," Tiller said.

"He's right," Greta added. "Parthenogenesis. Spontaneous embryonic development. A lot of animals can."

"Virgin birth," Tiller said.

Greta nodded. "Something like that."

"A portal to the past," Tiller said.

"Partho-whatever-the-fuck, that thing's a demon dragon," Scott said. "I'm all for killing the bitch and going home."

"We can't just go kill her. Not without bullets. We need to know more about her first," Greta said. "What can you tell us?"

"*Argentavis*," Tiller said. "Giant teratorn. Related to it anyway. Probably doesn't feed the same. Probably isn't the same. Fossils have been found from the Andean foothills to the Argentine pampas. But that would be a different species. Maybe we call this *Wyomtavis*."

"Kind of don't care about the name," Greta said.

"So we got a dino-condor, a supernatural mother-fucking-canyon that Tiller's family got connected to somehow, two stuffed mice, a bear head, a goat-fawn, fizzers and fish-walkers, oh, and a bison and ghosts," Scott said. "Not to mention the threat of other ancient creatures. Anything else, besides the fact that Tiller wants us dead? Come on, Greta. We need to get to the goddam quads."

"You think you can kill the bird, or run away?" Tiller said. "No one can run. You think Zollers is alive? Or Bill Cherry? Doubt either escaped. You learn the hard way sometimes. This whole canyon is a bed of vengeance. The creatures and us? We're just caught in the middle. Ain't any of us evil."

"Speak for yourself, asshole," Scott said. "Pretty sure that sacrificing your friends constitutes the dark side."

"Still want us to die?" Greta asked.

"I don't know about any of this anymore," Tiller said.

Just then the goat-fawn got up, dragged itself close to Scott, and collapsed.

"Man, get away from me," Scott said. "Creepy little bitch."

The goat-fawn ignored him, rested its head on its legs.

"I don't understand," Greta said, "bringing us and the cattle here to sacrifice. All for what?"

Tiller cleared his throat. "To live . . ."

"To live what?"

Tiller seemed to be listening.

Greta started listening too. Fizzers could be heard near the opening, shuffling around, hissing and spitting, maybe chewing on something, *a piece of a calf*, she thought, then repeated her question.

"To keep this canyon ours," Tiller said.

"So that the government won't take it?"

"Maybe."

She knew what he was saying between the lines—he and his dad *wanted to live forever*.

"I'm saying, we just kill the bird," Scott said.

Tiller groaned. "Doesn't work that way."

Just then a horrendous scream from the limestone canyon.

"That bird is insane," Scott said.

"It wasn't the bird," Greta replied.

"What are you talking about? Wasn't a calf."

"Vultures don't have vocal cords," she said.

"Maybe the mother canyon," Tiller said. "It knows the calves are almost gone."

"What happens when they're dead?" Greta asked.

"The bird will take the rest of what the canyon is owed. You, the cows. Me if I don't get away. My protection is almost gone. Not supposed to stick around. If I had some of the paste that Dad used on the taxidermy, it might fix me up. But Dad told me not to bring any. It's only for . . ."

"Maybe Bobby didn't want you to get away," Greta said.

"What about your little deer-goat thing?" Scott asked. "Can you tell it to distract the bird so we can get to the quads?"

The goat-fawn turned its head toward Scott.

"And go where?" Greta said. "We can't outrun the bird to any kind of wifi. And then we'd have to outrun it again just to stay safe."

"You want to die in here?" Scott said. "That huge bird is the only one eating. I don't even have any water. Unless you still do."

"Let's think about this." Greta tossed him her bottle. "How does the bird operate, maybe we can use that knowledge against her. *Her*, right?"

"Just a guess." Tiller shifted his weight and wheezed.

Still thinking, Greta could see the glyph stars clearer now, the painted bird too. She wondered if someone sat in here once with the same problem, then she tried to think how they might have solved it. "We need to understand how she flies, her wing load, her nest," she said. "How she takes off and lands. Maybe she's a glider. Maybe she needs something high to jump from to even fly. Maybe she has limits to what she can carry."

"If it can pick up a calf, it can pick my ass up," Scott said. "Doesn't even matter anyway. It can just hold us down and pull our faces off."

"Maybe she exits that hole some other way over a large cliff," she said, "then comes back through her den, flying back out the front."

"Hell of an assumption," Scott said. "You got some

dynamite? We can blow her the fuck up, eat teratorn nuggets all the way back to Ten Sleep."

"If we don't figure this out, we're going to sit in here and starve."

"Good," Scott said. "If anyone's starving, it's me while you two throw yourselves into its den."

Greta ignored him. "She can't eat too much, or she won't be able to fly. She's just killing."

"*Just?*"

"It's not overeating," Tiller said. "And she's not working alone. It's the canyon. It's the past. The *mother past*. This thing is smarter than you and I. She was in my grandmother. I seen her in Bernice's eyes a thousand times. The canyon is cunning, ruthless, and would rid the world of people, if allowed."

Scott let out a groan, then: "Isn't that what you're doing?"

"What happened to Bernice?" Greta asked.

"Don't know."

"Time and space are an awful bitch," Scott said. "Maybe we can get away while it digests Tiller."

"Do you know what condors do when they eat too much and need to fly all of a sudden?" Greta said. "They void their entire stomach contents. They vomit."

"So?"

"I don't know. Fun fact I guess."

"Look, I want a helicopter gunship," Scott said. "I want the cavalry. I want some surface-to-air rockets to take out that feathered cruise missile." He looked at the goat-fawn. It hadn't lifted its head for some time. "You didn't answer me. Will this, or them, or whatever protect us in the hole, cavern, cave, wherever the bird flew? Or maybe back down the trail?"

Greta felt something strange just then . . . like the air in the room shifted . . . She grabbed the stuffed mice from her pocket. They'd stopped moving. Their legs crumbled in her palm. The fur seemed to collapse, wilt. She let out a gasp, wanting to cry. "They're gone," she whispered, heart hurting, then she slipped their remains back in her pocket.

"Twice dead," Scott added. "Guess that answers that."

"Their protection was always limited," Tiller said. "I was supposed to get away before the goat-fawn died. Along with other taxidermy you never saw, it was only supposed to protect you from the things she birthed and to guide us here. It's what Dad learned to do to ward off the power of this canyon . . . the *magic* . . . the same that cattlemen stole . . . my family stole . . . But this protection changed. Something in you did it, Greta. I think they gave you extra protection. Maybe they want you to live and for me to die since I messed things up. Maybe they want the contract with my family to break."

"I have a feeling you fucked that arrangement a long time ago," Greta said.

"You don't understand family duty," Tiller said. "You don't know what's been expected of me . . . I hate that I can't be what my old man wants . . . but how am I to help it? I'm not him, will never be him, not completely . . ."

"Which is what?" Greta asked, wanting to give him a lesson on family duty, something she'd both succeeded and failed in.

Tiller was quiet for some time, then cleared his throat. He didn't get a chance to speak.

"You know what?" Scott interrupted. "How do we know Tiller even got all the bullets? He's been lying since he called our asses to come work for him. Probably planning to steal back the money he paid us."

Tiller didn't say anything.

"Solid question," Greta agreed, then to Tiller: "How do we know you got all the bullets?"

"You don't." Tiller winced loudly this time. "Want to go look?"

"Daylight's nearly gone, and it doesn't sound like she's finished killing the calves," Greta said. "Why are you hurt anyway? What's wrong?"

"Got bit."

"You only now tell us?" Scott said.

Greta wondered aloud: "By the goat-fawn?"

"Your bear head. When I was stealing the bullets. Apparently, it latched onto you in ways I don't understand. Was protecting you from me, though it should only have been protecting you from her, from monsters. I think the bite is infected. I need . . ."

"Chewed on by a decapitated bear," Scott said. "Doesn't get any better. Lies don't get any weirder."

Tiller turned on a flashlight, pulled open his tattered coat and lifted his blood-drenched shirt. His pale skin, ghost-washed by the light, revealed a partial bite, not horribly deep, but purple-red gashes dripped blood down his side. All the skin around the bites had inflamed into red-pink welts.

Greta still didn't tell them she saw the bird picking up a dead calf that first day of the drive. Sure, maybe she—*the bird*—was supposed to stay in the canyon, but that wasn't happening either, yeah? Maybe the contract had already changed, was always changing, and this time *this* canyon, or bird, had the upper hand over people, even the Tillers. Either way, no one was getting out anytime soon, not out of this room, not out of the canyon, and not far enough away.

Night fell while they still debated, and with it, the remaining light. For hours all Greta could hear was breathing and the killing of not just the calves, but the cows, most of which they could hear stampeding in every direction, a few up the switchbacks.

The herd was lost.

And that hurt, like losing Hannah.

There was never meant to be a cattle drive. They were never meant to get farther than this spot. And now Greta had to figure a way out, and about all she had to help was a skittish friend, and a bear head. And for the night at least, she and Think Tank were separated—if he was even still *alive*-dead. Could he be? She'd never even seen him snap those jaws. And that made her suddenly think that maybe the bear head had been biding his time, saving his remaining energy, or magic, for moments like this. And maybe, just maybe, Think Tank still had something left to give.

And while the taxidermy had protected her, their magic, she knew, wasn't keeping the bird away from the herd. Not anymore. The canyon needed blood, and was taking all it could get. At least for the night, whatever was left in the goat-fawn was keeping the fizzers out of this place, though she could hear them *fizzing* closer now and then, knocking at the door.

The People

The People, whose tribal name shall remain unspoken, came down the frigid western coastline of what sixteen thousand years later would be called North America, in canoes made of overlapping bark and whale tendon.

Fires burned in their boats within insulated baskets, keeping them, their children, and their pets warm. They constantly foraged along their journey, eating mostly shellfish and seal meat, though sometimes they caught flightless sea ducks, roasted them on shorelines, and strung feathers on elk and other mammal hides that they used as garments. Sometimes they scraped and cut flesh from beached whales and used the fat to soothe aching joints and rashes. And then cut into whale heads for their yellow oil and some of them smeared the balm on their skin, or used it as grease on torches, or sprayed the sticky substance from their mouths on fires, and then sang to their ancestors to reveal the journey their children would one day take to the interior, for they knew that moment would come, that time moved both slow and fast, perhaps together like stars sliding with the curve of the milky night sky.

Soon, even more of the People arrived. They made shelters among ice floes where seals, shorebirds, flightless ducks, crabs, and mollusks were abundant. They frequented a similar area farther south, a mile inland from an island, and built more shelters there, and stayed during the rains to watch the seaside snow melt. That was the spring they noticed forests growing along the waterline, not just inland, and observed small warblers fly in to breed and nest during the spring and part of the summer, then leave with their young, and return again. This happened twice per year, and wasn't only warblers, but so many other birds coming and going, heading south, or heading north, generation after generation of them, always so hungry, eating every berry, seed and insect they could find. And this happened offshore too, seabirds eating anchovies or sardines, depending on the season, and sometimes the horizon was filled with loons and shearwaters and sea ducks, even endless streams of fat pigeons, and other times the birds would disappear, and parts of the year many flew north in great numbers, including clouds of colorful parrots, and other parts of the year many species flew southward. And some birds were always there, the tiny plovers, the cormorants, pelicans and oystercatchers. And sometimes the People ate the larger birds, though they didn't take more than they could eat, and respected the nests, and never took all of the eggs, and sang to the little ones after they hatched. And they were also haunted by these animals, saw ghosts in them that reminded them of their People in the far north, and in this way were haunted by their ancestors who also ghost-walked among them like shadows in the fog or darkness, and stood naked outside their shelters and stared, eyes black, mouths open, smoke exiting nostrils, tongues black and shiny. And those ancestors sometimes stole members of their tribe and carried them into frigid waters, drowning them.

Two hundred years later the People knew every cove and inlet and storm shelter, and knew the land many days and nights into the interior. During this time, the People still made canoes in the same manner from downed trees and beached whale skin and tendon, and they patrolled the waters, and because the frigidness of all the seasons still lingered, they burned wood down to coal in their boats, the young attending to the fires, sometimes dogs in their laps, and foraged the coastlines, though sometimes they saw their ancestors standing in a line in the water, beckoning them to enter and never return.

Sometimes mammoths the size of tiny bison, but much wider, with round heads and long nose-trunks followed them when they explored the shores, bounding along, curiously grabbing at their faces and tickling their ears, singing in strange honks like the geese that sometimes filled the sky. Children called these pygmy mammoths *snoutytrunks*, and some became pets, living with The People many years. And then it seemed only a few more were seen briefly far inland, and then their tiny kind were no more, though there were the giant shaggy mammoths with fatty humps on their backs, and the shorter-legged mastodons with flatter heads, and both could be any color of bark or earth or clay, and all bellowed like angry mountains and whales, and the males were violent and crushed some of the People, who hunted their kind.

Some of the People's shelters were completely covered in mammoth and mastodon furs, and the beds sometimes were of the same thick hides. When the People killed a male, there would be an especially abundant feast, and they raised the meat to the stars and told stories of milk and abundance, and left some to rot for their ancestors, who still lured some of their numbers to drown in the sea. And it seemed some of these ghosts would reappear far inland, including that of a young woman who hovered in the sky above their canoes, and some saw men paddling in one of the boats after her and they got swept over a waterfall after the ghost, and those men were no more. And then she was seen again in the village, not flying, but eating the face of a young child, then carting the corpse to the sea.

The People felt that the sky and heavens had allowed them bountiful seaside harvests, which gave them hope for fewer turbulent storms. Sometimes the grey could last not only through winter but most of the summer, and the rain and snow could be murderous, especially since they believed the storms and cold were what brought their ancestors, who would visit their dreams, or appear like dark trees in the snow, mouths dripping with black blood, who repeated amid their gurgles: *Wait for boats from the south, from an unknown tribe, that is when your new journey must take place. You will know.*

The People also fed on mussels and abalone through the years, thinking the sea's nourishment would help prepare them for an eventual journey, possibly inland, that this nourishment would increase their numbers, and connect them to the ancestors they abandoned long ago. They continued to forage blubber, skin, and oil from beached whales, which they found by the musky death scent on the tides that came to their nostrils like a hurt in the ocean. They said whales cried close to shore when their dead washed up, and the elders thought the whales maybe knew their ancestors, or maybe some were their ancestors hiding prophecy. The

People wailed with the pods, and afterward, some of the tribe would swim into the sea and be nevermore.

More glaciers and ice cracked and broke, glittering like sapphiric jewels. This was where waters rushed into the sea, close to the constant melt, where nearby forests spread across hills and mountains, their tree lines filled with exuberant birds. There, rodents scurried into holes, and foxes snatched them by their tails, and bears mostly ate fish and berries, and slow-moving giant sloths consumed almost more fruit than any other animal. The sloths were easy to hunt, and stood like towers of stone, and quickly disappeared from the land. There were also giant squish-snouted bears, and big cats with fangs like curved boneknives, and towering flightless birds that the People hunted for their eggs and meat. Amid all of this, many deer and elk, camels and small horses drank water from ponds. And nearby, where the People lived, they built pits, and gathered around them, and burned bones and flesh, and discussed their affairs and the arrival that was destined to come.

One day, two canoes came from the south, having paddled for months and months. The elders, upon seeing these strangers dragging strange boats ashore, worried these weren't their People fulfilling words carried from the past.

The elders didn't know the squarer shapes of these canoes, the way their strange bark lay in the water or rested on land. Nor did they recognize the color of the boats and the curious trees from which the hulls were constructed. Nor did they recognize the odd shape of the travelers' short-cut hair, the paint on their chins and shoulders, all so different. Some elders thought these men and women must be *the dead journeying back to them*, because before they arrived there had been two strange sightings. Some of the

People's ancestors appeared above a seal colony swarming amid school of fish in the surf. Arms to their sides, blood poured from eyes and nostrils before these floating spectral women descended into the swells and sank. The same dead women appeared later in the village by rising from fire pit flames, and said,

They are almost here.

And the People thought then that maybe many of the dead were going to arrive. But these strangers were flesh and blood and didn't leak gore and understood the ancient language from *before* still spoken by elders, and convinced the People that they'd paddled for months, *chased by ghosts*, and had carried with them a portion of an ancestral mother-prophecy, and said that it must be carried into the interior of the land, farther than they'd traveled along and *between* shorelines.

The elders put their trust in these strangers and held a great meeting and feast where it was decided that a few of their number would venture along the rivers for many suns to find what the strangers called the *mother-den in the great canyon*, where the elders hoped were fewer glaciers and warmer air, for this was close to the time of no-ice, of forest blankets and veinlike waterways. More trees were waiting to be born, the elders reassured the strangers, telling them that flowers were blossoming in jeweled prairies and petal-filled mountains.

Even so, the elders warned that while venturing northeastward any travelers would likely encounter frozen mountains, and must be prepared for *ice-land* journeys, and would have to cross glaciers pocked with crystal-blue chasms and waterfalls that fell to the heart of the earth.

The elders, hoping the dead would finally stop haunting

them, said they would send ten with the strangers. But the strangers shook their heads, said they would only travel back home, that those interior lands would be certain death, that they could not survive the *ice-lands*. The strangers said that where they were from there had been no snow and ice for many generations except in the highest mountains. They said their mother prophets told them others must be appointed, that those must be young and strong, and must build families to spread from this snowball earth from where the People live.

The People told the strangers that it was not a snowball earth anymore but a slush earth, and in parts even a dry earth, because the summers had grown warm, and everywhere the rocks and beaches held broken ice, if any at all. It melted into carpets of moss, and in some places, reeds grew thick, along with countless creatures and birds. Still the strangers insisted they must travel south again. It had already been an incredibly long journey, they said, then revealed the prophecy, a *gift*, which wasn't knowledge, but something they must protect. They said they'd come with nearly twenty boats, and lost most of them to storms and sea creatures, some on land as well, that many of their greatest warriors and hunters had been killed or drowned. Even attaining the gift in the first place had taken an entire generation of brave men and women to climb the clouds to a sky island and survive return journeys until they finally retrieved the gift.

The People's village, amid a cluster of rocks that served as protection against both elements and creatures, included many rock paintings and drawings, and right away their shaman scrawled images of the travelers, their boats, their stories, their gift. Then the elders said they would heed the strangers, honor them, and pull from their own warriors to make the journey. The elders then gave of the land to the strangers, and bestowed upon them bags of petals and seeds, and potent glands of various creatures, and in return, received the gift which had been bundled in several layers of llama hides.

The gift had to be taken to where a meeting of interstellar and earth-fires and floods and upheaval had taken place very long ago, a canyonland of long-dead monsters, where endless fire and death from fallen mountains and ash clouds had ravaged the land long *long* ago. The elders and the strangers both saw in their visions that this catastrophe had occurred three times, and that from them most of life ended and mountains were born and reborn, and that was where long-dead ocean beds once percolated with the beginnings of things. These visions contained strange green beads of life which flourished and wriggled even in asteroid craters that left great fissures in the earth, and these creatures were so tiny that they could not be seen unless beneath a large bubble, and some algae beads had been frozen in beds of rock and time, while other beads had grown and thrived and bore the fruit of life and transformed, sprouting lungs and fins, then hands and feet, and became the fish and birds and lizards, even men and women.

The strangers soon returned to their southern lands while the elders selected a young warrior woman, Pye'ta'wa'wawi, their most precious and adored hunter, to become a great tribal mother of the interior. The elders painted red suns upon her skin with dyes made from orange-brown pond-surface creatures heated with bear grease. Afterward, she beamed with brilliant star patterns, and was made the holder of the mother-prophecy and gift. Her lover, Večkwani, a fisherman and boat builder, was given a carved shell-hook necklace, and was told to help keep the mother-prophecy and gift safe. Both were appointed the leaders of the ten. Pye'ta'wa'wawi said she would also bring her dog, Mo'n, which sat and scratched a floppy ear for a long while, then chased a pair of small, husky horses, each with plump white bellies, dark red-brown heads, and short, spiky manes. Some of the children rode them. Mo'n barked and nipped and licked, then soon curled next to a bowl of coals that had been placed in the lead boat.

It was early summer when they left in four canoes with the gift, which they placed next to one of the fires, and began their long journey eastward on a meandering river.

Soon they lost one of the boats on river rocks, their rowers having to walk back toward the coast. They were never seen again, so dangerous was this land even close to the village. More boats were lost a month later, torn apart by the largest giant bear any had ever encountered. The bear stood more than ten feet tall in the morning light. Its striped, tan-and-brown head had a squished snout, long teeth, and claws that could tear heads from necks. The bear wandered into camp, mauled several sleeping men and women, eating much of their bowels, tearing into their crushed heads, feasting on brains and tongues. A young warrior, sneaking to the bear while it chewed grey matter, put a spear into its rib cage. Even so, the bear ripped the young man's head away, and after smashing boats, fled with the remains into the forest.

Pye'ta'wa'wawi, Večkwani, and Mo'n had protected the gift during the bear attack by setting out from shore in the only undamaged boat. Pye'ta'wawi wanted to stay and fight, as did Mo'n, barking and snarling, but Večkwani pulled Pye'ta'wa'wawi away, convincing her that the gift was more precious than any of them, that the lives of those being killed had already been given before any blood had been spilled. Mo'n followed.

They paddled away from the cries and screams and when they returned, found two maimed women who soon died. Pye'ta'wa'wawi agreed they still had to find the canyon and fulfill the mother-prophecy, and then told Wečkwani a secret, that she was with child.

And now she told him they must grow their family in the lands where the mother-prophecy would be fulfilled, and must arrive before the child was born. They wrapped their dead loved ones in skins, painted symbols of the shores of the afterworld on their bodies, and buried them in shallow earth with their favorite necklaces.

Then they tracked the bear into the forest, and found him dying. It could hardly lift its head or move, and Pye'ta'wa'wawi said she forgave him, and touched the bear's short squish-snout, and the bear groaned, wanted to growl, but couldn't. Wečkwani retrieved the hunter's spear from the beast's rib cage. Heartblood poured in a great gush.

They then cut out the liver, and took several claws, and some of its hide, then left the rest for the animals of the forest to consume. Then they found the head of the hunter who stabbed the bear and wrapped it in some of the hide to bury with the others, and trekked back to their bloody camp and broken boats.

Afterward, they talked to the shrubs and trees and grasses, asking them to grow upon the graves, to spread their roots between the bones of their brothers and sisters. And then they asked the sun to watch for their spirits, and begged the moon to guard over them too, and for the stars to watch over memories, to place them alongside those of their ancestors, to add them to the milk of star-heavens' long story, one that would take many lifetimes to tell.

It was here one of the ancestor's ghosts appeared. She bent unnaturally, frozen like an ancient, gnarled tree. The ghost bled from her eyes, and trilled and pulled out all of her hair, making blood pour from her scalp. Then she demanded they leave, and and said that she would take care of the dead warriors' travels. Another ghost flew from the forest over the river, and as the three set out, the other ghost stood on the shoreline, and the river ghost hung in the air, and both pointed to the east.

After several more weeks, navigating rivers through sections of canyons and mountainous terrain, Wečkwani asked if they were close to what Pye'ta'wa'wawi started calling mother canyon. He asked this every morning before they set out. For days she wouldn't answer until finally telling him how the elders held secret meetings with her, and bestowed upon her the sight needed in order for them to find the mother canyon's steep walls. She told him it was in the stars and the seasons, that the birds and animals would also hint at the way. She read their signs, listened to their calls and songs, watched their flight patterns, and dreamspoke with them.

The nights grew longer and colder, and as they traveled they began to notice more ice packing river shorelines and lakes. Sometimes entire glaciers bordered their path. Towers of ice dropped like falling mountains, and still they paddled around lake icebergs and snaked along fractured ridges and wind-scoured islands, paddling through skims of ice that connected river paths. They often slept on the frost-stiffened ground, sometimes constructing igloos of ice chunks, their faces reddened, lips cracked, and near to starving.

Soon portions of the landscape turned iceless, and Pye'ta'wa'wawi said they were within several weeks' walk of the mother canyon. There they abandoned their boat, which they hated to leave, for it had served them for many months.

They entered a wide, endless savannah filled with wildgrasses and trees, herds of zebras, camel, horse, and deer, and all manner of mammoths, mastodons, and sloths.

Pye'ta'wa'wawi tamed both a young camel and one of the small, stocky, dun-colored horses. She then spotted one of the stunted mammoths that her grandmother said children once called *snoutytrunks*, a cute fuzzy male filled with joy and curiosity. He honk-honked and begged for his ears to be scratched. The creature followed them for many days, and brought them fruit, and loved its trunk pet and scratched, and also to tickle and snort on Mo'n, which made the dog whine for more.

Pye'ta'wa'wawi spent several weeks teaching both the horse and camel to carry their supplies, and tried with the tiny mammoth, but it always wanted to play, even in the middle of the night, and soon wandered off to eat from a lush orchard of sweet-smelling fruits and was surrounded by sloths and deer, and they could hear its squealy honk-honk as they climbed through the valley, and were sad when they no longer heard it, though Mo'n's ears occasionally perked at an unknown trumpet. When that ended too the dog cried and barked, hoping the pygmy mammoth would come back and play.

The next morning they woke to the tiny mammoth at the edge of their fire. But this time something was off. It stood with its head cocked to the side, and tried to hop, but its legs were stiff. It had a deep slash in its side exposing ribs and pink meat and was missing half an ear. Along with that, its eyes were empty sockets, and its trunk was caked in an oily grime. Otherwise, it appeared to be the same creature. Mo'n growled and walked up to it, sniffing, and the *mammoth-thing* lifted its trunk, excited. Then Mo'n whined in both confusion and recognition, and sniffed and licked at the trunk probing her neck, and almost growled but didn't.

Then from the distance, an apparition appeared, an elder male warrior, then another, a woman carrying a spear, and beyond them, a line of *apparitions*, dark in the distance like statues of night ice, draped in the hides of the ancestral northern tribe. The closest ghost moved toward Pye'ta'wa'wawi without walking, and told her, *This is the last of our protection. We have created this creature anew to make balance against the canyon-den. She is the mother and may distrust you, but with this creature will protect you with death magic until the mother sees your worth. Be wary with who you share this knowledge*, and then the ghost, bleeding from his eyes like the others they'd seen, touched Pye'ta'wa'wawi on the lips with a blackened hand, and she took a breath and *knew*.

Pye'ta'wa'wawi and Wečkwani soon journeyed again, the dead mammoth following, but not always at their side. Mo'n strayed from the couple and walked only with the *alive*-dead tiny mammoth, which now stepped unnaturally, and tried to hop, then tried to swing its trunk and show its excitement as protector. And while the creature did not sleep, at night it curled on the ground, trunk flopped over Mo'n's haunches, the dog snoring after licking at the mammoth's wounds.

The travelers ate from the animals of the plains and sewed warmer skins for themselves, hides from a dead bison that fell off a cliff, for there was a chill now in the daylight, and deep grey skies, and the temperature dropped severely at night, and many areas again became covered with thin layers of snow and ice, and low thick glaciers they had to cross, while also seeing that the *great thaw* happened here the way the elders said it would. Though winter hadn't fully arrived, they knew it would be severe, yet believed the next spring and summer would reveal even more of an abundant land.

After a bright fire-colored hummingbird with a throat of orange jewels landed on her hand, Pye'ta'wa'wawi said they were finally close. She and the tiny fire-bird were in conversation for several long moments, the bird's needlelike tongue flicking, as if speaking or tasting, and then it desired nectar or sleep, and flew off, never to be seen again.

They built fires at night in a perimeter as best they could, and sometimes found little caves to protect themselves from bears, dire wolves, and giant cats, though they knew these creatures wouldn't prey on them, not like the bear that had killed their brothers and sisters. They would often see the squish-faced bears gnawing on bones of sloths and bison, while so many birds passed in the sky that they turned grey afternoons black as night. Pye'ta'wa'wawi said many of the birds had been birthed from mother canyon.

A few weeks later they found a canyon entrance covered in ice and snow. Pye'ta'wa'wawi said this was the sacred place. The tiny mammoth seemed to know it, and had lost more of its skin and the rest of an injured ear, though nothing fell out of its side, and that was because a patch of hide had been sewn on, keeping its mushy insides sloshing in its belly, which seemed about to burst.

Pearled rises and cliffs loomed like rock clouds, and Pye'ta'wa'wawi led them inside with Mo'n, the tiny *alive*-dead mammoth, the camel, and the horse. Not far inside they lost their camel to a hungry lion. Mo'n tried to fight off the beast, but Pye'ta'wa'wawi called the dog off, and they made their escape farther into mother canyon.

The horse loved Mo'n even before the lion attack, but now whenever the two slept, it was with the dog curled against the horse's side, twitching with dreams while the mammoth, stiffer in its steps, could no longer lie down, so stood guard.

A few days later they found a set of switchbacks from an ancient trail that led to a cave in one of the canyon's fractured, ice-covered rises. Outside the entrance stood a leaning stone tree, and a portion of what once was a nest. Pye'ta'wa'wawi said they must enter, and so Mo'n whined, and Wečkwani lit a torch, and they let the horse go, though it stayed by the entrance where they built a fire to ward off wolves and lions. The mammoth continued by their side, now dripping a blackish fluid, skin sagging from bone, reeking of death.

The hole itself bore deep through limestone, then opened to a cavern, where protruding from walls, fossils of ancient corals, squid, clams, and marine reptiles glistened in torchlight. Here, a giant squish-faced bear huddled in a kind of nest surrounded by bones. Pye'ta'wa'wawi, within weeks of giving birth, waddled up like a silent, pregnant cat and speared the bear in its sleep, and as she did, her unborn child's heart thumped rapidly inside her. Afterward, she sucked the bear's blood and thanked the creature for its life and wisdom.

Deep in the cavern they built another fire, where they unwrapped the gift, which had miraculously not broken. They'd kept it warm for months, a colorful giant egg the hue of a pale winter sky with bright wisps like rain clouds. And they surrounded the egg with hides, and Mo'n pranced around the shell like a happy mutt, and the tiny *alive*-dead mammoth tried to lift its trunk with excitement, but could hardly twitch its sagging appendage.

The mammoth-thing, in a pool of its own black liquid, let out a rattle from its withered throat and tongue. Mo'n whined at the mammoth, then lay next to the egg, and licked the shell lovingly.

Pye'ta'wa'wawi sensed the mother canyon's presence, and *her* need, just like Pye'ta'wa'wawi's, to give birth, though the canyon's was months away. Pye'ta'wa'wawi sensed the urgency to communicate of the mother canyon, which soon accepted Pye'ta'wa'wawi as another powerful mother of the canyon, and both knew that if the tiny mammoth that had guarded them were to melt away, all would be safe. Now knowing this, Pye'ta'wa'wawi walked up to the tiny mammoth-thing, and still wasn't afraid of the creature, or its sagging skin and bony eye sockets, its skull exposed from patches of skin having floated away. She sang to it about the love of hummingbirds and people and dogs and mammoths, and brought her hand over the head of the mammoth-thing without touching, and could feel the eager hum inside it, and then the magic began leaving the creature, and then, still singing, she took a torch, and set fire to the body, which went even more rigid and seemed both relieved and full of joy.

Mo'n again cried, this for their second parting.

The canyon witnessed this.

A few days later the egg cracked from the inside, and then shattered altogether, and a vulture-like nestling the size of Mo'n stumbled out. The dog cried enthusiastic whine-barks, and soon the two were best friends, and over time the bird grew its feathers, and then its body grew and grew, and more feathers appeared, and all this time Pye'ta'wa'wawi and Wečkwani struggled to bring enough food for the chick.

One day the bird, now a massive fledgling, figured out how to flap its enormous wings because Wečkwani had manufactured wings out of bones and hide and tied them to himself and practiced flapping alongside the bird. Watching Wečkwani, the bird hopped and ran and fluttered its wings, and soon began branching from rock to rock, and after some time doing that, fledged and soared.

Not long after, the bird could fly right out of the cavern, and started bringing food to share—fawns and goats mostly—though at times, they hunted together as a family.

And then Pye'ta'wa'wawi gave birth, and swaddled the child close, and after some rest, they hunted as a family once again, the baby tight to her chest, the bird startling herds of deer, and Pye'ta'wa'wawi and Wečkwani hid with Mo'n, then ambushed and took home a carcass, while the bird carried another back to a roost upon the stone tree, and ate.

Eventually Pye'ta'wa'wawi realized something different about the bird from any other creature. Besides its enormous girth—the bird had grown to the size of a mastodon—the bird could speak to her through its thoughts. It told her long stories about its ancestors, birds upon birds upon birds for many generations, and said that it knew how to bring other ancient animals back to life, but that those could only exist in and around the canyon, for mother canyon, which the bird also *was*, would soon watch over their birth. This was a special place at the heart of the world, it said, and though the world had many hearts, this was one of those sacred places.

And so Pye'ta'wa'wawi made a pact with the bird and the canyon, a sacrifice that meant caretaker, and they agreed this would occur once every hundred or so years, timed with the canyon giving birth, and with that would come a flourishing of life that would remember past life, ancient life, violent life like that closer to the beginning of things.

Then the bird said mother canyon would live in harmony with the many animals of the savannah, and basins, and mountains, and all the birds, and the people that would come, like the baby that was now part of Pye'ta'wa'wawi and Wečkwani. And the bird said it loved this, and Pye'ta'wa'wawi loved this too, and Wečkwani worshipped his family and said he also loved the canyon and bird.

Then Pye'ta'wa'wawi was told that her great-great-grandchild would find an egg similar to that which was brought, and that that grandchild's great-great-grandchild would have a great-great-grandchild who would find another egg, and that this would carry on until there was no longer anything in the world worth remembering.

And then Pye'ta'wa'wawi said, *We are the rememberers.*

The Tenth Sleep

They waited for the sun to rise and again had little rest. The familiar stench weighed heavy, and only now, after it felt like days had passed and every moon-silvered speck dissolved, did cracks of morning light appear, revealing hints of cave stars and the shadows of where others sat. Greta had succumbed to a kind of near panic while sitting in the cold dark, heart thumping in ear canals. Her head filled with memories of Hannah and the Pope as if both stood just outside the cave, whispering for her to join them.

When not dreaming, she could hear fizzers skittering over rocks—their slavering mouths bubbling and popping—and random wails of trapped cows, then sometimes the thudding of wingbeats followed by the screams of a dying creature. Sometime during the night the calf cries ceased, though other trapped cattle could be heard falling to the monster bird and fizzers.

At some point Greta's body went numb. She felt alone and lost, forgot about time, about the dark. Even the rot and the scent of stone and dust became part of her numbness—she wondered if she'd smell

anything again. Amid that, a terror, a fear, her abdomen in knots, both cramps and nausea.

And then from somewhere deep within, a will to live blossomed as if from a tiny shimmering light illuminating her heartblood. By the time morning light spilled into the cave, she felt like she could try to think, to use this remaining time, which could be her last, to maybe meditate her way into something she could use to survive all this, to escape this trap.

Her life had always been about running away from something, she knew that now. Her response to Hannah leaving her was BBQ chips and Netflix, then after pulling that late shift at the Ribs N Go and slapping rib-slick hands away, was drinking with workmates at the Lope until last call. Then rinse and repeat.

It was a last call when she'd first seen Hannah. They didn't talk but then that very night Hannah stood outside her apartment in the rain like something from a movie, a pale ghost, but also so pretty, that plain-hot pretty. And that hair so black like ink got painted into the air around her scalp, hanging long and wet. And she had indigenous features, Greta didn't know how to explain them, but knew, maybe part of it was her full lips, the shape of her eyes and face, all that ink-black hair, though could that explain those perfect eyebrows in that porchlight? That was just skill at shaping, yeah? And this not-so-perfect twenty-something had been out there for at least an hour, wouldn't even knock on the door, and wasn't wearing a raincoat, just let that water come down on her plaid coat, the one Greta now wore. And that was the thing. Greta realized it wasn't Hannah's disappearance she feared the most. It wasn't even the bird, not that it didn't terrify her. That mega-sized condor wasn't good or bad. This was about fear *before* all of this, before the cattle drive, before the *monster* monsters.

It wasn't the Pope either. He wasn't the bird. He wasn't the canyon. He wasn't Hannah. The Pope had stopped being Greta's problem years before his corpse got dragged across that lawn. She only wanted to believe he was haunting her. She let what he'd kept saying while he was alive get under her skin, when he was already powerless, had been.

It was something else, wasn't it? This uncertainty in her gut, the twisting of her own knife, always finding herself in situations she came to regret, like loving a person who ghosted her, like taking on a cattle drive when she could have done something else with her time. Like dropping out of college and not going to her dad's funeral. All these choices added up to piles of regret. And that began pre-Hannah. That kind of pain made for an invisible life. It was why Greta couldn't help her mother drag a corpse, why she rejected close friends, *herself*, everything. Maybe that thing inside her was a monster too, maybe was the *monster* monster. She thought about what her mother once told her: "You never find opportunities to better yourself. Why do you do this? Your father worked his whole life and always improved. Even when white America beat him down every chance it got."

He beat me, Greta had wanted to say.

He beat all the desire out of me.

What was my America anyway?

But then that line her mother said when she dragged him, that phrase morphing in her mind, changing a little this way and that: *I dragged him, he was in the sun, so many flies . . . he was dead dead dead . . . so I pulled him by his limp arm.*

So now Greta wondered if she could partially blame

anyone else? Her mom? The Pope? The people who oppressed him, who helped make him? Was she supposed to feel sorry for her brown father? How about those faceless colonizers? Sure, she was angry at them. Those same people eyed her every day—Tiller in a cave of stars. And now she was trapped in this cycle, she realized, one that started before she was born, long before the Pope, maybe somewhere deep in a village, somewhere north of Mexico City, maybe five thousand years before it became Mexico City. Maybe ten thousand years before that. Or maybe three million years before that on an African savannah, stone tools and teeth the only remains from some forgotten primitive war, or serial killing, before it was all buried and rained on then buried again with sharp rocks, hide, and bone.

And then she heard Tiller groan. She had plenty to groan about too. And then she thought about her future again and wondered if this was what everyone did when facing death? Realizing you're ready to beg for that one chance to restart it all? You'll make it all better, you *promise*. You'll use brand-new jumper cables. The sparks will be so perfect this time. *No need to punish with giant birds and hungry bear heads because you're going to make it right. Second chances are what America's all about. Yeah? You'll be laser focused*, she told herself. *Clarity and direction will win out. You'll have a bear head to help this time, maybe a lucky fizzer foot.* Then she asked herself: *Why did it take this happening to find the desire that had already been stripped by faulty spark plugs in my American Dream? Was the Pope this cruel?*

If she escaped all of this, she would continue her Hannah mission. The biggest clue had been sewn in her coat all along. Hannah must have known she'd wear it until that plaid thing became a stinky mess. But what now? Get on her knees and just beg for it all to go away? She couldn't do that. Wouldn't change the fact that she was in this cave with Scott in his constant panic while Tiller cried about some little bear nibble.

Call the number on the key, that's what she'd do. Break the code on the mystery. And whatever good or bad the mystery held, that wouldn't matter. Because that would end it. Then her path would be clear. She wouldn't be *that* girl anymore. She wasn't.

Even now she was only vaguely aware that Scott crawled over to her. She could smell his breath—she didn't want to smell his anything, or herself, or that rot. Not Tiller either. Not fizzer butt. *Nothing.* Except maybe Think Tank. She missed him.

"I'll see what's up," Scott said. "Wait here." And just like that, she didn't protest, so Scott left to check on the bird, the fizzers, the cows, the calves, on the deadened sun, on whether or not the moon hung above the canyon in the morning light, whether starmilk poured around the blood-rose edge of dawn.

Why hadn't she gone too? Why did she need to sit in the dark with someone who wanted her dead? Had she really been this way her entire life? Why didn't she beg him a second time to stay?

Greta started replaying how she'd been living her life, how she always said, *I'm gonna do this or that, then have this other thing to fall back on.* Downside was, she'd focused on having just enough skill to fall back on nothing, and that was the problem with doing anything. If you focused on what to fall back on, you'd never go after what you wanted. And what she really wanted was more than getting out of a cave, away from a canyon, away from *my fault* memories.

She could be someone important, and that meant to herself. She knew why she hadn't helped drag her father, and that's what hurt. She'd let her mother do the hard part. That's something Greta was never willing to do: the hard part. All of the work that would make her something in this world, even if it meant some kind of father-care, mother-care, self-care while she got there.

She tried to stop thinking about all the bullshit, focusing on the present again, wondering whether the goat-fawn, its hollow body soaking up the darkness of this place, would drag through sparks of light, come curl next to her. But it wouldn't. She could hear Tiller's labored breathing, but no movement from the creature that had protected her one last time and led her into this place. Then again, it led her to Tiller. In her confusion, she waited, even as the light turned golden, until she became vaguely aware that Scott hadn't returned.

Had he finally run? Crept down switchbacks to the quads and hightailed it? She hadn't heard a distant motor. Then again, maybe he grabbed some water and made his way on foot, far away from this slaughterhouse.

She then noticed something odd, that the goat-fawn had spilled to its side. It didn't breathe, had never breathed. But that absolute stillness told her it wasn't going to move again. Whatever protection the creature had to give had finally been expelled.

It really was just her and Tiller. His skin had turned pallid. She thought he resembled the figure she must have dreamed on the ridge that first night, a grey thing under the moonglow.

"I can't feel my pulse," he said. "I'm cold."

Greta hated him, wanted to leave him to rot next to the goat-fawn.

She thought about Bill Cherry's boots, about Scott's possible corpse splayed on a rock. Then, *Think Tank*. What was in DNA that made people and monstrous things—which maybe were one and the same—want to decapitate someone, or in this case something as precious as a bear? She knew why she was thinking about that bear head. She needed that grizzly fluff more than ever. She didn't feel or sense, or whatever—not that she believed she had some kind of power, but *maybe she did*—that the bear head had experienced its second death, though she couldn't be sure. Could she? At the same time, she knew she needed to escape the cave, that she couldn't just leave Tiller. She had to get him out too, no matter how awful he was. On her feet now, she shuffled across the small room, felt his face, his skin clammy with infection and sweat. "You have to get up, crawl out with me or you'll die here."

"I can't."

"Come on," she said. "Scott's not coming back." She tugged on him, and he moaned:

"I said . . . I can't."

"Move it," she said. "Or I'll drag your ass."

Greta pulled hard at his elbow. He groaned but he moved with her across the cold stone and pads of dirt. "Better out in that sick air, than in this tomb." She ducked then kicked out and crawled into the crevice, hoping a fizzer wasn't waiting for her. Her whispers sounded loud as horns: "Keep up with me, all right?"

She could hear him shuffling on his elbows, wincing, making guttural noises while she squeezed and crawled ahead of him. Hungry, tired, and scraping her knees and elbows, she lay exposed to the buzzing, gloopy fizzer chorus permeating the canyon. A mooncold eye peered from the morning wash while dawn lit the canyon like some kind of pink-orange alien landscape of walls and spires and odd trees, including the fallen petrified tree above. Two fizzers scratched at nearby dirt and lifted their blood-covered snouts as she got to her feet. They'd been feasting. One spit out a little round calf ear that it had been chewing on.

"Come on, let's go," she whispered to Tiller, helping him up. She could see him clearly now in the dimness, his paled face, that grimace, blood soaking his shirt and coat. Even his arms and hands were covered in red.

The fizzers surely smelled the bleeding and snorted.

"But those things," Tiller said.

The fizzers stared and popped their mouths but they didn't attack.

Greta stomped a boot and they skittered away, buzzing and crying. "Still scared chickens," she said. "Looks like they got their fill anyway."

It was slow going down the steep switchbacks. A few of the roadrunnery-type birds perched on rocks eyed them, then ran when they got close. Everywhere, bits of hide, legs, blood. She could see fizzers feasting on parts, as well as other smaller creatures she'd never seen, nibbling at leg bones and hooves—a buffet of skin, tendon, and cartilage. These smaller bulbous-eyed creatures were covered in spotted reddish fur, some with patches of greenish feathers, all gnawing and slurping, wary of Greta and Tiller. Some licked blood off rocks.

Tiller started whispering to himself as he leaned heavily

on Greta's shoulder. He slipped to a knee more than once. "Just leave me, all right? Run if you can. I can't breathe."

"I'm not doing that," she said.

Then a scream. Greta knew it couldn't be a bird without vocal cords making that sound. The shriek vibrated the air, shook the ground, pierced her ears. She wondered if it could be the mother canyon releasing tension, maybe the pact, like an earthquake that haunted every hundred years, though maybe not, maybe this was the canyon crying, or angry, maybe communicating somehow, this language that could only be a scream, which you could only feel and fear.

"We don't have much time," Tiller said.

"Why? What's going to happen?"

"The canyon always takes what she's owed."

"Isn't it time for that to stop?" Greta kicked at one of the bulbous-eyed creatures. It scurried off. "No one has to owe anybody."

Tiller's breathing soon became more labored. "It's not like that."

"Why don't you try me?"

Tiller leaned nearly all his weight on her. "My family has taken everything."

A row of fizzers soon started to follow along rocks, some even on the trail. They smelled Tiller's weakness. Everywhere there were flies, so many more than she'd seen anywhere on the cattle drive, though there wasn't a living cow in sight. She hoped some got away, then swatted a fly off the back of her neck and nearly dropped Tiller in the process.

"This goes back hundreds of years," he said.

"Meaning?"

"My family took everything from this place. All the

people, the animals. The prairie. They cut down most of them forests, took those birds, as many as they could, and anything else like them. I'm sure they got shot out of the sky. That's in some of the family stories, though maybe not true. I don't know what's true anymore.

"I do know they'd taken so much that something happened—this new contract with *her*—and they was killers and a hundred or so years later used a man named Tom Horn to help with some of that. And I bought into it too, always did, because something got hold of us once they stole this place, and said, *If you don't give back from what you took, then you'll be gone too. The payment is blood, a lot of blood. That's the contract. Blood for life.*

"The land said this, cursed us, said we would be the ones to strike a new bargain, *the bargain*, and if we didn't, then mother canyon said she would creep back over everything, the prairie, beyond. Maybe take over this whole stupid world. And we would be trapped in it, and live forever up in that cavern. You think I wanna become her servant, caretaker, or whatever?"

"What do you mean blood for life?" Greta asked.

"A longer than normal life span."

Greta knew she was right. *Immortality. Maybe. Or all of this was bullshit.* They were quiet for some time, focusing on descending to the main trail, not falling on the steep curves, and keeping their footing on slippery half-dried pools of blood being licked at by fizzers and other creatures.

Nearing the bottom, Tiller groaned, almost fell, then said, "You don't believe me."

"Nice story." Greta kicked a rock at some fizzers, which scattered them into the rocks where they hid and complained. "I don't buy it."

"You heard the scream. You seen what she unleashed. You seen the things Dad makes, how they come to life. And you seen the blood being taken. There is a balance here. And my family, you, me—we're all in the middle of it."

"Sounds to me that along with everything your family took, they also stole some kind of ancient magic? Maybe compromised that knowledge? Wasn't his to begin with."

"Wasn't only Tom Horn or those cattlemen. Sure, the greed of men played its part. It was Grandma Bernice. She was taught by some now-dead cattleman, who taught Dad how to preserve the dead, how to make them come alive . . . how to make them protect . . . She got obsessed with this place, been coming since she been a little girl to talk to mother canyon. Dad says the two conspired, that Granny got filled with the fire. Said she killed her parents—I don't know it for a fact—but Dad said all my cousins, even distant ones, and their families, died in a barn fire before I was born.

"They were having some kind of celebration, some were finally gonna travel to where they could maybe use that power to live for centuries.

"And Granny, she locked those doors, set the walls to fire, and burned her own blood kin. Everyone turned up deader than a mackerel. Anyway, she taught Dad all that magic, that's what protected us."

"But she's not here," Greta said. "Not that I've seen."

"She ain't nowhere," Tiller said.

"Why doesn't that feel like the truth?"

"You never believe anyone or anything," he said.

They were at the quads now, the area slick with blood and bits of hide. Half a cow lay close, but what struck Greta beyond the violence was the absence of all those sounds she'd grown used to: mama and baby cows complaining, squirrels and birds chirping and warbling, the occasional distant scraping scream of a Red-tailed Hawk. They'd been replaced with the cries, pops, and buzzes of fizzers and other strange animals, not to mention that shriek from the canyon that she'd heard a few times now.

Tiller leaned against his quad, far from Think Tank. Greta handed him some water. He took a drink and let some of the liquid trickle along the sides of his mouth.

Greta searched for any sign of the monster bird. "Have to say," she said. "I don't know what the truth is. I mean, look around. This all feels like a big, awful lie. So don't blame me if I can't trust your declarations of honesty."

She took a drink too then rifled through ATV compartments for bullets. While she did, Think Tank silently snarled. She stopped and stroked behind his ears, happy to see him move for the first time, and more than that, was glad he might still bring some kind of protection now that the mice and goat-fawn were gone.

This time when Think Tank snapped his jaws she gave his ears a little pinch. "Stop that, now," she said. "You've done enough damage to the mean man. You know I missed you."

"I hate that bear head," Tiller said.

"Yeah. I know."

"I'm gonna die from this."

"Worse ways to go," she said.

"I know you hate me."

Greta couldn't find a single bullet. "How far to the next gas cache?"

"There isn't one."

It was then she realized Scott's quad hadn't been taken. She feared the worst, sighed, then opened his toolbox, pulled out a socket wrench. She then grabbed a thermos, positioned it under the quad.

"What are you doing?" Tiller asked.

"Stealing oil. Scott can ride double if we find him. I think he's up there somewhere." She pointed to the cave opening.

She torqued the drain plug, started catching as much oil as she could. She filled most of the thermos then re-plugged the cap, screwed on the lid, wiped the cannister down with an old shirt.

"Now what?" Tiller's voice slipped back to a whisper.

"My rifle is missing," she said. "Maybe he found a couple bullets. I wish he was on his way out of the canyon on foot, trying to be silent. More likely, as afraid as he was, he still went back up to kill that thing."

"The canyon's going to take what she's owed either way."

"You keep saying that." She loosened Think Tank. The bear's eyes swiveled, his jaw opened slightly. She pet him again. "I just don't see things your way, Tiller. Never really did." She grabbed a strap, then said to Think Tank: "Don't know if this will be more uncomfortable than how things already are, but I need you." Think Tank felt light in her arms, though unwieldy as she pulled a strap around his forehead, and another through his mouth. She was happy he didn't try to bite her. She connected the straps and head as best she could. Think Tank opened and closed his jaws.

"You're taking that?" Tiller said.

She then strapped on her Think Tank backpack, the bear's marble eyes facing outwards. She could feel him snarling at Tiller. This wasn't pretty, but she could carry him this way. If there was any protection from the canyon's monsters, this bear head was it. She took a deep drink of water, shoved some jerky in her mouth, then started toward the switchbacks.

Tiller struggled to pull himself up. "Take me up there."

"Going to find Scott if he's there." She chewed. "And maybe take care of that bird, or make it someone else's problem. You'd slow me down."

"That's not how this works."

"Get on your quad, Tiller." She swallowed. "Try not to pass out and fall off. Drive somewhere safe. Tell your dad whatever you want. It's over."

"He's probably here."

"Good, he can come say hello." She grabbed a flashlight and matches, turned to him one last time. "Get out of here. Don't get eaten."

She started up the switchbacks, expecting a bullet any moment from Bobby Tiller right between Think Tank's eyes or hers. Exhausted from lack of sleep and food, she made her way up, passing piles of cow ribs and heads. She could feel Think Tank furiously biting at air, which knocked her off balance several times. "It's all right," she said while a herd of a dozen fizzers now fought over a cow's hind flank. Another dragged a head, and another tore into some leftover innards. Many snapped their bloody jaws at her. Then more fizzers came, along with dozens of the buggy creatures, all tearing at picked-over meat. Any little creatures blocking her path, she stepped on or kicked downslope.

A few switchbacks higher, she'd stopped to catch her breath when out of nowhere a coyote leapt among the fizzers. This dog wasn't like any she'd seen. It didn't move right, didn't growl or yip, was missing an ear and had half a tail, and behind it stomped a taxidermy deer. A swarm of bees trailed it like a cloud, pouring from its mouth. Both the coyote and deer lunged and trampled after the fizzers, scattering them. Above the fray, an orange taxidermy cat, its notched ears laid back, pawed at some of the bugs. The cat soon snatched up one of the bug-lizards, eyed Greta, and ran off.

Having scared off or killed some of the fizzers, Greta watched the coyote sit on a rock, its head titled in silent howl, while the deer just stood there, its hide undulating with bees, clumps gathering around its neck. The cat then appeared underneath the deer, the bug still in its jaws. And then a taxidermy chinchilla appeared and stole the bug right from the cat, ran along the shadows, and did flips like some kind of circus creature, and the two ran off. And while that happened, a strange dead possum covered in toads came out of nowhere. The wiry-haired critter hobbled over to the deer and lay down at its feet, and the deer stepped an inch closer to it, like they knew each other, and the possum laid its head down like it was about to have its second death the way Greta's wedding mice crumbled in her pocket. And they were joined by a broken-necked jackrabbit that also seemed to gaze at the possum. Then Think Tank kind of nuzzled, and Greta turned so they could see each other as if one last time.

She pushed past them toward the nest hole, wondering if she should have said bye to Tiller for good the way she let Think Tank say goodbye. But that would have been too sentimental. His dumb ass had wanted her killed and got her into this unreal mess to begin with. And if Scott was dead, well, she knew why she really dragged Tiller's ass out of that cave of stars, somehow, he would pay for it. And if Bobby were really around, maybe he needed to be the next

Bill Cherry, whose truck she realized was her way out, if he hadn't crashed it. *If* she could get to it. She could hot-wire it even if his keys were lost. She was sure of that at least.

And then something twisted inside her while she huffed up the trail, ready to dive for cover from Bobby or angry fizzers. She began to pity the bird the way she pitied Condor 832 and its long journey to Wyoming, this solitary thing from the past that no longer knew this world. She wondered if the bird could adapt, or if it only knew to consume and protect, to wield its need to kill on behalf of the mother canyon in this perpetual cycle that circled back every few generations. Then again, Tiller seemed to think the bird was the canyon. And that made her think again that maybe the bird needed to be gone for good. And if there was an egg in there . . .

The warning of a thing, she thought.

The birth of a thing.

The death of a thing.

And so on.

Then it occurred to her this wasn't only about the bird or mother canyon. This was also about Tiller's family. Maybe they owed the canyon their lives now. Maybe she simply owed it some respect, maybe some goddam conversation, woman to woman, or maybe the mothering she gave Think Tank. Maybe she could figure out which rock to scratch to make the canyon like her. Maybe the canyon already did. Anyway, whatever Tiller thought that he or his family owed, or were owed by, the canyon, she had to assume this was going to end with two or more dead people, a dead prehistoric bird, and the hope that she might prevent this from happening again.

Then she heard the canyon scream again. A wail she couldn't explain. The shriek emanated as if from another dimension, another time, another being, or beings. As if the ground and limestone cursed their way into some big hole in the sky, while infinite screams rained down. The fizzers all went silent. Many scrambled, clueless, trying to find the source of the sound. And then the scream was gone, and the fizzers, many of which hid, started to poke their heads above rocks and make their grackle-like buzz-pops.

She heard the scream twice more by the time she reached the petrified tree and nest. "Don't listen," she said to herself and Think Tank. She could feel the bear head wriggling in agitation. *Good*, she thought. *Keep protecting me. Won't you please keep protecting me?*

Before she reached the opening, two fizzers scooped up some calf remains, then darted off. The rocky path otherwise lay covered in blood, bone, ears, teeth, bits of hide, and legs. A couple of calf heads remained, and Greta wondered whether their eyes would move, and mouths chew imaginary food. The rest, gone. Dragged off. And the smell, that reek, that breath from the hole where the bird entered with her prey, poured an acrid wind that blew from the belly of the earth.

The hole itself loomed darker than night, a sky empty of stars, moon, and nebulae. She could feel Think Tank shifting harder now, jaws twitching, opening. Something in the bear head had switched, she thought. She could use that, even though this was Bobby's doing that swirled within the taxidermy, magic that was never his. Wasn't that alchemic substance originally from the canyon? An enchantment old as time, dug or born from the limestone itself? Did that make the idea of it any better? Just how far did this hole reach anyway? And should she really care to find out? Like, how far did you have to go to find the magic? Was it in a vein like gold? Growing like quartz or other gems? Part of some clay or fossils? Maybe from ground-up bird bones or feathers or something else altogether. Maybe a fungus. Maybe some words you had to say over some ingredients you could buy at Home Depot. She didn't know, but believed that whatever it was, maybe Think Tank was hungry for more of it. Or maybe Think Tank simply hated this goddam place.

Then she entered the dark. All sounds of fizzers and other creatures went quiet. Inside, only the bright glimmer of limestone walls both reflecting and absorbing her flashlight beam, which also revealed the blood-path, sometimes piles of innards, bits of hide, a tail, a hoof, and something like a tongue, no, was a tongue, which wormed over other bits of flesh and rock as if searching for its mouth. Greta shivered. Her beam lit the pink sloshy muscle as it slithered, but the light couldn't yet penetrate deep enough into the tunnel where the teratorn had flown, deep, downward, possibly to where it was birthed, where Condor 832 may have been, where thousands of other birds, and bears, and god knows who and what had crept throughout the eons. They had come to feed, or be fed upon, or maybe to even debate the mother canyon. *Guess we know who won those arguments.*

The walls here, filled with wormed and spiraled fossils, created biovermiculations that made her dizzy. Everywhere the chalk-colored limestone walls seemed to move, though those movements had ceased millions of years ago. And there were bats too, wings twitching, bodies hanging in clusters and lumps from where the vermiculation was most mesmerizing.

"How far we going?" Greta whispered to Think Tank, or thought she did, she wasn't sure. She wanted to heave from the smell of rot and shit—because there was so much dung here too. She covered her mouth with a hand, had lost her handkerchief, tried to breathe through the cracks between her fingers. The stench slipped through heavy and putrid in her chest.

Then the walls stopped glimmering in response to the light. She couldn't see limestone but fur, endless fur, so much hide lining the tunnel. Everywhere, skins of the dead, pelts of everything this bird and likely those birds before it had killed. Claws, mouths, snouts, mummified human heads, clumps of human and animal hair and skulls, every inch decorated with hide and bone trophies, *maybe not trophies*, she thought, just a different kind of nesting material than what she'd found in that toppled petrified nest. That had been the *ancient way*. This was different, and still very old, like some carnivorous mammal, a weasel or wolf, had built a den, not a typical nest. A *burrow*. Like an owl burrow, only, this for a giant bird, perhaps more weasel-like due to using its victims to line its entrance, its home. And by the looks of this, its home had slowly been constructed through the ages, piled upon and used again and again. Greta could see where calf hides and blood had dripped even a thousand years ago. Mama cowskins too, all hanging in the cold. Necks and ears protruded from hides. Even some gutted fizzers splayed like decorations. Wool also, and deadfalls of bones, giant tangles of them. And halves of skulls in various states of rot, some dried out, some liquidy with eyes, staring a kind of judgment:

Why would you come, why should you leave?

Greta realized this path downward had been coated in bat and bird waste for eons, and the scat of whatever else had lived here: scaly things, giant things, fur-covered things, big cats, bears and sloths. Giant birds like the teratorn. A beak the size of a car. Bats the size of humans. Maybe, people. And all this shit and fur and some other rot filled her lungs with particles from the present and past, made her light-headed, feeling like this was a fever dream, and okay, sure, it kinda was, but she wished the goat-fawn and mice had been *alive*-dead longer, much longer, so they could hear her say, *Yes, I hear you, now save me so I can restart, kick-start my life, turn it around, turn it all around into something different*, though she was at least glad to have Think Tank strapped to her, squirming in anticipation for something, she didn't know what.

She thought she could set this part of the cave on fire and just run, allow all of this fur and bone to burn. It wasn't a bad idea. But then remembered she had to find Scott, couldn't just leave him like Bill Cherry in his boots. Besides, she couldn't be Scott, a friend willing to leave her—if that's what he did. She was better than that, she hoped. Would a fire even solve the problem? Might send the mother canyon-birdplane-teratorn-thing into a frenzy. Best to be quiet. Best to not start fires, not yet. Not until she saw where all this led. Along with that, something drove her to go deeper, to see what this tunnel might reveal about the birdplane, the past, even herself. She hoped the creature was asleep, worn out from so much killing. And maybe all the birthing and killing meant the thing was already dying.

She made her way along walls of thicker pelts, careful not to touch them, glancing to make sure nothing hung there besides hides, legs, paws, and hooves. She didn't want to run into anything that might be ready to pounce. And so far at least, nothing did, and nothing blinked from the walls, or slithered besides that slithery pink *tongue*-thing she'd stepped over.

And even though Think Tank felt warm to her back, and that wind blowing towards her was full of heat and rot, something about this underworld chilled her cheeks and neck. Even her insides felt glacial and numb. Bones crunched under her feet from tiny dead creatures. Human bones littered the path too, and she bent and touched one and it felt like ice. Skulls lined the walls. Rib cages lay open like traps, arm and leg bones hung like words in unknown languages, tibias lay separated from fibulas, appeared like spectral hyperborean ice carvings.

Amid the entrapment of the den: countless human artifacts. Canteens, pairs of pants and leather garments, a hundred-year-old cowboy hat, pairs of glasses, a black belt, a watch, boots, a more modern hat. Then, hanging as if on the end of a giant web, Bill Cherry's blue-mottled head, mangled and swollen almost beyond recognition, half eaten mouth in a dead man's grin, remaining eye partially closed. She could see another familiar head in the shadows. Zollers, just enough red hair and skin remaining to tell. *End of movie, yeah?* Then a rotting rifle from yesteryear. Items that made her wonder, cattleman or sheepherder? Likely both. Likely anyone. And then a crumpled indigenous-made dress, strings of beads, and farther ahead, points made of obsidian, arrows, some broken, strings of decorative bones, a broken spear, and weapons she didn't understand. Tools from the far distant past she could only think could be scrapers, cutters, bannerstones.

Soon the tunnel dropped steeply, and the ceiling expanded upward. She descended into a layer of mist that wrapped her legs, that soon reached her waist. The burrow lining held something familiar here. She stopped, a wide-eyed form stared back at her, head next to a calf head. She couldn't tell at first whether it was alive or dead, just there in the wall as if it had just been dragged and hung, eyes on her, unmoving, and when Greta started to pull the light away from its eyes, that narrow face, blood-covered, blinked, and was gone.

She could feel Think Tank really biting now. Something was here, or had been, and it wasn't the bird or Scott. She hadn't a feeling who or what, and was afraid that, whatever it was, it could be the mother canyon, or maybe one of the many ghosts she'd seen in the prairie now coming to get her. All the while she remembered the bird too, and was afraid of stumbling into its bill, or it snatching her in its talons, the thing tearing her apart.

Just ahead, another form, massive and shadowy. She wondered whether it might be alive or . . . Think Tank's jaws snapped and nearly knocked her over. All she could think to do was hiss. Then the bear head calmed in a sad kind of way, she realized, because this had been familiar. This was his body that she saw. His frozen, broken, headless corpse, stuffing half-ripped out, dropped in the tunnel, two legs missing. Greta felt a sadness too. Think Tank probably wanted to stand up, swipe a paw, but couldn't, was helpless with her, biting through the tunnel mist, and could only release a silent growl-cry.

She wanted to stop, to say something. But what do you say to a bear head that just spotted his own body? *The bear was dead.* Think Tank. *Dead.* His body and head. Everything. Dead. She whispered, "I'm sorry," and slipped out of her Think Tank backpack and knelt and stroked his ears over and over. And Think Tank seemed to know, seemed to calm for the moment. And so she cooed and snuck her shoulders back into the straps. "We have to keep going," she said.

She turned off her light when the den came to an opening, a drop-off into a larger cavern with several small fires burning throughout. She hadn't even smelled the smoke that rose and disappeared out some natural vent, she didn't know where. Shadows danced on the chamber walls amid the red-orange light, flickering upon the cavernous room's many shifting formations, including a towering limestone mound at the room's center, some kind of speleothem that had dripped into existence over the ages.

Another shadow loomed in front of her—close or far away she couldn't tell at first, then realized as her eyes adjusted to the dimness, the form was atop the mound, that perhaps a nest was there, one similar to the mostly petrified nest outside the entrance. Beyond that, other cavernous holes, maybe exits, maybe other fur-lined burrows that bore deeper. Greta couldn't tell if she was seeing chasms amid piles of detritus, or strange shapes cast on the rock by the firelight. She squatted and again unhooked Think Tank's straps, let the bear head roll off, and carefully set him upright, so he could watch everything through his marble eyes.

The room appeared brighter now. Fingers of limestone reached upwards, speleothems protruding below and between bones and fur, including one small round patch halfway up that distant mound—as if bubbling outward, a mineral different than the limestone—shimmering pale green and blue, opaline. And in front of that and the main mound, carcasses piled like the mountain of bones she'd once seen, halves of foals and goats and calves, every kind of bone upon bone upon bone, though on the main mound, she could see now, there sat the bird, birdplane, the *teratorn*, having been that dark shadow, and now she thought, her eyes even more adjusted, it must be sleeping. Or at least, didn't feel threatened by her arrival.

She could see a way to climb down now, ledge to ledge across slippery limestone, bits of bone and fossil, perhaps even a mastodon tusk to step over amid a sheepherder's finger bones. Maybe even a way around that mountain of bones.

Only at this moment, when Think Tank's jaws snapped, did she feel something in her back. When she turned, it wasn't who she expected. Not Bobby Tiller at all.

"I see your ghosts," Greta whispered to Tiller, nostrils filled with the bitter scent of death, one eye on the half-awake preening teratorn picking at a primary wing feather, the other on him. Down below, shades crept around the mountain of bones, echoes of people, ancient peoples, and some more recent indigenous that must be Crow, Arapaho, and other tribes. Some gazed up at the bird, others picked through detritus. And there were the settlers too. Sheepherders and their families, and cattlemen too, she assumed, and with them women, boys, girls, a woman holding a baby—the baby now drifting from her—some of the others floating now, feet dangling over bony protrusions. *These ghosts*, Greta thought, *or maybe real people living forever, trapped here, have been in this room a hundred years, others, thousands and thousands . . .*

"Weren't as hurt as you claimed," Greta said.

Tiller held out a small metal container half-filled with paste resembling black shoe polish. "Prolongs life and heals . . . to a degree. Every time you use it . . . you lose a little of yourself . . . Only, wouldn't have got to it if you hadn't helped me. Was out of my mind in that cave, didn't even think I . . . didn't think I was that wounded . . ."

"How'd you keep so quiet?" she asked.

"Tracker's tricks."

She sensed fear in Tiller, an uncertainty in his voice, she didn't know how she knew this. He'd been lying all along, about everything. The entire cattle drive had been a lie. His friendship had been a lie—if they'd even been friends at all. For all she knew he'd been slipping that paste into her food. And now here she was kicking herself that she didn't leave him in that cave of stars for the fizzers to eat.

She didn't know what to say about that container, his lies, or his intentions. "It was your dad who built these fires," she said.

Tiller sweat, face still ghostworn, maybe that bite not completely healed like he claimed—then again he did say you lose a bit of yourself with that paste. Maybe parts you don't want to let go of? Everything about him was grey and shadowy, as if he were about to transform into one of the cavern's shades. She stood back several feet, thinking: If she punched him right in his bear bite, maybe he'd collapse. She'd push him right off the ledge.

"Thought you didn't want this anymore," she said.

He turned on a flashlight, motioned toward a small opening to her left that she hadn't seen. "Go inside. Bird ain't gonna attack. Not yet anyway. Besides, it won't go in there."

She didn't know where he could be taking her, but the room wasn't far. Seemed they were at a dead end, until she spied an opening, where they slipped inside to see all kinds of bones and pelts, and on the walls hanging there, three forms, one of them headless. She didn't know how, but the bodies were attached, maybe glued somehow, to the wall, maybe stuck partly in the limestone itself? She wasn't . . . couldn't be sure . . . and what she did know, though could tell . . . these weren't taxidermy . . . these people were . . . have been . . . alive.

On the left, a woman, old, *so old*, and indigenous, wearing skins, shell piercings in her face. Grey hair, long and silky, as if recently washed. The beauty in her was unimaginable, timeless. In her eyes a liquidy youth, and deep knowledge. She gazed intently upon Greta with both rebelliousness and sorrow, and seemed to be whispering something to herself.

"That old savage goes all the way to the beginning of this place," Tiller said. "Canyon says she grew too weak to continue the pact, so cattlemen, my family, and that man hanging there with them, tricked her and her kind, and severed the bond." He then shined his light on the floor where an ancient dog lay dead. "That wasn't there before. Maybe was hers. Anyway, one of my relatives put her here like this, so we threw Granny up next to her. Tried to kill old Bernice but didn't work too well. She got too much of the magic in her. We cut out her tongue a long time ago. That slippery thing crawls around these tunnels somewhere, wanting to reattach itself likely so she can speak her nonsense again."

Next to the ancient indigenous woman hung Bernice, whose black eyes seemed from some godawful pit beneath Hell, a kind of mother-evil in them. Greta couldn't keep eye contact with them for long, as if they'd win her over somehow, make her do things worse than she could imagine.

Bernice appeared not even middle-aged, wore a tattered pale blue dress. She had thin black lips and her Cupid's bow came to two sharp points. A good portion of her upper throat was open, exposed. She bore into Greta with privilege and ferocity as if she thought she'd always been queen of this place, maybe the prairies too, until Tiller and Bobby took out her tongue and strung her up.

"Bernice said she'd hand this to us when the time was right, but she weren't ever gonna do that," Tiller said. "Not for a second. She roamed in here wanting to live forever, talked about killing every last one of us, even setting the canyon loose. We kept finding her with a bloody mouth from feasting on bats and whatnot. Not that she needed to eat. She . . . wanted . . . the *blood*. Half of them sheepherder ghosts down below was part of her immediate family. The Johnsons. Means they was my clan too . . . Surprised? Got my own mixed blood same as you. They got led here by that man hanging next to her. He got a history too, and no head as you can see. So now you know the truth. I got that defiled blood in me. Ain't a soul who knows besides you."

"You don't know a thing about mixed blood," Greta said.

Next to Bernice, a cowboy of some kind, and on the ground below his feet, a leathery mottled head, eyes wide and staring, lips trembling and spitting. His cheeks were blue-grey-green and withered like he'd lived and died, then lived again. Maybe over and over. A bluish pus came out of his mouth, opaque and glowing, and he had a giant mud-caked mustache and a hatred in his pupils that gave away his ruthless cowboyness.

"That there is Tom Horn," Tiller said. "Famous friend of cattlemen, bona fide rustler and buffalo hunter. Found his head in here, eyes staring, lips moving like he always got some shit to say. Nothing comes out his mouth other than that godawful pus. Bernice said he'd like to have been president of these United States..."

"That right?"

"It is... And now you got a choice..."

Greta didn't want a choice, but she answered anyway. "Sure. I like choices. What do you want? Song and dance? Think Tank doesn't do karaoke." She searched for a way out. They were in the dark. The bird was close. So much blood was everywhere, and those *people* hanging on the wall—were they even human anymore? Would she become one of them? She didn't want to cough up blue *pus*-bile or be tacked up next to Bernice, skin fused to limestone. Could she run? That bird would grab her before she fled ten steps. Tiller might kill her too. Bobby was likely around, though maybe Tiller already stuck his old man to some other wall.

"You changed the pact," he said. "Ain't a single soul done that since them people on the wall done it. And you did that because the canyon chose you."

"I didn't get chosen to do anything."

"You got powers I ain't seen."

"That's a bit delusional."

"We can be partners, Greta, carry this on. You and I."

"Live forever on a wall next to you? Next to Bernice and a headless cowboy? That's something to look forward to."

"You'll live in the ranch house. Beautiful views. Plenty of shopping. Mama always loved buying new clothes and walking around downtown with her imitation Starbucks from Dirty Sally's."

"That so? Or what?"

"Or you can die here, today."

Greta was horrified, disgusted. She'd rather let that bird

peck her brains out in one instant crush of bill against skull than allow Tiller to have any ownership of her. "You think I have powers?" she said. "Keep dreaming."

"You do."

"If so—and let's just pretend for a second that I do—it doesn't have a damn thing to do with this canyon, or your family. You know what it might have to do with? I'll tell you. It might have to do with cleaning out all this toxic shit that's been happening because of people like you for I don't even know how long. So, yeah, even if I did have powers, I wouldn't need to join you. I wouldn't need to be a part of this canyon, or to fix your life, or your family's legacy. Everything that's going on here . . . isn't coming from me . . . this is the result of the violence of the past, of this earth, of something that happened here a long time before those people got hung on that wall. And this canyon that wants to give birth and requires blood payment? Maybe like every woman I've ever known *she* just wants to feel less pain. Maybe she needs to be a part of this planet, and has felt a bit left out. Maybe she doesn't want to be bound to you, or me, or anyone anymore. Maybe everything she's been giving you has been lip service, and she didn't even realize another way out. Maybe she just wants to go away, crumble, to be no more. And maybe in doing so, maybe this *birth* was her last shot to give the planet a little bonus, something not seen in I don't know how long. So, if you think I have power, it's just because I figured out something you couldn't about us girls. So maybe you need to let go. Maybe you need to let her do her thing whether that's live, die, or whatever. And whatever it is, count me out."

Greta was terrified about standing up to Tiller. Terrified and cold and numb and overheated all at once. But it felt right, and that was something she hadn't done much of in her life—*something that felt right*. Sure, she talked back to a lot of people. But not when it came to serious threats. Not when it came to life or death. And she was tired of letting other people walk on her, tired of not standing up for herself. Now she'd told someone off in a terrifying hole that felt like the violent and maternal center of the earth. She'd done something right, without Hannah, though maybe it was kind of with her. Maybe wearing her old plaid coat, with her key pressed inside, was Greta's way of channeling some of that Hannah energy.

And then came the scream. It let loose so loud that it brought Greta and Tiller to their knees. Greta realized in that moment who was screaming, that this sound emanated not from the limestone or rocks or a ghost, but from the origin of the human connection with this place, this ancient indigenous woman stuck on the wall. *Pye'ta'wa'wawi. That's her name.* Greta didn't know how she knew, but Pye'ta'wa'wawi had been an integral part of the canyon for millennia, had been fused to it in ways Greta could never understand, and she'd brought something called the gift thousands of years ago. Greta also knew this wasn't a scream of terror, but of having gone through so many contractions with this place. It was a scream of warning too, of rebellion, of having been part of and—in a way only Pye'ta'wa'wawi could understand or even release—of having witnessed and birthed so many creatures over such a span of time.

Greta quickly jumped back up. Tiller was on his feet too, screaming, though Greta could hardly hear him. He aimed his shotgun and flashlight, and meant to murder Pye'ta'wa'wawi in front of her. And then she knew this was also why Tiller forced her here, because he wanted her to see him do it, see him destroy Pye'ta'wa'wawi once and for all.

Greta knew *this wasn't the way.*

Without thinking, she dropped her flashlight and rushed Tiller, and before he could swing the barrel. She shouldered him, and he and the gun went flying.

Then something else happened. Some creature had been with them, something she hadn't seen, or maybe had? Something disguised in all this rot and darkness. *A naked grey form.* A taxidermy woman. No hair. Skin open in wounds all over her body. She stepped from the darkness. Eyes like human eyes, but not, not real, couldn't be real, could they? Because these orbs were glowing, or reflecting fire, or were bioluminescent somehow. And either way, must have been the eyes staring at Greta from the hides in the tunnel.

No blood spilled from this emaciated skin-thing, only . . . wood and plastic beneath open flaps where the glue hadn't held . . . and it was moving, and missing some fingers, toes, part of a hand . . .

This skin-thing, this monstrous *woman*, fueled by some kind of anger that Tiller's magic couldn't dispossess, hissed and pounced on him in front of Greta. Pye'ta'wa'wawi stopped screaming to watch this struggle, to maybe intently see who or what could win out in these subterranean depths.

The skin-thing scratched at Tiller's eyes with her remaining fingers, and bit at him. At the same time, a black tongue slopped from the side of its mouth, burning Tiller, the skin-thing's acidic mouthslime pulling skin and flesh from his right cheek.

"Mother, get off me. Stop! Stop!" Tiller screamed, knocking the skin against the slick limestone.

The skin almost seemed to be stuck for a moment, then peeled itself, herself, away, eyes aimed at Tiller, a magic fury in them.

Greta knew then that Tiller and Bobby had done horrible things long before she agreed to this cattle drive. But for how long? Months? Years? Who else had they killed in their quest for eternal life?

And then Greta thought, if the goat-fawn was a nightmare, this skin was a night terror, though somehow, she also knew this monster was on her side, and wanted Tiller dead for his crimes, for his betrayal.

Greta watched in horror as the skin moved toward Tiller, while he backed away from his mother's partial hands that reached for his throat, her withered lips mouthing hisses that maybe expressed her love for him, her hatred, or both. Either way, the skin, Greta could tell, intended to end Tiller, and those skinny grey fingers aimed to dig into his neck, deep into his arteries as if knives meant to spill his dirty blood.

Tiller, about to be grappled, picked up a rock and suddenly gazed at the skin like she was his mother again, like he might grab her hand, like they might walk out of this hell into the big sky country and make amends. He seemed about to drop the stone, then didn't. He slipped in close, smashed the rock against her head over and over until what was left of her became a pulpy mass of folds and blackish slime.

During this, Greta grabbed his shotgun and tried to fire it, but for whatever the reason it jammed, or had never had any bullets, and by the time she tossed it and picked up her flashlight, his mother already lay still.

Tiller stood over the mass of integument that had once been his mother, who he, or his father, or maybe the two of them had murdered and turned into taxidermy. She could see Tiller hardly moving now, while the faces on the wall, and the head on the ground, watched.

Tiller set the rock down, face dripping blood, and held out his hands to Greta, as if this murder had been some kind of peace offering. Bernice stared hateful through black eyes then looked to Greta and smiled. Pye'ta'wa'wawi watched with a kind of knowing, while the dim eyes of Tom Horn appeared lost and disoriented. All seemed unfazed by this death, by any death.

Why is Bernice still smiling? Greta wondered. Maybe Bernice knew that something from herself had festered in Tiller, though could the old woman forgive him for pulling out her tongue and hanging her? Maybe she took joy in thinking Greta would kill Tiller. Maybe she just wanted to see death, any kind of death, knowing this had partially been her doing, fueled by some malevolence inherent in her DNA. Either way, Greta was sure that Bernice, like Tom Horn, was better off where she was.

Tiller tried to staunch the bleeding from his face. He opened the jar, dabbed his fingers in the paste, and hissing in pain, slathered it right on the wound, which instantly started to bubble and heal with new tissue, replaced just as quick by a dent, a hideous scar.

All the while, Greta tried to think what to do, backing away.

Now he moved closer, inch by inch. "It won't just be birds that will terrorize," he said. "If you don't join me, life will flow from this place like the world has never seen.

Creatures from the past no one should know about. It will be more terrifying than what you witnessed. Worse things can come out of here."

Bernice seemed to really smile at that.

Pye'ta'wa'wawi's eyes clearly disagreed.

"You don't know," Greta said.

Tom Horn's eyes didn't care, just watched. He was just a head, a withered brain, eyes, a bubbling mouth. If Tom Horn had anything to say, he couldn't say the words anyway, and maybe, Greta thought, *didn't care*.

"Visions. Images. Stories," Tiller said. "I do know."

"From who? Your grandmother?" Greta nodded to the wall.

Bernice grinned.

Greta watched Tiller limp, his ankle somehow twisted, she hoped broken, and all the while thinking what to do. So she talked. She knew how to do that. "No wonder you don't trust this canyon to play nice," she said. "Look what you did. This mother canyon knows it's probably the other way around: she doesn't trust people, probably doesn't trust the actions of any human except for Pye'ta'wa'wawi: devastation by countless settlers, colonizers, ranchers, all tearing at the land, ripping out trees, trapping animals from her creeks, killing any new monstrous creatures, burning at her soul by shooting every monster bird out of the sky, and killing the non-monsters by the tens of millions. Maybe she understands how the world might have an angry last line of defense in *her*, a Wyoming canyon, a place with a tenuous contract with humankind. Maybe she can't make up her mind whether she hates the world, or if she wants to risk everything."

"You wouldn't know."

"Where's your dad?" she asked, then found her way to a lower ledge, still keeping an eye on Tiller, thinking maybe she wanted to go down below where the ghosts prowled.

"This is how it goes." Tiller was out by the ledge into the main cavern now, Think Tank furious beside him. "The son takes over. We become the taxidermist; we learn the art of protection from our father, or in his case, from Bernice. And there were others, but they're gone now. We're what's left. We bleed the land out in the streets of Ten Sleep, in the prairies and canyons, and right here in this place. I'll teach my children the same."

"I thought this was about preserving family? Guess I should have realized more of the truth when you told me how Bernice burned everyone," Greta said. "Is there anything you say that isn't a lie? Clear now that you hate your own dad."

He ignored her. "The canyon requires one more." He swung his good leg and kicked Think Tank over the ledge, furry jaws snapping.

"No!" Greta cried. This startled the bird, its eyes on her, wings ruffling, giant bill parting as if hungry.

Think Tank rolled to a stop on a lower ledge.

"Bird only wants you now," Tiller said.

"I think that *fuckerpuff* wants whatever she wants." Greta started climbing down toward the bear head.

The bird lifted off, settled back down, eyes on her. It was massive, sitting upright, wings folded. This thing was all fuselage, feathers. And that bill, like the jaws of some kind of massive backhoe, that top mandible curving downward over the lower bill in a massive hook that could easily pull leg from torso, or act as a wrecking ball . . .

"You'll die down there," Tiller said.

"Try me," was all Greta could say, think to say, operating on pure anger now, trying to duck around a spire of ancient cavern sediment, then not slip on the wetness, since there were so many bones and bits that she thought she might twist an ankle like Tiller or fall and impale herself.

The bird's wings flapped, though the creature didn't leave her perch. Greta could feel the wind from the wings and wondered why the bird didn't come closer.

The bear head, she thought. *Think Tank.* The bird couldn't move near the talisman. She could destroy the body, carry it, but something about the head maybe . . . about being close to it for long . . . because that magic protected Greta. The teratorn could try to destroy a talisman, but maybe couldn't destroy all of one, especially a grizzly-sized, super-sized taxidermy, and definitely not a person who bonded with such a talisman, not until . . . maybe . . . the talisman lost its magic. Maybe the magic had to wear off, fade, and maybe Tiller wanted it to fade because he still needed her to join him? And until she did that, she was still the bird's enemy—though was she? And how would the bird know, or care? Was *she*—the bird—really that smart? *Had to be.* Thing was, she trusted that bird's intelligence way more than she trusted Tiller or that damn smile on Bernice's face.

Greta gave away her position by flashing her beam near the bear head. Tiller's light shone above her, he wasn't coming down, probably couldn't. He was afraid of the bird, of something, maybe too wounded to climb down. Maybe that paste shit didn't work on tendon and bone, only on flesh and skin.

Either way, her insides squirmed. She didn't want to think of being picked apart by that bird. And she didn't want to go back up to Tiller and be his business partner or whatever. She would be trapped if she did that, unhappy, and worse, would become a monster.

Hell. Fucking. No.

So, yeah, forget both options.

From her vantage she could see something else too, movement among the speleothems, a shadow, then a faint voice nearly drowned by the rustling of giant feathers and all the ghosts digging around, picking through detritus.

Grettaaa.

Needles pricked her arms and neck. It wasn't the goat-fawn. Couldn't be. That thing was never getting back to its feet, couldn't have one last hurrah . . . Unless . . .

Before she could move, she was pulled by a hand toward a shadowy crevice.

Then: *It's me.*

He'd said her name. Him. *Scott.* She'd never felt so relieved when she saw his face. She wondered how he'd gotten so far, why he hadn't returned to where they'd hid.

Agitated by Tiller's light, the bird flapped and lifted off, this time revealing something oblong and bright beneath it.

The gift . . .

An egg, Greta thought. A colorful giant egg the hue of a pale winter sky with bright wisps like rain clouds.

Another egg. Another bird. More parthenogenesis. The rebirth of a species. This wasn't going to wait a hundred years at all. Wasn't this what humans had always stolen over and over for these creatures, their ability to bounce back, to be viable again? So, what if this species was to return to populate the world again. It's what people wanted for themselves. *A rite of passage.* To *become*. Only problem, humans always had the propensity to become the bigger monsters.

Maybe this creature simply wanted to live. Though maybe she was still somewhat bound, and perhaps the egg, that gift, wasn't bound to anything? Maybe that's what could make this canyon spirit go away: let something live that everyone through the ages thought should die. Greta wasn't sure, but that egg might be more special than the giant bird. That could be its future.

"Did you see that egg?" she asked.

"I don't care," Scott said. "You need to kill the bird."

"I kinda like the bird," Greta said. "How about kill Tiller instead?"

"He has a shotgun."

"No bullets or jammed—though I shouldn't have tossed it. He's half-dead. I'm not so sure Bobby isn't lurking around here."

"You can shoot him," Scott said.

"You have a rifle?"

"And four bullets."

"One for each of us," Greta said.

"Not funny," Scott said. "The bird though. We need to kill it. End that damn thing."

"Didn't think to shoot the bird while it was preoccupied?"

"Need you to do it. Please take the rifle."

"Why me?"

"Because you're a better shot."

"And you think the bird is going to die with a couple shots?"

"Just take the rifle." Scott pushed it toward her. "Do it."

"I don't want to."

"*Please.*"

When Greta reached for the rifle a light shone in Scott's eyes, something that hadn't registered before, not until her hand shoved right through the weapon, Scott's ghost-image now dissolving.

Her heart sank.

The sad silvery glow in his eyes dimmed. And now the rifle dissipated completely, while Scott's form, mouth wanting to say something else, slipped into a dark vapor.

Greta knew her time was limited. She had to get out.

Scott was gone. Now Greta had no one to trust, no one to rescue *her* besides herself.

The bird was still the biggest threat. Bigger than Tiller, bigger than Bernice and that wicked smile. Or even Bobby, if he was around somewhere.

Greta dragged Think Tank close. Those jaws stopped moving some time ago, the marble eyes no longer rolled. Not even a twitch. She had to do something, but what? She set the bear head in her lap, could hear Tiller above cursing at himself.

Think Tank didn't move. "I suppose you're not going to protect me anymore." She stroked the ears, scratched its snout. "Is that really all you got?" She went for the ears again, started massaging. "Come on . . . Come back to me . . ."

Then the tiniest movement. A nose twitch. "There you are," she whispered. "I liked you better when you were biting people." She kept scratching. The bear seemed to yawn. "I need one more favor, though not sure what I'm doing. Kinda faking it right now."

Nearby lay the thermos. The one thing Greta had done right was placing the container out of reach, someplace Tiller or his dad wouldn't look—inside Think Tank's mouth, stuffed in his cheek. She was lucky they hadn't lost it with all that jaw snapping, but Think Tank pulled through, kept it in his cheek like a wad of Big League Chew bubblegum.

Once Tiller kicked him and his head bounced off a couple ledges, the container slipped out. Luckily it hadn't rolled far, or into any crevice. This time Greta lodged the oil-filled container deep in Think Tank's brain cavity. The bear head didn't fight back, maybe didn't have the energy. Then she strapped the head to her back, tying the straps that were still loosely attached, and set off toward the cavern floor.

"Tiller," she called out. "I'm going to get out of here. You can stay if you want."

When he didn't answer she knew he was likely on his way out, stumbling toward one of the ATVs. Or maybe was busy murdering the three hanging within that room. He seemed to want to be the only one who lived forever. She sure wasn't going to join him.

The bird watched her, cocked its head to the side, curious, that saucer-sized eye on her every move. Terrified, Greta thought that if it had wanted, the bird could have already scattered her insides around the limestone formations, maybe left her in parts on that carrion mountain. "You're not mean or hungry," Greta said, then tried some of that magic that worked on Think Tank. "You're a *good* girl."

On the cavern floor now, Greta had more than enough light—flickering and dancing, it made the bird appear even more monstrous than it was. She then scrounged around for loose, unignited kindling, and when she had enough, tucked the sticks under an arm. Next, she pulled a glowing half-burned log from the fire, and made her way toward the limestone speleothem hill where the bird perched.

Even though she stepped carefully, she slipped on blood, hide, and bone, and fell, burning her right leg with the log, scraping her entire right side. Angry at herself for falling, she patted Think Tank and re-strapped him, picked herself up, then gathered the spilled wood, searched for a foothold and climbed, glad the bird hadn't been so startled as to pull off her head.

"I can't blame you," she said to teratorn. "It's Tiller, his family, this canyon, though I'm not sure you can blame the canyon, especially if you're a part of it, or were?"

Think Tank slowly opened and closed his jaws.

Then Greta saw something, not the bird, a rocky shoulder several feet below the bird on the side of the speleothem, something she'd suspected when glimpsing the shimmering pale green-and-blue earlier. It didn't appear to be part of the limestone formations, though sediment had formed around it, maybe tens of millions of years ago? Longer? It wasn't all sedimentary rock, she could see that. Part of it was . . . no, not a meteor. Maybe a fragment from something bigger, maybe part of the dark primitive asteroid that crashed sixty-six million years ago, that somehow exploded all the way from the Yucatán.

Chicxulub.

It destroyed life. It created life.

Was Chicxulub the mother canyon?

There was no way to remove it. Well, no way she could know for sure, though J.A. Maynard would love this—he'd probably have a theory right away as to what it could be, and that might completely counter what Greta was thinking. Either way, this *rock-thing* likely wasn't formed when the limestone formed, just like the surrounding fossils in parts of the walls weren't born into limestone, or into sediment, but were the sediment that hardened into limestone. Those fossils had been living, breathing creatures that died, their bones and whatever caught in ocean-bottom muck, becoming part of it, so much death having rained down to Davy Jones's locker, and then over millions of years, something, some acidic chemical, and water, ate through this calcite or whatever, and formed a vast system of caverns, every grain perhaps a skeletal fragment of some marine foraminifer or coral, or microbits of other things, monstery things, and then drained, and then still wettened over time, forming the cavern's many columns and towers. Perhaps that asteroid chunk, or chip, had been hurtling through space, and because of its impact, broke apart, and maybe partly melted, and smashed its way here, an interstellar fossil, a piece of space-time, and also a dinosaur killer, and maybe had within it all the magic that the Tillers possessed, and maybe was the spirit of this place beyond what this bird could ever be. This, she thought, had to be what they pulled from to make their living taxidermy.

Here she built her fire, breaking and placing sticks above the ember, which soon enough, after she blew on it again and again, caught the kindling into a nest of flame.

All this time, the bird watched. Its head, now that Greta was close, blinked its curious eye, that third eyelid membrane closing horizontally, the eye itself giant like those of the sea kraken of lore, glistening with that nictitating membrane, which made Greta want to run a finger over it. A blaze glowed in the bird's giant retinas, and that machine-like bill could scoop parts of Greta not meant for scooping.

There was life in this creature. Greta could sense her wonder, her fear. And that apprehension and uneasiness,

Greta knew, came with the survival instincts of all birds, to fly, to eat, to chase, to defend, to do whatever it might take to not die and live on in the Neverland of earth. Greta just wished the bird feared her enough that she, or they, could maybe escape.

Something about that rock, she thought, had maybe created a supernatural link between this bird, or its distant relatives, or this species anyway, and the canyon that trapped both animals and humanity in ways Greta would never understand. But she knew this connection needed to come to an end, so that perhaps she and others wouldn't.

Instead of climbing down she clambered the last several feet, banking on Think Tank staying charmed long enough for her to do her next trick, which was all to make this bird understand that Greta meant the creature no harm.

She stood before the giant bird. The teratorn could kill her, crush her, pluck her apart, rip muscle from bone. She could sense the bird considering that very idea, its head jerking closer, then pulling away.

"All right, you," Greta said. "Move your pájara ass." Close enough to touch its feathers, she clapped at the bird. It didn't move. She clapped again. Stomped and clapped. She asked it kindly to move, tried ordering. Begged. Waved her arms.

The teratorn didn't budge.

Then Greta had an idea. She turned so the bear head faced the teratorn.

The bird took a step back.

"That's right, good," she said, now seeing the egg again. She took off her, no, Hannah's plaid coat, laid it out, placed a chunk of hide on top, then carefully lifted the egg, watching the bird watch her, then placed the birdspawn on the hide, adding what appeared to be stuffing but seemed more like human hair, wads of it, around the egg, and wrapped it all together in the coat, making sure the bird could see the great care she was taking. She caressed the egg. Cooed like she'd done with the mice. All the while she talked to the bird, tried comforting the giant creature, telling her she wouldn't hurt her baby. "I won't. Your hatchling will be safe, so safe." Before she carefully lifted the foot-tall egg, she added, "It's going to be all right. You need to have a future away from here."

The bird flapped its wings in complaint, stretched them wider than plane wings. But also maybe, Greta hoped, the bird was displaying its understanding of what was happening.

Greta lifted the wrapped egg, held it in front of the bird, which gazed at her like she might be reading Greta's mind. Greta then started down to the fire; the bird flapped again, opened its bill.

"I'm not going to put your egg in the fire." Greta set the wrappings carefully against a rock while she unhooked Think Tank. She felt the faintest twitch. She hugged the bear head like an old friend, said, "Thank you," kissed him, and was about to place Think Tank on the fire when a voice called out from the ledge at the tunnel exit.

It wasn't Tiller. It was *Bobby*. One of his eyes was gone, replaced by scar tissue.

"Stop!" he yelled. "I know what's in there. Drop that head on the fire and you won't live a second, let alone forever. Forget seeing your family again."

Greta thought about Hannah. Could see her face clear as anything like the day she met her. Greta didn't think about her own mother except for a fleeting second. She could live without seeing her again and quickly blocked the image.

But Hannah? She was *family*. Greta could see that smile hovering in the firelight, and knew Hannah was with her whether or not she ever called that number on the key.

Then the bird flew over to Tiller's dad, and perched. The creature really was graceful, and lovely, and terrifying. Bobby wasn't afraid of the bird at all, and ignored the creature. They seemed best friends, allies. Greta's heart drained itself into her stomach. She wasn't going to get out of here.

She was going to die.

"Don't know why my wife didn't drag you to the bird," Bobby said, "or why that bear head stayed animated so long. But time to go. You're done. It's over. Your blood's meant to stay here."

"Where's Tiller?" Greta asked.

"Boy wasn't ever gonna live forever."

"He never knew all the truth, did he?"

"Of course he didn't. *I am the canyon.* Not the bird. Not my mother. Definitely not my son. And maybe one day—"

It was then the bird leaned over and pinched Bobby's head from his neck. It came right off along with a long strip of spine, muscle and skin. Blood gushed and spurted in several quick bursts, then his corpse fell, legs kicking and twitching, hands opening and closing.

The bird dropped the head out of its bill, Bobby's mouth still moving, face covered in crimson mucus, and the teratorn plucked off an arm then talon-crushed the head into a pulp.

The bear head no longer moved in Greta's hands. Gently, she set Think Tank on the fire. He caught flame, like some creature long ago that helped protect travelers who journeyed to the canyon's heart. Greta's mind flashed to a tiny burning mammoth while she stepped back.

Bear fur popped, wheezed. Think Tank's snout lit like a log.

The bird quietly watched, then flew back to the mound like a flickering shadow.

Greta grabbed the egg wrappings and made the climb back out. Once she'd reached the ledge she turned briefly one last time, waved the bird her way. "Come on," she said. But the teratorn didn't move. "Come on!" she called again.

Greta couldn't wait and started off, nearly tripping over Tiller's corpse. A knife protruded from his eye, while his neck had been cut through tendon and artery. She didn't bother to grab the shotgun he retrieved, but did pause to snatch his wallet and shake out several hundred-dollar bills.

She started back down the hole at a fast gait and soon heard the explosion and nearly fell with the egg. She wondered if the bird died. She wanted her to live, same as she wanted to live. At the same time, she knew it might be easier this way. Then came a rumbling, and Greta knew something in the cavern had given way, that time, the past, all of the canyon's history had lost hold of itself when that chunk of asteroid maybe got dislodged, maybe broke apart again.

Smoke billowed above her. She knew the tunnel was ablaze now, that all of this might soon be a blackened hole filled with fragments of the past, and that even so the canyon might still flourish, but without the Tillers at least, without Bernice and that Tom Horn character.

Greta hurried her pace, could hear moans from the walls, from beneath the hides, from behind her. Still, she kept on with the egg, didn't look back, refused to stop or even wipe her eyes from the smoke burning them.

And then, after what felt like forever, she found herself

outside the hole under the night sky. Stars blinked and she thought of those third eyelids, how the teratorn had watched her wrap and lift the egg. She thought of the bird maybe flying into the moonless night air, while all those ghosts scattered, and Bernice and Tom Horn caught fire, Bernice screaming tongueless, Horn angry and bursting in his own crematory; and then maybe Pye'ta'wa'wawi, in all her frailness and beauty, welcomed the devouring element, and joined the spirits of the land in some forever dance.

Though the night air outside the cavern was filled with stench, something about it seemed fresh in comparison to what Greta experienced in the tunnel and cavern. She sucked air, and while she did, noted no giant shadows over the cliffs, no teratorns or other beasts. Not even fizzer buzz-pops or little things creeping about.

Soon bits of burning, floating ash spewed from the hole, and a joyous howl-cry soaked the air. Greta made her way down the switchbacks and knew she'd heard a final wail. Careful to not drop the egg, she kept it warm against her chest.

Though her legs were jelly when she reached the quads, she mounted Tiller's and fired it up. She used straps to hold the egg wrappings against her body to keep whatever was inside warm.

Somewhere on the trail, she found a way to forgive herself for not being able to save Scott, for the possibly dead birdplane, and for the many choices over the years that had left her numb. She no longer felt that way. Tired and hungry, every nerve ending felt alive, radiating a kind of electricity through her skin that kept her awake, determined. She'd never felt this kind of awareness, this kind of sensitivity. She could feel distant cries and howls amid the grumbling ATV and her own inner thunder, and somehow felt life swirling inside the egg too.

Maybe the canyon weakened, maybe it could no longer hold back the life it hid. Maybe that life would never reappear. Could be that's what that scream had been all about. Could be that Pye'ta'wa'wawi had found herself and that was all that was needed. She was finally released with the canyon.

Then she thought about what other eggs she might find were she to poke around, enough to transform the world? Someone might go back, if the world found out about her egg, about this bird, about any phone videos and photos. She knew that much. Nothing about this world would stay the same, not as long as whatever was in the canyon, or in the egg, continued to live.

She soon found Cherry's truck, the keys still in it, door wide open, no sign of struggle. Probably was carried away while taking a leak. She left the ATV and drove that pissgreen truck eastward, clouds of dirt kicking up in her wake. Several miles outside the canyon the buffalo appeared, and Greta knew magic *still* existed. The buffalo walked with her for a mile or two, and then it too stopped, and Greta braked to watch it curl into a ball on the ground. Next to it, she could see the jackrabbit. Both seemed deep in slumber.

She arrived at her car torn on what to do. Though she turned on her heater to keep the egg warm, though she risked her life to take the egg from the bird, to carry it all this way, she now considered smashing it.

No one would know. *No one would ever know.*

She could just leave it, whatever was inside would slowly die in the night, maybe by morning. Maybe a dog or a coyote would come eat the embryo, though maybe the embryo had grown to a chick already.

Would there be more birds? More creatures? Would there be more anything if this egg's life ended? Should she assume that some kind of prehistoric, ancient life would pour from the canyon? What if this was it? This egg? This fragile thing.

What if this wasn't a bird at all?

"I guess whatever you are, boy or girl or whatever, you're coming with me," she said, and took a moment to include some Marvel gear she stole from Scott's trunk to add to the wrappings. She pulled a Miles Morales hoodie over the whole thing. *Better this way.*

Then she piled Scott's comic book collection in her trunk. *Best to not leave that to the wolves.* She soon pulled onto Cottonwood Street, aimed toward the highway.

She planned to get to J.A.'s. He'd know what to do as long as she didn't accidentally destroy the egg between here and there. After that, she didn't know. Maybe find the desert. New Mexico, Arizona, or California. Maybe work a while. Maybe go back to school. Though probably not. Probably not that at all.

She'd make that phone call first, yeah?

She'd do that soon, very soon. The number was on the key. Didn't matter. She'd already memorized the damn thing.

Acknowledgments

Back around 1972, *this* three-year-old scrawny city kid from San Jose, California—to the horror of my mother—snuck out his bedroom window. It was pitch black when she found me in the neighbor's garage, or I should say, when my neighbor did and called her. I was under his car in the dark, trying to figure out how to get out of this mess since the door to his kitchen shut, and the garage door already had too. Didn't realize I was the quiet mouse, the ghost haunting him, watching, listening. Eventually, he heard some cat in his garage, *me*, that dumb dual-ethnic kid; and lucky he was a good man—because people are usually good, but not always—and that was just one occasion of me slipping out that bedroom window. Guess I didn't always sleep? Maybe needed to see the world, however big or small? Anyway, thanks to that neighbor for being a good man that day.

Sometimes Mom would find me on the corner of Candler Avenue and White Road, which was really close to Story Road. I now live down the block from Story Street, so maybe this means something, possibly the supernatural force in a name? Anyway, sometimes I'd escape with the family dog, Candy. We'd creep to the corner, sit and watch cars, and this could be any time, day or night. She was my protector, and now I think me and this tricolored dog spoke telepathically. Can't remember, though maybe she knew something I didn't about the power of thought. And so, I thank her for being with me. Because of her I didn't have a fear of animals then, or the dark, or much until Dad started to tell us about Bigfoot. Dad being a trucker and all, guess I thought he was some kind of explorer of the wilderness, that maybe he packed out of that petroleum eighteen-wheeler, hauled that flammable liquid on his back over mountain peaks, all the way to that blistering howl in the dark. I think I figured he'd heard it a few times, saw those wild lantern eyes peeking around a redwood. Said he'd seen *things* anyway, always believed him. And while Dad can be seen in the bear's father and Greta's father, I took the name "The Pope" and some extra meanness from Obed Silva's painful 2021 memoir *The Death of My Father The Pope*.

We didn't travel much but Aunt Patty lived near that huge volcano near Redding, which I guess is close enough to Bigfoot country, close to those dots on the map of sightings, like that Patterson-Gimlin footage taken north of Willow Creek. Guessing all of that area is Sasquatch land, especially the strip malls and movie theaters, definitely the minds and imaginations parked at tv screens blasting *Animal Planet*. Anyway, Aunt Patty, black shoulder-length hair, wide-faced, *her-way-or-the-highway* always on her lips, was married to Uncle George, a white blind man (both long dead). She owned a gift shop above Shasta

Dam in the Visitor Center. I stared out the big theater windows down at the spillway feeling I was on top of the world, that maybe I could soar like an osprey, slide down the spillway on my Big Wheel, ride that concrete like Evel Knievel. Aunt Patty sold deer feed in her tourist shop. Just outside the entrance, always a herd hanging around. Anyway, that deer feed, oats maybe, and being that I was curious and fearless about animals, and my parents really never paid much attention to where I wandered until it was too late, this time I set my eyes on a fawn, and carrying my cup of feed, reached out, started petting that soft fur, right on those starry white spots.

Then I took a hoof to the chest, *crack*, knocked the wind out of me. Lucky it wasn't my face since I was so low to the ground. Thanks, *mama deer* for your careful aim, for not trampling me while I lay on my back seeing spinning yellow stars. And thanks Dad for the few trips we took to those cryptid wildlands. And thanks Mom for picking me up after the deer attack. Though you've both been gone nearly thirty years, I remember with gratitude.

That day I learned animals were something to be feared. They had lives, hierarchies, families, limited patience, a mean streak, a protection spell or two. And I remember something else from one of those trips to the Redding area. A taxidermy grizzly in the town of McCloud, that street-front covered in snow, that monster bear scary as anything even in still-life mode—that full snarl, paws skyward—had no idea it had been murdered and stuffed. Thank you, bear. You've always been Think Tank in my dreams.

While on a trip a few years ago I met retired Carroll

College Geologist and Fullbright Scholar, Ray Breuninger. I'd met him after inquiring at Birds & Beasley's in Helena about area birdwatchers. The shop owners told me about the Tuesdays, a group of birders that Ray called B-listers. They were A-list birders to me in their rag-tag caravan that explored nearby hills, canyons and plains for birds. Ray, in his eighties, and me half his age, struck up a friendship. On a non-Tuesday I picked him up for an adventure. When I asked where I was driving, he said, "To a mountain of bones." We drove near Scratchgravel Hills, then some gravel road to see Bobolinks, then into a canyon over a metal bridge where an Eastern Kingbird perched. Within moments of parking—*everywhere*—bone chips glistened like shells. Then larger chunks of bones, then skulls, pelvis bones, spines, ribs. Pelts too, decomposing things. And then, a mountain of bones and hides, carcasses—halves and wholes of creatures like the world got turned inside out—elk, cow, coyote, pig, sheep, goat, dog, horse. We both stood mesmerized.

While we drove through the canyon he talked about geological processes, the forming of the land, including how life itself had been embedded in the sedimentary canyon rock in beads of early life. These *strings of beads* once lay in quiet water more than a billion years ago—sometimes in crude net patterns—but had become preserved as molds or flattened biconvex lens shapes. He told me how people shot at him while he searched in nearby North Hills for them. And he told me that he'd been one of the discoverers of these earliest life algae bead strings that formed 1.5 billion years ago. He later sent me his paper "Depositional Environment of *Horodyskia*

('String of Beads') From the Early Mesoproterozoic Greyson and Spokane Formations of the Belt Supergroup, Near Helena, Montana, U.S.A." Thanks to Ray for everything. Not a far stretch to see some of him in the character J.A. Maynard. That name itself was inspired by John Arthur Maynard, long retired CSU Bakersfield historian, a favorite professor in the early 1990s who passed in 2022 after a long battle with Lewy Disease. I can still hear him imitating some old editor, always singing in my ear over the phone, "Don't get fired!" His imitations during lectures were legend. He wrote, *Venice West: The Beat Generation in Southern California* (1993), and on his office wall, a photo of himself in his khakis—he served in Army Intelligence in Germany during the Vietnam War—having just slept on the lawn of one of poet Dylan Thomas's historic homes.

Two UC Riverside Palm Desert Low-res MFA Program professors influenced *Ten Sleep*'s early chapters. Thanks to Stephen Graham Jones (no longer at the program). He helped me first understand Greta when *Ten Sleep* was only a novella. He particularly liked my line about undulating cilia and said that I fooled him about that finger of metal that tears into Greta's tires, thinking a monster was coming from below, not above. He recommended episodes of *Yellowstone*, and of course Mark Spragg's *The Fruit of Stone* (2002), from which I created a glossary of layman's terms regarding Wyoming landscapes. Thanks to director/professor Tod Goldberg for the idea to begin the tale with Greta dragging those two-hundred-and-six bones.

More thanks: Can't recall the artist, but don't know what I would have done without stumbling onto a bizarre taxidermy goat-fawn created for an art exhibition. That image inspired all kinds of story ideas. *Gretaaaaa*. Thanks to SocksnFoots for constantly getting Warblerdemon out of hard spots. We shall make our way through the dark lands of Diablo again.

When it comes to the many folks behind the scenes of *Ten Sleep*, I need to first thank editorial duo Editorial Director Diana Pho and Associate Editor Viengsamai Fetters. They took my mess of a manuscript, saw the good in it, and provided guidance, enthusiasm, and support. They watered the gardens of *Ten Sleep*, and from that grew characters, story, and *myself*. Thanks for letting me push back on prairie dogs, bears and snoutytrunks. And thanks for the kind of experimental freedom I thought this book could manifest, especially in its tough-to-nail-down structure. Much gratitude to copyeditor Rayne Stone for being the most knowledgeable human on the planet. I sweat bullets every rare occasion I used "stet." Thanks to Brynn Metheney for weaving the best kind of magic with moody and creepy cover and creature illustrations. And none of this could happen without the full team of awesomeness: Thanks to Cassanda Farrin, Kelsy Thompson, Adrian James, Lou Malcangi, Shannon Gray-Winter, Martin Cahill (watch for his books!), and Kasie Griffitts. Additional thanks to the incredible Kensington management team, and the awesome extended Kensington team! Steven Zacharius, Adam Zacharius, Jackie Dinas, Lynn Cully, Vida Engstrand, Matt Johnson, Tracy Marx, John Son, and Joyce Kaplan. And can't forget to thank the sales team at Penguin Random House for all their enthusiasm and hard work!

A big thanks to my immediate family. Bits of Reina, Sue and Edie illuminate the voice of Greta. And Jordan and Ben seem to be chasing each other in that cat and chinchilla's playful antics.

Finally, thanks to Jane for choosing the interior and cover fonts—part of my thanks to her for listening to me read from *Ten Sleep* every morning while I developed the story. I owe much of the story's inspiration to her. She told me about a taxidermy shop outside of Ten Sleep, Wyoming, blood trickling into the street. I'd never even heard of the town. She'd attended University of Wyoming and has told me many high-country tales. I know a cowgirl lives inside her, maybe with the spirits of adventurous women from her storied ancestry. We saw that prairie dog town at Buffalo Jump, and we thanked every yip-dawg back then. At its visitor center that rattler headed right for my ankle until a volunteer said, "Sir, get over here, *now*." Even my sandwich sprouted legs and ran. I was maybe a second away from something hot pouring into my body. That little slithershaker was inspiration for the bites to *the skin* in *Ten Sleep*. Jane also told me about the taxidermy convention she once had to cater, which got me to thinking. And she told me about Star Valley, from where her friend Miles escaped. Thanks Jane. Here's something I love without question. We always hold hands at the movies. We always go to sleep so warm.

DISCUSSION QUESTIONS

These suggested questions are to spark conversation and enhance your reading of *Ten Sleep*.

1. How many western fiction tropes can you identify in *Ten Sleep*? Of those tropes, how many have been changed, modernized, or subverted in some way?

2. What makes Greta a powerful protagonist? What are her flaws? How does *Ten Sleep* use Greta's ethnicity, gender, and sexual orientation to challenge traditional notions of who should be the main character in westerns?

3. Greta's memories of her girlfriend Hannah seem to haunt her on the trail. How do you think her relationship to Hannah guides Greta's thoughts and actions throughout the novel? Do you think she and Hannah will eventually reconcile? Why or why not?

4. Animal chapters are included alongside Greta's story. What purpose do you think they serve in the narrative? How do

these animal experiences add to or parallel aspects of Greta's journey?

5. Taxidermy creatures are also prominent in various ways. Some may have a mysterious but haunting presence, like the Goat-Fawn. Others, like Think Tank, have their entire lives pre-taxidermy told as part of the story. What role do you think each taxidermy creature represents in the narrative?

6. Themes of family and community permeate *Ten Sleep*. For instance, the prairie dogs serve as one example of shared knowledge and defense in the face of danger and loss. What do the other characters—such as Greta, the coyote siblings, the owl, the Tillers, the wedding mice, and Think Tank—teach us about family community, trauma, and healing?

7. Are both Mother Canyon and the giant bird one and the same? What do both symbolize?

8. How does *Ten Sleep* resist ideas of settlerism and settler colonialism?

9. How do the different motivations of Mother Canyon, Pinkie Zollers, Tom Horn, Greta, Mother Buffalo, The Ghost Train, Hannah, Scott, and Tiller provide commentary about American attitudes, ideals, or beliefs?

10. In what ways are The People connected to the plot of the story? Why do you think it is important that Greta have a vision of burning prehistoric taxidermy?

11. Should Tiller, Scott, the sheep herders, and the other human characters suffer the fates that they do? Why or why not?

12. *Ten Sleep* uses the "final girl" horror trope as part of its resolution. Did you agree with its use? Why do you think the concept of a "final girl" is so prominent in the horror genre?

13. *Ten Sleep* is an eco-horror tale, as is Nicholas Belardes's first novel, *The Deading*, where nature has become a nightmare of humanity's own making. How are both books similar in this way? How are they different?

14. At the end of the story, Greta saves certain things after leaving the canyon. Why do you think each item she chose was important to take with her? What do you think happens to her afterwards?